STEFAN INSPECTED THE DEADHEAD ACCESS UNIT.

It was entirely physical, meant for a failure in his connect. There was no screen. He wouldn't be able to see anyone, but he would hear them, and they would hear him. It would have to be enough. He typed in his emergency access code to the Open Court.

"Access denied," a mechanical parody of a woman's voice said. "Invalid code."

Maybe he'd typed it incorrectly. Stefan tried again. And again. "Access denied. Invalid code," it said each time.

The Open Court was refusing his call. . . .

THE POLITE HARMONY OF WORLDS
series by
VALERIE FREIREICH

BECOMING HUMAN

As a sub-human spy probe, August gathers intelligence from the inner corridors of the Harmony of Worlds' Grand Assembly. As a confidant and lover, he reports to the Electors—and holds their most intimate secrets. As a clone of a traitor, his days are numbered because of flare—a genengineered condition that always calls for termination. Now a catastrophe, which only August can avert, threatens to disrupt the Harmony of Worlds forever. But first he'll have to decide what to trust—his tarnished instincts or his growing hunger to become human.　(453964—$4.99)

"Impressive."—New York Times Book Review

TESTAMENT

Since the days of the slowships, every man and woman of the now quarantined planet could recall the memories of their female ancestors . . . every man except Gray Bridger. Bridger has spent his entire adult life trying to escape Testament, for he is that rare genetic throwback—a singleton, who holds no memories other than his own. But the powerful Bridger matriarchy has its own plans for Gray, a destiny that could crush his dreams . . . or make him the most important man on the planet.　(454596—$5.99)

"Compelling, original."—Locus

from RoC

THE
BEACON

Valerie J. Freireich

A ROC BOOK

ROC
Published by the Penguin Group
Penguin Books USA Inc., 375 Hudson Street,
New York, New York 10014, U.S.A.
Penguin Books Ltd, 27 Wrights Lane,
London W8 5TZ, England
Penguin Books Australia Ltd, Ringwood,
Victoria, Australia
Penguin Books Canada Ltd, 10 Alcorn Avenue,
Toronto, Ontario, Canada M4V 3B2
Penguin Books (N.Z.) Ltd, 182–190 Wairau Road,
Auckland 10, New Zealand

Penguin Books Ltd, Registered Offices:
Harmondsworth, Middlesex, England

First published by Roc, an imprint of Dutton Signet,
a division of Penguin Books USA Inc.

First Printing, October, 1996
10 9 8 7 6 5 4 3 2 1

To my son,
Jared

Chapter 1

"Welcome home," her Hosts had said, but from her arrival on Earth, Beatrice Whit was a visitor and not a member of the community of Earth, set apart by her skin, her song, her history, and her mission. She belonged to the Ship.

Beatrice eased her way through the crowd of boisterous tattooed men and women, smiling when they noticed her but averting her eyes whenever she could. They danced and drank and devoured tidbits served by gleaming artificial servants. They chatted endlessly, trying to make the trivial profound. The people were giants; she used their massive bodies to play hide-and-seek with her guard, Kaim Pritchard's man. It was a game she couldn't win permanently, but the party gave her an opportunity to break free for a while.

The low, stone ceiling was a comfortable contrast to Earth's oppressively bright open sky, though the air smelled like tsampa left too long on the heat. A dim tunnel led farther underground. She made it her goal.

No one was ill. In another week or two, when they were sure, one of her three fellow Travelers might propose that they call the Ship to Earth. Since she was the youngest, Beatrice had decided not to be the first, though she yearned for the call to be made. At night, when she lay alone in the high, hard bed Pritchard provided, the beacon whispered tragedy into her thoughts. Tragedy and guilt. These rowdy clansmen, like the graceful Ropans with their stratified, new feudalism, were creations of the Ship, remnants of a civilization destroyed on a whim of the Friends; they struggled, often self-consciously, to reconstruct what they had lost, and had produced their Assembly.

She slipped into the dark. To be alone was wonderful, but it could not be wonderful for long. It was time Earth had friends. Beatrice reached for the beacon. There were tears in her eyes when she found it.

Stefan Acari sensed the Assembly at the edge of his mind but didn't reach out to it, although connection had the seductive fascination of an alcoholic's next prospective drink. Instead, he wiped sweat from his face with a crumpled napkin and looked around the subterranean ballroom for the host of the Waterman Clan party, John Denning, the clan president.

Thin, wailing music from stringed instruments played by live men, not mecas, echoed eerily off the limestone walls, intensifying the volume of noise and providing a very imperfect reason to dance, although about a quarter of the crowd danced anyway, in a jumpy, self-indulgent style that led to a collision as he watched. They danced as couples; none of the clansmen solo-danced with an Assembly phantasm. In fact, no one in sight wore an Assembly accessing band or full cap—typical of the isolationist Northern Sister Continent.

He smiled at a woman who was smiling at him. She approached, too close for a stranger in a sweltering room, but manners in the Sister Continents often seemed crude to a man of Stefan's Ropan sensibilities. He forced away his regional prejudices, as well as the automatic guilt at admiring a woman other than Liada, his wife, and made a courtly bow. She was young and pretty, though any true beauty was, for him, lost in the whirls of tattooed lines highlighting her eyes and her bare breasts. Customs differed; the Assembly held the regions of Earth together.

"I'm so thrilled to meet you," the clanswoman gushed.

That was an unusual opinion. Most people were wary of the Open Court and avoided Open Court Judges; they didn't understand that their secret misdeeds were usually petty and dull. "I'm honored to be here," he said. Surely she had mistaken him for someone else.

"How do you like the party?"

He glanced around the cave once more. Lit by the dim, yellow lights strung by the caterer's mecas, the crush of tattooed naked flesh gave the party the appearance of a frenzied orgy to Stefan; he tried not to stare. Augmented stalactites and stalagmites ringed the room's outskirts with flickering lights. Food and drink were unimaginative but plentiful. Judged by their laughter and smiles, everyone else was having an excellent time, though to Stefan the atmosphere seemed heavy with the sweet-sour odor of perfume, fresh beer, and the fecund dampness of the caverns. His smile felt stiff. "A cave is a unique place to hold a party," he said. "Appropriate for a clan that works underground so much."

"Tell me about parties on Numerica."

"I've never been to one."

She gaped, puzzled.

If she had assumed he was a Numerican—probably because, unlike native clansmen, he was fully dressed—that meant Numericans were present at the party. He surveyed the crowd more thoroughly and noticed a knot of people in a corner of the ballroom. Just visible through their bare backs was a small contingent of guests who, like Stefan himself, wore more clothing than the garish, wide short pants, body scars, and body tattoos that constituted fancy dress in this part of the Northern Sister Continent. "My name is Stefan Acari," he said, bowing gallantly to the young woman. "I'm an Inlander from Ropa and a Judge of the Open Court, but not an interstellar voyager, I'm afraid."

"Oh." Immediately, her attention wandered. She did not give her own name.

So much for his charming self, Stefan thought. She wanted an exotic, not an important man. "Are all four Numericans here?" he asked, trying to maintain the conversation so he would not be alone.

She nodded without looking back at him.

"Interesting, isn't it," he asked, "that the Assembly

doesn't contain any information on the launch of the ship that established the Numerican colony?" It highlighted the discontinuities between the present and the Old Modern Age.

"Oh, the Assembly." She dismissed the principal unifying force on Earth with a wave of her heavily tattooed arm. Stefan smiled. He liked the Sister Continents, but their insularity could be maddening.

She stood on tiptoe, trying to see beyond her clansmen mobbing the Numericans. Their arrival on Earth a few weeks earlier had astonished everyone. Records of the colony had apparently been lost during the turmoil of the Great Deaths, which killed off the Old Modern civilization; the Numericans' huge, uncommunicative ship in orbit around Jupiter was a mystery they refused to discuss. Theory and experiment of Earth claimed no living thing could traverse the unreal space beyond light speed travel, but the Numericans apparently had managed it.

"I've heard that they came from here," she said, turning briefly to Stefan. "The Numerican colonists. It shows in their name. Numerica was founded by the Amercans who lived right here in Old Modern times." The intertwining lines of her facial tattoo became more pronounced by her happy flush.

Ropans took less pride in their kinship with the Old Moderns. The Old Moderns had been sinners who'd brought the five Great Deaths upon the world; the Amercans had been the greatest sinners of all.

A clump of giggling women, neglected at the moment by their men, separated, some moving toward a drink-bearing meca and others toward the musicians. Their dispersal revealed John Denning. He was holding court before a group of clansmen, smiling with the radiance of a natural politician installed in his element.

"Excuse me," Stefan said. "I see John, and I need to thank him for the invitation." He bowed slightly, hesitated, then, when the clanswoman seemed not to have noticed, he walked away, skirting the crowd, detouring around clusters of people, avoiding dancers and conversations, heading to John Denning.

Denning's arms moved in broad gestures. His tone was hearty, although the crowd's noise prevented Stefan from hearing clearly what was said. As Denning listened to one man, he repeatedly nodded, but his gaze ranged through the room, and finally his attention fell on Stefan. "Judge Acari!" he called, as though surprised by Stefan's presence.

Stefan bowed, though it was a Ropan, not local, custom.

Denning made some low, humorous remark. His audience, smirking, glanced toward Stefan, then quickly turned aside as they saw that he was observing them, but not before he flushed. Large social gatherings made Stefan uneasy; he could not help but wonder how many strangers knew him intimately from his dumps into the Assembly. Then Denning strode past the others and came to Stefan. "Glad you're here," he said, leaning close enough to be heard over the party's noise without shouting. "I wasn't sure you would come." His tattooed face was shiny. He smelled like a laborer after a long day outdoors.

Stefan moved farther from Denning. "Reject an invitation from a serious contender for President of the Northern Sister? That would hardly be politic." He smiled, however, liking John Denning. Despite Denning's pride in being a wild clansman of the Sisters, visible in his scrolling, swirling, abstract facial tattoos, John Denning was a well-educated and intelligent man. Stefan even suspected Denning had a moral center beneath the pragmatism of an effective politician. Besides, the invitation had been a godsend, Stefan's excuse to leave home and Liada for a few days, and gather his thoughts on divorce.

"Relax," Denning said. "Tonight you're just another guest. Dance. Have something to drink. Tell everyone back in Ropa that the Waterman Clan knows how to entertain." He clapped Stefan on the shoulder. "Anyway, since when has a Judge of the Open Court needed the goodwill of a local politician?"

"Not so local. You managed to get the Numericans to attend your party."

Denning cast a sidelong glance toward the Numericans. "It wasn't entirely my doing." His grin seemed forced; his tattoos made him look fierce. The tattoos and scars meant something, clan signs and whatnot, but Stefan didn't know how to decode them.

A servameca bearing drinks opened a path through the crowd and the Numericans were momentarily exposed. Stefan saw two of them. They seemed formal where the clansmen were eager; they moved back like reluctant dance partners as the clansmen squeezed forward. Even in the cavern's weak light, their complexions—what was exposed past their long-sleeved shirts and long pants—were perceptibly more golden than was usual, even in Greater Chen. Stefan recognized the Numerican leader, Charles Syne, from the early, excited newsbriefs. Then the crowd closed around them again. "What are they like?" Stefan asked.

Denning shrugged. "I've barely spoken with them. My contact's been with their liaison." His voice dropped and his mouth puckered in unsubtle distaste, then he beckoned a passing humaniform servameca and took a freezeglass of flavored water from it that, by the tint and foam of the water, looked identical to beer. He sipped while scanning the room over the rim of his glass. Across the room, a clansman waved at Denning. He waved back, smiling, and leaned close again to Stefan. "Someone in the Open Court should take an interest in the Numericans," he whispered.

Their conversation would be in the public record next time Stefan entered the Assembly and made a dump, an immediate, automatic deposit of the contents of his mind. Privacy was a polite game, a lie, even; Stefan's reserve was a defense he had adopted because of the dignity and social distance it provided. Nevertheless, Stefan lowered his voice, too. "You want an Open Court investigation of the Numericans? Why? What's your grievance? Something political?"

Denning didn't answer; he gestured graciously at the waiting servameca. "Help yourself."

Stefan rid himself of the balled-up napkin and took a freezeglass of beer. He studied Denning, but the tattoos hid whatever clue to Denning's motives he might otherwise have found. Earth's first interstellar visitors were very interesting guests, but the puzzle of their existence and survival during a faster-than-light flight was a question for scientists, or perhaps historians, not a matter for an Open Court Judge. Stefan itched to consult the Assembly for information about them, and about Denning, but refused to give up the temporary privacy provided by his failure to have made a recent dump. In any event, the Assembly wouldn't know much. The Numericans were new to Earth, while Denning was an Assembly peripheral, an adept, but not one who made dumps. "Sorry, John. I can't help you, anyway. I can't investigate even if there is cause." Stefan stiffened in an unconscious and inadequate attempt to deny the tug of the connect against his mind. "I've gone nominal."

Denning grimaced in surprise and took a step back from Stefan, like a doctor beginning an examination. "No one goes nominal who's been an active ticker as long as you," he said. "You won't leave the Assembly for long."

"I won't do a dump."

Denning stood motionless, observing Stefan, perhaps checking his last file dump. Denning's stillness contrasted with the frenetic movement of the dancers beyond him, and emphasized how rarely Denning himself was stationary. Usually, he seemed to do several things simultaneously. His eyes roved, his hands moved, he fidgeted, yet it all seemed part of his informal, jocular style and the overall impression wasn't of rude inattention, but of repressed energy, so that his listeners were grateful for the attention he did settle, even fleetingly, on them.

A gang of rowdy, clearly drunken, men called to Denning in singsong rhyming slang so dense Stefan couldn't understand it from outside the Assembly, despite his fluency in Northern Sister languages. Denning waved at them. "Voters," he said, excusing himself from Stefan. "Have a good time; be sure to meet the Numericans. We'll talk later." Then Denning left, swaggering toward the men in the exaggerated local style of assertive manhood.

Stefan sipped his beer. He preferred wine, but anything cool was welcome. The cave's ventilation was inadequate for the number of people present. The early summer disease forecast for the Sisters had been clean. No new cases of Tremblers, Red Death, or Hives had been reported in Bowl, the nearest town. Ordinarily, Stefan wouldn't have given the close atmosphere a second thought, but the party had an edgy pressure, as though too many secrets were confined in too small a space. The overheated air formed a slight haze where it contacted the cool stone walls. He imagined viruses hovering, and an outbreak starting here.

He was getting a headache from the thick, dank atmosphere, and a sense of hollow loneliness from the crowd. He felt inside his mind for the Assembly like a man patting the wallet in his pocket, to know it was there, but withdrew before connection. Comforted by its presence, he missed the rush of entering it fully. Denning's comment reinforced his own fear that he couldn't control his craving: *No one goes nominal who's been an active ticker as long as you.* Without the Assembly, half his brain seemed to be missing.

He meandered through the room and spoke in passing to several members of the Waterman Clan, admiring their party, and declined an invitation to dance with Marta Denning, a hefty, hard-working woman who was the clan treasurer as well as John Denning's wife. Older, married women, like Marta, covered their upper bodies, but facial tattoos and scarification still gave them a savage, not matronly, look. Stefan moved in a slightly downward direction, since up would have meant out and, however much he longed for the cool, forested hills aboveground and his comfortable hotel in the nearby town of Bowl, it was too soon to leave.

He pretended to study the glittering, augmented stalactite formations, and walked away from the party's center. The air cooled pleasantly as he moved down and farther from the crowd. He drained his glass. Well-set, a servameca was immediately there to take it and proffer another. He refused and went closer to the edge of the lighted area. No one seemed to notice.

A moist, clayey smell drew him deeper into the cave; it was the fragrance of recently turned, rich soil, new and yet old as the land. He followed a concrete path, which looped, shutting him off from the party. The human sounds became background noise. Cool air moved against his sweaty skin; he shivered. A glowing red sign ordered visitors to halt, but he went cautiously forward, willing to continue as long as faint shadows indicated shapes.

Denning had specifically invited Stefan Acari, not requested the presence of an Open Court Judge. They'd occasionally met on Court business, most recently at an intervention by the Open Court in a riparian rights decision of the Central Sister's Land Local, and had dined together several times. It didn't amount to a true friendship, though it was sufficient rationale for this invitation. Mysteries surrounded the Numericans; Denning apparently wanted to bring the Open Court to bear on them, but informally. Why? Stefan guessed that Denning's interest in the Numericans had hidden significance. He assumed such intuitions originated in the Assembly and came through his implanted connect, yet he hadn't entered the Assembly for weeks; perhaps he was wrong. It didn't matter. None of this was his concern if he didn't enter the Assembly. As long as he was nominal, he had privacy, but he couldn't be a Judge.

At the farthest edge of the shadows, directly ahead in the darkness, was a large shape. Stefan considered, then went forward more slowly, straining to resolve the shape into something he recognized, deliberately scuffing his feet to warn of his approach. It moved; he guessed it was someone seated on a bench. Every mind had a particular resonance, like a mental fingerprint, which was detectable by the Assembly. Since the Assembly continually skimmed everyone's surface mind—though it could do nothing more without voluntary connection—it could match an individual in the geographic vicinity with its records to identify the person. Only tickers—or the Assembly Adjusters, who were entirely and constantly integrated into the Assembly system—could command the Assembly to perform a geographic search, not peripherals or the general public. A few weeks earlier Stefan would have done so routinely, without giving it much thought, but a search required him to connect. He wouldn't. That would initiate a dump.

He stood, rubbing his thumb across the smooth amber stone of the heavy Acari estate ring, curious to discover who else had left the Waterman Clan party, but hesitant to interrupt.

A woman's voice asked him to come forward. She sounded glad of his arrival, but not as though it were a rescue, and had an accent that he couldn't place. "Don't let me prevent you from going on," she said.

He smiled more easily than he had at the party, though she wouldn't be able to see him. "I can't go farther without equipment, at least a light," he said. "And this part of the Man Mouth Cavern system isn't especially interesting or the land local wouldn't rent it out for parties." As he spoke he advanced until she was only at arm's length, though she still was no more than a vague, solid shape against the scarcely brighter darkness.

"Man Mouth? Are we likely to be digested?"

He forced an audible chuckle, like a considerate man expressing appreciation of a joke to someone blind. His voice seemed rough and insincere following hers. She spoke like an accomplished singer, in well-modulated tones of perfect pitch. The rise and fall of each syllable was fully realized. "Man Mouth is a corruption of an older name," he said, "from the English Speakers' Empire—locally, the Amercans."

"Ah. You're quite erudite." She emphasized the slight rhyme as if to tease him.

Stefan smiled at her gentle mockery; there was no sting in it, only a shared pleasure in their companionship. "Just pedantic. And I read a guide provided by my hotel."

She laughed with the beautiful sound of an instrument running up a scale. "You're not from this area, either?" she asked. "I see you're fully clothed, not covered with scars and paint."

"I'm from Ropa." He echoed the mild disdain for the clansmen implicit in her tone. "You see very well in the dark." It was a question.

"All of us do. I'm a Traveler."

He hesitated, then asked, "You're one of the Numericans?"

"We prefer to call ourselves 'Travelers.'"

"Of course." He struggled for something clever to say, but was hampered by his inability to see her expression or sense her mood from body language, and by the knowledge that she probably could see him. That made him shy, and her beautiful voice made him reluctant to speak.

"Join me here, looking out at the darkness." He heard her pat the bench.

Feeling his way cautiously, so as not to land on the ground when he sat, but equally careful not to brush against her, he lowered himself onto the bench. It was sized for lovers, barely adequate for two, but she didn't shrink away. He clasped his hands around a knee and leaned back. Despite their proximity and his strained staring, he saw nothing of her face. Her fragrance was slight, a hint of perspiration and a whiff of soap, but no perfume. He remembered the Waterman clanswoman's effusive questions and was unpleasantly conscious that anything he asked about Numerica would certainly have been asked of her before. The Travelers had been reticent.

The silence lengthened and became difficult to break. The darkness had a velvet texture, but no shape. His mind tried to find patterns; failing, it tried to make them. Even her excellent night vision could have seen only cold stone walls. He glanced back toward the party and saw a faint, florid glow around the curving tunnel that was the warning light, then he stared ahead like studying ocean waves or mountains, as if there was something to be seen in the emptiness. It was more peaceful than the party, silent and complete in itself. It didn't wait to be filled. Perhaps his unease had been because the party was a perversion of the purity of the cave.

"It's beautiful, isn't it?" Her voice was tender. "Like being on the ship in unreal space, entirely without light or stars. Or here, in a dark sky at night, or deep, dense water. Pure. Raw. It draws a person inside. You felt it. You came."

Her voice was lightning, allowing him, for an instant, to see what she felt. The darkness had seemed bleak until she spoke. Her description came from her tone more than her words and startled him into a déjà vu. He knew exactly what she described: freedom, yet purpose. He'd felt it on the Assembly's edges. Embarrassed by his unexpected emotion, Stefan spoke lightly. "It was more of an escape, for me. I came here for the coolness, and for air that didn't smell as though it needed to be washed. There were too many people, and too much exposed skin." That was superficial, after the intimacy of their rapport, yet told more about his outlook on the party than he usually revealed to anyone outside a dump.

Something, a flash from her teeth or an almost inaudible sound, made him certain that she'd smiled. He realized by his pleasure at that small success that he was flirting. The woman was merely a voice in the darkness, yet he felt he knew her, and wanted to know her better. He was sure she was honorable, unlike Liada. Her voice radiated honesty and humor; a person's voice was the clearest expression of truth.

She touched the back of his hand. "Mine was an escape, too."

He could flirt with her if he wanted; Liada had forfeited the right to his fidelity, and if he stayed nominal, no one would know what he thought and did. It was only fair and necessary, however, to tell this woman the full truth, despite the possibility it would end their conversation. He straightened his back. "I'm Stefan Acari, a Judge of the Open Court." Since she could see, he extended his hand in the local greeting gesture, inadvertently brushing his fingertips against the soft sleeve of her blouse. She slipped her hand inside his. Hers was small, with narrow fingers and clipped nails. Her skin was unexpectedly cool, and the flesh was smooth and dry. The Numericans—the Travelers—were somewhat transformed, he'd heard, by life on Numerica. He wished he could see her.

"Beatrice Whit." She withdrew her hand. "Have you come to judge us? The Travelers?"

He imagined a wary, wry smile, and was surprised at his ability to imagine the face he had not yet seen. Liada was more beautiful, he guessed, but beauty was shallow. Nothing physical showed in the Assembly and speaking with her alone in the dark reminded him of that. Besides, Beatrice would have a more interesting face, a visual counterpart to her lively voice. "I'm here at John Denning's invitation," he said. "I'm not sure why I was invited. Perhaps to meet you, but the clans have a tradition of using courts for political purposes, and he's running for President. He may have accusations against an opponent he wants to share with me."

She touched his arm, a brief, light contact that substituted for an apology or was encouragement. "You're open with your opinions, Judge Acari. What if I'd been John Denning's wife?"

She didn't understand the breadth of the Open Court's power, or the privacy he'd given up to it, either. Denning already knew Stefan's opinions. "I've met Marta Denning; she couldn't fit on this bench," he said. "Anyway, she might agree. So might John. The clans are proud of their boldness, and claim straightforwardness is truth."

She laughed. "Will you accommodate him?"

"No. A Judge of the Open Court can only work

through the Assembly and I won't enter it just now."
He wouldn't discuss Liada's infidelity with even so empathetic a woman, but she was a stranger on Earth. It
was likely that she didn't understand clearly what he
was. "The Open Court is the Assembly's judiciary; its
authority isn't from the regional governments. Because
of the Assembly's capabilities, we don't require the usual
formalities of the common courts. There's no court-
house, no legal technicalities or strict procedure. Our
concern is fairness, not law; justice, and not jurispru-
dence. If we find an inequity that the common courts
can't resolve, or an injustice no one else will investigate,
or prejudice that interferes with reason or truth, then
it's our responsibility to inquire and judge. The initiative
is on each Judge. There is no appeal from our decisions.
They override those of any other court. Independent
Defense, the Assembly police system, enforces each
Judge's rulings. Since a Judge's power is so broad, to
prevent misuses of authority, Open Court Judges are
accountable for their honesty. We're tickers."

"I'm sorry, Judge, but I don't understand what makes
a ticker, though I've heard the word." Her comment was
apologetic but her tone expressed that she had a nebu-
lous grasp of the concept and had formed an unfavorable
opinion of it. She continued, speaking too quickly, obviously ill at ease. "When my ancestors left Earth, there
was no Assembly—so much is different from what we
Travelers expected!—and the Assembly seems peculiar
to us. It's everywhere." Her distaste showed when she
used the word *Assembly*.

His hands grasped the cold edge of the bench tightly.
The stone was gritty, with a thin layer of sand that dirt-
ied his fingers. "The Assembly is a machine of brilliant,
unprecedented design. We use it for communication and
information storage instead of Old Modern Age computer nets. It's better, and it's much more. The Assembly
is the world's great good, the blessing that followed the
Great Deaths; it unites all people into one."

"A world government?"

He shook his head, then remembered. "No. It doesn't

govern. It lets us know one another; it creates trust. The Adjusters exist to keep it functioning—it's located in the Southland, and so are they."

"Antarctica?"

"Yes." He knew the old name from his friend, Romaric Ezio. "It works like a human mind, making connections idiosyncratically; when people connect, they do it through code commands delivered by their directed thoughts focused through an Assembly band, cap, or an implanted connect. The Assembly is especially sensitive to emotion. Some people are more adept than others. The adepts with implanted connects are called peripherals. Everyone, but especially adepts, adds inconsequential bits of emotion to the stew of Assembly information."

She was listening closely. Her breathing was synchronous with his. "That's how a ticker is different," he continued. "We're peripherals, but the Adjusters have chosen us again. Each time we connect, we add our consciousness into the Assembly as a file accessible to the general public—a dump. There is a deposit of the contents of a ticker's mind, all his thoughts, actions and, of course, emotions, each time he accesses the Assembly: for information, to work appended, to make a call, or even just to check the Assembly's keeptime. It's involuntary, immediate, and unavoidable. All Open Court Judges are tickers. The mind isn't a perfect recording device, however; with time, memories do become muted, and rough edges smoothed, but a ticker has no privacy. Neither does anyone else, while they're with him."

Beatrice didn't respond immediately, and when she did her clever voice was guarded, emphatically neutral. She'd understood. He was not now explicitly judging her or the Travelers, but he was always a Judge and a ticker. "That is a great responsibility," she said. "A difficult occupation."

At least she had not said it was a great power. "Tickers are chosen by the Adjusters; I didn't have a choice, myself," he explained, although it sounded like an excuse. "It's an honor. Tickers get their name because we're the heartbeat of the Assembly."

"And if you don't want to be?" she asked as he paused.

"The only alternative is to go nominal and never use the Assembly. I'm doing that now, leading the life of a deadhead—that is, someone so mentally disabled or incompetent that he can't connect. It's inconvenient. The Assembly becomes a habit, and I miss the ... pleasure of connection." He felt he was giving the wrong impression. "It is my privilege to be an Open Court Judge, not only a duty. It's important to protect those the common courts don't, to do something for the world. It's what the Assembly is."

"They were right to choose you. You have a passion for justice."

He shrugged, feeling blind and therefore stupid. With her voice so detached, he had few clues to her emotion. She disapproved of him or of the Assembly. Was there a difference for a ticker?

Unable to see her, unable to feel her presence through the Assembly, she was a blind spot, a hole in his perception he wanted to fill. After speaking of it, he ached to connect with the Assembly. Its warmth would envelop him. He longed to play God, to have a hundred million minds appended to his; he wanted to know he wasn't as alone as, separated from the Assembly, he felt himself to be. It was too soon. Stefan's son, Tepan, shouldn't have to know the full force of his bitterness against Liada, Tepan's mother, unrelieved by the passage of time. He didn't want Tepan to be teased because of Stefan's inability to control and cool his anger. Then, too, Stefan simply wasn't ready for everyone he met to know that he'd been lied to, cheated upon, and betrayed by his wife.

Beatrice sighed and moved her feet against the ground, adjusting her position. "You expose yourself to protect others." Beatrice's tone was analytical. "Your thoughts aren't your own."

He felt as he did after arguing with Liada, drained

and sad. He shouldn't have expected Beatrice, who'd gone into the darkness for solitude, to understand someone for whom solitude had, for years, lasted only until his next dump. "My mind and my thoughts are my own," he said. "They simply aren't private. The Assembly doesn't control me, but if people couldn't inspect a Judge's mind, they wouldn't accept Open Court decisions. Often, they're unpopular, or they wouldn't have been necessary."

"I understand," she said. Her tone had warmed a bit. "It's a great burden to place on anyone."

Embarrassed by her sympathy, Stefan remembered the ghastly first years after he'd been made a ticker. He might have died from drinking, drugs, or suicide had it not been for the support of friends, particularly Romaric. The inability to do anything without it being known had been appalling for an adolescent. "I should return to the party," he said. He brushed grit from his hands off against his pants and stood. "I apologize for interrupting your meditation."

"You didn't," she said, "and I would like you to stay. I'm not anxious to go back to the party; it was difficult enough to slip out. We're always watched." From slightly troubled, her tone became amused. "A bit like your life, I suppose."

He smiled. "Perhaps."

"Tell me about yourself, Judge Acari."

"Stefan, please. And I dislike speaking about myself. It generally is unnecessary."

She laughed. So did he. "Have you entered the Assembly?"

"No." She was emphatic. "The Assembly is unnecessary."

Every normal human on Earth connected with the Assembly. To avoid it meant isolation from human contact, human knowledge, and human civilization. The Assembly commanded trust. Some claimed the Assembly was overused, but only the UN-Assemblers, the covert radicals of the Sister Continents bent on destroying the Assembly, claimed it was unnecessary. He struggled to find a less controversial topic, and one that wasn't personally invasive, but Beatrice found one first.

"Have you heard anything recently about a new illness?" she asked.

Health Reports and the weather: safe topics. He was grateful that women were so clever with small talk. "No, thank God. It's been a quiet year, except for the drought in Ropa." He sat down again.

"We didn't see much of Ropa," she prompted.

Without realizing beforehand what he intended to say, he found himself describing his home, the Acari Estate, telling her about the orchard dedicated at Tepan's birth, of a plan to drain a marsh because, for the first time in living memory, there was no surplus farmland, and of how the tenants' wives made lace, and the men kept honeybees and raised pigs, products they sold collectively, with his own produce, in Paris or Blin. He refused to allow his estate manager, Drom Hanzin, to charge a percentage for the service. She clearly was no farmer's daughter, but he didn't ask about Numerica. He fell into the rhythm of answering questions anyone else would have found unnecessary. More relaxed than he had been in weeks, he recognized his embryonic infatuation with Beatrice. He was nominal; he could enjoy it. Whatever John Denning's reason for issuing the invitation, Stefan was glad he'd left Acari to attend the party.

Darkness made Beatrice homesick for the Ship. In retrospect, Shipboard life had been innocent. After several weeks on Earth, none of the Travelers knew whom to trust among their Hosts, and therefore trusted no one, certainly not their liaison, Kaim Pritchard. Like everyone they met—Kaim Pritchard had his own agenda, but his was probably that of the Assembly Adjusters.

She liked the Judge. He seemed genuinely to have been met by chance. His reticence concealed sadness, but once he overcame his shyness—encouraged by her own intimate, warm tone that was almost song—and began to talk, his sadness lifted. He didn't see as clearly as she did the tension between his desire for human intimacy and the horrid particulars of his naked life; he rationalized his existence. Beatrice feared that she did the same thing. Oddly, as his sadness lessened, so did hers.

Since he asked few questions, she relaxed her vigilance. He responded naturally to the fragments of song she inserted into her speech. His near understanding of song made him a comfortable companion, too.

The Open Court seemed a great perversion; every Judge must absolutely be a good and decent person, then they were abused and used as illustrations of the good the Assembly could do. No one grasped that these Judges were already trustworthy without the Assembly, which only distorted their lives. The act of intervention in injustice had such brave simplicity. The Judge could tell himself that he did only good. What could she and her Friends say? That so far Earth had suffered no new sickness? Kaim Pritchard's Assembly Health Reports were apparently true.

As he spoke, Beatrice listened to the Judge's words and the subtle affection of his tone; she wondered how the Judge would pass judgment on their mission—on her—and she sighed. She missed her innocence.

Beatrice sighed. Stefan's throat was dry; he'd talked too much. "I apologize for boring you."

She patted his knee. "You haven't. You've made me appreciate the Earth better than I had. All we usually see are these formal parties."

The cave had become intimate. Her breathing was audible, as if they were hiding their heads under the same blanket of darkness. Alarmed by the strength of his reaction to Beatrice, he automatically strove to suppress the emotion. "We should return to the party. They've probably missed you." He stood.

She immediately stood, too.

The puzzle of the Travelers had come alive for Stefan. He wondered about Numerica, and Beatrice's long, frozen passage through unreal space—hadn't a newsbrief speculated on a workable stasis inside the ship? Would she have told him more if he weren't a ticker? He wished he could filter his dumps beyond the limits of the physical privacy screen. He knew the argument: a Judge must be above suspicion. The Open Court was vital to the well-being of the Earth, but what did they do in Numerica? He didn't ask.

Without speaking, they walked separately around the bench.

Something scuffed the ground deeper in the cave.

"Who's there?" She sounded concerned.

"An animal?" he suggested. There were cave-dwelling creatures, putrid, white-fleshed things.

"No, someone's been listening."

Eavesdropping on an Open Court Judge was pointless, but Stefan didn't mention that. He heard another sound, closer, although distances were deceptive among bare rocks, without light. "Show yourself," he called. There was only silence.

"Someone is there," Beatrice insisted. He heard her shuffle a step toward the sounds.

He reached out his hand, impulsively, to restrain her. "Wait." His fingers closed around her arm just below the elbow. She was thin. He thought of his son, Tepan, who was only four, and smiled because her clean, neutral smell in the dank cavern had reminded him of putting Tepan to bed, still damp after the nurse gave him his bath. "Wait. Are you being followed?"

She drew a deep breath. "Constantly. Our liaison is really our guard."

Strain as he might, Stefan saw no one. A man might stand a meter away and be invisible, but such a man, if he wore infrared or collected-light goggles, would be able to see them. The Travelers were important. They made the world larger by bringing news from beyond it, but agents of change were never universally welcome. "Guards aren't necessarily a bad thing," he said. "We should return to the party. You're safer in public."

"Yes, of course." She started walking. Her hard-shod shoes tapped against the stone ground; they sounded annoyed.

Stefan lingered behind. She noticed and waited. Because she was between him and the ruddy glow from the warning sign, Beatrice was a faint shadow. Suddenly, another shape darted toward her. "Drop!" he yelled, running forward to intercept her attacker.

Beatrice fell to her knees.

The second shape hesitated a half meter from Beatrice, and only rushed away as Stefan arrived. Stefan's outstretched fingertips, trying to grab the other, skimmed a bare arm. He felt raised cicatrix, a patterned line of intertwined scars around the attacker's wrist, then the other man escaped toward the party. Stefan started to follow.

"No. Don't." Beatrice was breathless. She clutched at Stefan. He helped her to her feet while trying to spot the man. Stefan's fleeting impression was of someone large but thin, though even that view could have been distorted by the darkness. He was probably young; he had moved lightly. "Are you all right?" he asked. Beatrice was trembling. She came only to his shoulder.

"I'm fine, now." She released Stefan and brushed her clothes with her hands, inhibiting the physical comfort he, in any event, hesitated to give. "Thank you." Her voice was composed.

"I'll go after him." Briefly, Stefan considered an Assembly geographic search to identify the intruder before he was lost in the party crowd, but with Beatrice unhurt and the aim of the man so uncertain, Stefan wasn't ready to dump. Any dump just now would prominently feature Beatrice, who craved solitude even in the children's Assembly access. Tepan's happiness was more important.

"No, please don't bother," Beatrice said. "I doubt he meant any harm."

"I didn't see a weapon," Stefan agreed. Still, the incident was strange. If there was any purpose to it, perhaps it was a warning, but of what? From whom? To whom?

She dropped her voice. "Please, don't mention this to anyone."

He frowned at her naïveté. "I'm afraid I can't promise that."

"Oh!"

"But I won't be making a dump any time soon." With Beatrice, he had managed to forget Liada; now thoughts of her surged back like an oily tide onto a clean beach.

Beatrice touched his hand. "That will be fine. I simply didn't want our liaison to lecture me about leaving the group. He can be unpleasant."

John Denning disliked the liaison, too. Stefan didn't comment. They walked toward the party. When they were near enough to the red warning light for Stefan's eyesight to be more than imagination, he studied Beatrice while she would think herself unobserved. She had the physique of a boy, with arms a bit too muscular for her narrow shoulders and a solid, compact body that nevertheless, by its awkward stance, failed to look full grown. Her breasts were only a hint of fullness, more contrast with the smallness of the waist—her least boyish feature—than an independent attribute. Her face was visible only in profile. Her lips were parted in an expression that could have been anything: reticence, dismay, fear, or even the startled opening for a kiss. He wanted, with an unreasonable intensity, to know this woman better.

She turned and he lost his view of her face. Her shoulder-length hair shimmered crimson in the light. She sighed again—he supposed she was thinking of their return to the crowded party—and slipped her arm through his, as Liada might once have done, for comfort and as an artless claiming. The assumed familiarity pleased Stefan. After a fumbling start, they strolled side by side. She didn't flounce, or lean on him, or brush against him. He wanted her to like him; it made him tense.

At the edge of the light, where vision was easy, Stefan looked down. She looked up without releasing his arm. She was a jaundiced goddess: large-eyed, pale-haired, with a refined, undecorated face, and younger than the other Travelers he'd glimpsed. The yellow complexion of the Travelers suited her, reminding him of the golden patina on an ancient madonna. She smiled without showing teeth, and nodded ahead; attending the party was her duty, not her preference.

Beatrice's grip tightened as they entered the ballroom. Nearby, her fellow Travelers remained surrounded by avid questioners who jostled for position like ants around a sugar candy, but this time Stefan noticed other men scattered at the party's margins who didn't crowd the Travelers, or dance, or talk. Their attention was discreetly oriented on the Travelers. Guards, he supposed, who had undressed in the local clansmen custom, but who lacked body paint, tattoos, or scars. Except for that, he might have concluded that the eavesdropper had been one of her guards.

Clansmen spotted Beatrice. They advanced, smiling. A meca detached itself from a temporary service wall and approached, carrying a tray of warm, chocolate desserts. Sweat, which had dried in the cool, unlit cave, formed again on Stefan's forehead and back. A social smile automatically tightened on his face. Beatrice squeezed his arm.

Near the Travelers, John Denning was arguing with a man whose back was to Stefan, but who was dressed in high Ropan fashion—overdressed, in fact, so that his elegant clothes seemed pretentious. Denning's arms made broad gestures; he pointed a finger at the other fellow, who responded with an assertive move forward. Just then, Denning spotted Beatrice. He broke into a grin, put his hands on his hips, and said something that seemed jaunty and faintly disdainful to his overdressed adversary.

The man turned, saw Beatrice, hesitated, and then did a broad double-take. "There you are!" He approached Beatrice with outstretched arms, as if he intended to embrace her. She moved against Stefan as though physically seeking his support against the fellow's advance, then the man dropped his arms in an affected exclamation. His every gesture seemed part of a charade, which made every gesture appear mocking. "I've been wondering where you were. I was about to dispatch a search party," he said.

Stefan was unable to place him, yet his voice, together with his exaggerated mannerisms, struck a chord of unrealized recognition. It felt uncomfortable and was an unusual experience for an Assembly ticker.

The new arrival hadn't so much as glanced at Stefan, but when he turned on him, without awaiting Beatrice's reply to his overwrought greeting, he seemed already to recognize him; he was a ticker who'd done a geographic search. "Stefan Acari," the man said in the tone one scolds a naughty child. "I didn't know a Judge was here. You haven't checked in recently with the Open Court."

Stefan bowed perfunctorily. "Have we met?" People were gathering, and this posturing dandy was giving them a show.

"Kaim Pritchard," Beatrice said. Her tone was determinedly neutral. She dropped Stefan's arm and stepped away from him.

"I'm the Travelers' liaison, appointed by the Assembly." Pritchard bowed too low, making the bow sarcastic. Rising, he brushed a lock of his curly reddish-brown hair from his high forehead. He had freckles, a snub nose, and the body of a wrestler. "Thank you for returning Beatrice to me, but I'll take over now. It's my job, Per Acari. I'm not landed, so I need one."

Once he had been identified as a Judge, use of Stefan's Ropan court title—Per, or Lord, Acari—rather than his judicial one, was an insult, one the clansmen wouldn't understand, but clear between Ropans. It was made vulgar by the man's offensive chumminess. The name, Kaim Pritchard, meant nothing to Stefan, and why the Traveler liaison should insult him was a mystery. Meanwhile, this Kaim Pritchard, while speaking in the local language, had the clear accent of an inhabitant of Zona, the Ropan forced settlement zone where the diseased and impaired had once been segregated. It made him easy quarry if Stefan chose to target him for personal invective. Stefan glanced at Beatrice. She seemed uneasy, so Stefan only nodded politely at Pritchard, who from his mocking smile, knew precisely what he'd done and said, and forced himself to be gracious. "No one tells the Open Court what it may or may not do, Mr. Pritchard, but I take no offense, since I'm presently nominal."

Pritchard brushed at his hair, then he bowed once more, to a proper, not ironic, depth. "And I apologize, Per Acari. We should begin again, without old wounds between us."

After Stefan's own disavowal of his status as a Judge, the social title had become tolerably suitable, but it grated. And *old wounds*? "Do I know you?"

Pritchard's face became empty, as though he'd gone deep into the Assembly. Where had Stefan ever come across an Assembly adept from Zona?

"Poupey," Stefan whispered as, abruptly, he remembered. The name Kaim Pritchard had meant nothing because the charity student had always been called Poupey—doll, or puppet—for his falseness and pretensions to nobility. Sometimes he'd simply been called Pou, louse, even by Lycee tutors. A "grace and honor" charity student was, at best, uneasily accepted in a school for the sons of Ropan aristocrats, but Poupey worsened his situation with lies, affectations, and blatant social climbing. He'd been insufferable after he and Stefan were coincidentally chosen as peripherals at the same time, using his new connect and adept abilities to send nasty or fanciful pseudonymous messages and expecting Stefan to keep his secret. Stefan had, though Romaric Ezio, Stefan's best friend then and since, had discovered it. He'd briskly and thoroughly put Poupey in his place by publicly ridiculing him, telling him that Stefan's Assembly aptitude was irrelevant, whereas Poupey should cling to his, as it might provide him with employment, likely his only chance at it since he was unfit for anything requiring trust independent of the Assembly. That must have been what Poupey—Pritchard, rather—had meant.

Pritchard had heard his nickname. His eyes hardened, but he made a wry face and spoke with exaggerated humility. "Thank you, Per Acari. It is a great honor to be remembered by a man like you, who has done so many kindnesses."

Stefan colored. Romaric had continued to belittle Poupey until Stefan had shamed Romaric into stopping, unfortunately, also in public. It had been a low point in their friendship. Thereafter, Poupey had been ignored, even shunned, by Romaric's friends—most of the school. Even the other grace and honor pupils had avoided him. Soon after, Stefan had been chosen as a ticker. By the time his life resumed a modicum of balance, Poupey had disappeared from school. To the extent that Stefan thought about it, he had assumed Poupey had been intimidated, physically or verbally, into leaving. If that was so, the incident was minor, schoolboy bullying, but it was the kind of inequity the Open Court, on a larger scale, was meant to prevent. Stefan knew it spoke poorly of him that he had stayed largely oblivious of Poupey and his problems. Embarrassed by his adolescent self-absorption, Stefan bowed to Pritchard, very low and sincerely. "Mr. Pritchard, I apologize for any offense I may have given, now or in the past."

"Such nobility of spirit," Pritchard said to the gathered clansmen. "Thank you, Per Acari."

Stefan frowned and took a step forward. Enough was enough.

"There you are, Stefan," John Denning said, coming from behind Pritchard. "Monopolizing the pretty lady." Denning had a drunken grin on his face, though Stefan knew Denning hadn't been drinking. Denning performed a sloppy salute at Beatrice, who stiffened and drew farther away. "And look, Kaim, we've found our missing guest. Here she is, safe and sound."

Pritchard looked between Denning and Stefan. "That tunnel entrance should have been blocked. You wildmen nearly caused an interstellar incident." He snapped the words hard and fast.

Denning grinned at the derogatory epithet for the Northern Sister clans. "Wildmen?" he said. "Tonight we're cavemen!" The four of them were the center of attention—even the music had stopped—and the growing audience laughed, in part at Pritchard. The other Travelers huddled together, isolated and temporarily unattended by the crowd. Smaller and slighter when compared with their clansmen hosts, the three Travelers—two men and another woman—looked like dressed-up children taken to an adult party.

Stefan spoke mildly but pointedly. "What kind of interstellar incident, Mr. Pritchard? Beatrice simply took a walk." Did Pritchard know about their encounter in the cave? If so, how?

"What does it matter now?" Denning interjected. "She's safe."

"Yes. Safe." Beatrice sounded suspicious of everyone.

"Beatrice should not have been unescorted." Pritchard gazed sternly at Denning, then turned to Stefan. "Per Acari, the Numericans are my concern, not that of the Open Court, and certainly not yours. It worries the Adjusters, and me, when you sequester Beatrice. No matter how attractive you find her, recall that she's a guest of Earth. Please act accordingly, without further abuse of your social rank or its presumption of honor."

Outrage froze Stefan in place, that this nixt mirko, Poupey, should impugn his integrity. "I shall remember what you've said, Nixt Pritchard," he said coldly. It was Ropa's lowest form of address: nixt, nothing.

"So. We understand each other."

Beatrice stepped between them. "Thank you for your concern for my welfare," she said gracefully to everyone. "Truly, I'm fine. Stefan, I enjoyed our talk. And, Kaim, we only found each other. Judge Acari didn't spirit me away. But if you would accompany me back to my friends, I would appreciate your help." She extended her hand to Pritchard.

Pritchard glanced at Stefan and, as he took Beatrice's arm in much the same way Stefan had held it, he smirked as though he had won something valuable.

Stefan was sure Beatrice's sweetness to Pritchard was counterfeit, intended to deflect him from Stefan. He didn't fear Poupey or need her help. As Pritchard drew her away, moving with grace despite his broad frame, Stefan followed.

"No." Denning's heavy arm fell around Stefan's shoulders, restraining him under the guise of steadying himself. "They know your soft spots. Don't go after him without knowing who he is."

"I know him." Stefan tried to shake Denning off, but the clansman politician had a powerful embrace.

Denning's voice was urgent. "You don't know *what* he is. Listen. Pritchard belongs to Independent Defense."

"I'm not afraid of ID or him. He's a policeman; he works for the Court." Stefan finally jerked free of Denning's grasp. Denning staggered as though truly drunk. Nearby, someone chuckled and called out. Denning winked, but when his clansman approached, Denning waved him away.

"Your being here upset Pritchard." Denning sounded pleased.

Denning had invited Stefan to come. Stefan hesitated. Across the room, Kaim Pritchard was fielding questions directed at the Travelers, answering many of them himself, and bantering with the Waterman clansmen with the easy assurance of a native. He even gestured like a clansman, his feet planted widely apart with his hips thrust forward as Denning might have done. Stefan recognized the result of constant, low-grade contact with the Assembly. Pritchard stayed close to Beatrice.

Denning lumbered clumsily into the path between Stefan and Pritchard. "Listen. He's not just ID, he's traceless."

Stefan turned back to Denning, surprised. "Only the Adjusters are traceless. Shadow-men are tales to frighten children."

"Be frightened," Denning said. "And be careful." He clapped Stefan on the back, then walked off to rejoin his party.

Beatrice pressed her cheek against the cold window glass of the stuffy coach and stared out at the night sky. Its texture was thin and rent with holes compared to the plush darkness of the cave. Ground lights charted the human presence on Earth; star lights promised something more vast. It was that vastness she missed. On the

Ship, the window to unreal space had opened onto eternity. On Earth, something always blocked a longer view.

The limousine was comfortable. The four of them sat two and two facing each other—Beatrice beside the Fox, with Charles Syne and Mariyo Emit across—but Kaim Pritchard had joined them in the compartment. His jump seat was between Charles and Beatrice.

Charles traded blandness for Kaim Pritchard's veiled threats. She tuned them both out. Pritchard wanted information, of course, and was getting more difficult to put off, but tonight she refused to let herself worry. She stretched her legs against the ache of Earth's gravity. She still wished for the slightly lighter weight she'd carried on the Ship.

The Fox hummed an interrogative, directed to Beatrice.

Kaim Pritchard stopped harrying Charles. "Tell *me* about it, too," he said, affecting pleasantness.

The interrogative was too easily interpreted by their Hosts, particularly adept users of the Assembly. She didn't answer. On the Ship that was the safest response to threats, to pretend the stranger ceased to exist. It was natural to Friends. She didn't stop gazing out the window.

Pritchard was persistent. "Beatrice, I was worried about you. These wildmen are dangerous. I thought one of their native isolationists had harmed you. Please don't wander off alone again." He tried hardest to be agreeable when speaking to Beatrice, and ever since his confrontation with the Judge, he'd been particularly attentive. He was staring at her now, and would certainly continue to pester her unless she answered. After a moment he asked another question. "Why did you slip away from the party with Acari?"

Beatrice wondered why Pritchard disliked the Judge, as she had already labeled Stefan Acari in her mind. It suited.

"He's the kind of man who considers himself better than others," Pritchard continued. "You heard him, calling me names. An Inlander."

It was odd, Beatrice thought, that human speech was

fraught with pretensions of logic while the human mind was so better suited to registering emotion. No spoken human language was without the germ of song, a certain resident emotion conveyed in word usage or tone, irrepressible since human thought was dependent upon it. The word *Inlander* for instance. When he said it so derisively, Pritchard shouted his own feelings of inadequacy. She recognized who had begun the quarrel. Pritchard had baited the Judge—they had a shared past—then he'd been angry with John Denning for defending the Judge. Beatrice didn't trust Denning either, however. With Pritchard, one couldn't be sure, but Denning lied.

She wished the Judge was with her. His reticence and sadness had resonated in counterpart harmony with her own. He also was a special category from others, with grave duties to perform. She smiled at her reflection in the window, recognizing in herself the yearning to confide and obtain absolution.

The Fox touched her hand. A good friend, he seemed always to know what a sigh meant.

Beatrice leaned back and sang what she couldn't speak aloud because their Hosts were listening. To unattuned human ears, her sounds were formless, wordless, and odd; there was no rhythm and no clear semantic subtext. Their Hosts, Charles claimed, would never decipher song without their help; two generations passed on the Ship before their ancestors had used it. Certainly, their Hosts hadn't understood song so far. Nevertheless, Beatrice privately speculated about how close the emotional context of song must be to the integral management commands of their Assembly, making song potentially accessible to talented Assembly adepts, like Kaim Pritchard or Stefan Acari. The grammar was the same. Why not?

Beatrice sang of the tension in the crowded cave, of the silence in the tunnel, and of the man she'd met. The Judge's lack of personal camouflage had immediately struck a sympathetic chord in her. She sensed his very mixed desire to continue without the Assembly and yet to have its satisfaction—after all, it was a kind of song—

and the satisfaction of performing his duty. Her song echoed the Judge's voice, a quiet composition of self-confidence, uncertainty, and interest, just at the edge of his own singing. *I liked him* was the thrust of what she sang. *I wish him well.* She wished they hadn't sat so dangerously close.

The Fox didn't face her as he answered; song required only vocal contact, not direct address. His song was a brief reassurance. *No one is ill yet.* Honesty made him add, *So far as we know.*

There might be no illness. Or illness might already exist, hidden from them by Pritchard. The Assembly Adjusters could suspect their mixed gift to Earth.

Beatrice turned away from the window. Pritchard had been studying her face. "You like him," he said accusingly.

"He's clean enough to be able to judge and have his judgments accepted," she finally said.

Pritchard turned quickly to Charles.

"A wonderful party," Charles said dryly. "Thank you."

Beatrice looked outside again, glad of the night to hide the unfamiliar landscape. Forests were an acquired taste. She listened to the sound of the wind passing across the metal surface of the car and to the distant hum of the beacon. The deaths would begin soon, if they were to begin at all.

Chapter 2

When Beatrice looked at Kaim Pritchard, she didn't see a man, just a fleshy extrusion from the Assembly that commanded him. He knew everything about the Earth. He could speak every language; he knew every bit of specialized knowledge, as if information was a module attached to his brain. His competency was oppressive; his goodwill was a lie. She had hoped to avoid him. Usually he was lethargic in the morning.

"Where are you going?" he asked in a raspy whisper. "The others are still at breakfast." Pritchard cleared his throat, covering his mouth with his hand, and winced when his head moved. He rubbed his temple with his inside right wrist. He had dressed with less care than usual, and the faintly striped blue pants contrasted strangely with the pattern of his shirt.

Beatrice didn't answer. She went to a wall of windows overlooking the rear of their residence, Hilltop Lodge, outside of Bowl, and studied the misty morning. The sky was more gray than blue, and the damp air was as clammy as the cave the previous night. A slowly swirling opaque fog obscured most of the grassy field. Beyond it, the hilltop forest had become invisible, except for the treetops, which seemed to float above the ground, defying gravity. She didn't miss the trees. The forest had seemed messy and random. Its density gave the impression that the trees were walls encircling a prison. If so, Kaim Pritchard was the jailer. The Judge liked trees, however, and Beatrice had determined to give them another chance.

"The sun will burn the fog away," Pritchard announced from just behind her.

He was always right.

She walked away from him again. This central area of the main Lodge contained meeting and dining rooms, offices, and Pritchard's suite. On either side of the main Lodge, two attached wings of long halls with closed doors—the residential areas—extended diagonally, partially enclosing the grassy yard. Beatrice and her fellow Travelers used a few of the rooms. The rest were vacant. The emptiness reminded Beatrice of a massive dying off, like a view into the world just after the ravages of the Great Deaths. Pritchard's men stayed in an older, smaller building that lay between the two newer residential wings, and just in front of the forest.

The Lodge was thick-walled and heavy in appearance, like a fortress, except for the two glass walls of windows. To leave Pritchard, Beatrice went to the front window wall. Another open space, this one paved for vehicles, was also bounded by forest, except for the driveway. Nothing was visible in the fog but for a two-man patrol walking rounds close to the Lodge.

Pritchard came up beside her. "With the Assembly, an adept can feel a person approaching long before he's visible. You're safe inside our perimeter."

Except from you. Beatrice didn't speak her mistrust aloud. The Earth authorities wanted information. The caution that had protected Beatrice and her fellow Travelers had been created by the Ship's imposing presence beyond Earth's reach, but it was wearing thin. That was expected. The Friends on the Ship had planned that when the time was ripe—about now, when Earth authorities lost patience and it was too late to quarantine the Travelers—the Travelers would explain their mission, but because the real authority on Earth was the Assembly Adjusters and not the regional governments, an explanation was something Beatrice and her fellow Travelers had realized they must not give. Pritchard was the Adjusters' agent; he'd demand one, forcefully, once the Adjusters gathered their nerve.

Beatrice turned away from the fog drifts and glanced around the lobby, where she and her companions had spent endless inactive hours. Because of the outdoor gloom, the high-ceiling, timbered Lodge lobby was lit by electric lights. The illumination fell in scattered patches that only accentuated the overcast outside. An alcove contained a series of deadhead caller accesses. Through them, with Pritchard's permission, the Travelers had sometimes spoken with others of their Hosts without entering the Assembly. It had seemed desirable, both to Pritchard and the Travelers, to quell Earth's fears of the Ship and them. Beatrice's plan—reluctantly agreed upon by the other three—was to use a deadhead access to call the Judge this morning. They needed to sidestep Pritchard to discover the medical situation; she instinctively believed the Judge could be trusted. Kaim Pritchard, however, was capable of hiding an epidemic.

"You want to place a call?" Pritchard asked, following her glance. His breathing was labored.

She didn't respond, although with Pritchard alerted, she doubted she'd have an opportunity to call.

He grabbed her wrist when she would have turned away. His grip was hard. "To whom?" he demanded. "Stefan Acari? The Open Court is dangerous to anyone with secrets."

She couldn't resist. "That's why you were hostile to him? To protect yourself?"

Pritchard scowled, which was at least an honest reaction. His sometimes helpful attitude was a veneer. His pleasantness was an invention. "I know Acari. He's not the worst of them, but he's an Inlander. They won't take a meal with a nixt mirko, or speak directly to one. Most would die before letting a doctor who's not certified as clean touch them. They're vermin who took over Ropa because they happened to survive when others were dying the Great Deaths." Pritchard jerked her arm to emphasize his point. "Stay away from him, Beatrice. He'll only hurt you."

There were times when Pritchard was capable of authentic emotion, when Beatrice saw that he may once have been a child, someone's lover, or something other than the Assembly's pawn. This was such a time. He'd been hurt. She didn't believe it had been the Judge who hurt him, yet he identified Stefan Acari with those who had. He was jealous because she had spent time with the Judge and enjoyed it, as they both knew she did not with him. "That's not true of Judge Acari," she said more gently than she usually spoke to Pritchard. "I saw him eat and drink, like anyone. He was civil to you when you were rude to him."

"He's married," Pritchard said quickly. "And he never strays."

The Judge had not mentioned a wife, though he had talked a great deal about his son. She had assumed his wife was dead.

Pritchard saw something in her face. He released her arm. "You see? You can never trust one of them; they'll always disappoint you."

She shrugged and rubbed her arm where his fingers had bruised her. "We only spoke briefly."

"Then why call him now, Beatrice? Talk to me. You know I don't mean you any harm, but we have to know how you came to Earth, and why. Why keep secrets? Bring your ship into Earth orbit. Let us meet whoever is inside. Please. Talk to me." He reached out to touch her again. She pulled away immediately. Pritchard didn't know how to touch without making the contact feel like a restraint.

"What did you talk about with him?" Pritchard glanced out the window as though someone had called, and there was a slight delay before he continued. "What were you going to tell him today?"

"Nothing." She regretted her silence; she should have explained their mission to the Judge.

Pritchard began to cough, grimacing when it didn't immediately stop. It was a dry, shallow, hacking cough that sounded more irritating than alarming, but went on and on. He covered his mouth with his broad, freckled hand. He was perspiring, though the room was cool.

Frightened, she stepped back from him. He hadn't merely had a hard night. Kaim Pritchard was ill.

"Sorry." Pritchard struggled to catch his breath.

"I am going to call Stefan Acari. Now." Beatrice started determinedly across the wooden lobby floor. She and her fellow Travelers must learn how many people were ill and whether the illness was new.

Pritchard chased after her, wheezing. "The deadhead access won't work." His voice was hoarse. "From now on, the only caller access from this Lodge is by cap or internal connect. All four of you arrived with implanted connects. Why won't you use them and enter the Assembly? Beatrice, talk to me."

She stopped. He caught up. Light from a nearby table lamp lit his face. His freckles were prominent, and seemed more plentiful than usual.

"You can call Acari," he said, "but you'll have to use your mind and not your hands. Don't worry, Beatrice. You don't fully enter the Assembly to make a call. The connection is superficial."

He lied so easily and well she couldn't hear it in his voice, but the Adjusters wanted Traveler knowledge, and they'd steal it if given the opportunity.

She had seen people connect to the Assembly using the thin, flexible caps. Some closed their eyes and held their hands clasped together as they bowed their heads, like praying. The Assembly was a false god, a perversion. Bands were smaller, and used only for limited access, such as calls, but Pritchard didn't offer one of those. It wouldn't matter, anyway. She had an internal connect; they'd take what they wanted from her mind. "No," she said.

Pritchard smiled sourly. "I wish you would, Beatrice. As for Acari, he's leaving. He has space reserved on the early transoceanic Throw to Ropa." He rubbed his forehead again. His eyes were bright and slightly bloodshot. He coughed and tried to clear his throat of phlegm, but the attempt sounded like a prelude to vomiting. His eyes watered. He was worsening as she watched. As though embarrassed by his human frailty, he didn't look at her.

She couldn't have met his eyes, anyway. Kaim Pritchard was ill, and it was almost certainly her fault.

He made a long, grinding sound, then spat a glob of bubbly yellow sputum, flecked with red and black, onto the carpet. Beatrice made a small moan that wasn't song.

"Sorry." Pritchard sounded better. He began to clear his throat, then thought better of it. He hesitated before speaking, and began slowly. His voice was soft, to protect his throat; despite the words, it wasn't amicable. "Beatrice, I'm not your enemy," he said. "There are those who'd hurt you to get information about your ship. I won't do that. But leave the Open Court alone."

She looked down at the bloody sputum. The Fox made a habit of walking the woods, to expose himself, if necessary—he saw it as his duty. She'd accompanied him once, after they'd first arrived at the Lodge. "I'm going for a walk outside, alone."

"No, don't," he said, reaching for her arm again. "It's not a good time. You'll get lost in the fog."

"How could I, with your guards everywhere?" Her tone was acid. She evaded Pritchard and quickly walked out the door. She stood for a moment trying to gauge her direction, then set off determinedly toward the hazy forest.

Stefan watched the meca roll into his suite and close the door behind itself. Its black-glass finish shone with the perfection of a mirror. Essentially ovoid, it had protuberances at "shoulder" height for attachment of cleaning appliances. They looked like arms and made the mechanism humanoid, like a headless man. Humaniform serva-mecas were even more disturbing.

What operated the meca? Not the Assembly. Only human minds could connect. This thing was a mindless agglomeration of fabricated parts and inflexible logic, an antiquated throwback to Old Modern times. Such machines, although expensive, were popular among the clans. Even deadheads could use them, or those who chose not to connect, including nominal tickers, like Stefan. Bowl was as convenient as anywhere on Earth to avoid the Assembly.

He watched as a device that was part brush and part vacuum cleaner extruded from the meca. The black shape moved with pauses to adjust and calibrate, but then began to dust the surfaces as efficiently as any human. Judged by its work alone, the meca seemed rational. Without the Assembly, he sometimes felt no more alive than that. Would he become accustomed to this half-life existence?

There was a knock on the suite's outer door. "Stefan?"

Stefan touched the meca's control button. The brush and vacuum arrangement rose back into its body; the mechanism went dead, as if he were God taking a human life. Stefan opened the door.

"Stefan?" Denning smiled hesitantly while peering into the vestibule. "Is everything all right?"

"Fine." Stefan bowed slightly—it was more of a nod—then moved aside to let Denning enter the gloomy suite. The foggy morning sky didn't shine much light through the window. He hadn't bothered with lamps, and the meca didn't need them either, so the room was dim.

Denning went into the sitting room as though he knew the way; Stefan followed. The suite was the best in the hotel; the hotel was the finest in Bowl, but the town was provincial. Stefan's rooms included the large entry, a sitting room, a dining area, and a bedroom, all decorated with falsely aged wood paneling, thick carpets, and stiff fabrics in somber, intricate patterns that, Stefan had realized during other visits to the Sister Continents, locals mistook for splendor. This suite's color scheme consisted of variations on the color blue. It was not well-designed to lift one's spirits.

Denning glanced into the bedroom. "I half expected the golden girl," he said, with his usual irreverence. "There are two men and two women, but they're not couples. If she broke free of Kaim Pritchard again, it looked like you had a chance with her."

Denning was joking, but it wasn't funny. "I'm married," Stefan said.

"But not happily."

Denning's casual, unexpected reference to Stefan's private life as public knowledge felt particularly ugly. "What do you want, John?"

"I couldn't do that," Denning said. "I couldn't be a ticker."

Perhaps it was an apology. "Name one politician who could," Stefan said coolly. The dark room was too intimate, and reminded him of the darkness he'd shared with Beatrice Whit. Stefan had awakened remembering her. He had been happy in her presence, at peace despite the fact that he was self-exiled from the Assembly. His first thoughts had been of maneuvering an opportunity to see her again. He knew, though, that he must not do it. His infatuation with Beatrice, a Numerican, especially juxtaposed with his anger at Liada, would humiliate Tepan, and Stefan himself, when he eventually connected and dumped. He had to put Beatrice out of his thoughts. He felt a flash of resentment at the necessity, then repressed that too. There were manual lighting controls built into a table unit. He raised the lights to their brightest setting and sat in the most comfortable chair.

Denning sat, too, in a chair perpendicular to Stefan's, which caused him to face the window. He didn't immediately speak, but seemed to observe the fog obscuring portions of Bowl's main square and the buildings around it. He was dressed for business, in a shirt and loose jacket. Clothing seemed to have affected Denning's attitude; he didn't smile. He had pulled his hair back; it was thinning. Denning's facial tattoos were not as prominent as they had been at the Waterman party, when he'd probably applied cosmetic enhancements, but they still made him inscrutable. The tattoos were black and red lines on his paler skin, like tears flowing down from Denning's eyes; some tears were bloody. Stefan waited.

"Brace yourself," Denning finally said. "You spent time alone with the youngest, prettiest Numerican. Anything to do with them is popular—you saw my clan. People can't get enough; expect to have the utilization rating of an entertainer for your next dump.''

Such as it was, a Judge's privacy depended upon being of only marginal interest to most people. Popularity couldn't have come at a worse time for Stefan. "Thank you for the warning," he said, "but I won't be making a dump anytime soon. I told you so last night."

Denning leaned forward and placed a hand over Stefan's knee. "If you manage to beat the odds and stay out of the Assembly, then I'm glad for you, Stefan. You're entitled to privacy, though I'm sorry about your timing. I need you, and so do the Numericans."

Chary of Denning's intimacy, Stefan twitched his leg; Denning removed his hand and settled into his chair, spreading his arms across its back.

"I'm not a voter, John. Save your campaign pitch. If you have a reason for the Open Court to be involved here, then ask formally for a Judge to be sent. I'm not available."

Denning shook his head. "You have a secret. I don't believe you've been bribed. I don't believe you've done anything that the rest of the world needs to know. It's something personal. Have you considered using a web doctor? One of them could build a pocket to keep memory of your secret out of your Assembly dumps. The Open Court—the entire Assembly—would be better off for having retained you, whether or not it's technically illegal."

Stefan was interested despite himself, and unwilling to admit it. "You rationalize illegalities very easily."

Denning grinned. "I'd never make a good Judge, that's true, but I'm a good judge of men. Stefan, I like you. You're honest. You believe in what you do, and do it well. A politician knows how rare that is. So don't lie to yourself. A ticker's physical privacy screen doesn't extend very far and it can't cover your feelings. You think you've accepted the Assembly dumps, but you really haven't. Few men can, and those men are hollow. Despite your resentment, you won't stay nominal.

You're addicted to the ticker's rush. What's it you call using the Assembly? Playing God? You'll connect eventually; it may as well be now. We need you."

Stefan's connect tugged at him with increasing insistence as he thought about it. He'd never been so long outside the Assembly. Perhaps Denning was right. In some sense he really did not want to connect—to dump—and was using Liada's infidelity as an excuse. But Denning was also right that eventually he would. He wanted to believe his return would be because the Open Court's work was worthy, not from expedience or addiction.

Denning kept talking. "Pritchard was not too happy to discover you at the party last night. You have a reputation, Stefan, and to my way of thinking, it's a good one. Since I don't trust Pritchard—or the Adjusters who sent him—I hope you'll stay."

"What don't you trust?" Stefan studied Denning, realizing for the first time the depth and sincerity of his anti-Assembly opinions. Stefan had supposed them mere political rhetoric, since isolationism was popular in the Sisters.

Denning crossed his legs. "This area is a backwater, and yet our land local was *asked*—ordered by the North Sister Federal Council, really—to play host to the Numericans. The Council takes its orders from the Assembly, meaning the Adjusters. Why send them here, when every region is eager to have them? Why us?" Denning removed his arms from the chair back and leaned forward, closer to Stefan. "I think the Adjusters plan to blame the clans for something. The Open Court—you—could stop them."

"Blame you for what? This isn't enough for a Court inquiry."

"That isn't all." Denning stretched again, unable to sit still. "How's this? The Waterman Clan has been burdened with new, unreasonable demands because of the presence of the Numericans." Denning raised his hand in a gesture that was partly a protestation of honesty, and partly an attempt to prevent Stefan from interrupting. "They brought a parasite to Earth. A barnacle. The sewer system has become infested with them. They're hard to loosen once they're encrusted in a pipe."

"Clogged drains? You need more plumbers, not a Judge."

"The cost has fallen on the Waterman Clan. That isn't fair."

"Raise the fee you charge. They're not enemies; the Travelers are your cousins, descendants of people sent out from the Sister Continents before the Great Deaths. Your own clansmen say so."

"Too many people died too quickly to keep a cultural continuity; we aren't the Amercans, however much we pretend." He laughed. "Anyway, I know history, too. History doesn't make men cousins."

Stefan sighed. "You want to use the Travelers' presence to criticize the Assembly. Find a different campaign issue, John. The Assembly is honest and I don't share the Sisters' xenophobia."

"Just Ropa's snobbery. And I'm not a xenophobe, Stef."

Stef. From a tattooed wildman, the intimacy was offensive. Stefan got up and went to the window, away from Denning. There was an uncomfortable justice in Denning's remark. Denning wasn't a xenophobe, while Ropans, even Stefan, were snobs regarding the clans.

"You're interested in the Numericans," Denning continued, pretending to be oblivious of his own rebuke. "Just ... explore. Your questions have to be answered, unlike those of a local politician."

Stefan faced him. "The Travelers don't own anything; their shuttle disappeared under the ocean. They're wards of Earth. They couldn't compensate the Waterman Clan for the cost of unclogging pipes, even if I ruled they had negligently caused a problem."

"They have the secret of faster-than-light travel; they have that ship. What are those worth?" Denning crossed his arms against his chest and waited.

Stefan came back from the window and glared at Denning. "That's it, then. You want me to force them to tell their secrets." Stefan's sudden anger came from nowhere in his consciousness. He remembered Beatrice speaking of darkness as a friend; he would protect the Travelers from forced revelation, from anything like his compulsory dumps. "They haven't committed any crime. However much the people of Earth might want to know something, they can't simply take all knowledge as their right. The Assembly can't have everything it wants. The Travelers are entitled to their privacy and their secrets."

Denning's tone was warmer than his words. "I hadn't realized you'd become an UN-Assembler." The UN-Assemblers were terrorists, mostly from the Sister Continents, violent opponents of the Assembly. As Stefan immediately objected, Denning cut him off. He gestured loosely with his hands, like a lecturing teacher too polite to point. "Never mind. Of course you're not. It was a joke, a poor one. But your attitude is dangerously naive. You should have privacy. No one really needs to know your secrets. The Numericans are something else again. One way or another, they're going to tell us about their ship and Numerica. The Adjusters will act, and to be perfectly frank, they'll be right. It isn't a matter of the Assembly, but of the security and future of Earth. For the Numericans to arrive from the stars in that great hulking ship and tell us nothing is ... unacceptable. But please. Pritchard brought the Numericans to my hometown for a reason. The Adjusters don't like the clans, or me, and we would make excellent scapegoats. Stay awhile. The Open Court could be our only protection. Stefan, I'm afraid."

Denning seemed sincere, but he didn't stir as Stefan observed him. "You know more than you're telling me," Stefan said.

"No, nothing. But I have a politician's instinct for when something isn't right."

"And I have a Judge's instinct for knowing when I'm being used. Sorry, John, but the Open Court doesn't stand guard duty, and as I've said several times already, I'm nominal." Stefan walked back to the window, glanced outside, then came back to Denning. "There are only four of them. Hardly a threat. Why doesn't everyone leave them alone?"

"Pritchard is traceless. If you care about the Numericans, Stefan, then ask yourself why a man so unaccountable for his actions has been placed in charge of them by the Adjusters." Denning stood, facing Stefan directly. "Last night you seemed to know each other. What was Pritchard like then?"

Poupey, the charity student, had been untrustworthy; as Kaim Pritchard he was a traceless, direct agent of the Adjusters, with custody of Beatrice. Then Stefan realized he was getting caught up in Denning's conspiracy fantasy. "John, the Open Court is part of the Assembly. Why do you trust it?"

"I'm not sure that I do," Denning said. "It's you I trust. But I see I haven't convinced you. Well, Pritchard will be glad you're gone. He'll be able to do anything he wants to anyone."

"You're exaggerating the powers of Independent Defense, John."

"And you're underestimating the power of the Adjusters." Denning walked down the short hallway to the suite's exit. Stefan followed and at the door, Denning turned around. "Stefan, promise me that if the clans are blamed for anything to do with the Numericans, you'll return to Bowl and investigate. Please."

John Denning, as important a man as lived in the Northern Sister Continent, was afraid. "Of course, John."

After Denning was gone, Stefan stood for a while at the window. Bowl was shrouded in white gloom. He felt as though his mind was wrapped in the same mist. The Assembly awaited him, just beyond his consciousness, but for once Stefan wasn't sure connection would clarify anything. The Throw to Ropa would leave before there was sunlight.

One advantage of the Sister Continents was the prevalence of deadhead caller accesses. A clerk in the hotel lobby directed Stefan to a bank of separate booths in a room set aside for that purpose.

The unit had a keyboard, like deadhead accesses in Ropa, though it had an odd arrangement of keys, not alphabetical, making it difficult to use. He turned on power in the interface unit and read the explicit instructions printed to the side of a large, empty frame. The local system improved on even the best Ropan model, which had only a flat, two-dimensional screen for viewing the other party to the call. The clans' model provided a holographic display inside the frame. On a real call, using the Assembly through a connect, a caller could hear, see, and even smell the called environment. Callers were virtually present with each other. Stefan would miss that impression of real life, but the call would be a better substitute than in Ropa.

The Assembly's grammar required certain formulas or codes before calling through a connect. The deadhead access made that unnecessary—calling instructions were installed into the mechanism—but Stefan had to consciously suppress recalling the commands, they were so natural for him; otherwise, he would have entered the Assembly through his connect and dumped.

Then there was the matter of personal call codes. Like a recipe, a call code was composed of necessary ingredients, but personally spiced. For family and friends, the code was individual and intimate, a composition of words and emotion-laden images that seemed to create the essence of the person in his mind, and which led to a completed link. Since his codes were mental images, he could no longer use them. For when a deadhead or a stranger called, there were long number-letter strings assigned to each person or business; Stefan had difficulty recollecting them.

He pecked at the keys, fuming at the method's clumsiness. Mistakes would be a constant problem. Finally, he heard Drom Hanzin's voice; a moment later Drom, Stefan's chief steward of the Acari estate, appeared in holographic miniature inside the frame. A peripheral, though not a ticker, Drom had an implanted connect and didn't need a cap. In Bowl it was morning, but at Acari it was midafternoon. Drom was outdoors; the sun was so strong that it made Stefan squint when he stared into the hologram, as the instructions advised. There were no clouds in sight. Dust rose from the stone drive. The only green was the line of dull evergreens along the visible portion of the drive. They needed rain.

"Will you be returning home soon, Per Acari?" he asked. Between them, use of Stefan's court title was entirely proper.

"Would delay be a problem?"

"No, sir, but your wife has asked me several times." If Drom suspected marital tension existed between Stefan and Liada, he was too professional to show it.

Stefan smiled. For once, Drom could not know his employer's psyche; Stefan's thoughts and problems could only be guessed. For now he was like other men. "I plan to return on the Throw later this morning. I'll be in Paris tonight."

The hush around Drom was unnatural. Sound transcription during even a normal call missed softer noises, so there were no birdcalls, no distant shouts, no susurration of wind through the evergreens. Background sounds didn't exist. This call was only slightly worse than usual. "Drom. Anything else?"

"We've begun drip irrigation, tapping into our water reserve."

"A good idea." It was a choice that, on most estates, the lord would have made, but because he was a Judge, it was Drom's choice, not his. An Open Court Judge who was also an Inlander needed an excellent steward, an independent one who could even, when necessary, be secretive—as by his position, Stefan could not be—for the greater economic benefit of the estate, but it rankled. Stefan nodded curtly, ready to end the call.

"Shall I inform Pera Acari that you called, Per Acari? Or neglect to mention it?"

Drom was prying. Did he know about Liada's infidelity? Stefan frowned. "I'll call her." He broke the connection without a parting word, by pressing a key on the machine.

Usually, he savored the sensations of the swirling void that was the vacant interface between mind and Assembly. It had never felt entirely empty to Stefan; he perceived a distant universe, possibly the Assembly files and functions, possibly the multiplicity of engaged minds. The Adjusters, who had made a complete and permanent joinder with the Assembly and who adjusted its operation whenever necessary, must reside in those margins, too, while at rest. It could be that it was their personalities that clung to this unreal place where he had often lingered. Through a connect, the Assembly held a multiplicity of emotional tones, depending on the day and the files with which one was connected. On this fringe, the mood was always one of sadness, though of such overwhelming scope that it was glorious. As a deadhead, a nominal, Stefan felt none of this. The call simply ended in silence.

He sat, head bowed. He didn't want to call Liada. Quickly, before he could change his mind, he tapped in the code to his house, not to Liada individually. She wouldn't be wearing her cap, but the reading room of his house was integrated into the Assembly in a similar way to that of deadhead connections, though a true deadhead couldn't use it. The holographic image displayed was of his empty reading room. The call alarm would have rung throughout the house. She would know it was him.

A door slammed upstairs. The noise reverberated through the Assembly's unnatural hush. Stefan settled into the chair in the deadhead caller access, trying to get comfortable. He failed.

Liada hurried into the reading room. "You're staying away longer than *you* expected," she accused, staring at Stefan's favorite chair, where the Assembly had automatically installed his image.

"No. I'm coming home on the next Throw."

She scowled, apparently unhappy that her nastiness had been too hasty, and turned away. The wall she faced was paneled in a dark, polished mahogany, but above the mantel molding, between two matching, glass-doored cabinets displaying eight generations of courtesy gifts from tenants, there was a beveled mirror in which he saw her reflection, but not his own. The deadhead access he was using was too crude for that.

Liada had the face of a sophisticate, with dark, straight, fine hair so black it made her pale skin ghostly. She never went outdoors in daylight without a wide-brimmed hat. Her small, red mouth had thin lips, often pressed tightly together as though preventing the escape of any indiscreet sentiment. She rarely showed her teeth, even when she smiled, which was uncommon, anyway, in Stefan's recent experience, though she must have smiled for someone. He had believed her face looked weary, but Romaric had claimed she had dangerous eyes. That had been on the morning of Stefan's wedding, and immediately after that statement, Romaric had smiled and congratulated Stefan, heartily, his attention lingering on Liada's womanly hips in the close-fitted red wedding dress.

Stefan had considered himself lucky. The marriage was inevitable, having been arranged while they both were children; his luck lay in having a bride so beautiful, rich, and clever as Liada Zehn, since he'd been a younger son, not heir to Acari. Liada's hips had thickened very little with the birth of Tepan, but lately they had thickened again. Until she'd told Stefan she was pregnant by another man, however, he had not noticed. Instead, lately, he watched Liada's hands. Her fingers were long, pale as her face, and the nails tapered like swords, in the current fashion, to a tip she polished in red. During arguments they would be motionless, often clenched, but once unsheathed—when she pointed them at Stefan—they did not rest until a wound had, in some fashion, been inflicted. "Aren't you going to apologize for leaving without saying good-bye?" she asked.

"It's never done any good. You aren't less angry afterward."

"You're only polite when it's of some benefit to you?"

It would be easy to be drawn into an argument. She seemed to try to provoke them, while Stefan wanted to have as little to do with her as possible, within the confines of their hollow marriage and the existence of their son.

She turned back, seemingly facing him. The delicate gray silk of her thin, clinging tunic flared from midthigh to midcalf. As she moved it swirled prettily, exposing the lavender undercolor. She might have dressed up to be conciliatory, since she expected to greet him in person in a few hours, but the tunic emphasized the expansion of her waist. She wanted him to ask who the father of her child was. He knew it as much as he knew anything about his wife, and refused to give her that satisfaction. "You're always so smug," she said.

"Smug men are happy, Lia. A smug man doesn't have an unfaithful wife." He took a breath and stopped before he said more. The inadequacies of their marriage were as much his fault as hers. Because he was a ticker, because he'd known that what he felt would be broadcast in his dumps, had he restrained himself from loving her as he had restrained so much else? Had the Assembly made him *unable* to love? Yet he had been betrayed, if only by her weakness.

She twisted at the waist, then back, an indecisive, girlish motion. "We need to talk."

"No, we don't." He supposed she was concerned that he would turn her out. Foolish as he would look—the cuckold—her position was worse. He could rightfully retain her dowry and Per Zehn, her father, might well refuse to take her in. Was she frightened? Her hands were limp, held at her waist as if she felt ill, or to protect it. He dreaded exposing his private life to everyone who cared to follow his dumps—litigants, gossiping locals, Acari friends, and Acari enemies—but then it would be over for him, while her entire life could change with a divorce. The grounds, the choice, were his.

"I saw you at that party." She loaded distaste into her inflections so heavily that he was reminded of the subtlety of tone in Beatrice's voice. "It was in the newsbrief.

You had one of those Numericans, a scrawny woman, hanging on your arm. You were smiling."

He felt an urge to justify his pleasure in Beatrice's company to Liada, but stopped himself in time. He wouldn't let her innuendo soil his brief encounter. "Maybe you're right; we do need to talk," he said. "We can't go on like this."

She bit her lip. "What do you mean?" she asked. "You could stay nominal; you're strong enough."

"I'm not nominal for your benefit and I won't stay nominal forever," he said. "I want to see Tepan. Please call him down."

"He isn't here." She flounced, showing off what had been a voluptuous figure, and still was to any but knowing eyes. "Stefan, stay nominal; then we can be together the way it should have been, as a private husband and wife. We can put this incident behind us."

"I don't think that's possible, Lia. I have a duty to the Open Court. Where's Tepan?"

"We'll talk when you get home," she said firmly.

"Where's Tepan?"

"At Ezio. With your *friend*, Romaric."

Stefan cut the connection. He used Tepan's personal call code and was instantly connected, since his son, as a minor, had no choice to decline his father's call. Stefan recognized the nursery dining room at Romaric's estate.

"Papa!" Tepan cried out, kicking back his chair at the table and extending his arms to be picked up by the image of Stefan that the Assembly had caused to appear. When well-set, Assembly calls were seamless, and Romaric's entire residence was elaborately integrated into the Assembly network, since neither he nor his father or grandfather had ever been peripherals. Aside from the sudden appearance, as if he'd magically been transported, there were no standard visual cues indicating Stefan was not actually present.

"It's a call, Teppy," Romaric's eldest son, Frey, said with the condescension of a ten-year-old addressing a much younger child. Romaric now had five children, one born every two years, as if he kept a regular appointment with his wife.

"I just wanted to see you, Tepan," Stefan said. Back in his deadhead access booth, Stefan moved, and in Ezio estate he appeared to kneel to his son's height. He hungered for a hug, which was impossible. Tepan, with a sheepish glance at his idol, Frey, had already lowered his arms.

Tepan's own nurse, Rezya, was standing near a screen—it showed a garden scene—that hid the entrance to the nursery kitchen. "Is he well?" Stefan asked.

Rezya, one of Liada's latest in a succession of apparently unsuccessful hirelings, curtsied and blushed. "Of course, sir."

Stefan wanted to know how Tepan had spent the day, what he had studied and played, the details of the clever things he'd said and done, but to pester Tepan or his nurse for information might embarrass them and would certainly interrupt the meal. Already, Romaric's six-year-old was throwing peas at his two-year-old sister. The Ezio family nurse was glowering at Rezya, as if she were to blame for Stefan's disruptive presence.

Tepan solemnly asked Stefan to stay. Stefan shook his head. "I can't. I'm coming home, though; I'll be there tonight." He hesitated, then added in a lower voice, "I love you."

Tepan smiled, then glanced at Frey—Romaric, though a good friend, took little interest in his or any children, so Stefan's involvement was Tepan's one superiority over the older boys. To diffuse it and forestall teasing, Stefan said a few words to Frey, inquiring after his schoolwork and the scores in the local football league, before ending the call. He had to pack and get to the Throw field. There wasn't time, he told himself, even to attempt to place a call to Beatrice.

"Welcome home," the Hosts had said. As Beatrice rushed away from Pritchard into the misty field, her every perception emphasized the alien nature of the surroundings. She ran toward the side of the Lodge, where the Fox often began his solitary walks along a gravel path, but the pavement had been invaded by wriggling, reddish-brown worms. She had to go slowly or squash them. The air smelled of the worms and moist soil. As if the mist had deadened sound, there was nearly total silence. Then, as she left the pavement, the ground became uneven and spongy underfoot, improperly alive.

This wasn't home. Home was her niche in the Ship's human shelter. Home was the smell of boiled tsampa. Home was Eyni, laughing at something witty she had sung, or sharing a lament for the dead. Home was where a person went when she needed comfort. Home wasn't terrestrial.

Moisture from the dewy grass soaked her thin slippers. Sogginess between her toes felt dirty. The wet slipper rubbed against her left heel. Occasionally, the slippers squeaked.

She saw the path through the fog as she got closer, but not far along it. Strange as the world was, however, she wouldn't return to the Lodge. Pritchard, who had quickly understood the Travelers' limitations, would expect her to creep back. She went on.

Pritchard's cough might be a minor cold, or the result of too much conversation shouted over the party noise. His freckles might just be freckles, and not symptoms of internal bleeding. It could be coincidence, and humans might now be resistant to the pathogens the Travelers carried. Beatrice didn't believe it. Pritchard had spent too much time too close to them. The only question was the severity of his illness. Had she killed him?

She rubbed her skin, feeling its slick texture, just slightly softer than human. This bit of the Friends hadn't reacted to Earth. Neither she nor any of her fellow Travelers was sick. Those were good signs, yet they increased her guilt. Better if illness went both ways.

Beatrice reached the forest path. The fog worsened inside the woods, as if the tree branches caught and kept it. Trees rose from vapor-shrouded ground like scraggy brown columns irregularly arranged. Their leaves were grayed by the mist, as though a white fire had charred them. The fog ceiling was lower than the treetops. The horizon was the edge of the farthest tree still hazily in sight. The world was limited and latent. It frightened her in the way no Kroni aboard the Ship ever could—she didn't understand it.

She continued forward anyway, stubbornly unwilling to turn around. The path was clearly visible because the white gravel stood out against the darker ground. She wouldn't lose her way.

Stagnant rainwater had puddled in old ruts made by horses' hoofs. This was a riding path, but none of the Travelers had trusted a living creature as a vehicle, so Pritchard had sent the beasts back. Beatrice went slowly, but she kept on. There was nothing to do in the Lodge but avoid Pritchard. The Fox said the path ended in a waterfall. He claimed to like the woods. The Judge did. In the cave, when she had called trees obstacles, he had said they were majestic, but these shapes around Beatrice seemed like ancient, defleshed bones. The woods felt abandoned.

She stepped over puddles. Her feet scuffed the gravel. It made no sense that she didn't want to be heard, but soon she was tiptoeing, although that hurt her toes when they pressed against the sharp stones. She wished she'd waited for the Fox. Even Pritchard might have been an acceptable companion, a liaison between Beatrice and nature. She smiled at the image, then remembered his cough. Only time would tell.

On the Ship, diagnosis excelled, even when there was no cure. A person knew if he was ill. *Blessed are the dead,* she sang inside her thoughts. *Blessed are those who can still be reached.* It was an old lament, as old as the Friends' travels, a cloak for the dead. When the full community of the Ship sang, each remembering their own loved ones, the lament was a chain binding the dead to life, uniting the races who traveled together under the auspices of the Friends. Humans sang alongside Kroni and Flin, though they had no other common ground. The lament gave grief sound; like much song, it was emotion vocalized. Individual words were less important than pure meaning. Eyni, a Friend, Beatrice's best friend, said it was shared grief that had founded song. Grief gave thinking beings a reason to sing: to console one another.

Eyni. Beatrice shivered, though she wasn't cold. Eyni would not have liked this fog. He would have run back to the Lodge and laughed about his cowardice. Pride was not important to a Friend.

Beatrice's face tensed from her strained peering forward, trying to see what was ahead; her hands were clenched fists, close at her sides. Something moved in the brush. "Hey!" she called. There was no answer, but that didn't mean she was alone. Pritchard's guards had to be nearby, yet she felt the same sense of menace she had when the eavesdropper in the cave had passed her. She was sure the Judge had saved her from something foul.

A Judge. She and her fellow Travelers were also judges, or maybe not; they were testing devices, measuring sticks—even, collectively, a liaison, a bridge built to determine if the two separate shores were able to support the weight of contact. Or they were murderers, entirely cold-blooded.

Someone was there.

Beatrice went faster. She imagined humans running from the Friends in misty woods like these. They hadn't been friends, then, only incomprehensible monsters come to steal people from their homes, their families, and possibly to take away their lives. Of course, the Friends let the ugly, terrible Kroni capture their samples. Kroni, the friends of the Friends, never showed empathy, yet they sang, too. Those first captured humans had hated the Ship; they'd left diaries, required reading before this mission. Their lives had been short as disease after disease struck them. Only the hardiest and luckiest survived: Beatrice's ancestors.

The Friends had their own instinctive imperatives. Strongest of them was the hunger to reach out. Humans expanded and conquered; human societies grew. The Friends joined. They embraced and included. Their methods could be equally brutal, but the intentions differed. She couldn't judge them. She was not only a product of their actions, but now a party to them. Would the Judge call her arrival on Earth immoral? Someday, she would ask.

The fog moved. Some patches were thicker than others. As she walked, a heavy cloud paced her. She wondered how far from the Lodge she had come; without sight, there was no distance. She began to hum a child's song, simplistic and placid, but it was so incongruous here that the effect wasn't calming.

She heard running water and recalled the Fox's description—a waterfall and a stream. She understood the heavier fog. Understanding brought composure. She hurried. She'd visit the waterfall, then leave.

Ahead, a lattice-work bridge gradually separated itself from the mist. A tall man leaned against the rail, like a companion she might have kept waiting. She went up to him, pleased. To see anyone, even one of Pritchard's men, was preferable to suspecting an invisible watcher.

The bridge was narrow. He didn't move aside for her to pass, although he glanced at her, so she stopped beside him and leaned against the rail herself, looking down over its side. The sound of moving water was pretty, but the stream was lost in low-lying mist.

Neither of them spoke. Beatrice inspected him more closely. He wore bulky glasses that covered a good portion of his face, probably devices to see through the fog. His face was tattooed. Pritchard had begun hiring locals.

"My friend says there's a waterfall," she said to break the silence between them, which had become ominous.

He turned to her, moving slowly. He seemed very large. His black vest exposed bare, brawny arms. Raised lumps of scar tissue made patterns near his wrists. "So?"

She gave him a big, nervous smile. "How far is the waterfall from here?"

"Farther than you're going." Another man spoke—a man who had apparently followed her and come up from behind. Shorter and stockier than the first man, but also tattooed and wearing the same heavy glasses, he stayed just off the bridge.

She looked over the rail again, judging the distance down, and decided she could make the jump since it was into water. She knew menace when she heard it; these men would harm her.

As she was willing herself to go over the rail, the second man said, "You're coming with us."

Beatrice turned. She felt childlike in comparison to them, but she'd faced down irate Kroni on the Ship and wouldn't let mere men intimidate her. "Sure," she said cheerily, and seated herself on the rail. "First, can I try your glasses?" She pretended to glance at the man near her at the rail, and twisted around in order to reach for his glasses.

He stepped back to keep her from grabbing them. That wasn't her intention. Instead, she raised her legs and let herself fall into the stream. As she fell, she screamed. These men could not be Pritchard's, but Pritchard's men couldn't be far. Her voice didn't seem to carry in the mist.

Stunned by the sudden cold and the harsh impact of her body against the water, she gasped, then held her breath as water covered her. Her right arm and both legs scraped against rock she hadn't seen from above, but not so badly as to break them. Her water-soaked clothes weighed her down, but the fast-flowing steam pulled her along with its current. She struggled, then her face was above the surface. She stayed silent, trying to orient herself while keeping her head above the water as she was dragged along. She didn't see the bridge, or either of the two men, but she heard them shouting at each other. They weren't far, and they seemed to be coming closer. She wished she could swim, but could only let the water do its work on her.

A splash and curses. They were following; the smooth sound of graceful movement through the water told Beatrice they would catch her. She thrashed her arms, trying to increase her speed away from the bridge, but it was hopeless. She only managed to slow herself, and somehow got her face underwater.

A hand grabbed her ankle, then yanked her. She kicked, but he didn't release her. He towed her backward. Underwater still, she couldn't breathe. Her right side scraped against a rock. Desperate, she forced herself to stop fighting. Her head came out of the water, then she was upright, on her feet, secured by an arm around her chest. She coughed, trying to catch her breath. Water dripped down her face. Her drenched clothes clung to her. She shivered. The water was shallow enough that she supposed she might have been able to run through it and escape, if only she'd known. If only they hadn't found her.

The man turned her roughly to face him. Through the watery veil of her hair, which she couldn't push aside because the man was restraining her, she saw the second man wading toward them. On him, the stream was only waist high. He held something white in his hand.

She was still gasping for breath, but managed to ask, "What are you doing?" She realized they wouldn't understand; she'd asked in song.

Her immediate captor shook her violently. "Stay still! No noise or I'll have to hurt you." He pushed his heavy glasses up onto his forehead. She didn't recognize him.

There were others in earshot who might help her. She took a breath and screamed.

He slapped her. Her head pitched back; her face stung. Her nose was bleeding.

The second man reached them. He extended a white cloth as if she should examine it. She tried to duck away, but the first man gripped her hard, pinching her waist; with his other hand, he yanked on her hair and pulled her head back. The second man pressed the cloth against her nose and mouth. It stank. She turned her head, but her first captor held her. The world trembled, blackened, and then was gone.

Chapter 3

Marta Denning couldn't run quickly, but she did run, crossing the pavement of the Throw field like a bouncing ball, hopping from impact to impact with force but not grace, her time in the air gradually decreasing, the distance traversed lessening. She was walking before she reached the gate, but her effort had been sufficient. The Throw to Paris hadn't boarded; the gateman had held the passengers, certain, as was everyone watching— and they all were—that such exertion implied an urgent, weighty cause.

Stefan had recognized her from halfway across the field and known she must be coming for him. He tried to sink back into the crowd of clan and Ropan businessmen. Tourists took a zep; the ballistic Throws were for those to whom time was important and cost wasn't, but even businessmen were eager for entertainment after the lengthy delay. They turned to Stefan, exposing him as Marta Denning approached with a directness bred of desperation and fatigue. Reluctantly, he came forward.

"John," she huffed. "John." She pressed her hand against her chest above her heaving bosom, as though that could help her catch her breath. At least she was fully clothed.

"John sent you?" Stefan supplied the missing words while trying to avoid providing additional drama for their listeners.

Marta nodded, without seeming satisfied.

Stefan had already refused Denning. He was about to comment on Denning's nerve in sending his wife on this last-minute appeal, when he noticed that Marta was crying. Her flushed face, as she gasped for air, was wide-eyed and frightened, not merely nervous. Tears dripped down her tattooed cheeks.

"Please," she whispered over the sound of her own hard breathing. She came a step closer and shook her head, impatient with her own physical inadequacies. She glanced toward, then away from, the other waiting passengers in mute appeal.

"All right," Stefan said. He took her arm to lead her out of earshot of the others.

"I can't hold the Throw for long," the gateman warned. "We're already a long ways behind schedule."

"I understand," Stefan said. He led Marta back the way she'd come, toward the fence meant to keep casual visitors away from the boosting Throw. He didn't go far. He didn't want the gateman to presume he was staying in Bowl. Marta's fleshy arm quivered in his hand; he let go. "Marta, what is it?"

She had recovered enough to talk. "John. He was taken into custody—detained they say, for questions." Her eyes implored him to understand more.

John Denning had been denied assistance from the Open Court and then arrested. It looked too conveniently coincidental, except Marta didn't seem to be acting.

"They took him, then nothing," she said. "He's dropped out of the web—the Assembly—like he's *dead*. I tried to call you on his priority." Marta was babbling, and her clan accent had thickened.

"Who arrested him? Why?"

"Don't know," she wailed. "No one said nothing, except it was on authority of Independent Defense!"

"Pritchard." Stefan needed Marta to pull herself together, but assuaging the fears of excited women was not something at which he excelled. He patted her arm. "Marta, please. Where did they take him?"

She shrugged, and tears pooled again in her eyes.

Courts were prominent in the Northern Sister, and they had unique local rules. "Have you demanded the body location?" Stefan asked. The demand had a specific formula. No one could be held in the Sisters without the relevant local authority stating where he was being kept, and why.

"Couldn't," she said. "They say John's outside their jurisdiction."

Stefan hadn't left Bowl quickly enough to escape his duty.

"Hey!" the gateman called.

Marta grabbed Stefan's hand. "John always said to call *you* if there was trouble. Help him, please!"

This was what the Open Court was for. This immediacy, requiring instant intervention, was only part of it, of course, but the adrenaline charge coursing through Stefan, the questions he knew that must be asked, the plan of intervention already being outlined spontaneously in his mind told him that now—this moment—he had to decide whether or not he was a Judge. A nominal would walk away. A friend could only sympathize. A Judge of the Open Court would enter a preliminary intervention.

He felt the Assembly press against his mind like an errant lover. If he went in now, the truth about his marriage would be known, but then the revelation would be over; he wouldn't have to avoid the Assembly. *But will I ever get out of it?* a small voice inside his head wondered. And what about Beatrice? She disapproved of the Assembly; he was sure of it. Would she despise him?

Marta dabbed at her eyes. "Please." Her tone was deferential. She was begging his help because she trusted him to be a Judge. Clearly, she loved her husband; the most Liada might once have felt for Stefan was a modest affection. As for Beatrice, to her, their encounter had probably been just a pleasant conversation.

He should never have come to Bowl. He had no business here, except as a Judge. He'd known it when he came. So had Denning.

Denning. Ultimately, all justice was personal. He couldn't betray John's trust in the Open Court or in him. He couldn't leave a man he knew and liked to Pritchard's questionable mercy. He couldn't respect himself if he acted selfishly when he might prevent an injustice.

Stefan connected with the Assembly. It flooded his mind, so that for a moment he was unaware of real life. Immersed so deeply, he was not a Judge; he was not Stefan Acari; he was only a ticker, a heartbeat of the world inside. It was going home in a way returning to Liada could never be. The Assembly gave him license to play at being God.

Faster than conscious thought, Stefan's mind dumped into the Assembly. He was unaware of the process, making it deceptively painless.

He could reach for anything he wanted to know, and know it. The Assembly codes were a grammar that was entirely natural to him, as much so as retrieving his own memories. There was no center, and yet nothing was distant. Information existed at every gradation and degree. He was within it, part of it, a cell within a body of immense size. It was the greatest joy possible, and the deepest sadness. He remembered it now, though it was too much to recall or fully imagine while immured in fleshy limits. He was everyone, the unconscious consensus of a billion psyches. He was no one in particular. He was the depth of the Earth and the innermost center of life. It was inconceivable that he had ever considered withdrawal from this.

His attenuated individual thoughts echoed unnoticed at the borders of all the minds in contact with the Assembly. His emotions formed a fundamental module affecting the Assembly's nature, and thus their lives. He played God in a dollhouse of earthly size.

Stefan Acari. The Assembly seemed to call to him, as it always did, or else he separated himself from the rest; there was no knowing. It was said that Adjusters were simply the ones who never came out. Stefan thought of this separation as his self-song; like the theme of a larger work, it was his core, a composition that had emotional meaning beyond the simple fact of designation.

It took great effort to gather himself together into a whole after so long without connection. He wanted to revel in the pleasure of impersonal omnipotence, but there was work to do. *Here I am.* And he was. Once identified, to himself as well as the Assembly, Stefan rode the Assembly the way a man rides horseback, aware of the personality and will of the beast he rides, but setting their course.

The Assembly's psyche seemed more powerful than he remembered it. On its outer fringe, there was the sadness he always sensed, but it reached deeper than it had before. Inside, where the work was done, emotions varied like the weather, but there was an enduring temperament, as if each contact left behind a ghost that had coalesced into a soul. He had mentioned it to Liada. She'd laughed and claimed he had anthropomorphized an appliance, as though the Assembly was a giant meca. Thereafter Liada had sometimes referred to the Assembly as "Stefan's other wife."

Geography inside the Assembly was a matter of connections, not movement. The Assembly's grammar was emotional, and from a human mind, that meant images—subtle ones, given in a series—though an adept knew, as most people did not, that there was room in the grammar for improvisation. Nevertheless, the basic forms of command, the images that affected the chemistry of his brain and sent the Assembly into action, were as habitual to him as blinking. As he issued the necessary commands, they triggered a change in his perceived Assembly surroundings, making the Assembly more analytical, and a colder place, where work was done. This was what laymen saw, but it was not what Stefan craved about the Assembly.

No one absorbing his dump could truly know what he felt when he connected. Even in Stefan's own memory, lacking the immediate experience, the recollection was banal. Only another ticker understood, though peripherals, who connected nearly as fully but with fewer options for control, had some idea of it. Denning, a peripheral, called it a "rush," but it was more. It was life lived all at once.

"Will you help him?" Marta Denning was tremulous,

as though afraid Stefan had abandoned John. Only seconds had passed for her, but they'd been marked by Stefan's abstracted silence.

With the expanded awareness that came from access to the Assembly files and minds, Stefan viewed her as if from a distance. The low-level Assembly contact gave him broad insights and a constant shallow gratification that was an understated comfort of doing his job. He didn't delve into the available knowledge on Marta Denning, however. She was worried about her husband, and he wanted to set her fears at rest. Stefan smiled. "I already have. I just registered a preliminary intervention for an investigation by the Open Court."

She collapsed against him, sobbing with relief. Stefan signaled the gateman to leave without him.

"No willpower, eh, Inlander? You're back in the Assembly." Kaim Pritchard's snub nose wrinkled with scornful amusement. He had met them in a rather tacky public office labeled "Reservations." His manners inside his own domain—the scenic Hilltop Lodge, which the land local had given the Travelers—were even less pleasing, at least with regard to Stefan, than they had been at Denning's party. Pritchard glanced at Marta Denning, standing grimly beside Stefan, but didn't greet her.

After waiting so long to reenter the Assembly, relief from the constant tension made Stefan magnanimous. He was a Judge now, and not a private man; sarcasm was a sign of the speaker's weakness. Besides, Pritchard's eyes had a glassy, reddish sheen and he'd been coughing when they entered the office. He was ill; Stefan made allowance for it, though he stayed at a distance. Pritchard was not the type who would self-quarantine if he were contagious. "My information is that Clan President Denning's detention was done on your authority," Stefan said. "Where is he and why are you holding him?"

Pritchard chuckled. "Clan President," he said. "I'd say that's about equivalent to an Inlander's authority, wouldn't you, Per Acari? Except that the wildmen elect their leaders, unlike Ropans. Do you think you'd be elected, if your tenants could vote? How many people want a Judge to lead them? Or a man who can't control his wife?"

Stefan forced down the hot flush of shame; he could brood over the open secret of Liada's infidelity later. "Irrelevant, Mr. Pritchard," he said. Pritchard's blatant antagonism was probably an intentional attempt to obscure Stefan's just authority, although even the obnoxious were sometimes in the right. It was possible Denning's arrest was justified and his attempt to influence Stefan earlier that morning was a ruse. "The Open Court has intervened. It has authority even over you; I have that authority. Answer my question. Have you detained John Denning? And why?"

"How did she get you back?" Pritchard asked, gesturing loosely at Marta Denning. "Your Throw left hours ago."

The unscheduled delay must not have been recorded in the Assembly. It was one of those purely local inconsistencies meant, by its perpetrators, to save face for their clan. Perhaps Kaim Pritchard had made his move, arresting Denning, a bit too soon. No wonder he was touchy; he'd expected Denning's handpicked Judge to be gone.

"So the clans were covering up their incompetence," Pritchard said, apparently pulling the information from Stefan's dump.

Stefan reached out into the Assembly on a reverse geographic search, to identify the closed knot that would be Pritchard's access. Pritchard had an implanted connect and a unique, constant entrance into the Assembly—Stefan visualized them as doors. He wanted to be able to identify Pritchard in the Assembly. Stefan found nothing. He tried again. Nothing. Pritchard *was* traceless, even to a Judge.

"You see?" Pritchard asked softly. "I can read your mind."

Not only traceless, but able to sense Stefan's attempt. Pritchard could watch Stefan as if the Assembly were his eyes. It was greater access than a ticker had, as much as the Adjusters. Denning had been right about Pritchard's source of power. Nevertheless, two could play Assembly mind games. Kaim Pritchard, the nixt mirko from Zona called Pou, a louse, was the Adjusters' agent. There was no accounting for taste. Stefan collected every bit of contempt for others that a Ropan Inlander's life had instilled in him, however deeply he had suppressed it, wrenched it into his surface thoughts, and studied Poupey.

Pritchard blanched, which sent his freckles into high relief.

Stefan smiled and continued to highlight his disdain. "This is an Open Court investigation, Pritchard. You are obliged to answer. Independent Defense serves the Open Court. You'll obey me."

"This is a special situation. You have no authority over me."

"Nor you over me. Get out of my mind, unless you like what you're seeing there."

Pritchard seemed about to answer, then was stopped by a fit of coughing. It took time for him to bring his cough under control.

Marta Denning had meanwhile pushed a chair out of her way, going closer to Pritchard's position beside the window. She ignored the clatter as the chair tumbled noisily over, though it seemed to startle Pritchard. "Do you have my husband?" she demanded, low-voiced and intent on him. "Yes or no?"

Marta Denning was a short, overweight woman, certainly no physical threat to him, yet Pritchard hesitated, watching her almost warily, before turning from her and addressing Stefan, silently, through the Assembly, as though the two of them were on a call. "One of the Numericans has been kidnapped."

A detached contentment settled over Stefan. The investigation was acquiring a shape. Naturally the Adjusters, the Assembly guardians, were concerned for the Travelers. Pritchard had been given broad powers in order to protect them, but the Adjusters would have no reason to oppose Open Court involvement. "Which one?" Stefan asked aloud.

Inside Stefan's head, inaudible to Marta Denning, Pritchard said, "The one you can't keep out of your thoughts. The one you admire so fervently, and compare so favorably to your wife. And tell me, Inlander, how do you suppose your wife has enjoyed your latest dump? Your friends? Your tenants? Your dear little son?"

Except to be saddened that Beatrice Whit was the kidnap victim, Stefan barely felt the sting of Pou's offensive. What else could one expect from a nixt mirko? Even Pou's mental calling voice had Zonan inflections, and his method of attack was a vulgar and contemptible one, entirely in keeping with his ignoble background. Such persons were best ignored; a nobleman didn't tumble in the dirt at their bidding. At some level, however, of which Stefan was scarcely conscious, he disliked the role he was playing and the man he became, using every available means to achieve results. "What has the kidnapping of a Traveler—if it's even true—to do with Clan President Denning?" Again, Stefan spoke aloud, despite Pritchard's clear desire to keep information from Marta Denning.

Pritchard had turned slightly away while Stefan hammered him with arrogant venom. He turned back. "I have good reason to believe that the culprit is John Denning."

"What? No! That's a lie!" Marta shouted. "You know it, too, you bastard," she said to Pritchard. "If you do anything to John, I'll . . ."

"I control your husband's life," Pritchard interrupted.

Marta fell silent; she looked to Stefan.

Pritchard brushed his hair from his forehead. "I intend to keep Denning in custody until I know, with the Assembly's certainty, everything that's in his mind," he said. "Since he's a peripheral, getting into his mind requires his deliberate connection into the Assembly. So far he's refused. It must be a desire to hide unscrupulous dealings. But I'll break him, if I have to."

"He's torturing John. You've got to help him, Judge. Please."

"Show me your proof against John Denning, Pritchard," Stefan ordered.

"No," Pritchard replied. "Your investigation is superseded by mine."

"It's political intimidation, pure and simple," Marta said. "The Adjusters don't like John's opinions. That's all. John hasn't done anything wrong."

"I will order Denning's immediate release, and do so with the full power of the Open Court, unless you give me good reason why you are holding John Denning." Stefan stared at the overdressed Poupey, meaning every word and being sure he knew it. Lace cuffs! The outfit was ridiculous.

"Are you involved with these wildmen, Inlander?" Pritchard asked. "You were alone with Beatrice last night, and didn't enter the Assembly until just this hour, long after your meeting with Denning, during which a web doctor was mentioned." He smiled. "Were you really just sitting and waiting for the Throw? Tell me, if it was contested by the Adjusters' agent, do you believe your order would carry much weight in the Assembly?"

"Is that the best you can do, Pritchard?" Stefan said. "I'm entirely open, which is more than I can say of you. Shall we both be tested?" Yet the web doctor had been, briefly, appealing. Stefan twisted his estate ring around his finger, then realized he was doing so and stopped. He'd never liked wearing it.

"There are occasions," Pritchard said, "when the citizens of Earth prefer not to know what is happening, as long as they're assured it is well handled. They leave those to the Assembly police. In this case, to me." Pritchard moved his eyes beyond Stefan, to Marta Denning. "Some information is not public."

Stefan hesitated, weighing matters, and decided he would get no further with Pritchard while Marta was present. Pritchard and Marta had an antipathy that went beyond John Denning's arrest, as if they already knew each other. "You can leave," Stefan told her. It was an order. "Stay available. I may have questions to ask you, too."

She looked from him to Pritchard. Slowly, she nodded. "All right." She shuffled toward the door, stopped, and looked back at Stefan. "John hasn't done anything wrong, Judge."

Pritchard made a surly noise that became a cough, one that rose from deep in his chest and caused him to spit bloody sputum into his handkerchief.

Stefan bowed to Marta. "The Open Court is honest. You can be sure that my investigation will be thorough." Stefan walked part of the way to the door with Marta. "If John's innocent, he'll be freed."

"Don't make promises you can't keep," Pritchard said inside Stefan's head. His nastiness lacked deep emotion, but still had a smarmy ugliness.

Marta closed the door behind herself. As Stefan watched her leave, he wondered about her relationship with Denning, a powerful, attractive man who, unlike Stefan, had chosen his own wife. Why a fat woman of little formal education, pleasant but not extraordinarily so; ambitious, but only for her husband, not herself; hardworking, but more in the manner of a workhorse than a racer? Was loyalty so precious? He pushed that thought aside.

"She is an odd choice, isn't she?" Pritchard said inside Stefan's mind. "But an attractive wife has its disadvantages, doesn't it, Inlander?"

"So, Poupey," Stefan said aloud, "have you ever found a woman who would let you touch her voluntarily? Or do you prefer to rape them with your mind?"

Pritchard hesitated, then he laughed. "I can even feel what a strain it is for you to say that. You were the only one at school for whom I had any respect at all."

"A strain to be rude, yes. But I mean what I say, Pritchard. Tell me what happened to Beatrice, and why John Denning was arrested for it, or I'll enter an immediate order for his release. On the other hand, if you have reasons for what you've done, I will not interfere with you. I will even join your investigation and add my authority to yours."

"I don't need your help."

"Perhaps not, but you can't prevent me from providing it."

Pritchard exhaled—it was nearly a sigh. "Come here," he said. Pritchard was standing at the window. He turned to look outside.

Stefan was reluctant to approach an obviously sick man. Contagion was a lesson the Great Deaths had taught, and since three of the five original great plagues still existed, endemic in the population, though less virulent, it was a lesson that had not been forgotten. "What's the matter with you?" he asked.

"Nothing." Pritchard was sullen.

"Your eyes are bloodshot," Stefan said. "You coughed up blood. A hemorrhagic fever of some kind."

"It's not Red Death," Pritchard claimed. "I feel all right."

Stefan didn't believe Pritchard, but Stefan had survived Red Death. He was immune, though his parents and older brother had died. He went to the window, keeping his distance from Pritchard.

Stefan looked outside, following Pritchard's gaze. The trees in the nearby woods at the side of the Lodge still had a hazy look, as if the morning's mist clung to their branches long after it had vanished elsewhere. A party of armed men in drab clothing, but not uniforms, were exiting the woods, while a similar group seemed ready to go in. The two were conferring. They were too distant for Stefan to be able to see any but the broadest gestures, but they obviously hadn't found what they were looking for. Beatrice. No one was moving with more than deliberate speed. "She was lost out there?"

Pritchard nodded. He spoke through the Assembly, perhaps to protect a sore throat. "I told all the Travelers to stay inside, but she sneaked into the woods alone while I was working in my office. You saw yourself that she liked to wander. They all do. They often take walks along that path over there."

"Did anyone actually see her leave?"

"Unfortunately, no. The fog was heavy this morning."

Stefan watched the searchers. They moved efficiently. One tall, unarmed man was directing the others. He turned and glanced at the Lodge—seemed to look into their very window—then returned to giving orders to the men.

"They haven't found anything yet," Pritchard volunteered.

"Not even tracks?" Stefan let astonishment into his tone. "The ground is wet. Look at the mud they're leaving on the pavement." He pointed.

"I meant, nothing useful. There are tracks; they end at a stream. Apparently the kidnapers met her on the bridge and took her out of the area through the water. We're searching along the banks."

"With dogs?" Stefan hadn't seen any.

Pritchard turned to him. "My men know their business, Judge."

The mockery was back.

"I *am* a Judge," Stefan said, "not a litigant. I don't have a cause here, Pritchard, just an investigation." He gave the other man time to consider that while he himself took a step back from the window. "Has there been a ransom demand?"

Pritchard frowned. "No."

Not good, if anything Pritchard was saying was true.

"I'm not lying," Pritchard protested.

Stefan disliked Pritchard's voice in his head, like an inescapable mental whisper. "Have there been threats against them?"

"Nothing serious. A few crazies, already tagged by ID. The likeliest suspect would be someone connected to the UN-Assemblers. We suspect Denning is one of them."

And then there is you, someone connected with the Adjusters, who have taken upon themselves the job of dealing with Earth's interstellar colony. Stefan didn't need to speak aloud.

Pritchard chuckled hoarsely. "You've been talking to Denning," his voice said inside Stefan's head. "What proof do you have, except your arrogance and Denning's accusations?''

Stefan changed topics. ''Were there signs of a struggle?''

''Yes. And we've found one of her shoes at the edge of the water.''

''What about John Denning's involvement?''

''He was found here, on the Lodge grounds, about the time we realized Beatrice was missing.''

Stefan had assumed that Denning had been arrested at home, or at the Waterman Clan Hall. Puzzled, he slowly asked, ''Was he found walking the grounds?''

''No. He was in a coach.''

Stefan made a blunt sound of disbelief. ''That's all? He was driving to the Lodge and so you arrested him?''

Pritchard straightened from the tired, aching slouch into which he had gradually fallen. ''It's enough for now. You know it, Inlander.''

''I want to talk to Denning myself.''

''No. It would disrupt our interrogation.''

Stefan considered, then nodded. He would lose that argument. ''Can you tell me anything about the Travelers? What have they said about this?''

''I won't discuss the Numericans with anyone.''

''Travelers.''

''What?'' Pritchard spoke aloud.

''Beatrice told me they preferred being called 'Travelers.' Didn't you know that? You're their liaison.'' Pritchard didn't respond. ''I'm going down there.'' Stefan gestured at Pritchard's men near the forest's edge.

''I'll order my men not to answer your questions,'' Pritchard said, again through the Assembly.

Stefan studied Pritchard's clothing. He was casually dressed, but in the fussy style and bright colors of a Ropan dandy. Stefan usually wore black or gray, joined occasionally by somber blue. Pritchard wore pale blue pants, but his tunic, deeply scalloped along its edges and lacy at the wrists, was emerald green silk. The flamboyance struck Stefan as sad, the attempt of a nixt mirko, and a traceless, faceless creature of ID, to create a personal identity.

Pritchard heard the opinion. "I'm disappointed," he sneered. "I changed just for you."

The pitiable thing was that it might be true.

"Don't patronize me, Inlander!" Pritchard's voice was rough, as if the membranes of his throat were damaged. His face was red.

"Let's stop this, Pritchard," Stefan said in a conciliatory tone. "You're right; I don't like it either. Get out of my mind—I'll accept your word that you have—and let's behave civilly to each other. We both have a job to do: to find Beatrice, and get to the truth of her disappearance." He extended his hand in the local gesture. It seemed more fitting than a bow.

Pritchard looked at Stefan's hand. He didn't take it. "Each time you do a dump, you'll warn her kidnapers— Denning's accomplices—of what we know. You've received all the cooperation that you're going to get from me, Inlander."

Stefan dropped his hand, and stayed reasonable and calm. "I've worked on unfinished criminal investigations before. I can hold back from the Assembly during the detective phase. The importance of the Open Court is its impartiality, and between the kidnapping of a Traveler and your arrest of Clan President Denning, this is a very political case. You're going to need me, Pritchard, whether or not you like it. I'll stay out of the Assembly, if that's what you want, until you've finished marshaling your evidence. But meanwhile, I'm involved." With a certain melancholy, having relished his recent connection, Stefan gave the commands and broke free of the Assembly. For an instant, he felt very small, and lost.

Pritchard chuckled. His chuckle devolved into a cough. He shook his head as, coughing hard, he covered his mouth. His face and hands had more freckles than before; Pritchard was definitely developing a rash. Stefan moved farther back. When the coughing fit was over, Pritchard said, "I underestimated you. Not only do you wile your way into my investigation, but you even use me as an excuse not to make dumps."

"Mr. Pritchard, every word I've spoken is the stated position of the Open Court." There was no reason to continue the deprecation, since Kaim Pritchard could not get inside Stefan's mind, but their relative positions might still be useful, however distasteful it was to flaunt them. "I am a senior Judge of the Open Court, and an Inlander of Ropa. You are no one, and your actions can easily be disavowed by your superiors. If you obstruct me, then I'll publicly appeal to the Adjusters down in Southlands. We both know what they'll have to do." The ability to bluff was one benefit of having left the Assembly.

It seemed to hurt Pritchard to talk. "Conduct an investigation. You're right that I can't stop you, but I don't have an obligation to help you much, either. The Open Court is an anachronism. The Adjusters have begun to take a more active role in world affairs. When this is done, you'll see who it is that's in power, and who's disgraced."

Stefan walked away from Pritchard. He really was ill, but that didn't excuse him. "Beatrice was in your care when she was taken, Mr. Pritchard. It makes very little sense that she would be kidnapped by persons waiting on grounds—patrolled by your men—on the off chance that one of the Travelers would choose to take a walk on a foggy morning. It makes less sense that John Denning, president of the largest local clan and an aspirant for a major political office, would be lurking in his coach on the Lodge grounds with that in mind. It makes no sense whatsoever that an ID agent would reject, would recoil, even, from help offered by an agent of another Assembly-derived jurisdiction. Mr. Pritchard, I have tried. From now on, I must consider *you* my primary suspect. Interfere with me, and I will make an immediate new dump, letting every person on Earth know exactly what I think, and why."

Stefan nodded at Pritchard and left the room before the traceless nixt mirko could reply.

*   *   *

Stefan heard the Travelers before he saw them. He had walked about the Lodge, trying to get a sense of the place where Beatrice lived, and as he approached the open door to the Lodge's main dining room, they were impossible to miss. Their tone was human but their noises were not. More cacophony than speech, the sound was atonal and random, with no discernible pattern or beat, no tune, no harmony, no melody, no rhythm and no sense that it was speech. "What *is* that?" Stefan asked a guard stationed outside the door.

"That?" he said, with the faint superior familiarity with the otherwise unfamiliar gives. "They do it all the time."

"But what is it?"

The man shrugged. "Probably a game."

A woman's voice warbled. Before the sound seemed finished, she shifted into something approaching a yodel, then was silent. Another voice, this time a man's, twittered ridiculously. Someone whistled.

Outside with Stefan, the guard smirked. "It can go on for hours," he said. "I think they're crazy."

None of Pritchard's men had hindered him so far, so Stefan walked into the room. The guard followed, but protectively, as though the Travelers were dangerous, and he stayed near the door, hand on the butt of his gun.

The room was too large for their small group. Sunshine from the south-facing windows illuminated a few cobwebs around the high overhead lights set into the cathedral ceiling. Unused tables were stacked against an inner wall, but the worn carpet showed where they'd formerly been placed. Too many chairs were set at the table left available for their use, so it seemed as though a crowd had been there, most of whom had vanished. The residue of a meal for three was still on the table, pushed to the side. The plates were neatly stacked. Sunlight made the grease on them glisten.

Two men—Stefan recognized Charles Syne, the presumed Traveler leader—were comfortably sprawled with their legs extended over an extra chair. A woman, perhaps twenty years older than Beatrice, sat hunched forward, peering at hard-copy papers scattered between her and Charles Syne, making the table look like an executive's desk from the Old Modern Age. That anachronism, and its sordid association with deadheads and UN-Assembler criminals, reminded Stefan, uncomfortably, that these people weren't in the Assembly. They'd never been part of the great, ongoing plebiscite, nor had their ancestors. He went farther inside the room. None of the Travelers looked up. Stefan bowed and introduced himself.

The woman hummed to herself. The second man stood, walked past Stefan without appearing to notice him, and took a hot drink from the tarnished side of a stationary servameca. Syne stretched. Except that they were no longer making odd sounds, they seemed unaware of Stefan.

The man with the steaming drink blew gently on it, then set it to his lips. He decided against sipping it, apparently, and held it away from his mouth without having swallowed.

Stefan looked directly at this man, who was standing a meter from him. "I'm here investigating the disappearance of Beatrice Whit and the arrest of John Denning for complicity in it."

Nothing. These people could have been made of stone for all the emotion registering on their faces. These were Beatrice's people. The calm, refined, intelligent woman he had met, was one of them. She must have sometimes made similarly exotic sounds.

"I spoke with Beatrice last night," Stefan said.

The second man looked up from his drink. He studied Stefan in the way one examines a specimen, without expecting it to look back, or crediting it with intention when that happened. The woman stopped rustling her papers.

"What did she say?" Syne asked. After hearing their sounds, the altogether human voice and language were startling. Like Beatrice, he had a beautiful voice.

Stefan decided it was a test. "That she liked the dark.

She said . . . it was beautiful. That it drew a person inside." He stopped. It had been easy to forget with Beatrice in the dark cave, but having heard their odd
sounds and seen their peculiar behavior, Stefan was
forced to recognize that these three strangers were interstellar voyagers. There was more at stake here than the
disappearance of a woman, or the arrest of a prominent
man. If Pritchard's behavior regarding Beatrice's disappearance was evasive and ambiguous, perhaps it was
merely caution concerning a reaction from the ship. "I
mostly told her about myself," he said.

The man with the drink made a low, whistling sound
that ended in a click. Stefan shuddered. The Traveler
returned to the table and sat near Syne, but was no
longer relaxed. The two men made noises. The woman
returned to her papers, only occasionally contributing
a sound.

In daylight, the Travelers' amber complexions were
more prominent. He'd met Beatrice in a cave, and there
was something of the cave dweller in these people.
Large-eyed, with a kind of shimmering pallor, they were
made for dusk—they saw well in the dark. They were
small and slight. Together, they seemed to be a new race
of mankind, but four individuals were not a significant
sample. He supposed their coloring resulted from something in the Numerican environment.

Stefan pulled out one of the unused chairs at the Travelers' table, dragged it to a spot from which he could
face all of them, then sat down. They chanted something
brief and wordless, seemingly mindless, which ended in
a screech.

It was language. Bizarre, like nothing he'd ever heard,
Stefan was sure this was a conversation. He closed his
eyes and listened.

His initial impression didn't change. There was no easily recognizable format. He couldn't distinguish sentences or words. There did seem to be meaning, however,
just beyond his grasp, the kind of meaning that the unconscious mind creates without language.

Who were these Numericans? Why wouldn't they talk

to him? Why wouldn't they tell anyone about themselves? This was a mystery that the Adjusters had sent Kaim Pritchard to penetrate. Stefan guessed Pritchard had made little progress. Now one of the Travelers was missing and the Adjusters' agent didn't want him to investigate the disappearance.

Stefan believed in the integrity and the necessity of the Assembly. Local regimes varied; the Assembly was not an adversary of any of them, merely an unofficial but powerful alternative jurisdiction. It kept civilization together after the Great Deaths nearly extinguished humanity. It prevented regions from warring on each other. Would an agent of the Adjusters resort to kidnapping, so he could use stronger methods of persuasion on a Traveler without fear of retribution from the ship? Denning would say yes, but even just the question sickened Stefan.

Sunlight warmed Stefan's face and brightened the darkness through his closed eyelids. The Assembly felt very close, but there was no help for him through his connect. He thought of using it, just once and quickly, to contact Tepan, but decided not to make Pritchard privy to his thoughts again. Besides, Tepan had been at Ezio, and Romaric would protect him. Stefan opened his eyes, feeling as though he needed sight to find his way through what he wanted to say to these people.

"Do you suppose you can outwait us?" asked the second man. He finally was sipping his drink.

Stefan smiled. "I already have."

The man laughed. He made a quick, eager sound. He wanted to help; Stefan knew it.

"I want to find Beatrice." Stefan looked directly at the man, who was partly turned away. "Can you help?"

"You're the Judge," he said. He had a rich voice, and said "Judge" as a term of affection. "Beatrice mentioned you."

Syne made another sound, like a wheel skidding on pavement. An objection. The two men, with occasional commentary from the woman, continued making their random, unpatterned noises. The sounds sometimes overlapped; occasionally they stopped altogether. The Travelers didn't necessarily look at the speaker, nor the speaker at the listener. Not one word had been spoken in a language Stefan recognized, but he had no doubt that they were arguing about him.

The second man shifted position in his chair to actually face Stefan. "My name is Paul Talley," he said, "but Beatrice likes to call me the Fox. She thinks in archetypes; we all do, a bit."

Syne made a hollow, booming noise. The Fox turned away. He made a sound that caused a chill down Stefan's spine.

"Kaim Pritchard has arrested John Denning, your host last night. He says he's responsible for Beatrice's disappearance," Stefan said. "I know Denning. Not well, but enough to doubt he kidnapped Beatrice." Raw belief didn't constitute proof, even in the Open Court.

The Travelers met his gaze this time, as though despite their lack of cooperation, they felt no guilt and had nothing to hide.

"I won't stop my investigation just because there is a convenient target, nor if I find an inconvenient one. But I could use your help. Anything you know." Stefan waited.

The Fox raised his cup, making it a screen hiding his lower face. "I take a walk in the woods," he said. "Alone. Nearly every day, at approximately the same time. With Pritchard's knowledge."

"And that of all his men," the woman added.

Syne nodded slowly. "Beatrice left breakfast to call you; later Pritchard told us she had been kidnapped."

"I heard them talking in the lobby," Talley said.

Stefan straightened. "Pritchard and Beatrice?"

"Then the glass door slammed." Talley stood. His cup was empty. He walked to the servameca.

Stefan hadn't noticed, but the Travelers had fallen silent and were watching him. Pritchard couldn't probe these people through the Assembly. They had to be physically observed. Constantly, oppressively scrutinized.

Pritchard's men weren't only guards, they were spies. He looked; the guard was in the room, listening.

The Travelers had cooperated with him; they hadn't done as much for Pritchard. Despite the situation, Stefan felt an absurd pleasure. He had been trusted by people who were as near to alien as anyone in his experience. In addition, it had not been lost on him that Beatrice had planned to call him. She might have told Pritchard.

"Thank you." He got up, bowed, and started toward the door without expecting any response from the Travelers. They didn't bother to speak the obvious; social niceties were absent. Still, there was something more he wanted to say. He turned back. The Travelers were no longer watching him, but they would hear. As would the guard and, through him, Pritchard. "I like her, too," Stefan said. "Very much."

Chapter 4

Beatrice was determined to survive. She was sick. She was delirious. Her body ached. Death is the great privilege of life, Eyni had sung, quoting Friends' philosophy at the death of Beatrice's mother, but Beatrice had remembered her mother's fight against that privilege, how she had resisted it with every ounce of her will and strength. Beatrice had sung the lament with Eyni, but she knew she would someday resist death, too. It was a human trait.

Whenever her thoughts were coherent, Beatrice remembered her capture. It had become irrelevant, however; they had taken her just as she became useless to them. Pritchard had been sick, and she had run guiltily away; possibly her dunking in the stream had hastened the sickness, but Earth had infected Beatrice. Now, she would recover or she would die, but meanwhile, she could not be questioned.

She wished she could see her skin, or touch it, to know how it was reacting to the native pathogen. Her skin—Eyni's skin—was the second half of the test of contact. She couldn't check it, however. She couldn't move at all. Immobilized as though her brain had been disconnected from her muscles, she felt the burning, cramping, stinging, paralytic spasms as her limbs demanded that she move and she couldn't satisfy them. Phantom pain, but agonizing. Her neck wouldn't turn; her lips wouldn't open for scream or song; her eyes wouldn't close. That symptom made this disease entirely new and quite terrifying.

She longed to close her eyes. Nightmare images assaulted her mind like forced hallucinations she couldn't prevent herself from seeing. They left her confused and frightened. They didn't end.

There was one way left for her to communicate: the beacon, which cried its warning to the Ship and other ships. Her fellow Travelers might know of her paralysis and listen for her. Beatrice reached out to it, hoping it would be the Fox at the other end. She remembered how he had nursed her in the human shelter, where Friends could not come, when she sickened with a spiking fever caused by something brought aboard after contact with a world of Friends. As she had wanted then, she needed to know she wasn't alone. Talk to me, she sang inside as she reached out for the beacon.

Reached into nothing. The beacon was gone. Her fellow Travelers must have called the Ship.

Stefan discovered where John Denning was being kept when Pritchard's guards wouldn't let him upstairs in the older building. "How do I know you aren't holding Beatrice Whit up there, too?" he demanded, although he had expected to be turned away from Denning's cell.

The guard's answer came from Pritchard, who had followed Stefan's survey of the Lodge and grounds all afternoon, using the guards' eyes to track him. "Don't you trust the Assembly?" the man sneered with Pritchard's inflections.

Stefan could almost hear Pritchard chuckling. "I trust the Assembly," Stefan said, "but not any agent of it who uses another human being as a puppet." Stefan looked directly into the man's eyes, reaching for contact with him and not Pritchard. The guard turned away.

It was disgusting. Pritchard moved his awareness from man to man, riding them and changing mounts, as though men were transportation for Pritchard's psyche. The Adjusters apparently had uses for agents like Pritchard, but as far as Stefan was concerned, Pritchard had forfeited any moral authority. The essence of morality—and certainly the core of the ability to judge—was empathy. Somewhere in life, Pritchard had lost any vestige of it.

"Mr. Pritchard wants to speak with you before you leave, Judge Acari," the guard said in his own voice. He still wouldn't meet Stefan's eyes.

"How is John Denning being treated?" Stefan hoped that the guard, who had in all likelihood been humiliated by Pritchard's intrusion, might tell him the truth.

"Fine." The guard was noncommittal.

Was it a weakness in the man, or a weakness of Stefan's, that Pritchard's appropriation of another person's body affected them so differently? Stefan would have fought it with all his will.

Denning's prison was in the smaller, older building, separate from the main lodge and its two wings. The building also housed Pritchard's fifty or so men. Denning was heavily guarded. Probably, if there was any logic whatsoever in holding him, the protection was necessary. They were in clan territory, where John Denning was popular. His clansmen might decide to use force to free him. That was probably Pritchard's excuse for excluding the local authorities, including the police in Bowl, from the investigation. They were all clansmen. Aside from whatever news Marta Denning spread, the abduction of a Traveler hadn't been announced, nor had John's arrest made the newsbriefs. That silence felt wrong. The Assembly was a means of disseminating truth; censorship was something truth abhorred. It also seemed extremely inefficient for catching the kidnappers. Suspiciously so.

Stefan walked back across the grassy field between the buildings. Dozens of windows faced it, including the large windows of the lobby. He felt eyes on him like they were bugs creeping up his back. Beatrice's room faced this direction. Stefan had examined it carefully, but had not found any sign of her personality there. Clothing, all originating on Earth, had formed the larger part of her belongings. Toiletry items and a few hardcopy newsbriefs, which he had taken with him to peruse later, had constituted the rest of her personal effects. The Lodge contained rooms filled with gifts sent to the

Travelers by citizens of Earth, but Beatrice had not taken personal possession of any of them.

Pritchard's private office was just off the lobby. Its door was open and no clerk or guard was stationed outside, so Stefan walked through the doorway without knocking. Unlike the rather plain Lodge, and the shabby room where he had first met with Stefan and Marta Denning, this room had been recently redecorated—the carpet showed signs that furniture had been rearranged or changed—and it was sumptuous. Apparently the public antechamber of a suite, since a half-open door led to more personal, but equally ornate space, the room was filled with magnificent Ropan antiques. A tall standing desk, the kind used for estate or household subsidiary records not collected in the Assembly, was lavishly carved with flowers, and hares chased by foxes. It belonged in a lady's sitting room. Two matching oversize loungers, upholstered in yellow silk, were there for reading and record-keeping. Since for an Assembly adept like Pritchard, or Stefan, reading, research, and records usually meant partaking of the material via the Assembly, a reading chair needed to be comfortable but not necessarily well lit. The room's only lighting was from an elegant, if rather baroque, silver floor lamp placed incongruously just in front of the window. The place looked as though it were furnished with random loot stolen from a nobleman's estate.

Pritchard was alone, reclining on his side in a lounger, but his bent, cramped posture was that of a man in pain. It was a sympathy-evoking image, and hard to reconcile with Stefan's aversion to Pritchard's Assembly practices. For an instant, he almost excused Pritchard's misuse of his subordinates as a temporary necessity, then Pritchard spoke. "You don't have much experience with women, do you, Inlander?" he said.

Stefan wished Pritchard would stop calling him "Inlander." It wasn't even a form of address, only a reference or definition. He knew Pritchard was attempting to irritate him; the attempt was a success. Still, he need not let Pritchard know it. "I want the hard-copy transcripts of your interrogation of John Denning. Since it has all been outside the Assembly, it can all be put into text."

"She's a heartbreaker," Pritchard said.

"I understand that you were the last person to see Beatrice. You hadn't informed me of that fact yourself."

Pritchard blinked and looked up at Stefan. In the dusky twilight, Stefan saw that Pritchard's freckles had coalesced and become bruises. His face was slightly puffy, too, as though he had been beaten. "I wasn't discussing Beatrice," Pritchard said. "I mean Liada. Your wife. She's a beauty, Inlander. Gorgeous. I remember your friend, that bastard Ezio, saying so when we were all in school. I think he was jealous. His fiancée was a dumpy woman, a few years older than any of us, as I recall. You don't really understand what a woman like Lia wants, Inlander. You think that if you're a good man, then she'll love you. Women aren't like that. They want to feel they're at the center of your thoughts. But, then, even if you weren't so stupidly honorable, you couldn't lie. You're a ticker."

Stefan stayed absolutely still. He had to, in order to keep himself from physically attacking this shameless, loathsome, baseborn stain on humanity, this Poupey, leering over Stefan's mental images of his wife. Pritchard was ill, he told himself. Some illnesses affected the personality. Pritchard was the Adjusters' agent, for better or worse. This was a ploy to inhibit Stefan's investigation, and only showed Pritchard's own degeneracy.

"Do you realize how rarely you thought of her?" Pritchard continued. He waved his hand as if indicating Liada's infidelity. "Before all this, I mean. I would never make a mistake like that." Pritchard did not seem to be speaking to Stefan, but to himself, as if weighing his options for the future.

"You'll never have the chance." Stefan knew he should not be drawn into the conversation on Pritchard's terms, but it was impossible to resist. Stefan's mind was not a private place, and the physical privacy screen he was allowed, for decency's sake, was insufficient shield against this vileness. For the first time in weeks, Stefan was sorry for his wife, and felt guilty at what he might have done to her, however inadvertently.

"Don't be so certain," Pritchard taunted. "I've always hoped to meet her. I think I will, very soon."

Liada would never have anything to do with the likes of Kaim Pritchard, a nixt mirko from Zona. The idea, while repulsive, was also ridiculous. Stefan laughed, if shakily. "I want the hard-copy transcript, Poupey. That's an official request. And next time you try to distract me, don't be so obvious or so absurd."

Pritchard jerked as though Stefan's comment had been that of a puppet master pulling his marionette's strings, and he sat upright in the lounger. "There is none. We aren't keeping a record."

"Then start." Stefan had expected Pritchard's response, having encountered obstructionist behavior during other investigations. "Consider it an order from the Open Court."

Pritchard didn't answer. He seemed to pull into himself. He shivered. A sheen of sweat made his bruised face appear greasy. His green silk tunic was damp under the arms and along the side on which he had been lying. Perhaps it had been illness speaking.

"Have you been seen by a doctor?" Stefan asked. If Pritchard was unable to work, perhaps the Adjusters would send a replacement.

"I'm better; I've stopped coughing. It's just a headache now. Don't worry, Inlander, you're safe enough."

Self-diagnosis was dangerous medicine. Stefan had stayed a safe distance from him, near the room's entrance. "I'll come back in the morning."

"What did you think of their noises?" Pritchard asked, interrupting Stefan's departure.

Stefan hesitated, then turned back, sufficiently interested to be willing to discuss this with Pritchard, who had probably heard quite a bit more of the Travelers' sounds. "Obviously it's a form of communication."

Pritchard nodded. "How would it develop?" His voice was still husky.

"Something they designed to protect their privacy on

Earth?" Stefan hadn't had time to consider the issue of the Travelers' oddities before, but as he spoke he saw the fallacy of that. The Travelers' sounds were too peculiar. "It must be modeled after native Numerican sounds. It's . . . unearthly."

"There are limits on the human language ability," Pritchard said. "Restraints set by our biology and genetic inheritance. Our experts say this isn't human language. We've taped hours of it. Our best linguists, working fully appended to the Assembly, can't decipher anything. No vocabulary. No grammar."

Understanding hadn't seemed beyond reach to Stefan. "Then what is it?"

"I asked you. They rarely do it within hearing of strangers. Any insights?" Pritchard's tone was neutral; he was trying to draw information from Stefan without giving any away.

Stefan was vastly surprised that Pritchard would discuss the Travelers with him at all, however much he needed advice. "No, but it seemed familiar. I wonder how good your experts are."

Pritchard gave a brief nod. "I've wondered, too. None were even peripherals; linguistics doesn't attract adept students since language doesn't mean much inside the Assembly." He flexed his back without moving his arms, rolling his neck slightly like a man with an ache he can't quite reach, more at ease with Stefan than he had been, as though Pritchard required acrimony to break the ice.

"What do you think it is?" Stefan asked. "You, not the experts."

Pritchard observed Stefan. He lowered his voice. "Every Assembly adept who hears it thinks it's communication. If linguists don't, then there is something wrong with their science. But they were looking at human language. Maybe the Travelers aren't really human."

Startled, Stefan's first thought was that Pritchard was joking, but he looked entirely serious. "I don't believe that. They're obviously human. Their ancestry is from Earth. What proof do you have for an idea like that?"

Pritchard continued to watch Stefan, but didn't answer.

"Nothing? Then it's not only wrong, it's silly. They're human. It's probably what I first said, that the sounds have something to do with Numerica."

Pritchard shrugged, very slightly, but it effectively conveyed that he disagreed with Stefan. "Beatrice had quite an effect on you," he said. "More than you let yourself recognize." It sounded like advice.

Enough was enough. "Good night, Pritchard," Stefan said, and walked out into the lobby. He ordered one of Pritchard's men to call a coach to take him back into Bowl.

"But, sir, didn't you want to see Mr. Denning?" the guard asked in surprise.

"What?" Stefan had just been refused entrance to John Denning's jail. Fifteen minutes later, and Pritchard had changed his mind?

Pritchard tottered out of his office. "I intended to have a light supper now," Pritchard told Stefan. "Then I planned to check on Tom Chantry's progress with Denning."

It was a taunt and a test. How much do you want to see John Denning? Enough to dine with a nixt mirko? Stefan had no objection to Pritchard's social status, only to his person and his obvious illness, but too much was at stake to be fastidious. Good manners were the best revenge. He bowed deeply. "You are the only other Ropan I know in Bowl," Stefan said. "I would be honored if you allowed me to join you for dinner."

Pritchard smiled like a pleased child, missing the satire or not caring. "An Inlander begs a nixt mirko to dine with him only when he wants more than a meal. I tell you plainly, Per Acari, it won't do any good."

Beg? Stefan didn't understand Pritchard's game of favor and insult. It wasn't rational. His illness had warped his thinking. He had, however, trapped Stefan into insisting on the meal by making his honor depend on the sincerity of his request. "Frankly," Stefan said in a low, more personal tone, "I'm confused by these clansmen and the Numericans, tired of tattoos and noise. I'd like to dine with a fellow countryman." He used the Ropan term, making the self-described nixt mirko into a compatriot. It was asinine, but a man of superior breeding could always twist honor to suit his purposes. "However," Stefan continued, "I could not possibly impose on you unless this . . . business was out of the way first, so that it was clear that our dinner was based on mutual esteem and the fond memories of our schooling together and not, as you have suggested, on any base motive."

Pritchard's glassy red eyes stared like those of an animal, then he nodded. "I see how you've achieved your reputation for integrity," Pritchard said, but his bitterness was rueful.

Stefan and Kaim Pritchard exchanged brief, polite smiles, and walked across—back across, in Stefan's case—the yard to the older building. They went slowly and in silence. Pritchard walked as though his entire body ached, and Stefan did not try to hurry him.

The old building was musty, as if until recently it had been unused. Pritchard led the way through his men, then upstairs and down a corridor lined with a series of closed doors. Former prison or former hotel, the dreariness was the same.

"That was true," Pritchard said abruptly. "When we were at school, I wanted your respect. Your friendship. I admired you."

Nonplused, Stefan didn't answer.

"Your friend. Romaric Ezio. He was a pig," Pritchard continued. The effort of walking was making him wheeze. "He wouldn't let me near you. I never knew why you liked him."

Stefan was grateful they'd arrived at Denning's jail so he didn't need to reply to Pritchard's odd confession. A single guard stood outside a room in the middle of the row; it was the same man who had been downstairs earlier, and been used as Pritchard's mask and Pritchard's voice. The guard stepped aside for them without a word having been spoken aloud. Pritchard opened the door, and passed inside first.

It was a standard hotel room of the cheaper sort and made a flimsy jail, but no one with an internal connect could hide from the Assembly. Painted an old pastel shade that had deteriorated into brown, the room contained a spring-mattress bed without a headboard or covers, one worn, upholstered blue chair, and a plastic table with a built-in capstand. A tall, wooden chest of drawers, with two drawers missing, and a ceiling lamp completed the furniture. A doorway opened onto a bathroom. There was a window; it was open, but that airing hadn't rid the room of the stench of vomitus. A recent puddle of it lay on the floor beside the bed.

A man without a weapon stood at the window. He had a look of greater competence than Pritchard's other guards; he was watching Denning.

Denning lay on the bed, turned slightly away from the window, with his knees bent and his legs pulled up in a loose fetal position. He was naked. His arms were strong, but there was a sad, middle-aged flabbiness about his waist and hips that Stefan hadn't noticed at the party. His forearm covered his eyes. He didn't move when they entered.

"Anything, Tom?" Pritchard asked the interrogator.

"No, sir. Not yet."

Except for his color, and the rise and fall of his chest, Denning might have been dead.

"He has formidable defenses," Pritchard said in a raspy voice. "Peculiar, in a supposedly innocent man. Tom is my best agent, though. I'm sure we'll get in."

Tom stared at Denning for a moment. Denning groaned and tucked his legs closer to his chest.

"What do you think, Tom?" Pritchard asked jovially. "Could you break a Judge?"

Tom glanced coldly at Stefan, but didn't answer.

"It might become necessary. He's unbribable, you know. Too noble and too rich." Pritchard laughed as though he'd told a joke, then went to the far side of the room. As he passed the bed, Pritchard slapped the soles of Denning's feet. "Sit up," he ordered. "You have a visitor."

From admiration to threats. Stefan didn't try to understand Pritchard.

Denning moved his arm. He blinked. His eyes teared as if unaccustomed to the light, and they didn't immediately focus. His tattoos stood out against his pallor. His lips were bleeding where he'd recently bitten them. He looked nothing like the self-assured man who'd visited Stefan that morning, but he didn't look as abused as Stefan had feared.

Beyond the indignity of nakedness, there was little physical harm being done to John Denning. The pain was behind his eyes, the attempt of Assembly adepts to break forcibly through a semipermeable connect into a man's mind. Even that seemed to have been only lately begun. Tom wasn't fatigued. Denning had—rather too obviously—been fed during the afternoon. His clothing was neatly folded, in a pile on the table. Nevertheless, Stefan wished he could have intervened to prevent this interrogation. Denning's stubbornness would, in the absolutist logic of ID, give his arrest the appearance of legitimacy. "Hello, John," he said.

Denning raised his head like an old man. He recognized Stefan and his mouth twitched in a shadow of a grin. "Stef," he said. Immediately, he winced and his head fell back against the mattress.

"I apologize for the wildman, Per Acari," Pritchard said.

Pritchard had hurt Denning on Stefan's account. "No matter." Stefan's mouth was dry. "Will you leave me alone with him?"

"No. You've stopped entering the Assembly and he hasn't let us into his head. He might say something useful, which we'd miss if no one was here to listen."

Pritchard was too accustomed to the Assembly to bother using the mechanical eavesdropping devices Stefan had seen clansmen turn against one another, or he was too arrogant.

"You have a secret, John," Stefan said quietly. "I

don't think it has anything to do with the reason for your arrest, but your refusal to open now seems suspicious." Stefan nearly smiled, awful as it would have been in these surroundings, because the parallel with Denning's earlier admonition to *him* was so close. Denning's eyes met Stefan's. "John, enter the Assembly voluntarily with me. I give you my word, and pledge the Open Court, that your secret will be kept safe. I'll arrange it with the Court. You're a peripheral and entitled to privacy. Even I can keep secrets. I'll ask the Adjusters to block it in my dump."

"Them." Denning turned his head away as he winced. Clansmen tried never to show pain.

"Whatever political act you've done and hidden isn't worth this much suffering," Stefan said.

Denning tried to grin. "Yeah." He glared at Pritchard like a man betrayed.

"Just connect, and we're all done." Pritchard glanced at Stefan and smiled slightly.

"Go to hell," Denning said.

Denning gasped, then covered his eyes again. Tom, the interrogator, was staring down at Denning from across the room.

"Stop it!" Stefan looked at Pritchard. "Stop him."

Denning's body relaxed as the attack on his defenses slackened. Stefan went closer, ignoring the stench. "Marta reached me just before I boarded the Throw to Ropa. You have a loyal wife, John." Pritchard's subordinate chuckled. Denning alone, in all the world, couldn't know about Liada. Denning and the Travelers.

"Marta," Denning said softly, with affection, but also with a hint of a question.

"She's fine. She's free. Listen, John. Eventually, they'll break you. They always do. Tell them what they want to know. Show us that you're innocent. Show *me*."

"Can't," Denning muttered, uncovering his eyes.

From his expression, Pritchard's man Tom Chantry was straining at Denning like a leashed greyhound in the presence of a rabbit. Stefan's interview might have been a pretext for battering harder at Denning's mental gates. Pritchard, however, was not working Denning personally, and Pritchard was the likeliest to be able to succeed. Of course, Pritchard was ill. In fact, he appeared in worse shape physically than Denning, except his dignity was intact and his mind wasn't under siege.

"May I ask, Judge Acari," Pritchard politely said, "just why you feel so strongly that he's innocent when his actions contradict it? Do you have some evidence you're not sharing with me?"

"Someone on your staff is involved," Stefan said. "Denning couldn't have known Traveler habits."

"My staff. *My* staff." Pritchard spoke to Denning, as if sharing his pretended dismay with his prisoner. "Judge Acari, I think that you suspect me. It isn't so. As it happens, my staff did contain traitors. I hired two local men to patrol the farther grounds. Wildmen, recommended by your friend here, Clan President Denning. Both have disappeared—we can't find them through the Assembly. They're dead, or their connects are gone. Their intake interviews were clean; clearly a talented web doctor suppressed their true motivation. Web doctors, again." He sighed falsely. "Perhaps we should ask your friend John more about the web doctors he knows."

Denning tried to sit up. "Easy, John," Stefan said.

"We suspect that these people communicated outside the Assembly, using radio-wave devices," Pritchard continued. "The locals like mechanical toys. The continent is gadget-ridden."

"Even if the two men were John's clansmen, you still have no reason to hold John."

"I have his failure to cooperate. But this is accomplishing nothing." Pritchard gestured at the door. "You've seen him, Per Acari. The interview is over. We were on our way to dinner."

Stefan glanced down at Denning, whose watery eyes were watching Stefan, and wary. "Tell the truth, John. Now, while I'm here, so it can't be twisted. Beatrice Whit, the Traveler, is missing, presumed kidnapped. Did you order it?"

"No," Denning said, glancing sideways at Pritchard. More strongly, he repeated, "No. I didn't order the woman kidnapped."

Stefan believed him. Pritchard's two missing men could be anything: fantasy, plants to implicate Denning, or Pritchard's own, closest associates.

Denning stretched out his hand. "Tell Marta I'm all right," he said, whispering as though he'd hide his request from Pritchard.

Stefan nodded. "I will, of course."

"It's time to leave, Judge," Pritchard said irritably.

"Tell them you want me, when you can't take more, John. I'll be here. I'll enter a judgment. If you're innocent, you *will* go free." He walked hurriedly out of the room and waited in the hall as Pritchard lingered a moment, perhaps instructing his henchman in forced entry into other minds.

When Pritchard came out, Stefan immediately asked, "How long do you estimate until you've broken into Denning's mind?"

"There's no way to know."

Stefan was quiet as they walked out of the staff building and back to the main Lodge, mulling what he had just seen. "Move him to a clean room," Stefan said. "Let him dress."

"Is that an order, Inlander?" Pritchard seemed amused. He was walking even more slowly than earlier, however, as if the visit had taxed his strength.

"A suggestion." He glanced sideways at Pritchard. Sweat beaded Pritchard's face, glistening purple in the dying light. "It's a question of respect for your fellow men, Kaim."

Pritchard stumbled on the uneven ground. Stefan caught his arm and kept him upright. Pritchard sagged, letting Stefan support him. His body felt hot. Despite the queasiness he felt at contact with disease, Stefan continued to aid Pritchard until they entered the main Lodge. "About dinner . . ." Pritchard said.

"It's late," Stefan quickly interrupted. "You're not well. I'll certainly understand if you cancel it."

"A postponement? If you don't mind, Judge?"

"Not at all." Stefan bowed. Pritchard's illness emphasized his origin in Zona. Stefan was relieved he wouldn't be honor bound to spend more time with this insecure, rootless nixt mirko. He couldn't decide whether or not the interview with Denning had been staged, let alone what that might mean. "I hope you're better in the morning," he told Pritchard. "I'll see you then."

Pritchard sank into one of the lobby chairs. He didn't speak, but by his expression, Stefan doubted it was because he was working in the Assembly.

Beatrice realized she was wrong. She wasn't ill, this was torture. Her captors wanted information and they were pulling it from her helpless mind.

Drugs, not fever, made her delirious. The images she saw were external, part of their questions and not horrors produced by her own mind. In fact, the images weren't horrible, it was their assault on her, her forced participation in viewing them, that made the experience a form of madness. She couldn't move. Restraints held her in place. She controlled neither her body nor her mind.

When her thoughts were clear enough that she could think about what was being done, the procedure reminded her of testing vision. An image would be shown, then it would change, and all the while her brain would flash with hot pinpricks of thought, emotion, or physical sensation—a measurable reaction. There was no passage of time, except her weariness. They had her and it wouldn't end until they wanted it to end.

Again and again, she tried to reach the beacon. She couldn't imagine how two of her fellow Travelers had been convinced to call the Ship; she was no longer certain they had been. The silence when she listened for the beacon was persuasive, but she knew her friends. They would not have done it; they had been chosen for the Earth mission in part for their stubbornness.

If they hadn't, then who had called the Ship? No one else on Earth knew how, except possibly the Adjusters and they would never do it. Earth had been swaddled by the Assembly like a baby who never outgrew its diapers.

There was another explanation. Her mind was gone. Her capture had so damaged her that she could not reach the beacon.

If that was so, she was useless to the mission. If it was true of the other three Travelers, then the mission was dead. The Ship would leave without her. Welcome home.

Stefan stared out the coach's open window, reflecting on his proper role in this investigation while idly watching human-driven vehicles weave in and out of the meca lane, passing his coach in hopscotch fashion while attempting a faster progress than was either safe or legal; his meca-driven coach lumbered on. The clans adored mechanisms almost as much as they did speed. They practically worshiped their Amercan ancestors, making ruined skyscrapers—admittedly, they were impressive—into shrines. They ignored the sins that had brought the five Great Deaths to the Old Moderns, forgot their greed and lack of honor. The clans made them heroes and used the Assembly less than any other region, disregarding the good it did. They refused to see that their much higher rate of violent behavior was a direct result. Still, Stefan liked visiting the Sister continents. Among the clans, he was camouflaged by being an outsider; his dumps weren't watched as entertainment.

It had been a long day. Unlike the morning, the evening sky was clear. Trees cast long shadows across the road. If Marta had been even a few minutes later reaching the Throw field, he would already be home. He twisted the estate ring on his finger. It never felt right there. Death had given Acari to him. His true home was the Open Court, an ideal of justice. It depended upon the Assembly, however. What if Pritchard was an accurate reflection of the Adjusters? Stefan relaxed against the plush seat and, from experience, forced such thoughts away. Stray ramblings disappeared in his dumps.

Buildings replaced the trees as the coach entered Bowl. Its evening atmosphere was hushed. Bowl was a new town, although it existed near the site of an earlier, Amercan place. Not a tourist town or governmental center, Bowl was merely a pleasant working community and a clan hub. At Bowl's outskirts, the coach passed a large park in which uniformed children played a game with an odd-shaped ball. They ran from side to side and even into one another. He'd seen the game before; the clans claimed it came down to them from the Amercans. The children made Stefan wonder if Tepan had heard of his parents' troubles. Had Frey teased or protected him?

Bowl's main avenue was wide and pleasant; not many inhabitants were afoot and vehicles were fewer than they were outside the town. Stores with glass windows artistically displayed their wares. A few shops were closing, but most had another hour in their day. Stefan leaned forward. "Change Order," he said loudly, though he knew that volume was unnecessary; the meca wasn't deaf. "Take me to the Waterman Clan Hall."

"Acknowledged." The coach's mechanical voice was a woman's.

The coach passed Stefan's hotel, which was set back from the town's main square, then a number of spare, plain buildings, the local clan halls. They entered another square. Stefan didn't know they'd reached the Waterman Clan Hall until the coach stopped. The Waterman building was larger than most, but no more grand.

"Judge!" a man called as Stefan alighted from the car. "Judge Acari!"

He turned, surprised, since he knew almost no one in Bowl.

A plump, smiling fellow came forward; his balding head looked especially bare because of the quantity of closely drawn tattoos across his face. He seemed vaguely familiar, but outside the Assembly, Stefan didn't recall him. The man extended his hand. "Paine Quinn," he introduced himself. "We've met, Judge Acari, but it was some time ago, on that water rights case along the Colorado; I was one of the mediators, before you were involved. I thought you came to an excellent decision. Oh, by the way, I'm the clan's chief administrator, and a friend of John's. But I wasn't at the party last night. Someone had to mind the store." Quinn shook hands vigorously, in the clansman manner while he chattered on, and led Stefan forward.

"Yes, of course," Stefan said.

Paine Quinn never stopped talking. "We—the entire clan—want to thank you for trying to help John," Quinn said as he brushed aside a tall, tattooed, half-naked man who was guarding the Waterman Clan's door. Quinn ushered Stefan into a busy lobby. "We're all worried about this Pritchard fellow. Seems a nasty sort. Turned away the police chief—wouldn't even let him in the Lodge." Quinn was a smaller, less accomplished version of John Denning. John didn't jabber or gush. "Marta's in the Great Room. I suppose you want to see her?"

Stefan nodded, and followed Quinn into the Waterman Clan's Great Gathering Room.

Marta Denning was seated alone on a wide, padded bench while her solicitous family and friends hovered nearby, ready with sympathy, support, and food. The tableau reminded Stefan of the wake he had attended, three years earlier, for Mikel Warring, then the president of the Northern Sister, who had died in office. The clansmen had been jockeying for position in the new order opened by the untimely presidential vacancy even as they expressed an unseemly—by Ropan lights—depth of sympathy and grief to his widow. At least this time there was no corpse to which homage was due.

The room, which had been buzzing with low conversation, quieted, and Denning's clansmen watched Stefan suspiciously as, alongside Quinn, he advanced on Marta, their substitute martyr in John Denning's absence. Stefan bowed as deeply as he would have at the Oblander's court in Paris. Satisfied with his show of respect, the clansmen resumed their own conversations.

"Any news?" Marta asked eagerly.

"Mr. Pritchard hasn't said much more than what you

know." Stefan wanted to discuss John's condition in private, to minimize an overreaction by the volatile clansmen.

"That they're torturing John, trying to squeeze open his mind." She had no such concern, apparently. Her hands rested on the bench as if they braced her body. It caused her posture to seem aggressive, but her expression was steady. "Judge Acari, do you believe John is innocent of kidnapping that Numerican?"

Stefan scanned the room. The contrast with the party of the previous night was a matter of demeanor. The clansmen wore slightly more clothing—many seemed to have come straight from work—but they were subdued, not dancing. There was drinking, and most were nibbling at the abundant food, which this time was spread along a table rather than served by mecas (although there was a meca that occasionally removed waste or clutter), but conversation was somber. The tone was angry, not merely worried. He didn't want to provoke them. "My investigation is in a preliminary stage," he said, "and it's Open Court policy not to make factual statements except by the Judge's dumps, and never to render a judgment until the final order."

A tall man pushed forward. "But that Assembly man claims John kidnapped a Numerican?" he demanded. "Why would John do it?"

It was the central issue. There was no reason for John Denning, or any clansman, to kidnap a Numerican Traveler. Murmurs of agreement sped through the room. Stefan remembered the ship, waiting above and perhaps listening to the Assembly. "I can't comment."

Those near enough to hear frowned. Their regional courts were better than most, and were public. Speaking slowly, watching his words as carefully as if he were formulating a judicial ruling, he spoke to Marta, but also to all of them. "No evidence I've seen indicates that Clan President Denning has done anything for which he should be detained. However, the authority holding John is the Assembly's Independent Defense. It is granted more leeway than other agencies because it's observed by the Adjusters. As a Judge of the Open Court, I do promise you, however, justice will be done."

Marta looked down, hiding tears. He sympathized. His position did not allow him to express it.

"What use was it to call on the Open Court?" the tall man demanded of Marta. "You shouldn't have brought in an outsider."

"She didn't," Stefan said. "An Open Court Judge is not an outsider anywhere connected to the Assembly."

The man grimaced, shifted his weight without changing his position, then squinted at Stefan. "To hell with the Assembly."

There was silence from most listeners, but scattered throughout the room clansmen muttered approvingly. No one appeared shocked. They waited for Stefan's reaction.

"Rejecting the Assembly is foolish, but it's your right," Stefan said mildly, "as long as you don't interfere with others' use. Right now, though, the Open Court is the best protection John Denning has." Anyone who succeeded in life came to terms with the Assembly eventually. They all knew it, but clansmen blustered.

The man came closer. His dirty hands were those of a laborer, but he spoke like an educated man, despite his attitude. "Go home. We'll take care of ourselves. We can free John without help from a man who can't keep his own wife from playing around."

Marta watched Stefan through shrewd, narrowed eyes that still glittered with tears for her husband.

This was worse than being taunted by Pritchard. Stefan gave up a private life for a world filled with people just like these. He served them and cherished them inside the Assembly. Copies of his mind circulated like the latest fictions in order to protect them, and yet they were numb to the fact that he was human, too, and callously used what they learned about him—learned while he provided plainly unbiased justice—to attack him. Inside, he seethed, but he let the cold persona of the impersonal Judge perform. "If any extrajudicial action is taken, that self-help will be severely punished. I will make certain of it. But the Open Court will not stop, and I will not leave, until my investigation of John Denning's arrest is completed."

Marta Denning had struggled to her feet. "Judge," she said. "Thank you for staying to help John."

He inclined his head toward the door. "May I speak with you alone?"

She walked with him, her hand resting on his arm, escorting him graciously from the room, giving him her approval and attempting to undo the disrespect. Her courtesy didn't warm his disposition. It was ridiculous that a Judge's dignity required her support.

"Thank you," she said when they reached the lobby. "I needed an excuse to get away. That's John's kind of setting, not mine."

"Who was that man?"

She sighed. "Orion Nash, President of the Woodmaker's Clan. I apologize. I can't control those men the way John can. Orry can't help his rudeness; he's ignorant."

There were fewer people present, but the lobby wasn't private. The man guarding the outer door opened it as if to encourage Stefan's departure. "I do need to speak with you." Stefan lowered his voice. "I've seen John. He's fine."

Her face lit up. In her joy Stefan saw that two decades earlier, Marta Denning might have been pretty. She'd never been a beauty, like Liada, but there was a liveliness about her that her plumpness hid. She lacked Beatrice's grace, and her voice was sharp and thin, but Marta Denning was devoted to John. Respect for that let Stefan shed some of his rancor. "Then he's alive," she said. "I was so afraid Pritchard had hurt him. Come up to my office. Tell me everything."

She led the way past an open stone staircase to a small elevator. It took them to the third floor, the building's highest, where the air felt unnaturally cool. The Waterman Clan used air-conditioning. While doing so wasn't prohibited, climate manipulation was rare, and generally limited to situations of scientific, sanitary, or medical need. The cold had driven the humidity from the atmosphere; it was refreshing.

The third floor contained offices. The largest, with an open door, looked like a shared administrative space; others were marked with names. Paine Quinn's was directly opposite the stairs and elevator. Stefan couldn't help thinking of him as the clan's combination publicity man and bouncer. Marta's office was the farthest from the elevator. Her name was printed on the door without a title, although John's had both his name and the word "President" in large gold letters. The doors were closed, but Marta let them both inside and flipped a switch, turning on bright ceiling lights.

Marta's office was cramped because its central feature—apparently a heavily modified deadhead caller access—was huge. The oversize holographic display frame was propped up on a plain wooden desk. Stefan walked closer and inspected the unit. The keyboard was mounted on a shelf below the desk. Like the one at his hotel, the key arrangement was not alphabetic. The microphone, for auditory pickup and use as a receiver, was more prominent than in the hotel access. Blank paper was loaded into an attachment on a plastic ledge to the side of a squat mechanism. More paper, wrapped in colored translucent plastic, was stacked on the floor. A spiral-bound stack of thick hard-copy printout was on the corner of the desk. An upright, extrawide, cushioned chair was behind the desk. Wooden cabinets lined an entire wall. Only a small area under the window—it overlooked a ground-floor courtyard garden—was furnished with comfortable chairs for use during Assembly connection, though that was usually the most significant office equipment. There were no caps or capstands in the office. Stefan had heard rumors of "closed rooms," into which the ever-ambient Assembly was unable to extend. Curious, he reached out and immediately sensed the Assembly, like a flirting girl, teasing him, waiting to be kissed. He stopped just short of connection. He would enter the Assembly after completing this investigation. The ability to connect and the delay in doing so were both satisfying. He didn't stop to consider why. "I have a friend who would enjoy this very much," he said, thinking of Romaric Ezio. "He collects books and antique information systems."

"This isn't an antique," she said. "We use a computer system, modeled after the Amercans'. Most of the clans are moving to them now, to keep their privacy. We don't trust sealed Assembly files."

"I see." No wonder the Adjusters were uneasy about the clans. This secrecy didn't bode well for the Sisters' continued integration with the rest of Earth. Stefan swallowed hard, imagining a global war. They had been common during Old Modern times; Earth needed the Assembly.

Marta sat down at the desk. She glanced at a two-sided miniature of John, Marta, and their three children: a serious young man and two smiling younger girls. Stefan hadn't met them.

Stefan turned one of the chairs near the window so that it faced her. The chair was made of wooden slats and was too low, so his legs stretched out uncomfortably. He guessed Marta didn't use it; she would have had difficulty getting up.

"Tell me about John," she asked.

Stefan told her that John was under guard, and that they were trying to get into his mind, but that he was strongly resisting. She listened with a mixture of pride and dread. He mentioned, while observing her closely, his offer of help if only John would let the Open Court— let Stefan—connect with him under a prior-approved secrecy seal. She nodded firmly, her lips compressed, when he said John had refused. "Let them prove he's guilty; he shouldn't have his mind invaded by anyone, even you, Judge, just to prove he's innocent." It was a common doctrine in the Sisters, and one that would probably have protected Denning in normal circumstances. "Beatrice isn't just anyone," Stefan said.

"Beatrice?" A meager smile moved across Marta's lips.

"The kidnapped Traveler."

"The ship hasn't moved since she was taken," Marta said. "As soon as I left that Lodge, I checked with the observatory. Nothing's changed."

"Interesting." Stefan wished he'd asked the Travelers if they could communicate with their ship, although it was unlikely they would have told him. "Did you know John came to my hotel this morning? He wanted me to stay in Bowl."

Marta looked down at her keyboard. "It was a risk," she said softly. "I warned John."

"What?"

She raised her head to look at him. "Inviting you here. It told Pritchard we suspected him and probably made him very angry. But John thought your presence was necessary to protect us."

John Denning had said much the same thing, but Stefan still found it far-fetched that they could have been suspicious of Pritchard's presence long before anything had actually happened to a Traveler. Of course, events had proven the Dennings—*possibly* proven them—right, but how had they known? The Sister Continents were full of conspiracy theorists distrustful of the Assembly, but Stefan hadn't considered John Denning one of them. "Marta, *did* John participate in the Traveler's abduction?"

"No." She looked right at him.

He nodded, but he didn't go on to tell her, as he had intended, about his suspicion that John's interrogation had begun just slightly before Stefan had been allowed to see him. "John was interested in the Travelers. Do you know why?"

"Who isn't? The faster-than-light star-drive. The possibility of seeing new worlds." She shrugged.

"Leaving Earth would mean abandoning the Assembly." Although the magnetic resonance that was the foundation of the Assembly had no theoretical limit, there was a practical one. Other magnetic forces could cancel or distort the force on which the Assembly was based. Tests had shown that the detailed Assembly information began to deform outside the Earth's outer atmosphere; much beyond the reach of the Solar System, even the Assembly essentials were gone. Those findings had prevented an interest in exploration from developing in other regions. Stefan wondered about Numerica. The Adjusters researched the Assembly mechanism, though they didn't tamper with the original brilliant design of the founders. Couldn't they build a second machine?

"So what?" Marta said. "For some of us, the Assembly doesn't matter. I can't connect. If I try, then nothing happens. I'm a deadhead." She spoke as though she relished the word, with a flourish in her tone, as though she was flaunting a withered or deformed hand to forestall a disparaging remark.

Denning's wife was a deadhead? "I didn't know." He should have suspected it when he saw the deadhead access in her office. "But you used the Assembly. You said you tried to call me."

"I used John's designation, and this." She patted her deadhead computer. "It's more than just a caller; it allows me to activate most Assembly functions in simulation, too."

His attention went to the miniature. "Your children?"

"Johnny is fine, normal. He uses a cap, not an internal connect, like you or John. Stacey and Kate will, too." She stared straight ahead and right through him.

He studied her tattoos. The differences from John's were minor, insofar as he recalled the details of John Denning's face. Were tattoos a matched set, like wedding bands?

"It was a head injury. An accident," she said, although he hadn't asked.

Marta was lying. Even without the Assembly to advise him, he knew that in the few cases where physical injury made the use of a cap impossible, those individuals also had other severe impairments. Nothing else was wrong with Marta. She had probably been born impaired, as were about 8 percent of all humans, but didn't acknowledge her congenital defect. Why had Denning married her? In Ropa, a deadhead wife would have been a major detriment to political aspirations. Perhaps in the Sisters it was an asset.

"You disapprove," she said. "You think that because you're a ticker, you're better." She indicated herself with a sketchy gesture.

"No. I don't." It was true. "In a way I envy you. You'll never have to choose between a public and a private life."

She smiled. "I married a politician."

Thrown off guard by Marta's disclosure, Stefan had let the conversation become more personal than he liked. "What about UN-Assemblers?" he asked. "Are they active in Bowl, or are there any other terrorists?"

"What do they have to do with John?" She seemed taken aback.

"They might have kidnapped Beatrice to get information about Numerica and the ship, hoping to use it against the Assembly."

Marta tapped her fingers against the wooden desk. "Terrorists blow things up; they don't get information. Besides, there haven't been any incidents here."

"If we proved someone else took Beatrice, then Pritchard would have to free John. The best thing would be to find Beatrice, safe and sound, and capture her kidnappers. Pritchard has concentrated all his efforts on John. He'll never find anyone else that way—or Beatrice, if John's innocent. The Bowl police should investigate. Unofficially, of course. You suggest it." Stefan got up from the awkward chair.

"There's one thing," Marta slowly said. "Did John mention the strange barnacles that we've seen in the sewer system ever since the Travelers arrived?"

The barnacles again. "I thought they were John's excuse to keep me here."

"No, they're real. Paine Quinn—you came in with him, remember?—has asked the systems engineers to find out how long it takes before our monitoring systems detect an accumulation. My thought was—it was my idea, right after I found out why he has John—that if we located new barnacles, we'd know where the kidnapers are keeping the Traveler. And if we didn't find any barnacles anywhere but in the system down from Tyler's Hill, the Hilltop Lodge system, then we'd know it was all an excuse and Mr. Pritchard still has her there."

The barnacles didn't seem a promising angle to Stefan. How quickly could the things infest a sewer system, even assuming that they were related to the Travelers? "Do what you can with it, but be discreet, Marta." She nodded and he turned to leave the office, then walked back. Marta's hands were poised above the keyboard. She set them down on her lap. "Pritchard claims that two men John recommended to him are missing. Disappeared at the same time as Beatrice. Local clansmen. Do you have any idea who they are?" As he spoke, Stefan gazed out the window, as if the answer to Beatrice's disappearance might be in the courtyard.

"I don't think John recommended anyone to Mr. Pritchard." Marta sounded like a housewife in a huff over unpleasant gossip. "It isn't something he would do."

"A politician?" Stefan turned back to her. "John didn't have any friends he would have liked on ID's payroll?"

She seemed confused for the first time during their conversation. "I don't think he was ever asked," she said after a moment. "He didn't like Pritchard, and it was mutual. That's why we called you."

"Well, ask the police, unofficially, if there are any clansmen missing from Bowl. I don't want Pritchard to know I'm behind the questions, so I'm depending on you. All right?"

She nodded. "Of course, Judge. Anything."

She was worried about John, but Stefan's new perspective on Marta Denning made him uncertain he could trust her. "One other thing," he asked. "Can you get a sample of the barnacles to me? I'll have it tested in Ropa to see if it is extraterrestrial."

She straightened in her hard chair. "We know what we're doing, Judge. Most scientific advances come from the clans or down south in Djenaro."

"Still. If you would, Marta." He didn't make it an Open Court order.

She nodded. "I'll tell Paine."

Less satisfied than he had been when he entered the clan hall that he knew what was going on, Stefan left the office. He took the stairs down to the main floor. The crowd in the Great Gathering Room was larger than before. He left the building without speaking to anyone.

Outside, the dark had finally arrived, but streetlights eased the night. He remembered the way to his hotel; it wasn't far, so Stefan started back on foot. The streets were busier; the evening was the time clansmen socialized. Many of them, of varying tattooed visages, were strolling toward the Waterman Clan Hall.

With evening a chill had entered the air. He rubbed his arms. Paper crinkled, and he remembered the hard copy from Beatrice's room. He pulled the thin, wrinkled throwaway sheets from his breast pocket and stood a moment under a light, reading: official Health Reports, worldwide and local, for the last three days. Why had Beatrice collected Health Reports?

Chapter 5

Drom Hanzin was prepared for calls at odd hours; he had a dummy. "Per Acari, what can I do for you?" the dummy said, and bowed to a servant's depth while doubtless Drom himself stayed cozily in bed back in Acari, where it was 3:30 A.M., yawning and rubbing his eyes as he spoke the words the dummy pronounced.

"Sorry, Drom," Stefan said. "What's the situation since this news came out in my dump?" Stefan didn't feel up to a scene with Liada. As he delayed his courtesy call to inform her of the postponement of his return home, he'd dined alone in the hotel restaurant. The execrable food had almost made him wish for a dinner with Pritchard, who would probably have set a good table. After the meal, he had settled on awakening Drom as the simplest way to fulfill his obligation.

Drom's dummy—fully and formally dressed, looking alert, well, and entirely realistic on the hotel deadhead access—hesitated, and rubbed its chin exactly as Drom might have done. The dummy was a good-quality design, well worth what Acari paid for it, despite the fact that its cost exceeded Stefan's salary as a Judge. The salary was symbolic, anyway, the smallest amount paid any Judge, since Stefan had not needed more. "It's gossip, Per Acari. It won't affect our bottom line." Drom hesitated, then added, "I'm sorry to hear it, though."

"Thank you," Stefan said curtly. He didn't want sympathy from a man he employed.

"Your wife has remained at the great house."

Stefan recognized Drom's circumspect method of asking instructions. "Is there something you want to say? Go ahead."

Drom's replica sighed. "I foresee the possibility of long-term problems. Matters of ambivalent allegiance, conflicting instructions. Precedence complications. What about this child? Decisions need to be made to settle matters as soon as possible."

"You believe I should repudiate Liada and disown her child."

Drom was uncomfortable. Even with the dummy intermediary, that much was obvious in his voice. "It would be easier. The status issues would be resolved. You have a son and heir."

Stefan frowned. To discuss such intimate matters with Drom, who necessarily kept secrets from Stefan, was bad enough, but Stefan suspected Pritchard was eavesdropping on every call he made. Independent Defense had the power to do it, and Stefan lacked confidence in Pritchard's ethical constraints, so he had decided to use Pritchard's eavesdropping to his own advantage. "I won't turn her out." Repudiation meant Liada would have nothing. Stefan wasn't blameless, however betrayed he felt.

"Per Acari." The dummy bowed Drom's acquiescence.

Liada would not be Pritchard's hostage, if Stefan could help it. Given Pritchard's interest in her, it was best if Stefan showed no interest at all, yet he couldn't act out of character. "Tell her that if she initiates dissolution proceedings against me, then I won't contest, and she can have a widow's portion. Or if she doesn't initiate, then file dissolution against her in the Oblander's Court within seven days. Offer a half-widow's portion."

"That's very generous," the dummy said. "Unnecessarily so. Per Acari, you may wish to marry again, and have other children. Since you do intend to end the marriage, her own statements provide a basis for denial of all comfortable support; I recommend repudiation, not divorce. Also, any offer should include all claims of the child. Meanwhile, she should leave the estate immediately for the town house in Paris."

"You've given this some thought." Stefan had expected as much. Drom's diligence was predictable.

"Naturally. I'm your steward."

His paid man was telling him how to manage his personal life. Though he'd called specifically for this purpose, and to deflect Pritchard, it galled. "This is because I'm a Judge," he muttered.

The dummy stayed silent.

"I don't care if you're in bed naked, Drom, making love with your wife, but I don't want to see another minute of this dummy. If a man tells me I should turn out my son's mother, I want to see his eyes."

The image changed. Drom, wearing a blue robe, was sipping a hot drink from a mug in the kitchen of his house on Acari property. Despite the time of night and the intensity of the subject being discussed, he appeared his usual composed self. In the past, Stefan had found that imperturbable quality reassuring. "I apologize, Per Acari."

Stefan was reminded of Pritchard's treatment of his men and regretted his outburst; he envied Denning's easy intimacy with his clansmen. "You know my name, Drom. After all these years, you've yet to use it."

Drom flinched slightly. "Stefan."

Stefan kept imagining Pritchard listening over his shoulder. "What do the tenants think of having a Judge as their Inlander?"

Drom passed a hand through his uncombed hair. "They're proud," he said. "It's an honor. But there isn't any advantage for them."

None at all, for anyone. "I could only have gone nominal and never entered the Assembly again. I wasn't offered a choice."

"We all understand."

Drom was a peripheral; perhaps he did. If so, Drom's bland, professional expression didn't show it. Stefan felt himself to be whining or making excuses. Inappropriate. "No matter. This investigation will be over soon; I have an idea where it's going." Let Pritchard hear that and worry. "I may slow down my work for the Court, afterward, and spend more time at home." Drom wouldn't like the interference if he did, but Stefan wanted to help Tepan through this period. Naturally, he couldn't mention Tepan aloud.

Thoughts of Pritchard reminded him of something else. "Drom, is there any illness at Acari now? Anything unusual in Ropa?"

"No . . . nothing on the Health Reports. Is there a reason you ask, Per—Stefan?"

"Just a hunch." At least with Drom Hanzin, Stefan had no obligation to explain more. "It's probably nothing."

"You have good instincts, sir."

Stefan placed his finger on the key to terminate the call. He hesitated, then said instead, "I'm sorry I called so late, Drom. Go back to bed."

"Thank you, Per Acari." Drom bowed to his image. "One other matter. Per Ezio asked that you call him."

"Good. Thank you." Stefan broke the connection, and sat a moment, pushing at the estate ring with his thumb. He glanced down. The amber stone reminded him of Beatrice; it had her coloring. He stretched, lethargic after the overcooked meal, then painstakingly typed in Romaric's calling code.

They released Beatrice from the imprisoning body-mold. The images had stopped. She had been left alone to stare at darkness. It was wonderful to see nothing. She pretended to herself that she was looking through the Ship's window, when suddenly, soundlessly, her cramped limbs were moved. Pain shot through her. Then there was light. She felt dizzy and sick. Her nausea passed and she struggled feebly on her own to sit. Someone swore but helped her, and for the first time, she saw her prison. It reminded her of the Ship.

There was a constant background hum. Mechanical, of a different timbre than the Ship, it was irritating until it receded gradually from her consciousness. Darkness,

a low ceiling, featureless walls, helplessness, and the
sense of exhilaration (although here it was unreasonable,
a product of light-headedness mixed with triumph over
fear) suggested the interface rooms, where humans first
met Friends.

She'd been an eager, ambitious, healthy child. She'd
gone alone. Her mother had led Beatrice out the door
through which she'd never before passed and told her,
in song Beatrice sensed was false, that there was no need
for worry. Then she'd left.

Beatrice had heard of the Friends. Those in the
human shelter spoke of them, often with disapproval. A
person could spend his entire life inside the human shelter and never see a Friend, or any other of the races
who inhabited the Ship—or rather, they would see one
only once; everyone was tested, but no one was forced.
The shelter was a truly safe haven from others, but those
who stayed constantly inside it had no purpose to their
lives; even as a child Beatrice had sensed it. Their needs
were met, freely, and they spent their time however they
wished: eating, sleeping, sex, or innocuous quasi-inactivity
interspersed with futile politics. Would she be one of
them, or one of those who came and went, leaving the
human shelter for the nether parts of the Ship?

The tall, gray door had clicked, locking itself behind
her. Beatrice pushed at the pad, which was supposed to
open the door for any—and only—human palmprints,
but the human shelter, where she'd spent her entire
young life, was out of reach.

The air in the interface room became heavier. Its new
smell made a bitter taste in the back of her mouth. Tears
dripped from her eyes, and her eyes stung. She wiped
them, but it didn't help. She spat, but the bad taste remained. She cried for her mother, but her mother
didn't come.

Even so young, Beatrice had been pragmatic. Review
of her usual emergency stratagems—shouting, crying,
and pouting—made clear that they wouldn't work without an audience, so she had hunkered down against the

wall nearest the door to the human shelter and waited for a Friend. Only then did one come.

Smaller than Beatrice, he had longer, whiplike arms and a head like a wrinkled melon, too big, too round, and hairless. He was a smooth amber-yellow color. He took one long look at Beatrice and screeched something she understood as distress.

"Me, too," she'd said miserably.

Eyni, as she'd later learned was his name, stopped and listened. He wailed, tentatively.

Beatrice shivered. She knew some song, as well as her own language, a derivative of Earth-english, but this supposed Friend wasn't singing.

They exchanged unintelligible sounds. Beatrice guessed they were being observed, which made her try harder to be patient and expressive. Eyni hadn't tried half so hard, he'd later admitted. Finally, he'd turned, marched to the closed door through which he'd come— opposite her own—and placed his flexible hand on the pad. *His* door opened. He left.

The door hesitated on its rollers. Beatrice wavered on her toes. As the door began to shut, she rushed toward it, but was too late to pass through. She glimpsed a large, dusky space with lots of people in it. People of all kinds. Without thinking, she put her hand against the pad for this second door. It opened again. For the first time, Beatrice entered the Ship.

"Welcome. Welcome home." Friends sang to her as she crossed the threshold. From these adults, she'd recognized the simple song. Larger than Eyni, but not as large as her mother or any of the human men, the Friends had overwhelmed Beatrice with their number and their strangeness. There had been humans among them, too, one whom she recognized by sight from the human shelter, but others whom she did not. They stood like shy giants among the Friends.

Eyni had run back to Beatrice. "My friend. My friend," he had sung, laying a claim to her that no other Friend would contest. Why did the Friends seek friends?

No human fully understood, but by coming to Earth, Beatrice had approved and joined their quest.

The Friends wanted friends everywhere, of every kind; they claimed it made them strong. Beatrice had taken an instant dislike to the Kroni, shuffling at the edge of the group greeting her, watching with their dark, hard eyes. Lean and toothy creatures, they frightened her, as they did most humans. There was no rapport between the species, except that each was a friend of the Friends. Still, the Kroni had inspired her first interspecies song. "I want to go back," she'd sung.

"Hey, wake up!" One of her captors slapped Beatrice's face. It stung only slightly. She blinked, groaned, and raised her arm to protect herself.

"She okay?" another asked.

Their voices were too loud. Like food after a fast, too much seemed to be happening to her at once. Beatrice whimpered and her arm fell back in the cradle that had held her.

"Come on," the first voice encouraged.

She tried to look at him, but the view didn't change. Her muscles weren't responsive to her wishes.

"Yeah. She's going to be fine." The same man put an arm under her back and raised her to an upright position. To Beatrice, he said, "Muscle relaxants. Nothing to worry about."

She recognized the voice as that of the man on the bridge. He sounded much friendlier. She could move her eyes, and she looked at him. He seemed young. The tattoos were new, with fresh, bright colors, not only the monotones of older clansmen. "Sorry about that," he said, as though her situation was something for which he could simply apologize. "The worst is over."

"We're going to ask you a few questions." It was the other man from the woods. Her captors were unspecialized. The muscle men were also the interrogators. No division of labor, the first sign of incipient civilization, according to Ship dictums. She giggled, dribbling saliva from the corner of her mouth.

"Why's she laughing?" the second man demanded angrily.

"Ah, leave her alone. She can't talk yet, and she's all drugged up."

An expert at determining intention from tone, a crucial skill on the Ship, Beatrice decided that neither was quite comfortable with his role. Kidnapping wasn't their idea; they were subordinates. She worked to form the word. "Pritchard?"

"We'll ask the questions," the second man said. To the other, the Boy, as she'd already mentally labeled him, he said, "Bring her the bowl."

Beatrice tried to help herself stay upright, but she moved in haphazard jerks, and only when she strained. She sighed, which made a raspberry sound and irritated her captors. The mind was a muscle of a different kind. She reached out for the beacon; perhaps her mind was less drugged.

Nothing.

If the beacon was down, and her mind was all right, then someone had called the Ship. Why ask her questions?

Meanwhile, the Boy brought a tray with a steel bowl containing a gray porridge. It smelled like the warm tsampa her mother had made on the Ship, and was the first food on Earth that reminded her of home. "Can you feed yourself?" he asked.

She lifted her arm. It shuddered clumsily, but it ended where she'd wanted.

"You'll spill it," the Boy said sympathetically. He glanced at the other man. "I'll feed her."

"Up to you." The man's tone was a verbal shrug.

They were in a cramped, cluttered room with a low ceiling. The room felt damp. She was cold, probably because she was naked, except for a blanket across her legs. It was night, she supposed, since they each had a lamp, the only light. There were no windows.

The door at the end of the room opened. It creaked. A third man stood watching them. He was tattooed, but he held himself more formally. "Have you started yet?"

he asked. His accent was different, but not Ropan or anything she knew. He was in charge.

"She's hungry," the Boy claimed, although Beatrice hadn't spoken. "She hasn't eaten real food, just that drip." He set the tray down, filled a spoon with the steaming, aromatic porridge, and brought it up to feed Beatrice.

Cooperation with the softer-hearted of her captors seemed wise. Besides, the almost familiar fragrance of the porridge had aroused her hunger. She lurched at the spoon and swallowed.

The newcomer said, "Well, hurry up. She wants this over." He left, the door creaking behind him. The sound was a metal on metal scratch combined with a whine, like a song of isolation.

"It'll be all right," the Boy said as he fed her another slow spoonful.

Beatrice heard his strained insincerity; they had let her see their faces. Who was *she*? And what had happened to the beacon?

An image inside the holographic displayer, Stefan's friend, Romaric Ezio, sat cross-legged on his huge bed with some of his collection of ancient hand-copy books spread around him. Wide-awake despite the time difference, Romaric kept what he called "vampire hours." To Stefan, the view was as if he were standing across the room, looking toward Romaric. "Ro?" Stefan said, moving slightly in his chair to bring his apparent orientation closer.

Romaric's black and ivory tunic was wrinkled and unbuttoned; a half-empty wineglass rested atop an unusually tall pile of heavy books on Romaric's left. He didn't qualify for an implanted connection to the Assembly, but his estate had full caller access throughout the private rooms; he needn't wear a cap to receive a call. He frowned at Stefan, and as his right hand flipped the pages of one of the books, his inattention caused a delicate sheet to tear. He swore, then seemed to look directly into Stefan's eyes, and swore again. "How could you do it?" Romaric asked.

Stefan knew what Romaric meant: Liada, and his dump exposing them both. But John Denning, and then Beatrice, had needed him; they had claims on him that no real judge could resist. "There was an emergency; I had to act."

After saving his place with a slender, black lacquer bookmark, moving slowly and deliberately, making Stefan wait, Romaric put the book down carefully beside himself on the bed. The deadhead access was only auditory and visual. Stefan smelled nothing but the lavender of the scented hotel deadhead access booth, but he remembered the musty odor of decaying paper that filled Romaric's rooms. It came from the hundreds of books lining open shelves built to house Romaric's collection. The horde looked like the library of a medieval monastery, except Romaric was no monk. "When they chose you for a Judge, they were right." Romaric cleared his throat, then covered his mouth while he coughed, as though Stefan was truly present in the room. "You made yourself a laughingstock, and for what? A wildman politician?"

Romaric Ezio was disdainful of everyone outside his small circle of intimates. An elitist rather than a mere social snob, he looked down on other noblemen, too, not merely commoners or non-Ropans. They'd known each other all their lives. "You're not the Judge," Stefan said mildly.

"You shouldn't have done it, Stef."

"Lia did it, not me." Stefan had expected greater understanding from Romaric. "Sooner or later the truth would have been known. I couldn't stay nominal forever. I *am* a Judge. She knew that when she told me."

Romaric shook his head. His look said that Stefan was being childish, or purposely obtuse. "She supposed you'd put your own interests ahead of these wildmen." He waved his hand, dismissing all fifty million inhabitants of the Northern Sister Continent with the gesture. "You should, Stef."

It was simple for Romaric to believe that a man's personal honor, his family, and his land must come first in his own regard, and that such an ordering of life was right. Romaric didn't consider it necessary to participate in the world's improvement. He didn't ponder the reality of strangers; he had never felt their living presence in his mind or tempered his convictions with a compassionate awareness of their existence. Stefan grimaced and glanced away, then was startled by the blank wall of the access booth; in a true Assembly call he would have seemed to remain in Romaric's presence. He quickly turned back. "She knew I wouldn't."

Romaric sighed. "Lia believes that if she could find the right lever, you'd give up everything—the Assembly, me, even Tepan—for her. She keeps searching for it, and you encourage her by trying, each time she disappoints you, to be a more conscientious husband, not because you care for her, but because you think you should. You two should have gone your own ways years ago."

"You know me so well." Stefan intended to be sarcastic.

"I do," Romaric said. "And it's because I don't pay attention to these dumps into the Assembly. The Assembly killed your marriage. You don't let yourself feel anything, because then everyone will know."

"She betrayed me," Stefan said softly, "and now you say that I'm at fault?"

"These things happen." Romaric shrugged. "They're worked out. Privately." Romaric picked up a book as if his statement derived from it, then set it back on the bed. His bed. Romaric and his wife, Maja, led entirely separate lives; Stefan doubted they'd ever spent a full night in the same room. Both seemed content with the arrangement.

Stefan listened to the repetitive ticking of Romaric's massive floor clock. For years Stefan had used the Assembly's constant keeptime, but thanks to his friend's tutoring, he could read the ornate, gear-driven face. Four o'clock. Tepan would be asleep; Ezio was a second home to him. Stefan wished he were his son's age again, without responsibilities, except to learn and let himself be trained. That was a dream, though; life had its perils and disappointments even at the age of four. This family disgrace—his mother's dishonor and his father's public betrayal of it—would shame him. "Can you keep Tepan there for a few days?" Stefan asked. It was the purpose of his call.

"Of course."

Whether or not Pritchard listened, he could do nothing to coerce Romaric Ezio, whatever anger he felt for his schoolboy nemesis, but Stefan needed Romaric to understand the urgency. "I want Tepan safe, Ro. No matter who asks for him, or what they say, keep him there, safe. Swear it. And if anything should happen to me, then you're his trustee and Acari's regent."

Romaric spat into his right hand, then extended it to where, on his caller's simulacrum, Stefan would be. Romaric would never violate their crude childhood swearing ritual. Stefan spat and raised his hand to grasp his friend's. "My word," Romaric said. As he covered the image of Stefan's hand with his own, thousands of miles away Stefan imagined a ghostly sensation of warmth. "Stef, that nixt mirko out of Zona was always unsavory; I assume this is because of him. Don't worry, he won't touch Tepan, even if he is the Assembly's Poupey now."

Stefan envisioned Pritchard hearing Romaric's casual contempt, the play with Pritchard's nickname: Poupey, puppet. It made Stefan uncomfortable, yet it was true; Kaim Pritchard wasn't his own man. "He may be listening."

Romaric grinned, and for an instant reminded Stefan of John Denning. "I always assume he is," Romaric said. "Him, or someone like him, working for the Adjusters. They distrust anyone who has his own opinions. The Assembly conveys information with the force of absolute belief. Belief is an Assembly function. Emotion, not thought or truth."

"The Assembly unifies Earth," Stefan chided him.

"That's true," Romaric said. "We don't have wars.

And the Health Reports are useful. I don't say abandon the thing, Stef. I know that without it the world would be more dangerous. But don't you think that we depend on it too much?"

"I'd like to think that I do something useful, true and, well . . . good," Stefan said.

"You do, but it's because of who you are, and not because of the Assembly."

"Without the Assembly, I couldn't do as much. You're being purposely stupid, Ro. Thoughtless. You say things you don't mean just to outrage people."

Romaric straightened, shaking the bed slightly. The wineglass nearly fell, but he caught it and drank. "Listen, Stef, don't be angry with me. I don't know how it is for a ticker, but for the rest of us, the Assembly deposits information without leaving room for deliberation, doubt, or discussion, the way there should be. The way it is in a book." He gestured at his collection.

"You're using the Assembly now. We couldn't exist without it." Stefan's tone was hard.

Romaric shrugged while idly toying with the cover of one of his books. "I know. Life would be different, and possibly worse for some people, but the Old Moderns managed. I'd survive, and so would you."

That was all that mattered to Romaric. Stefan remembered cases he'd judged, situations where, without the Assembly's protection, power alone would have ruled. "Spoken like a rich man."

Romaric shook his head. "You're the one who's insular, Stefan. You don't think about the Assembly nearly enough because it makes you feel so good when you connect."

Stefan flushed. "That isn't true."

"What? You don't feel the ticker's rush? You've told me so before."

Stefan said nothing. Remembering even the faded feeling of his entry into the Assembly earlier that morning gave a warmth that, while not orgasmic, was pleasurable and intense. "That isn't the point," he said.

Romaric had been watching. He nodded in understanding. "But then what is? Stef, just what do the Adjusters adjust? Truth? Can we trust people who act secretly and say it's for our own good?" He hesitated a moment. "Just remember who Poupey is, and that he, not you, is the Adjusters' direct agent. Remember that almost his first act on becoming a peripheral was to use what he learned to blackmail a woman into sex with him."

"I didn't know." Stefan was shocked.

Romaric shrugged. "Pou kept dogging your heels, trying to make something of the fact that you two had both been chosen. We kept him away." Stefan heard the reminiscence of violence in Romaric's tone and frowned, but said nothing. It was long ago and Pritchard had misused his abilities, as he was doing now if he was listening. "Finally, Pou was expelled," Romaric said. "The girl, and his lies. He was dipping into the Assembly to cheat on examinations."

"You never told me," Stefan said.

"After they made you a ticker, you had such a difficult time adapting to that damn Assembly, no one wanted to upset you. I only hope all this makes you reevaluate the Assembly. It's not as perfect as you think." He set down his glass and picked up a book; he shook it in Stefan's direction. "This is how human knowledge should be stored. Not injected into the brain on demand, fully formed. A man should have to digest facts for himself; I know you better from my own reading—my own perceptions of you—than I ever would from an Assembly dump. We need to think about how we use it."

"You're becoming a crackpot," Stefan said affectionately. Romaric hadn't changed when Stefan became a ticker and then a Judge, despite the public scrutiny to which their friendship had been subjected. His secondhand celebrity hadn't made Romaric any less a private man, because Romaric Ezio was unconcerned by anyone's opinion. That had protected Stefan, and kept him from being alone.

"Crackpot." Romaric smiled as though he enjoyed the name. "I prefer to call myself an eccentric."

Stefan laughed aloud, and heard the echo in the confined space of the deadhead booth. Inside the Assembly on a call, he rarely noticed anything from outside. Romaric would never understand the Assembly; it had always been an obstacle between them. To Romaric it was a foreign mechanism, requiring great effort to utilize. He found any connection more complicated than a call to be awkward. Not so Stefan. For him, using the Assembly was effortlessly natural. Inside was a protected place from which to think, one where his thoughts could be clarified, where he had instant, easy access to human knowledge and felt all of humanity around him. "It may be different for a ticker," he allowed.

"Your wildman, Denning, doesn't trust the Adjusters, either. He called them 'ice priests' in his last public speech." Romaric sipped his wine, then slyly added, "Maybe I'd like him."

"You? You would never see beyond his tattoos. Besides, Denning might make speeches, but he's a peripheral, part of the Assembly system."

"I didn't know." Romaric coughed once, then stretched and yawned. "How much does he actually use it?"

Stefan thought about Denning. He had obviously reviewed Stefan's own dump file in the Assembly. He was a proficient, flesh-pressing type of politician, popular in the Sisters where the Assembly was not. The party invitation had come by handcopy, not Assembly call, but Stefan had assumed that was done for effect, to impress him. "I don't really know. The Assembly is fairly easy to avoid here in the Sisters."

"Good for them." Romaric leaned forward. A pile of books spilled over, some onto the floor, but he didn't move to pick them up. "It's time you thought about leaving the Assembly. Denning thinks about it, despite being one of you."

"One of whom?" Stefan asked sharply. He'd never been lumped with Denning before, certainly not by Romaric.

Romaric lay back on his pillows. There were dark circles under his eyes. "People like you, Denning and little Poupey. It takes a certain talent to use the Assembly, at least, to use it easily and well. The codes feel random and artificial to most of us; they make no sense. But some people are receptive. You're chosen as peripherals, and if you're especially unlucky, as a ticker."

Romaric had not been chosen. "It's not intelligence," Stefan began.

"Of course not," Romaric interrupted. "Adepts are savants. It runs in families; Tepan's already better inside the Assembly than my sons, the tutors say. Personally, I think that it has to do with language ability; you always had the monkey's gift. If you're not careful, though, the Assembly will addict itself another dedicated public servant in Teppy. Better than recruiting from Zona, I suppose." He yawned and closed his eyes.

"I'll call again," Stefan said, ready to terminate the call.

Romaric ignored the offer. "I'm curious how these Travelers fit in. Beyond the obvious, of course, that they're outsiders and won't tell us what we want to know. Beatrice made quite an impression on you."

"She's interesting," Stefan said, defending himself against a tale begun in his own mind.

Romaric smiled. "I should have met them. Maja went to the reception in Paris, but I didn't bother. It sounded boring. That was before I began to study them, before the Assembly controlled their itinerary. Did you go?" He opened his eyes to look at Stefan, then rubbed them.

"No. I met them here. Ro, what do you know about the Travelers?"

"They're liars," Romaric said. He indicated the books, which surrounded him like toy soldiers on a sick child's bed. "The only Old Modern attempts to found interstellar colonies were performed in fiction."

Stefan, back in the deadhead access, stood up, causing his image to seem to move away from the bed. "The records aren't adequate. Too many died and the survivors were disorganized." His voice trailed off at the thought of the dark time that was the shared catastrophe of mankind, his civilization's central demon as well as its origin.

"You're wrong," Romaric said, as firmly as he had accused the Travelers of lying. "And so is the Assembly for accepting their fantasy. Use common sense. The Old Moderns had barely reached the moon before the Great Deaths; they couldn't have founded an interstellar colony."

"Use common sense, yourself. The Numerican colonists—the Travelers—are here. They arrived from space, and they're human. How else can you explain those facts?" Back in Bowl, Stefan was twisting his ring, but the motion was too small to register through the access. He recalled Pritchard's innuendo concerning Traveler humanity. That had been after his dump; no one else knew.

"Did you like the woman so much?" Romaric coughed again; his eyes were red and bleary. "Good for you. It's time you relaxed your self-control and felt something. Women are all liars, anyway."

Stefan flushed. "You're tired." He gestured at the door, the formal symbol of ending a call, then raised his hand to terminate the call physically. He stopped. "Or are you ill?"

"Something's going around," Romaric said. "Maja has it, too. Worse. A fever."

Stefan thought immediately of Tepan. "Is it serious?"

Romaric shrugged. "Don't worry, Stef. The children have been with their tutors, not much with us. You see, there are advantages to being a neglectful parent." He chuckled to himself and closed his eyes again. "Go on. It is late. I apologize for teasing you. I'm really teasing Poupey. Are you listening, Pou? Don't trust him, Stefan, and remember that he'll want anything you have. But since you've started, you may as well make the humiliation worthwhile and save that painted wildman, John Denning."

Her cell needed a window, Beatrice thought. She remembered the first time she'd seen the universe through one. The Friends had called it an "eye through the wall," and had seemed to enjoy it, though windows were a human novelty. They never understood the fascination of staring into the unfathomable depths of unreal space. They had never adopted the practice. With no years, no days, no measurement of time that was anything like human, just an interminable then and a fleeting now, the Friends didn't seem to grasp the concept of looking out or forward. Or perhaps, since song was really only a half-alien creole, Beatrice didn't understand the Friends' attitudes at all. But she missed them.

Stefan yawned, ready to go upstairs to bed, and pushed the key to disconnect. Romaric's room vanished, but instead of an empty display, the holographic field went glaringly white, the brightness of sunlight flashing off ice. Stefan squinted but had to turn away from the screen as he jabbed at the disconnect key again.

"Stefan?"

Stefan recognized the voice, although he had never heard it anywhere but inside his mind while connected with the Assembly. Its tone and timbre were precisely what he had expected. "Sir?" Automatically, he bowed, rising slightly from the chair. The Adjusters abandoned names when they gave up their physical lives for permanent connection inside the Assembly, nevertheless, each Adjuster remained an individual. Stefan had encountered this Adjuster before, and thought of him as the Amicus Curiae, the friend of the Court, for his seeming oversight of Open Court decisions. Other Judges had also encountered him. He was a respected presence, a wise advisor; Stefan had wondered if he had once been a Judge of the Open Court himself.

"Stefan. This is a delicate investigation," Amicus Curiae said. His voice had the sonorous tone Stefan would have ascribed to God. It filled the tiny room and echoed in Stefan's ears. Inside the Assembly, his presence had been much more equal and intimate. "You know something of what's at stake, Stefan, but not all of it. We know more, and what we know suggests that you should proceed, if at all, with caution."

"I cannot close a preliminary investigation without a ruling." It was plain fact. "I can't make one yet. I don't know the truth." Stefan's mouth felt dry. He had never spoken aloud with an Adjuster. His voice sounded tiny after that of Amicus Curiae.

"Truth," the voice intoned. "Not all justice is based on truth, as you have yourself found." Once, Amicus Curiae had placed a secrecy seal over a case where Stefan had issued a judgment based more on mercy than law. "We need to be certain you'll do no harm."

"What harm?" Stefan guessed it was the conversation with Romaric, the lateness of the hour, even in Bowl, and the sparring with Kaim Pritchard, but he felt immediately suspicious. He wanted specifics.

"More than you know. Stefan, connect with us. We can exchange information more efficiently."

"Sir, I can't dump." The Numerican ship was cause for concern, possibly even a menace, but the facts of Beatrice's kidnapping and John Denning's arrest still needed to be discovered. If Stefan connected, he would dump. Not only Amicus Curiae, but everyone would know what Stefan knew and suspected.

"We will protect your privacy," Amicus Curiae said, understanding Stefan's concern. "There will be no trace of you inside the Assembly proper. No one will receive any hint of this conversation, either."

Traceless. In the booth, Stefan frowned. "Sir, is Kaim Pritchard your agent?"

"He is ours." The voice hesitated, its echo dying, then it added, "He does what is necessary; so must you."

It was part reproof and part reassurance. Stefan disliked use of the royal "we," which even the Oblander avoided. The Adjusters did not command the Open Court, despite its being a feature within the Assembly, or so Stefan had always believed. Amicus Curiae was not his superior; he was part of the maintenance crew of a complex assemblage. Stefan knew that the blindingly white light was unnecessary, and the voice was a projection and enhancement meant to inspire awe. Had the tricks been fewer, they might have convinced him more. "Sir, with all due respect," Stefan said, "Adjusters are also human and fallible. A Judge's decision is his alone to make. Sir, the investigation is mine. I will not do anything to harm the proper interests of Earth."

"We know more than you about that ship; we need to know what you intend, since it can affect all of us. You must trust us."

Stefan tried again to look at the display, but couldn't. His eyes teared and all he saw was blazing, brilliant white, so intense it seemed that its edges wept colors. That angered him. The Adjusters wouldn't know it, since they could not now see into his mind, so he told them. "The Assembly doesn't have the right to know everything, about me or about the Travelers."

"Of course," Amicus Curiae soothed. "We trust you, Stefan, and hope someday you will be one of those who joins us. Before that, we must be sure that what you do now is right. Connect."

It was an order. He studied his estate ring. Light from the displayer made it glow gold. He knew a bribe when he heard one. Anyone who would offer or take a bribe was unfit to judge. Amicus Curiae was trying to influence Stefan's investigation. Stefan, despite the pleasure he took in the Assembly, had never wanted less to be an Adjuster. "No, sir."

"You refuse to connect?" It was the voice of an angry God. "You believe yourself more fit to judge this matter?"

A day, perhaps even an hour earlier, Stefan would have answered differently. "Yes, sir," he said. "And I do refuse to connect."

Chapter 6

Beatrice slept like death was on the other side of her rest, ripped awake by frequent nightmares. The last featured Pritchard. He chased her through the dim corridors of the Ship while leering Kroni watched and Friends laughed at them all.

She shivered herself awake. A blanket had been thrown over her and another was beneath her. Between them, she was naked as an animal. The blankets weren't enough insulation to prevent her warmth from seeping away into the dark.

The room was densely black and silent except, if she concentrated on it, for the steady mechanical hum. Unable to see much, her hand more a sensation than a sight, but she was able to recognize the interrogation table. She'd lain there in a temporary cradle while they watched her reaction to images, then they had used it as her seat when they fed her.

She moved carefully and sat, then stood, up. The floor was cold. It had a gritty texture beneath her bare feet, and the unevenness of natural ground. She curled her toes to lessen her contact with it. When she listened, she heard no breathing except her own, but elusive noises told her she wasn't entirely alone.

She draped one of the blankets around herself, making it into a dress, and was glad of the psychological protection it gave in this tense situation. The two men— the Boy had stayed away—had questioned her for hours, sometimes together, sometimes separately, asking things she wouldn't answer. She'd been confused, and therefore said nothing important since there was safety in silence. Her nakedness had been an extra source of misery.

Beatrice tried to consider rationally who had abducted her. Pritchard and the Assembly were her first suspect, but if it had been them, surely they would have conducted their interrogation in another way, using the Assembly.

The Assembly had been the Travelers' greatest fear. Its techniques were mysteries to them, but they had suspected their implants might make them vulnerable. These men, however, were tattooed locals. When they asked about Numerica, Beatrice realized that the Assembly and Pritchard were not her captors.

Beatrice felt the edge of the table, and climbed back onto it. She clasped her hands around her toes, trying to warm both extremities at once. She cleared her throat. The sound embarrassed her. It seemed loud in the dark, and replete with indecisive crudity. It also reminded her of Pritchard, and that he was ill. How would he fare? They didn't know yet if he would survive, therefore it had been too soon to call the Ship.

Rescue was her other concern. If Pritchard hadn't kidnapped her, then he might have mounted a rescue from these others, yet he was ill, and the Earth was probably in shambles after the call. Her friends were strangers on Earth, and while not precisely expendable, still all of the Travelers had been potential sacrifices; they might do nothing, even when the Ship arrived. Beatrice remembered the Judge, but Pritchard had said the Judge was gone. She hummed a bit of inadvertent song, a lament for the living that asked: What will become of me?

She could call no one without the beacon; she could depend upon no one for help. She would have to do the best she could alone. She lowered herself down from the table again. Her eyesight was good, but this darkness was profound. The only light was an exceedingly faint, all-around glow, as though the walls and ceiling were translucent and transmitted distant starlight. The door frame glowed slightly brighter. Moving with care, she slowly walked the short distance to the front of the

room, then went sideways to the door. She felt for the
knob and found it. The knob wouldn't turn. She pulled
it, though gently, trying to avoid noise that might bring
her captors. The knob wouldn't budge. What else should
she try?

The room held onto smells; the air didn't circulate.
Their sweat and hers, the astringent tinge of urine from
the pot they'd left, the fragrance of old porridge and a
faint trace of ozone all clung and combined on the
room's dark walls. They felt smooth, almost greasy, and
when she pushed on them, they were thin. It was an odd
kind of structure.

She had viewed the room during her interrogation.
The cradle in which they had held her trapped while
showing images had been partially collapsed and placed
on the floor. By the light of their portable lanterns it
had reminded her of a small coffin. That box, and another, larger, padlocked one were, together with the
table, the only furniture in the room; the men had taken
away the chairs they'd used during her interrogation.
Because of its small size, because of the darkness and
the lack of windows, it felt claustrophobically cramped.
On the Ship, her cubby was much smaller, but it had
been part of a large compartment, itself part of the
human shelter, and that but a modest portion of the
Ship. She had been free.

Naked, barefoot, and with no idea where she was
being held, she wouldn't know where to go if she broke
free of this cell. It was too dark to pace comfortably.
Beatrice sank down and squatted near the door, listening
for her guards. Not a sound. Did she dare pound on the
door to bring them? To what purpose?

Beatrice sighed. The Fox had probably been their target. He'd made a point of his availability, assuming that
eventually one of them would be taken. She'd been stupid to follow his usual path, stupid to be afraid of Pritchard's illness. Wasn't that why they'd come to Earth?

Beatrice sang a bit of cheery song. The cheerfulness
was lost and turned on her. It sounded desperate.

Abruptly, there was light. The walls and ceilings were

suffused with it. By its radiance, she could see easily. From outside her cell came sounds of human movement.

"Hello!" she called.

Voices spoke to each other. There were peculiar echoes. Something was dragged across rough ground. An aromatic smell she identified, from her time on Earth, as coffee wafted into the room, awakening her hunger. She hoped for more of the tsampalike gruel.

They would return. They would ask more questions. Beatrice had to decide what to tell them. With the Ship on its way, perhaps it was time to tell the truth.

A while later—it seemed a long while, but she couldn't be sure—footsteps approached. Beatrice got to her feet.

She considered jumping on them as they entered the room, but the idea was ridiculous. Her interrogators bumped the thin wall and twisted the doorknob, muttering to each other about its stubbornness, then it opened. The two older men walked into the room. They carried lanterns that gave them a spectral appearance.

"Move back," the man in charge said. "Away from the door."

"Afraid of her, Frank?" the other joked.

She was nothing, then, of which to be afraid. They were wrong, and this dank, close space was a good breeding ground for an airborne passage of a virus. "Something to eat?" she asked.

Frank shook his head. "Answer our questions first."

The door hadn't completely closed behind them. She moved back, as they'd ordered, but a bit to the left so she could catch a glimpse outside.

There was no outside. Beyond the door was a huge, dark space. The man who'd been the Boy's companion in the woods noticed her gaze and firmly pulled the door shut. "There's nowhere to go," he said. "It's a maze."

"How long have I been here?" She remembered only the one meal. She was hungry, but less so than she would have expected for the time she thought had passed.

"Never you mind." The Middleman between the Boy and Frank spoke a dialect that had a friendly sound, but his intonation was grim. She thought: This is the one who will kill me.

She decided to be honest. It was her best chance to survive. Once the Ship arrived, and the Friends came out along with Ship-born humans and perhaps a few Kroni—the Friends never understood the antipathy for them felt by humans—the Earth would know everything it didn't know now. Beatrice had begun to picture these three captors as renegades, outside the stream of information, who knew less than others did, despite their control over her. She had to bring them to comprehension; there was no reason to repeat her previous stubbornness.

"Tell us about Numerica. No more evasions," Frank said.

Beatrice clasped her hands, squeezing them together for warmth and relief of tension. How should she begin in the face of such ignorance? There was no Numerica. It was a lie. Pritchard had invented it. "Is Pritchard still sick?" she asked hesitantly.

The Middleman shrugged and glanced at Frank.

"We'll ask the questions," Frank said. He turned toward the door and shouted through it. "Bring us the chairs!"

"I'll answer whatever you ask," Beatrice said, putting humility and truth into her tone. "But first, I need to know what's happened to him. Just that." If Pritchard survived the virus, then the Ship's arrival would be all right. "Is he alive or dead?"

Frank and the Middleman looked at each other as though each was trying to discover the reason for her question. "She wouldn't want us to tell her anything," the Middleman said.

Beatrice understood, from his intonation, that the *she* was a different person from the *her,* Beatrice. So, who was this She, the person behind Beatrice's captivity? "She would want answers to your questions," Beatrice wheedled. "You'll get them, quickly and honestly, if you just tell me about Pritchard."

Frank shrugged. "Last I heard, the bastard's fine. You have something going with him?" He wasn't lying, but he didn't really know the state of Pritchard's health. "Is the Ship here yet?" she asked. "Who sent for it?"

"You said one question," the Middleman growled.

"Wait!" Frank sounded uneasily interested. "What's this about your ship?"

Whoever her captors were, they had nothing to do with turning off the beacon.

All life is risk, Beatrice thought. "If Pritchard is sick, then so are others," she said. "In Ropa and here. Wherever we've been. If Pritchard dies, so will some of them."

"You brought something to Earth. A new death." The Middleman sounded as if the matter were abstract. He turned to Frank. Beatrice couldn't see his face, but as he spoke his voice rose into outrage as the meaning truly penetrated. "She brought sickness here from Numerica! The bitch! She's infected Earth, and now the Ship is coming! Invaders! They're going to take over. And the damn Assembly is hiding it."

"What's going on?" Frank pushed the Middleman aside, and raised his lantern, the better to see Beatrice. "Is it true?"

"Partly, but it's not the reason we've come," Beatrice began. She and her fellow Travelers had conjectured that Pritchard knew about the illness because he had brought them away from the more heavily populated Ropa and Chen. He knew, because they had explained it, that the four of them were liaisons between the Ship and Earth. He certainly knew there was no colony of Numerica. She almost wished that she had been captured by his men. There was too much to tell these. She glanced at the unlocked door.

Frank grabbed her chin and forced her to look at him. The Middleman took a handgun from his belt and pointed it at her. "Tell me what the hell you mean."

It was hard to talk with his hand around her jaw. "Cross-contamination is a risk of contact for both sides. We were sent to see if contact is safe yet."

"Is it safe?" Frank stared into her eyes. His were dark hollows, entirely shadowed.

"We don't know. That's why I asked about Pritchard."

He released her with a gesture of throwing something away. She stumbled backward. Her blanket fell off.

Frank stared at the hand with which he'd touched her. He grimaced. To the Middleman, Frank said, "He didn't tell us a damn thing. Bastard!"

"Who?" Beatrice begged to know. "Please, tell me who you are? Why did you kidnap me?"

They ignored her.

The Boy banged open the door. He had brought the chairs.

"Get out!" the Middleman shouted. "She's infected with something she brought down from that death ship!"

Both men backed away from Beatrice. The Boy stood dumb in the doorway.

"Not that it matters," Frank said more quietly. "She's already infected us, most likely."

"Remember the party?" the Middleman asked. He glared at Beatrice. "My wife was there." He studied the gun in his hand.

"That's why he had us do his dirty work," Frank said, as if to himself. "Why he wanted to know how they talk to the ship."

The Middleman raised the weapon, aiming it at Beatrice.

"The risk is on both sides!" Beatrice said. Her voice pleaded for them to understand.

Frank slapped down the Middleman's arm, ruining his aim. "Who?" As though he was walking to the edge of a cliff, he approached Beatrice, but didn't quite reach her. "Who is on that ship?"

"Friends!" She shouted it. "Friends! No one is a stranger to them. They want to be welcome here." She rubbed her arm, where Eyni's flesh had become her own. "We do the best we can."

"Aliens." The Middleman swallowed hard. He seemed to have forgotten his gun.

Behind the others, the Boy dropped the chairs.

"Friends," Beatrice insisted. "The Friends are good." If they weren't, then her coming to Earth was unjustifiable, all the deaths were meaningless, and everything about her life was wrong.

"We have to tell her," Frank said. He was staring at Beatrice as though she were a sinister, alien creature, not a naked woman entirely in his power. No Friend ever looked at anyone like that.

"We *are* friends," Beatrice cried out. "They are. They want to protect Earth, but they want to know you, too." Contact with others was an instinctive imperative to the Friends. The only way to overcome their need for the synergy of association with strangers was the beacon. It had kept Eyni and the other Friends away until Earth was ready; they tried to be careful. She walked toward the kidnappers. "They want to be your friends."

Frank and the Middleman backed away, to the door. The Boy was gone. "Yeah, the kind of friends that sent you to make us sick before they come."

Stefan brought a physician with him when he went to the Lodge late the next day, Dr. Sidro Felipe, the primary care physician for emergency treatment from the hospital in Bowl. The hospital staff considered him a foreigner because he came from the far western shore of the Northern Sister Continent. In return, Dr. Felipe, a plain-faced man in a town of clan tattoos, seemed to have no liking for Bowl and its clansmen. He'd been eager to accompany Stefan.

"The wildmen respect only surgeons," Dr. Felipe said, spreading his long, thin fingers wide in a show of distaste. "Crude. If there's no blood, no cutting, these people don't believe the treatment can be effective."

People with grievances too often wanted the Open Court to intervene; Stefan refused to become drawn into Dr. Felipe's resentment of local attitudes. "I'm sure local opinion isn't different from that in Ropa; for so many illnesses, medicine can't do much but quarantine the stricken houses and pray."

"That's not true!" Dr. Felipe had a temper. "Good care always makes a difference. Tremblers is controllable. Red Death usually kills only the very old and the very young. If your friend has it, then yes, he must be isolated, but he'll probably survive. It isn't deadly to everyone, not anymore. The viruses have become less virulent, and we're the descendants of survivors."

"Both my parents died of it," Stefan said. "And my brother."

Dr. Felipe didn't miss a beat. "The Ropan outbreak fifteen years ago?" He continued, over Stefan's concise acknowledgment. "That was an unusually virulent strain. Even so, there were only two million deaths, worldwide. Our medical knowledge has ended the danger of anything like the Great Deaths happening again."

Only two million. Death had a different meaning to doctors, which was one reason Stefan disliked them. "I'm sure that's what our ancestors believed."

Dr. Felipe stared out the window for a moment. Short, very thin, and with dark circles beneath his eyes, shadowing his pockmarked cheeks, Dr. Felipe was an ugly man, and of a physical type unlike the people of Bowl. His fingernails were bitten. He hadn't smiled once since Stefan had met him. "We've made progress," he said. "A great many diseases from Old Modern times are gone. You'd barely know the names: syphilis, smallpox, measles."

"Fires burned out by something hotter." Stefan turned away, too. Sidro Felipe came highly, if grudgingly, recommended by his colleagues, and there was much to respect in any man who would willingly choose a profession that put him in the path of potentially untreatable, incurable disease, but his sour self-righteousness was irritating. He carped about the differences between himself and the "real wildmen" of the clans that populated the center of the continent as if ashamed of their mutual association in Ropan consciousness. Stefan disliked that attempt to better himself at the expense of others.

"The Health Report for Ropa is still clean," Dr. Felipe said. A peripheral, he'd probably consulted the Assembly once again. "Perhaps this is a statistical anomaly. I can't believe the Assembly would purposely hide an outbreak of disease."

Stefan had enlisted Dr. Felipe's help earlier in the day. It had been a hunch. Beatrice's collection of hard copy Health Reports had nagged at him. He recalled that she had asked after new diseases when they'd met in the cave. Pritchard was sick; so was Romaric, ostensibly a bad cold that Maja had brought back from Paris, where she'd met the Travelers. The Assembly's Health Report had indicated nothing going on in Ropa, but Stefan had asked Dr. Felipe to investigate more thoroughly. Dr. Felipe had ferreted out contradictory details. There had been a weeklong jump in Ropan mortality. Not much, only an extra 2 percent death rate than was usual, perhaps something to do with the drought. There were also a few reported cases of Red Death, though the strain seemed less virulent than usual. None of the reports was alarming, but Dr. Felipe had expressed surprise that his physicians' daily hadn't mentioned any of it.

"Perhaps the Adjusters considered a report unnecessary." Stefan watched the road. He had awakened to a sunny, quiet morning after the previous day's fog, certain he had made the correct decision in refusing to connect into the Assembly with the Adjusters, and yet apprehensive. The foundations of his belief in the Assembly had been shaken. Romaric had held the same antisocial opinions since adolescence; he'd once called the Adjusters "tickers with more tricks." Stefan tended not to pay him much attention, but the attempt of Amicus Curiae to influence him had forced Stefan to reassess the Adjusters. There was awe attached to them, but they were human, not demigods.

"You'll examine Mr. Pritchard and tell me what he has," Stefan said. "Then, possibly, you'll examine the Travelers."

"I'm looking forward to that." Dr. Felipe bit at a hangnail. "There's been nothing placed in the record about their differences. After so many generations of life in a different environment, there must be some divergence. It will be interesting."

"What about their coloring?"

Dr. Felipe shrugged. "It could be genetic, environmental, or disease induced. Anything. Have you noticed their slighter build? Is the gravity lighter on Numerica?"

"I don't know." Stefan had difficult questions. The first was why Pritchard wasn't looking harder for Beatrice. The local police had been ordered to watch the roads, rails, and other methods of transport out of the region only that morning; beyond that, Pritchard hadn't deigned to communicate with them. Pritchard was not managing this as a serious investigation. Stefan was more and more certain Pritchard already knew where Beatrice was hidden, but he needed proof, not reasonable supposition.

Their coach was stopped at the outskirts of the Lodge. A man leaned in, saw Stefan, then waved them on. They drove through the extensive, wooded grounds in silence. Stefan stared at the dense forest. Beatrice had not precisely said so, but she had implied that she did not enjoy the woods. He had spoken, for much too long, about the peacefulness of solitary walks in the woods on his estate, and of the graceful majesty of trees, but Beatrice had said—he tried to recall her precise comment—that trees were confusing and too randomly arranged. He had told her she would probably like formal gardens—he didn't, much—and Beatrice had laughed. He smiled, remembering, as he had smiled then. The road passed over the stream that had figured in Beatrice's abduction. Possibly she had walked the woods, and been kidnapped, because of him.

Pritchard was waiting for them at the Lodge's main entrance. He looked as though word of Stefan's arrival had dragged him from his bed. In daylight, Pritchard's face had purplish-red splotches but wasn't entirely bruised; his eyes were red. A hemorrhagic illness, definitely, but Red Death would have included vomiting and the changes induced by the partial dissolution of muscle and certain internal organs by now. Stefan left the coach. Pritchard clutched the railing at the top of the three short stairs as if it alone kept him from falling down, but he'd had the energy to greet them. Red Death would have had him incapacitated. "You think you're above everyone, don't you, Inlander?" Pritchard said in a gravelly snarl. "Even the Adjusters."

Had Pritchard been behind Amicus Curiae's approach? That could explain it. Stefan felt better; the Adjusters were simply poorly advised. "I only do what I think is right. Do you, Pritchard?"

Dr. Felipe came around from his side of the coach and was up the steps before Pritchard fully noticed him. "Who're you?" Pritchard was irritable. Stefan remembered his father's irritability and suspicion as he lay on his deathbed. Almost his last words had been an accusation. He'd blamed Stefan for murdering the family, claiming Stefan had purposely brought Red Death back with him from the university. The first to fall ill, Stefan had been the only one to survive.

"He's a doctor. Sidro Felipe. You need him, like it or not." Stefan was sorry for Pritchard despite Romaric's revelations. Good or bad, Pritchard was a man using strength of will to hold himself together. "You haven't reported your illness in Bowl or in the Assembly, have you, Pritchard?" Stefan signaled Dr. Felipe to proceed.

Dr. Felipe had put on the usual physicians' thin, white plastic gloves, but no mask. He was watching Pritchard intently, and frowning. He took Pritchard's arm as though to lead him inside, but Pritchard pulled away. The motion unsteadied Pritchard; for a moment he needed both hands on the railing in order to stand.

"The Adjusters know," Pritchard said angrily.

"I thought they did." Stefan felt grim. It had only been two days since Pritchard had attended the party in the close confines of the cavern. If this was Red Death, or something like it, he would have been infectious then. If the Adjusters had known about the illness at that time, they'd shown a reckless disregard for lives.

"You don't know anything." Pritchard pounded his right hand against the rail.

Stefan went closer. The red eyes glared. "Is it in Ropa?" Stefan asked gently. Anger was pointless; it was too late, but fear rose inside his chest as he thought of

Tepan, of Romaric, and even Liada. "Are any of your men sick, too?"

"Go inside," Dr. Felipe ordered Pritchard. He returned to the coach and pulled his medical bag from the side compartment.

Pritchard didn't obey the doctor. He stayed on the steps, looking down at Stefan.

Their eyes met. "Are any of the Travelers sick?" Stefan asked.

"Not them," Pritchard said.

"What do you mean?"

Dr. Felipe, carrying his case, returned to Pritchard's side. Pritchard glared at him, but was quiet. Afraid.

"You'll be all right," Stefan said. "I survived Red Death. You will, too."

"I doubt it's Red Death," Dr. Felipe said.

Doctors and their labels. Stefan ignored him. Pritchard's head hung forward slightly. He brought it up again, and looked at Stefan. His red eyes gave him the look of an animal, and his expression was wounded. "It's them," he whispered. "They brought it."

"The Numericans?"

Pritchard grinned. "No," he said cagily. "The Inlanders."

Dr. Felipe, showing admirable courage, placed his arms beneath Pritchard's massive shoulders and physically turned him around. The doctor glanced back to Stefan. "I'll inform the appropriate agencies once I know what this is," he said.

"I doubt you'll get through," Stefan told him. "The Adjusters are suppressing the information that there's an illness."

Dr. Felipe scowled, but then turned his attention on his patient. Stefan watched them enter the Lodge together. Pritchard moved stiffly. The man hurt when he walked; Stefan had seen that symptom before. He'd felt it. If there was Red Death, or a variant, in Ropa, if it was even now spreading through the Sisters, then why had the Adjusters suppressed the information? Fifteen years ago the Assembly had shut down every Throw line, every zep, every means of transport until the Ropan plague burned itself out. That was the best way of limiting deaths: confine them. Why wasn't the Assembly—the Adjusters who monitored it, or the doctors who advised them on such things—doing anything? Human stupidity, human prejudice, and human delay could magnify a disease's range and deadliness.

Pritchard said that it wasn't the Numericans. Stefan was glad. He had felt misgivings, wondering if Beatrice had something to do with a new epidemic, but perhaps her collection of Health Reports meant that the Travelers were concerned about getting sick themselves. Their ancestors had left Earth before the Great Deaths. They lacked the immunities acquired by generations of survivors.

Stefan didn't want to go inside the Lodge. The woods looked inviting; no one was searching them anymore, at least in this direction. There was no obvious path through the woods between the main road and the Lodge. He could walk and be hidden there.

A phantom lover, the Assembly had crept into Stefan's dreams during the night. He still felt its echoes, the siren song it left behind. The Assembly called as if it missed him, just as he missed it inside his mind. Alone, he was unable to feel the community of Earth. Alone, he was ignorant. However much the Adjusters might want him to connect, however much he wanted it himself, he could not answer. His duty as a Judge in this investigation prevented it. He was not sure he would ever be entirely comfortable connecting himself into the Assembly's web again. All the poisoned metaphors that he'd once dismissed suddenly seemed apt. There were secrets being kept. He looked up at the Lodge and felt again that the windows were eyes watching him, the compound eyes of an insect.

He felt the silky touch of his connect registering a priority call. The Adjusters? It could be anyone. If he concentrated, might he feel the difference between Liada's stridency, Romaric's irony or the feather touch of Tepan's love? He yearned to do as he had done automatically for most of his life, to reach out. He clenched his hands as if to prevent it, and walked into Hilltop Lodge.

They left Beatrice alone. The Boy brought her more porridge, sliding it along the rough ground after briefly opening the door. About a third of it spilled over onto the tray. He didn't respond to her greeting or her questions. Once the tray was through, he pulled the door tightly shut. His departing footsteps were loud and quick; he was running. They were afraid of her. She wondered if that meant Pritchard was dead.

Her legs pulled into a fetal position, she lay shivering on the cold, hard table. She could die. There were terrestrial viruses and bacteria that could kill her, but it was more likely that her captors would do it. She pictured the Middleman taking aim with his gun. First, they would confer with *her,* whoever she was, then they would ask more questions. Eventually, they would shoot Beatrice. Death would come to her alone. No one would sing a lament; there would be no cloak for her dignity. She'd known she risked death when she volunteered to leave the Ship, but hadn't truly understood that she also risked losing the balm of community.

Song was the Ship's lingua franca and the Ship's unity. Each race had its separate language and few could understand a language other than their own. Song was a gestalt beyond their separate logics. It let the strictures that chance wrought during separate evolutions dissolve into a communication that spoke directly to thought, and at its most basic, for all creatures, thought was emotion. On the Ship, it was easier to sing about death, or the joy of a particular event than it was to discuss spatial geometry; consequently, each race still used its own language and performed its own separate functions, once its members were trusted to work in the Ship. Humans, since there was no contact with Earth, were on probation. They stayed in their shelter, or toured the Ship as guests.

Song was only a Ship-wide pidgin language. It became

a creole between certain species: human and Friend, for instance. Beatrice had been able to sing fluently with Eyni. Their mutual grammar was passionate; they each worked easily within it, as did other humans who crossed the interface. Beatrice sang well enough to be invited to the Friends' separate shelter—the only shelter to which members of other races were admitted. The Friends didn't want sanctuary from others; they were the Ship founders, and they guided it.

"Do you trust them?" The human voice inside the Friends' shelter had startled her.

Beatrice, sitting cross-legged in the corner of Eyni's cubby, had looked around, then up. A tall human man, substantially older than her, was watching from across the stack. She only smiled, assuming she'd misunderstood the question, since to be inside the Friend's own shelter, he had to be a special, as she was.

He'd smiled back. "What's your name?"

She'd told him, though the human sounds seemed out of place. She, and all her friends, used only song inside the Ship.

"My guide through heaven," he said, and bowed.

Beatrice had never seen a bow before and had no idea, then, of what he meant. They did not bow inside the human shelter; they clasped hands. "Who are you?" She didn't know this man.

"Paul Talley."

Eyni returned from fetching water for them, but Paul Talley continued speaking to Beatrice in human. It was rude, yet Eyni didn't seem to mind. Paul Talley asked after some of the adults she knew, including her mother, who, he said, was his aunt. He lived inside the Friends' shelter, with his own, particular Friend. "I haven't been back in years," he said, referring to the human shelter. "If I returned, they'd breed me, since I've been in the Ship so long."

She politely covered her mouth with her hand, but a bit of song escaped anyway. It begged him to go on.

"Yes," Eyni sang. "But let me understand, too."

Paul Talley switched to song as naturally as Eyni ever

had, and he sang with a greater competence than Beatrice had acquired. He sat back on his heels, adopting the storytelling posture used inside the human shelter. "I'll tell both you children a story," he'd said. Later she learned he was a specialist in human matters, but then she'd bristled at "children" since she'd already begun to menstruate. "An old story from Earth, where we're going next," he'd said, giving her news she hadn't known. "A story about a fox and a lion." Beatrice couldn't recall the details with which he'd embellished his tale, the first of many he'd told over the many years of travel to the Solar System, but he had made clear the relative dangers of the two animals—neither of which she'd seen yet on Earth. The lion had seemed a very large and deadly Kroni, while the fox was entirely human. The first time the fox had seen a lion, Paul Talley said, he was so terrified he'd almost died of fright. Beatrice had looked at Eyni, and said nothing. The second time he'd seen a lion, the fox had been frightened, but he'd overcome his fear and managed to hide it. The third time the fox saw a lion, he'd felt brave enough that he went up to the lion and spoke as though they were friends. "Well," Paul Talley had said, looking from Beatrice to Eyni. "What do you think?"

Eyni sang his recognition of the story, and his boredom, as well as familiarity with this human man. Beatrice expected Eyni to wander away, but instead Eyni stared at Paul Talley in a manner which, among Friends, was aggressive, yet interested.

Paul Talley laughed; in song, he said something Beatrice would not have dared sing: that he wanted to talk to Beatrice alone. Eyni protested and complied in the Friend's manner—by walking away. Beatrice started to follow him, since her welcome in the Friends' shelter depended on Eyni, but Paul Talley caught her arm. "What do you say?"

"I say the fox was stupid. The lion was still a lion."

He'd smiled and released her. Later that visit, a Friend Beatrice didn't know, but one who ranked high on the Ship, asked her if she had an interest in training for a contact mission, the first return to Earth. She'd been recommended by Paul Talley.

Stefan immediately noticed the two Travelers in the Lodge's lobby, Charles Syne and Paul Talley, the Fox. Sunlight fell on their golden complexions, making them shine like gilt icons. They faced each other across a table, playing chess, directly in the path between the door and Pritchard's private office. Their shoulders hunched, they studied the board like old men, without looking up as Stefan's entrance cast a shadow over the board. Stefan watched their slow game for two moves, then said, "I'm here to see Pritchard. After that, I'll return to town."

Neither man registered that he had heard.

"I don't have any news of Beatrice, not yet." Stefan ignored their apparent indifference. It was bravado or a Numerican cultural idiom, but in either case, not an insult. Syne made a sharp, odd sound. He spoke, all without looking up from his game. "John Denning was moved. He's being kept upstairs, here in the main Lodge. South wing. Pritchard's ill."

Stefan nodded, then wondered if they even noticed. It didn't matter. They trusted him, even Syne, who hadn't at first. They'd never viewed a dump of his, and yet they trusted him. Syne had delivered a succinct report, and with no inscrutable noises. "I know about Pritchard," Stefan said. "I brought a doctor. The illness began with a cough, then a fever, and some internal bleeding. It seems similar to a disease we call Red Death, one from the Old Modern era; it was one of the five Great Deaths. There's still no cure and no vaccine. If any of you has the symptoms, or feels unwell, let one of Pritchard's people know, or tell me. A doctor does some good, or at least can ameliorate the symptoms."

Talley straightened. He made an interrogative sound.

"It may be a new variant of the old disease; it seems milder. No one is certain what it is, yet." One of Pritchard's guards was nearby, but not hovering.

"You?" Talley asked, or perhaps he only grunted, but Stefan understood.

"I'm immune; I survived Red Death." Stefan lowered his voice. "The Adjusters seem to have been hiding its existence from the general Assembly; I think they may have been concerned about frightening you."

Talley smiled.

"Thank you," Syne said quietly. "None of us is ill."

Stefan studied the board. Syne played a methodical game, but Talley had taken some extravagant chance and now was losing, or else he didn't play very well. "The disease may be in Ropa." Stefan spoke it like a question. He was wondering how he had known, from a sound very little different from clearing his throat, what Talley had wanted to know.

Talley searched Stefan's face without quite making eye contact. There was an awkwardness about his inspection, then he looked back at his game. "All life is risk," he said and moved his piece.

Was it a comment on the game or on the possibility of illness in Ropa? On life? Stefan crossed his arms against his chest and said, "There is such a thing as being too cryptic. Tell me about Numerica," he said.

Talley looked up, very briefly. "We can't."

Something in Talley's voice sent a chill down Stefan's back. "Anything at all," he said.

Neither man responded. Both seemed engrossed in their game.

"A friend of mine says you're liars," Stefan said. "He says an interstellar colony was an impossibility for the Old Moderns, just as it would be now, for us. Pritchard suggested that you're not human. The Adjusters are so afraid of your ship that they're willing to let people die rather than spread news of this disease." He heard the edge in his tone and forced himself to calm before continuing. "My concerns are smaller. I want to find Beatrice and determine who kidnapped her. Motive only matters to me if it helps me trace who has her. I want to know one thing about Numerica. Just one. Are there any barnacles, any creature at all, which you may have brought with you that could attach to sewer pipes and be used to trace Beatrice's location?"

Talley and Syne looked across the table at each other, clearly puzzled. Stefan's impression was that, whatever Pritchard said and however oddly they sometimes behaved, they were entirely human. Then they looked down at their game again. Talley moved his rook thoughtlessly. Syne made a chirping sound that ended in a screech. Talley hummed, then quietly said, "If someone can trace Beatrice using Numerican barnacles, then I recommended you allow them to do so and find her."

"I take that as a 'no.' " When neither man answered, Stefan walked away.

It was too soon to question the doctor. Stefan hesitated in front of a bank of deadhead access booths, then decided against calling Romaric. He would probably be asleep. It might be useful to see Denning while Pritchard was distracted, though. He went where Syne had told him. A guard was in front of the room, defining it as a prison. "Sir, no one is to go in," the guard said, but he seemed uncertain.

"I saw Denning yesterday. I'm on an investigation for the Open Court."

The guard seemed to withdraw briefly—not an Assembly adept, like Pritchard—then he was back and bowed. "Judge."

Pritchard was allowing him to visit Denning. Stefan went in, and closed the door behind himself, shutting the guard outside. The man didn't object.

The room was of a type with the previous one, a cheap single hotel room, but this one was clean. The bed was made with fresh linens and there was no odor of age or vomit. Denning was alone and fully dressed, stretched out on the bed. He sat up when Stefan entered, and looked much better than he had—tired but not under mental attack. Pritchard had let up the pressure.

"Stefan," Denning said gravely. "Thank you."

"How are you, John?"

"Much better, since you stopped them from questioning me." Denning was wearing his own clothes. They looked rumpled, but he had been allowed to bathe. His hair was still damp. "Can I leave?"

Stefan stayed at the end of the bed. "No. They'll be back. Eventually, they'll break you, John, as soon as Pritchard's well. So, did you do it? Kidnap the woman? Tell me the truth."

Denning watched Stefan for a moment, then got up from the bed. They were roughly the same height. "I didn't order that Traveler woman to be kidnapped." He looked straight at Stefan as he said it.

Stefan smiled. "I'm a Judge, John. I know careful wording when I hear it."

Denning glanced quickly at the closed door.

"We're safe from listeners."

Denning grinned like a man taking another into his confidence, but uncertain whether doing so was proper. "I haven't done anything wrong, Stefan. I swear it." He licked his right thumb, then pressed the damp thumb in the middle of three prominent tattoos: forehead and each cheek. Clansman honor, like that of children and Romaric, required physical expression.

"That doesn't mean much, John. Pritchard would say the same. Right and wrong are too personal. Did you have anything to do with it?"

Denning sat back again on the edge of the bed. "I don't mean any harm to the Travelers," Denning said. "I'm glad they've come; it might loosen the Assembly's grip. I think you're beginning to feel that grip tightening on you, too. It happens sometimes. A ticker goes farther in, and may even become an Adjuster, or—rarely—he gets disgusted and wants out. I always suspected that might happen to you. You're not cynical enough to be one of them. You don't want power. You and Pritchard, you're the reverse of each other. He's the kind that ends up one of the spiders, tending the web that holds us all."

Denning's rhetorical skills hadn't suffered during his imprisonment. "You don't answer direct questions very well. Just tell me why you were on the Lodge grounds when she was kidnapped."

Denning seemed surprised by the question. "Because he called me. Pritchard. He asked me to come."

Stefan pulled a chair close to the bed and sat down.

"I never had a chance to find out why," Denning added.

Everything Stefan learned about Beatrice's abduction, the Travelers, Pritchard, and Denning made the situation more complicated. He sensed Pritchard pulling the strings, even saw him at it, but couldn't prove it. Denning, once seemingly innocent, had become an enigma. Pritchard had arrested him, but wasn't pressing him—or anyone—for Beatrice's location. Denning and his clansmen were dishonest, Stefan was sure, but he wasn't sure how or why. He stopped himself, as he was accustomed to doing, from further speculation that might prejudice his thoughts. "You have an interesting wife," he told Denning.

Denning grinned.

"I'll tell her you're doing better." Stefan stood, went to the door, then turned back. "How did the Waterman Clan first become aware of the barnacles?" Stefan asked.

Denning barely hesitated. "Pritchard warned us to look out for them," he said, as if the matter were self-evident. "When the land local set them up at the Lodge; he said he wanted to be sure the sewer kept working." Lowering his voice as if to impart a confidence, Denning added, "I made it sound worse than it was; I wanted you to stay." Full of his usual energy, he got off the bed. "Pritchard wants to be you, Stefan. Rich, an aristocrat, and honest. Clean. That most of all. He envies you and can't stand for you to despise him."

"Pritchard should have been able to break you. He didn't. Why not, John? Was he really trying, or is this some game between you two?"

"I don't know what you mean. It's no game to me." The tattoos disguised his expression but from his tone, Denning was in earnest.

"I need to check on Pritchard," Stefan said wearily. He had accomplished nothing but to further confuse himself.

Outside, the guard watched Stefan more directly than he had before. "Get anywhere?" he asked.

"Pritchard?"

The man blushed, and didn't answer. Had Pritchard been using men as masks again? Stefan went directly to Pritchard's private office. Tom Chantry, Denning's interrogator of the previous day, was reclining on one of Pritchard's office chairs. His posture and closed eyes indicated he was busy with some work. Stefan waited. The man must know he was present. Eventually, Tom opened his eyes and nodded.

"You're the second in command?" Stefan asked.

The man stretched, obviously intending rudeness by his informality, and glanced at Stefan with a slow, dismissive smile. "It's not like that in ID, but yes. You can't use his illness as an excuse to take over our investigation. And I'm not Ropan. I don't give a damn about you, Inlander, and unless and until you connect with the Assembly, you might as well not be a Judge. Without a dump, you're irrelevant." He used Stefan's language, not the local one.

"I'll connect and make my judgment when I'm ready."

"I wouldn't hold my breath that the Adjusters will let you."

Stefan felt the Assembly as pressure inside his head. A few days earlier he had wanted to connect, and traces of the Assembly had been a balm. He didn't feel that way now. Instead, it was as if something threatening was struggling to get at him. He knew nothing about Tom Chantry except he was ID. Stefan twisted his estate ring around his finger. "Where are the interrogation reports I ordered you people to make?"

Tom tapped the side of his head. "Come and get them."

Stefan walked into the room. Tom quickly sat up and watched Stefan's approach carefully, as though he feared a physical attack. Stefan went past him and knocked on the closed door to Pritchard's suite.

Dr. Felipe called, "Wait!" from inside, then he opened the door, but blocked Stefan's passage inside. "I've called the hospital. They're sending a nurse and some supplies. I'm testing everyone in this place."

"Except the Numericans," Tom interrupted.

"We'll see about that." Dr. Felipe seemed to believe his authority was paramount.

"Is it Red Death?" Stefan looked over Dr. Felipe's shoulder, but the beige and blue room behind him was empty. Kaim Pritchard was not in sight.

"We'll see when I get results on the blood tests. Until I know what we're dealing with, no one comes near him but me."

"You think it's Red Death. I've had it; I'm immune."

"I *don't* think it's Red Death." Dr. Felipe shrugged. "Your immunity is uncertain."

Pritchard hadn't come out to dispute Dr. Felipe's control. "He's accepted being quarantined?"

Dr. Felipe glanced at Tom Chantry. "I had some difficulty managing him, so I put him to sleep. He thought I was drawing more blood. It was for his own good," the doctor rationalized.

"Fine," Stefan said, reminded of how much he disliked doctors. "I wish I'd thought of drugging him myself."

Chapter 7

There was a mob outside the Waterman Clan Hall, a mob of clansmen carrying militia-issue firearms. Stefan pushed his way through the crowd, pretending not to notice the muttered insults. Most were unintelligible native patois, anyway, though he heard himself called "a bare-faced bastard Ropan."

Marta was inside the lobby, in a tight group with Paine Quinn, Orion Nash, and a man in police uniform. Furious, and concerned about the mob, Stefan shouted over the noise. "This is not the way to help John Denning!"

They quieted and turned to him.

"Stefan!" Marta called as though greeting him at a party. "Judge!" She waved him to her side.

"John is fine," Stefan said firmly. A passage was opened for him, so he went to her. "You must not take the law into your own hands." He looked around, trying to get through to these people. "All of you, disperse. Go home."

"You don't understand," Marta began, but Orion Nash cut her off.

"We're not attacking the Assembly, or the Assembly's man—though we probably should. The Waterman Clan knows where that Numerican woman is being held. We're going to get her. That all right with you, Judge?" Nash taunted.

"We don't know *exactly*," Quinn protested weakly.

"Tell me what's going on." Stefan looked at the three men and Marta. Marta whispered something to Quinn. He signaled the crowd in the lobby; it began to move outside. Stefan went to Marta. "Tell me everything. Now."

"I tried to call you." she said, taking his arm and pulling him closer, and slightly away from Orion Nash. "Quinn's people found a new outbreak of the barnacles. We've traced it to the central Man Mouth system. We need the men to try to isolate the line it comes from, and then use it to find her."

Barnacles, again. According to the admittedly unspoken information from the Travelers, there were no such things. Whoever claimed there were might be Beatrice's kidnappers. Then again, John Denning had said Pritchard had begun the barnacle story. Even if the barnacles were a lie, they still could lead him to Beatrice. "This mob action is still inappropriate," he said. "The proper authorities should free her, not a wildman posse."

"This is the Chief of Police, Don Hill." Orion Nash indicated the uniformed man. "Good enough to satisfy you, Judge?"

The police chief looked at the ground, discomfited, then extended his hand to Stefan.

"Stop it, Orry," Marta said. "Don't make this harder than it has to be."

Chief Hill's handshake was firm, and his broad face, though heavily tattooed, seemed honest. Stefan nodded at the man, then turned to Quinn. "The Travelers were in the cave at your party. What you've found is meaningless."

"He thinks we're stupid," Orion Nash said.

The others ignored Nash. "No, Judge." Paine Quinn came forward of Marta. "We isolated the cavern's septic system for the party to prevent contamination. This is new, since we removed our buffer. That's how we found her so fast. She's there, all right. Somewhere in the cave. Trouble is, quite a few lines feed into the one where we found the barnacles since a lot of our fixtures also connect to old plumbing installed by the Amercans."

Stefan saw a look pass between Marta and Quinn. "No one wants that traceless ID man involved," Marta said, "so we have to act quickly and get out there and find her."

"Before Pritchard moves her," Orion Nash opined. "He's behind all this."

Stefan frowned and studied Marta, not Quinn. The loyal wife, the pitiable deadhead, she stood covered by her baggy, blue dress and her air of innocence. He didn't trust her. He also distrusted Pritchard.

"We need the men to help search her out," Marta said.

Search her out, as if Beatrice were the villain. Stefan gestured at the mob outside the clan hall. "I'm going with you to the caves," he said.

Paine Quinn started to protest.

"That's an order from the Open Court. But first, I want to talk to Marta alone, upstairs."

Stefan appreciated Marta's quick agreement. They rode the elevator to the third floor, side by side, in silence. It was slow. His anger at the clansmen needed a physical outlet; Stefan wished he had walked instead. He strode down the third-floor hall ahead of Marta, and went into her office alone. Her machinery was running, though he didn't know what it was doing. The holographic frame enclosed text. He didn't try to read the backward letters.

"Judge?" She patted him in a matronly manner as she squeezed passed him and went behind her desk. "How can I help you?"

"Marta, if those kidnappers are killed instead of caught, they won't be able to testify to John's innocence. Pritchard won't free him and I won't have enough proof to intervene. Your people are handling this rescue. If anything goes wrong, it will hurt John, and I know exactly who I will blame."

She studied him for a moment. "I understand." She sighed. "Why don't you trust us, Judge?"

Stefan wasn't certain of his reasons. "I'm being manipulated," he said. "I know it. It started when John invited me here. I don't know all the angles or the motives, but I will."

"The Open Court is a court of equity, not law," Marta said quietly. "Whatever you think of me—of us—I trust you to do right."

In the cool, climate-controlled air, Stefan realized that he was sweating. He wiped his forehead with a handkerchief. Marta, for all the weight she carried, looked cool. "Why not just tell me everything you know?"

She leaned with one hand on the desk. Although it brought her forward and closer, it was not an aggressive stance. "I can't. That bastard has John."

Pritchard was holding John Denning as insurance for the good behavior of the clans. "What is it that the clans are supposed to be doing, or not doing? Kidnapping Beatrice, or finding her?"

She shook her head, and gave a small shrug.

Stefan thought better of asking her about the web doctor John had mentioned; he didn't trust her enough. "We'll see, then," he said. He gestured at her equipment. "This can be used to make deadhead calls?"

"Of course." She stepped away from the desk. "I'll leave you alone. Call whoever you want. They'll be awhile getting organized, and I doubt they'll find that Numerican woman very quickly."

"Oh?"

She looked blandly at him and left her office, closing the door behind herself to give him privacy.

He sat down at the desk. As he entered Drom Hanzin's code, he realized that he was becoming accustomed to using a keyboard. Drom answered immediately; their discussion was brief. "Get Tepan back from Ezio immediately," Stefan told him. "There's a new illness, probably a variant of Red Death, and I have reason to believe Per and Pera Ezio have it," Stefan said. "Treat Tepan, and anyone from outside the estate as potentially contagious, but get a doctor to see Tepan right away. Keep Liada at Acari, too, unless I say otherwise."

Drom understood the stakes. He'd been through the last epidemic, too. "Immediately, Per Acari." He was again conventionally formal.

Stefan called Romaric next. He was in bed, but this

time, although he took the call, he had been asleep. "It's just a cold," he insisted. He didn't look as ill as Pritchard. Stefan hoped that his diagnosis was wrong. "Send Tepan home anyway," he told his friend.

Romaric waved a limp hand. "There was something I forgot to mention about the Assembly," Romaric said. "Why is it in the Southlands?"

"What do you mean?" The Assembly machinery was in the icebound southern continent because that was where the Old Moderns had built it. Assembly theorists said it had been put there to protect the workers from the ravages of the diseases. The Great Deaths had already started.

Romaric lifted his head and rested his weight on his elbows. His eyes were bleary, not red. "It was too far. Too cold. They wouldn't have built anything there unless that location was absolutely necessary. Why would it be?" He leaned to one side to free an arm and used it to point a shaky finger at Stefan. "They were hiding. Stef, there's something odd about what happened to the Old Moderns. That's who you should investigate. And don't trust any of them."

Stefan laughed. "I won't trust any Old Modern I meet, Ro."

Romaric made a cutting remark about Stefan's attitude that sounded merely grumpy. "Stefan, what I said the other day ... don't pay too much attention. We need the Assembly—it's who we are—but it's frightening to rely so much on something we understand so poorly."

Stefan smiled. "Get some rest. Have a doctor examine you." He terminated the call and sat back in Marta's chair. He stared at the screen, half expecting Amicus Curiae to reappear in blinding light, but nothing happened. The Adjusters had let his calls go through. Perhaps they'd decided it was too late to continue hiding an epidemic, or perhaps he was wrong and none existed.

Stefan stood and started to walk out of the room, then he turned and looked back at Marta's access. If the clans were using barnacles to track Beatrice, if they were the kidnappers, then there was a slim chance that Pritchard

and the Adjusters were entirely innocent. Pritchard
should be told of the rescue. Even if Pritchard was behind all this, it wouldn't do any harm to tell him. Pritchard was unconscious, however, thanks to Dr. Felipe.

Stefan returned to the desk and before he could
change his mind, he used the keyboard to send Pritchard
a textual message. *"The local police, with clan help, are
mounting a rescue of Beatrice Whit at the Man Mouth
Caverns,"* Stefan sent. *"Come quickly and assist them. I
will be there, too."*

The moist, earthy smell of the cavern was as Stefan remembered it. He could almost pretend Beatrice, rather
than a line of dour clansmen, was with him, but the
hard-packed, looping path they had walked together was
shorter than he recalled. The men quickly passed the
red sign and went farther into the tunnel. Their helmet
lights lit the bench on which Stefan had met Beatrice.
The bench overlooked a smooth, blue-white formation,
a frozen stone pond.

It was like walking in a park. The ground was level
and even paved in parts. Two by two they went up a
wide concrete stairway. "Convenient cave," Stefan muttered, though it made sense that their route wouldn't be
too far underground, and would follow Old Modern
paths, since it was the Old Moderns who had installed
the original Man Mouth plumbing.

"Shhh," warned a man behind him.

Stefan had been awake too long, though he had slept,
badly and briefly, in a folding chair. He was fairly sure
that the next day had dawned. Marta had been right that
the search hadn't gone quickly, yet neither Pritchard nor
any of his men had come by the time the Waterman
clansmen announced that they'd pinpointed Beatrice's
location. If the entire rescue was a sham, then it had
been well performed.

Helmet lights bobbed ahead on the cave walls like a
fractured spotlight, illuminating gray stone and occasional mud. Every one of them, but Stefan, carried a
weapon. He couldn't rationally object—they were going

to confront kidnappers, who were presumably violent
men—but Stefan found the formation of armed clansmen reminiscent of a firing squad moving into position.
Police Chief Hill, as he had sent them off, hadn't mentioned the need to take the kidnappers alive, or the necessity of protecting Beatrice's life. The only person Hill
had told them to safeguard was Stefan himself. Now,
there was no practical way of gathering the men and
addressing them, and no reason why they would listen
to a Ropan Judge.

The air cooled slightly, then no more, but Stefan's
fingers were stiff. The helmet they'd given him was too
small. He'd torn out the foam, and the plastic bumped
against his head and crushed his ears. His nose dripped;
wiping it on the dirty coverall the clansmen had supplied
was another discomfort. The coverall smelled like it had
been worn for days by a man who worked hard and never
washed. He supposed the rank coverall was meant to
discourage him; they had wanted him to wait at the cave
mouth. Caving in Man Mouth was not a gentleman's
hobby, Paine Quinn had said. A Judge could not be a
gentleman, Stefan had answered.

Nevertheless, darkness was disorienting and could be
dangerous. He stumbled once. The men didn't stop, and
he knew they would gladly have left him behind, but he
intended to be present during the confrontation with the
kidnappers. Stefan concentrated on walking, and the significance of their trek lessened as he thought only of his
damp feet, and where to place his hands, and strained
to see ahead. The kidnappers could not have brought
Beatrice anywhere truly rugged or far underground, but
Stefan began to suspect, as their march went on, that
the kidnappers had used a different entrance.

The men ahead gained distance on him. Their lights
were no longer close enough to brighten his way. Stefan
hurried to catch up, but managed to do so only when the
others stopped. They were leaning against the curved
tunnel wall, or crouched on the ground, as Stefan, and
those few behind with him, arrived. "Rest and eat something," a low voice said. "Last chance."

Stefan hadn't brought any food, only an extra light, but someone handed him a candy bar. He ate, after stuffing the litter into a zippered pocket. Its taste was wonderful. He simply enjoyed. He could have slept standing up. He thought he might. Inside the cavern, without access to the Assembly keeptime, he had no sense of how much time passed.

Stefan's feet were cold and wet. Mud was caked onto his shoes, and moisture had seeped in through the seams in the leather. "Damn shoes," he muttered.

Several nearby clansmen chuckled softly, with sympathy. This was his opportunity, Stefan realized. "I'm Stefan Acari," he said, "a Judge of the Open Court." Voices resonated oddly in the cave, as if the randomly changing height of the ceiling absorbed sound at the same time that the stone walls made it reverberate. Some tones vanished and others were emphasized. Stefan recalled Beatrice's expressive enunciation, perfectly controlled for the hard stone cavern, and modified his pitch so his words wouldn't carry beyond the men. "I met the woman we're here to free at the party a few nights ago. Her name is Beatrice Whit. She is a Traveler, a guest on Earth. Because of the kidnapping, John Denning is being held by Independent Defense."

Stefan felt his foreign accent being magnified by his near invisibility in the dim cave. Still, vision was the liar's sense; hearing was truth. Perhaps they'd recognize the truth. "I tell you, as John's friend and as a Judge, perhaps the only way to free him from Independent Defense is to release Beatrice unharmed and capture her kidnappers *alive* so they can testify to his innocence."

The men were silent. Stefan couldn't see their reaction, but felt as foolish as though he had delivered a monologue to the stone walls. The sounds of rustling fabric and groans told him they were preparing to continue. "Please," he said, "for John's sake, be mindful of her safety."

"You're no friend to John Denning," an unidentifiable voice challenged him. The activity stopped as the men waited for his answer.

The Assembly was a mind-sink, drawing out the contents of his mind; they knew what he thought of Denning from his dumps. "I have few friends," Stefan said. "Not many want to see themselves through the filter of another mind, and have that view of their lives made public. John Denning is willing to be seen. No, we're not friends, but I like and respect him. He invited me here and I came. I hope to free him."

No one answered or argued. After a moment, someone said, "All right. Up. Let's go." Stefan didn't even know which one was their leader, but he obeyed.

He reached for the Assembly contact and found its ambient signal even here, far underground. He toyed with it, playing at the Assembly's edges like a tongue worrying a loose tooth, without result but anxious and unable to stop. The better part of a day had passed. Why hadn't Pritchard's men come?

This time Stefan went near the front of the line and worked to keep up with their steady pace. Beatrice was ahead. He wanted to see her and assure himself that she was well. He moved like a sleepwalker, daydreaming. Their first encounter—it didn't seem as though it was the only time they'd met, and yet that was so—had been one of the rare occasions during which he'd been able to forget he was a Judge. Inexplicably, that forgetfulness had given greater honesty to his conversation, not less. Stefan's foot slipped on the cracked, muddy stone, jerking him into alertness. His first thought was of Liada, the automatic guilt he still felt at anything that might bring embarrassment to her, or tension between them. Then it occurred to him that with Liada he was always a public person. His sense of propriety intruded into every aspect of their marriage.

How must it be for Liada to see herself through her husband's eyes? His very mixed feelings toward her and their arranged marriage were unremittingly accessible. Her life was as naked as his. Tired and oppressed in the underground by the weight of the world above, for the first time since she had announced her pregnancy he understood, without ego or pride intruding, why she might seek comfort in the arms of a more private man. He didn't fault her. It wasn't fair; it wasn't right; it was just real life.

The lights ahead went out. "What's going on?" Stefan whispered.

The man next to him reached out and turned off Stefan's helmet light. "Up there."

That wasn't an answer, but Stefan stayed quiet. He strained to hear the other men, his only indication he wasn't alone in blackness so intense he might as easily not have had eyes. Careful to avoid stumbling or scraping his helmet against the low ceiling that had been his last sight, Stefan leaned against the nearest wall and waited.

The men were supposed to sneak as close to the kidnappers as possible, and then overwhelm them with numbers and surprise. It wasn't much of a plan, but their sketchy knowledge of the kidnappers' encampment, and the fact they knew only one way into it and therefore couldn't surround them, had committed the rescuers to on-the-spot decision making. Stefan wished he could consult with those ahead. They carried radios, with which they could contact Quinn and the police chief, but none of them was wearing a cap, so the Assembly was unavailable.

What about the Assembly? If Pritchard were implicated in Beatrice's kidnapping, Stefan supposed it could only mean that the kidnapping was an official, if secret, Adjuster-approved act. How far up the hierarchy should Stefan assign fault? The knowledge would come out in Stefan's dump; he would make one as soon as he knew more. Secrecy, antithetical to Stefan's understanding of the Assembly, was the Adjusters' weapon; yet the Adjusters weren't all there was to the Assembly.

The cave air was stagnant and smelled unclean. He rubbed his forehead to soothe the hollow twinge, like the dry socket of a tooth. Time passed. He heard soft traces of voices, but nothing definite, nothing entirely free of possible fabrication by his mind. "Anyone?" he said under his breath, when the specter of having been deserted in the dark was too intense for his rational mind to bear.

"Shhh," said a voice at his side.

The others were still present. Stefan hunkered down. His legs ached. His neck was stiff from stooping to avoid low ceilings. He closed his eyes. His mind glazed with fatigue. Time was a water torture dripping drop by drop into his head. It left a residue behind, fossilizing his thoughts like the stalagmites and stalactites which were water turned to stone in the caves. He had to free his thinking.

Stefan's head drooped. He jerked awake, aware he must have dozed. "Hey!"

"Shhh. What?"

"What's going on?"

A foot scraped as someone approached. "They went ahead," the other whispered. "They'll send for us when it's safe."

"No!" Stefan jumped to his feet. They'd tricked him, used darkness as a restraint while they did as they pleased. He might as well have stayed at the cave mouth as sit a tunnel away from the rescue.

He reached up to his helmet and fumbled for the light switch. Whatever wildman gadget the others had used to travel the tunnel, he had only normal light. When it clicked on, the brightness stunned him momentarily.

"Turn it off!"

Stefan swore in his own language. There were only three men left of the group of twenty. He started walking in the direction the other men must have taken.

All three scrambled to their feet. The nearest grabbed at Stefan, grasping the shoulder of his filthy coverall. "Stop. You'll get hurt and ruin everything."

Stefan yanked free and continued forward. With just his own, single light it was difficult to go quickly, especially since the ground had roughened; this wasn't part of any tourist trail.

Two men caught up and, between them, they seized Stefan on each side, stopping him from following the others. "Either you release me," Stefan said, without a useless physical struggle, "or I will enter a judgment against you for obstruction, this minute." Stefan felt fierce, and vindictively proud of it. He fully intended to do as he'd threatened. He would brave the Adjusters. He would lay before the people of the world his own suspicions and their causes without issuing a judgment. The world would be the court. It could decide if the Adjusters, or Pritchard, or the clansmen—if anyone—could be trusted. Irrationally, he was disappointed when they released him. He strode ahead and the others, without lights, followed like moths chasing a flame.

The tunnel curved. Stefan followed the bend, watching the ground and not the route ahead until he noticed that the tunnel had brightened. He stopped and looked forward. They'd almost reached a high-domed cavern. It was relatively well-lit, although its height was obscured by darkness and he could not see the far side. Five of the clansmen searchers were visible, apparently at ease.

Relief made Stefan smile; they'd captured the kidnappers. He trudged toward them, slowing since there was no urgency, and because he was tired.

From behind, one of his guards yelled, "Hey! We're here. The Judge!"

A clansman in the cave ahead turned, glanced down the tunnel to where Stefan had probably just become distinguishable. Others turned. Two went forward, out of sight. Something unintelligible was shouted; it sounded like profanity.

Sharp reports from gunfire rang out, echoing strangely in the tunnel so that their precise source and number were impossible for Stefan to determine. "No!" he shouted, and ran toward them.

Locked in her room, Beatrice heard new voices and hoped for deliverance. She pressed her ear against the wall, but was unable to make out more than murmurs.

There was no shouting, no anger, and not even much surprise in what she overheard of the muffled discussion. She returned to the table and sat on its edge, considering. Were these new men allies of her captors, or rescuers engaged in a negotiation? She felt she should know. These were her people, yet their language was not song. It was much more ambiguous than that.

She returned to the wall, and stood near the door, imagining her three jailers sending potential rescuers away with one excuse or another. She would be left to the mercies of these men, who feared and despised her. Perhaps rightly.

From the vantage of the Ship, Earth had seemed merely an overly large human shelter. It seemed to have no purpose. Beatrice had accepted that it was proper to bring Earth out of its isolation. The cost to Earth was no greater than the burden the occupants of the Ship routinely shouldered in traveling unreal space.

The greatest obstacle to contact, after the problem of travel itself, was that contact was not only between intelligences, but was between whole ecologies and environments. The Ship would meet not only humans on Earth, but all of Earth's organisms. So, too, Earth would contact not only Friends, Kroni, and other intelligent races, but also their cultures, their creatures, and most especially, their pathogens.

Some, even most, pathogens were harmless across species lines, but another strategy, the fateful one that made contact perilous, was hypervirulence. Certain viruses stay ahead of their own destruction by spreading to new species—by being ultra-contagious across species lines—and when they fall on virgin soil, with no immunities and no resistance, they kill ferociously, sometimes extinguishing entire species. The intelligence of the species is irrelevant. The Friends themselves were tough, since each prior encounter strengthened their general immunity. They also did what they could to control or cure diseases they would bring to a newly contacted world; they built a resistant population, but eradication of all threat was impossible.

The Ship also risked lives of its own, but the Friends did not ask permission before a first contact. "They're sending us," Charles Syne had once told her, but the Fox had smiled his foxy smile, charming and cynical.

"Who are we?" he'd asked. She knew. They were descendants of people the Friends had ripped from Earth as sacrifices to a longer, greater plan. Their mission was its culmination. The call had been given; the Ship was on its way. Right or wrong, her mission was done. She intended to survive it.

Beatrice surveyed the room. There was nothing with which she could cut through the wall and escape, but she could make noise. She seized the narrow end of the rectangular tray on which the Boy had brought her most recent meal. Gripping it firmly, she banged it against the wall. At the same time, she screamed for help.

She couldn't hear over her own noise. She didn't know what happened outside. When she stopped there was silence. As she was about to begin again, someone in the distance shouted. A moment later, there were shots.

She dropped to the floor as bullets whizzed through the hut.

The cavern had no color. Any pigment was absorbed in its immense size, which spread light from the kidnappers' lanterns too thinly, like watered paint. The men, the walls, and the kidnappers' structures were black or shades of gray.

To Stefan, the place looked like a wilderness encampment, but without scenery. Two huts had been constructed in one end of the huge chamber. Supplies were stacked neatly on the ground outside one, which had its door closed. A table and two chairs were set at the front of the other, closer hut. They seemed to have been dragged there from inside to enjoy a breeze; of course, there was none. This was a major establishment, a base inside the cavern, but it wasn't fortified, only hidden.

Two men lay dead on the ground near the chairs. Another body was half hidden among boxes and crates. Beatrice's kidnappers. Where was Beatrice? Stefan walked farther into the underground chamber.

A clansman caught up to Stefan from behind. "Are you all right, Judge?"

The shooting had ended. He shook off his guard without answering and went toward the victims. "What happened?" he demanded.

Several men from the rescue group turned. No one responded.

A low, mechanical hum vibrated throughout the room. It made his head pound. "Who's in charge here?" he asked.

"I am." A young policeman—he wore a star on his coverall—near the front of the group glanced once more at the dead, then walked to Stefan. He nodded curtly. "You were supposed to stay back," he said. "We have to keep you safe."

"What happened?" Stefan asked again. His impression was that as soon as his presence had been announced by his guards, this larger group of clansmen and police had shot the kidnappers. Without provocation. He hadn't seen who had shot first, but Stefan was fairly confident he had just missed witnessing murder.

The policeman glanced at the dead, at his own men, and only then answered. "We were talking to them. We'd surprised them, and there were only these three. Just the one in back"—he pointed at the third man, near the rear hut—"had a gun. They admitted that the Traveler was here, but refused to surrender her. Then someone in that hut started yelling and pounding. I told them to open it. The two up here refused and began a retreat toward the hut. One reached into his jacket. Jerry shouted that you were coming, then the guy in back shot at me. We shot back."

Murder or bad luck, it had been an enormous blunder to kill the men and directly contrary to Stefan's explicit instructions. ID or some other authority might determine if any of the dead were Pritchard's missing local hires, but the significance of that would depend on interpretation. The men who could testify had been eliminated.

"No one touch anything," Stefan said. "That's an order from the Open Court." Site investigation might reveal something useful. Beatrice was here; she might know who had taken her.

Stefan walked to the two dead men, glimpsing anonymous, scientific-looking equipment through the open door of the nearer hut as he passed it. The dead men had worn thin jackets and slippers, as if they'd been lounging at home. Blood seemed black, not red, in the dim light; it was everywhere. It had spouted from the chest of one man, soaking his jacket. His face was wet with the blackish blood, as though he had camouflaged himself for the afterlife. They had tattoos. Stefan knelt. No weapon was visible anywhere. Stefan closed the blind, staring eyes, the whites of which were gruesomely prominent because of the contrast with the blood; his hands were sticky with blood afterward, and smelled of death.

"Open the other hut." Beatrice would be inside.

No one moved to obey him.

Stefan stood. "Open it!" Concerned, he remembered the banging the policeman reported. Beatrice had tried to get their attention then, but there had been no sound from her since his arrival—since the shooting. He started toward the hut.

The lead policeman went to Stefan, blocking his way. "Sir, these men told us something about that Traveler that you should know." He took on a confidential, familiar bearing and came closer, dropping his voice.

Stefan imagined Beatrice bleeding to death in the locked hut. "You'll tell me later. Do as I say."

"Judge, I'm John Denning. John Junior, I mean. You know my parents." Denning's son glanced at the other clansmen, reassuring them with a brief, self-possessed smile in which Stefan saw the resemblance to his father, even as Stefan angrily realized that Denning's son not only had been allowed to participate in an expedition bearing on his father's arrest, but had led it. "Judge Acari," John Junior continued, "the kidnappers said she is a disease carrier. They discovered it while they were holding her. All of them, the Travelers, are contagious for some new plague. That's why they weren't hostile to us when we arrived here; they expected us to join them. We need to get this information out, and not through the Assembly. I think the Adjusters have been hiding it."

Stefan remembered his own suspicions.

John Junior nodded, and shifted the position of his rifle on his shoulder. His eyes were wide with credulous virtue. "I don't think they were lying," he said. "She's dangerous. We should leave her be until a doctor gets here."

Stefan studied the clansmen. They were all young, armed and restless. They would not obey him merely because he was a Judge of the Open Court. Independent Defense was not present to buttress his position. Stefan lowered his voice and spoke to convince John Junior, their leader. "We need her in order to free your father. This botched rescue was supposed to do that. You were willing to risk your lives then. Her ... illness doesn't change anything, if it's even true."

John Junior shifted on his feet. "My father wouldn't want me to do anything that would hurt the entire world." He spoke self-righteously, but his tone was honest.

Pritchard, half delirious with illness, had denied it, but perhaps the Travelers had brought illness to Earth. Stefan remembered the animal redness of Pritchard's eyes, and the pain behind them. Perhaps Pritchard was dead. The cave smelled of the dead men's blood, the same stink as Red Death's final stages. These men weren't cowards to want to avoid death. He wouldn't leave Beatrice alone, possibly injured, in the hut, however. "I'll do it." He moved around John Junior.

"One thing, sir," John Junior said, stepping between Stefan and the closed hut again. "The kidnappers claimed that the Numericans were making us sick on purpose. They have a plan, something about more of them coming to Earth. An invasion, spearheaded by the illness. Judge, I think these Numericans are evil, and maybe not even human."

It made a crude sense. An illness to soften the opposition, followed by an invasion. It wasn't wrong to refuse aid to an enemy. Stefan just couldn't believe Beatrice was an enemy. He knew her. He'd heard her voice in the darkness and couldn't believe she had come to Earth to kill and conquer. He could not believe that she had lied.

At the same time, true or false, the Assembly of Earth needed to be informed of these accusations. Though he hadn't reached a final judgment, Stefan knew he must dump. The Adjusters could not stop him in time to prevent it. Reluctant but resigned, as Stefan went toward the second hut to free Beatrice, he reached out to warn Earth against her. He used the commands that would connect him with the Open Court central depository and initiate his automatic dump; he steeled himself for the rush. Nothing happened.

The Assembly wasn't there.

He stopped. He took a deep breath. He tried again to connect, to call Tepan. It had always been instant and automatic, but he was unable to make even a simple call. Nothing. He searched for any trace of the Assembly. The pressure was gone. He was alone. The Assembly had vanished.

Chapter 8

Stefan may as well have recited nonsense verse; his codes didn't work; the Assembly was gone. He stopped walking toward Beatrice's hut and even closed his eyes momentarily as he strained to connect to the absent Assembly, but like a lost child searching aimlessly for its mother, his attempt was useless.

"Judge?" John Junior asked.

The Assembly no longer pressed against his mind. Why? Depth underground had never affected the Assembly before; besides, Man Mouth caverns were shallow.

"Judge?" John Junior sounded more concerned. "You're right not to help her. She isn't a victim, she's an invader."

"What?" Stefan remembered where he was, and that he had a duty to perform, irrespective of his inability to contact others via the Assembly. Beatrice was in the hut; he couldn't let her suffer. John Junior was in his way again. "Step aside," Stefan ordered him.

John Junior had a heavier physique than his father, and a round, pleasant face. He glanced from the hut to his men, then to Stefan. "She's dangerous." His tone tried to be firm, but sounded worried.

Stefan studied the young clansman. Without a cap of his own, John Junior wouldn't know about Stefan's inability to reach the Assembly. "Move, or I'll contact the Assembly police to arrest you for obstruction. I make the judgments here, Mr. Denning, not you."

John Junior glanced at his men once more, then moved aside.

Stefan walked to the third dead kidnapper. This man had held a weapon, as reported, but its safety lock was still engaged. The open, dead stare showed the kidnapper's surprise. Every shot fired in the cavern had been fired by John Junior and the men. "Do you know any of them?" he called over his shoulder to John Junior.

"No, Judge. They're strangers."

Yet Pritchard claimed his missing hirelings were locals. Stefan didn't pursue the thought. His head ached. He was confused by the loss of the Assembly. Unconsciously, he was repeatedly and fruitlessly straining to connect. When he realized it, he tried to force himself into mental relaxation, but was as successful as if he'd forced gaiety upon himself. He pressed his forearm against his eyes, then recoiled from the grimy coverall sleeve.

A spray of bullet holes laced the left front quadrant of Beatrice's hut. They were at the level of his chest, perhaps shoulder height on Beatrice. If she'd been at the front of the hut, she might have been hit. Her silence was ominous. He surveyed the clansmen and the position of the dead kidnappers. Some rescuer had fired very wildly indeed to manage to hit Beatrice's hut accidentally. Some rescuer. It hadn't been only the kidnappers who were dangerous to her.

The door wouldn't open. Though the hut was flimsy, a built-in tight-lock made the door its strongest part and none of them would know the combination. He shook the knob. The building trembled, but the door didn't budge. "Beatrice?" he called.

"Hello? Can you help me? Please?"

Stefan recognized her weak voice. "It's Stefan Acari, Beatrice," he called. "Are you hurt?"

"Shot. . . ."

He looked for something with which to force the door open and saw the dead man's gun. Blood was already congealing on it in the cavern's cool atmosphere. Stefan turned to John Junior, about ten meters behind. "She's in there, hurt. Give me your rifle," he said, then turned back, facing the hut. "Beatrice, are you away from the door?"

There was a shuffling sound. "Yes," she then said.

John Junior came to Stefan. "I'll do it." He aimed at the lock, but before he could shoot, Stefan slapped the gun barrel down.

"Not like that. You'll hit her again."

John Junior took aim more correctly and shot away the lock. The plastic door frame cracked, then the door swung open. John Junior hurried back and away, but Stefan went in.

For a moment he didn't see Beatrice. The hut's single room was unlit, and darker than the cave. A milky glow, the texture of an overcast, gloomy evening, came through the thin, plastic walls. There were no shadows. He spotted Beatrice on the floor partly behind one of two large storage boxes, and in front of a long table. She was on her side, supporting herself with her left arm. As Stefan entered, she raised her head. "Judge?"

She was clothed in a gray blanket, which had fallen away, partially exposing her. Her thin body looked like a bronze statue in the pale light. It was smooth and firm; her small breasts were accentuated by the flow pattern of the blood that had run across her chest. She watched him trustingly, her eyes wide as those of Tepan when he needed help.

Stefan yelled through the open door, "Bring a first-aid kit! Send in a medic." He went closer, trying to see where she'd been hit through the blood and gloom while avoiding offensive glimpses of her body. He didn't touch her.

"You came." Her voice was low, breathy, and not so controlled as he remembered it. She spoke as though it was Stefan himself she'd hoped for, not merely rescue. She'd tried to call him, her friends had said.

"A long story." Stefan knelt in front of her. "Now, how badly are you hurt?"

She moved her head, indicating her right shoulder. "No so bad," she said, but gasped the words.

Stefan leaned back so he could see through the open

door. No one was visible. The clansmen were keeping their distance. He remembered why and drew back slightly, then she made a small, hurt sound, a rise and fall of pain, as though it came in waves, and he ceased worrying about possible contagion. He reached automatically for the Assembly to bring help. Nothing. He sighed. He was on his own. "I need a first-aid kit," he said. "I'll be right back."

"Don't leave," she said. "Please. I'm cold."

Another blanket lay on the floor near the front of the hut. He brought it to her, then hesitated. It was cold in the cave, much too cold for her unclothed body. She needed medical assistance and to get out of the cavern, but the clansmen outside would resist if he brought her to them. "Can you stand?" he asked. "I'll help you to that table. You'll be warmer off the ground."

She nodded, and immediately looked to him for support as she struggled to sit. He didn't consider a refusal. She reached out with her good arm and he took her hand. It was cold. His fingers closed around it, moving spontaneously to warm her as he helped draw her up. Though careful not to touch the wound itself, Stefan found it impossible not to come in contact with her blood. It stained his dirty coverall. As he held her against himself her scant warmth seemed to warm him. She needed him in the most physical sense, for shelter from the cold, for help from pain, for the continuation of life. He braced her, almost carrying her, the few steps to the table.

Outside the hut, someone laughed. She shivered and brushed against the table, whimpering slightly as the impact sent a vibration through her shoulder.

Ashamed that he had caused her further distress, he tried to apologize, but she leaned closer against him in a palpable show of trust and favor. The tabletop was high off the ground for a person as small as Beatrice. Stefan lifted her and set her gently onto it. "I'll get a medical kit and come right back," he said.

Beatrice nodded without looking directly at him. She must have known that the others in the rescue party were avoiding her. Her humiliation angered Stefan for its callousness and reckless disregard for her life.

He hurried outside. The clansmen were gathered between the two huts. John Junior was speaking to them in a low voice. Stefan couldn't hear what was being said. Conversation stopped as he exited the hut. They were waiting for him, yet they had not bothered to examine the kidnappers' base. "I need a first-aid kit," he said. "You managed to shoot the kidnap victim."

"How seriously?" John Junior asked.

"She's bleeding and in pain. The wound is starting to clot and, barring an infection, shouldn't be life-threatening."

"Too bad," someone muttered.

Stefan looked, but couldn't be certain who had spoken. He was outnumbered, but wouldn't let the insult pass. "I don't want to hear anything like that again. We can't know if the kidnappers were lying. Meanwhile, you're letting a helpless woman suffer. I'm no medic, but I'd guess one of you is." They didn't answer; they also avoided meeting his eyes. "Then I'll do what I can since none of you brave clansmen is willing to try. Get a medical kit for me."

John Junior gestured at a man who then reached into his pack and brought out a white box with the traditional red cross, though in the cave, the cross was a dismal black. He handed the kit to Stefan.

"Have you come in contact with her blood, Judge?" the man, presumably a medic, asked.

"I'm not stupid."

"There are gloves inside," the medic said.

"Use them, Judge. Be careful of her." John Junior sounded as though he cared—he would be a good politician, like his father—but didn't order anyone to help. Stefan returned to Beatrice's hut alone.

She hadn't moved. If the kidnappers had spoken the truth, he was risking his life, but he went to the table and set the first-aid kit down. "My medical knowledge is limited," he apologized, "and I can't consult the Assembly." The stab of fear that acknowledgment sent through him made him reflexively try again to reach it. Nothing. He swallowed, forced a smile for her, then busied himself opening the kit. The gloves were on top. After he put them on, he realized how poorly equipped he was. He needed better light and sufficient water to wash the wound. He stepped back, contemplating his next move and feeling like a half-wit. He didn't want to leave her alone yet again.

"You'll do fine." She smiled, the patient reassuring him. Pain etched her face like clan tattoos.

"Judge?" John Junior was at the door. "I brought a lantern." The switch clicked as he turned it on and the hut was flooded with light so bright that Beatrice blinked and her eyes teared.

"Thank you," Stefan said, thinking better of young Denning, who stood indecisively in the doorway, studying Beatrice. Stefan moved slightly, to block his view of her. "I need to wash the wound before bandaging it, and my canteen's almost empty. Can you get me more water?" He removed his helmet and set it beside Beatrice on the table. That felt better, though he supposed he shouldn't have touched the dirty helmet while wearing the clean gloves.

"I'll get you water," John Junior said. "Did the bullet go all the way through?"

Stefan checked to be sure his first impression was right, then nodded. "Yes." The bullet had entered her back, and exited from the ragged chest wound. The drying blood outlined faint lines in her flesh, like veins on a stained leaf. There were none of the usual fine hairs of normal human skin. She was pale in the harsh light, bleached. Her skin wasn't amber, it was a ghostly white.

"It's not so bad, then," John Junior was contrite, but also excusing himself from the failure to help Beatrice. He left the lantern at the entrance and went for the water.

Beatrice and Stefan looked at each other. "Thank you," she whispered. "You stayed to help me." She reached to touch him, but inadvertently used her right arm and winced as it hurt her.

Stefan was awkwardly aware of his hands, as though they'd grown to twice their normal size, and that her rescue was botched, and that he had mishandled even his attempt to bring her medical aid. The loss of the Assembly worried him, but fatigue made even that catastrophe seem distant. It was probably his connect, or the Adjusters' doing and he lacked the energy to meditate on the consequences of either. He knew that she was thanking him for something that wasn't really true. He had stayed to help John Denning, and hadn't known of her kidnapping then. Her immediate captors, if not their superiors, were dead, and he still needed to find information that would implicate or free John Denning. "Do you know who was behind the kidnapping?" he asked. "The three men here are dead, so we can't find out from them."

"No." She sighed. "And after they knew about the plague, they didn't ask many more questions."

"The plague?" In her presence, he could not believe that Beatrice would commit an evil purposely. The Travelers' plague could not be true.

"Judge Acari?" John Junior called from the doorway. "Here's a nearly full canteen of water, and a clean cloth." He stood waiting at the hut's entrance for Stefan to fetch the water. Stefan touched Beatrice's leg through the blanket, then went to John Junior. "Ask her," John Junior said.

Whatever truth there was to the story of a Numerican plague, Stefan wanted to hear it while alone with Beatrice. He took the water and the rag. "Later," he said. He closed the door. It rattled in the broken frame. A shattered door wouldn't stop a virus, anyway.

"They're afraid," Stefan said when he returned to Beatrice. "Some story your kidnappers told."

"It's true," Beatrice said.

Stefan examined the canteen. It didn't sound full when he shook it. He unscrewed its cap and let it dangle on the chain. He covered the canteen's mouth with the cloth and tilted it, dampening the cloth. There wasn't enough water to rinse her shoulder. He would need to wipe the wounds.

"It's true," she repeated.

He had raised his hand to begin. His arm dropped to his side and he looked at her. "You didn't know what would happen."

She studied his face. "Stefan, we came knowing some of you might sicken. Some might die. How is Kaim Pritchard?"

Stefan went behind her, to the far side of the table. The entry wound was small. He used the damp cloth to cautiously wipe the area around it, careful to touch her only through the cloth. "I don't know how he is. When I last saw him, yesterday, he was quite ill."

"You might become ill, too."

Stefan heard the tremor in her voice and lightened his strokes. He could be contributing to her injury by his lack of medical knowledge. He had always depended on the Assembly to supply such information in an emergency. "I understand," he said. "There is disease on Numerica, and you're unable to come here without the risk of spreading it. It's a difficult choice." He was thinking of Numerican negligence versus human necessity, and the issue of the Numerican failure to warn Earth. However he tried, it was impossible to keep to the abstract while his hands stroked her bare flesh, and when, despite the dank cave atmosphere of the tiny hut, her fragrance filled him. No longer fresh and clean, Beatrice smelled of female warmth and blood, of her own sweat and fear, and also something sweetly odd and new. Her peculiar skin? The composition was erotic. Uneasy with his attraction to someone wounded and dependent, Stefan focused on details. Her hair, as he brushed it off her shoulder, was soft and very fine. He stroked her back with the cloth even where there was no blood, using a firmer touch and feeling her spine. She shivered.

"Stefan," she said, then stopped and didn't say more.

Gradually the white rag blackened with her blood. Her back was clean, and only a small ooze issued from the entry wound. He bandaged it with gauze and tape from the medical kit, though it would need to be redone as soon as they found a doctor. All the while, he knew she wanted to divulge something. He did nothing to encourage her.

He came back to the front of the table so he could clean the larger chest wound. Her fortitude was remarkable. The blanket was around her waist; her breasts were bare to him. The areolas were only slightly darker, as though covered by something translucent. She looked up. How terrible could her secrets be? He couldn't comfort her until he knew them. "Why don't you tell me about it?" he asked quietly. "I'm not in contact with the Assembly now."

"Of course not," she interrupted, obviously relieved. She reached out her good arm and touched the side of his cheek. "Stefan," she said. "There is no Numerica. There is only the Ship and our Friends. The Ship will be here soon. Too soon." She looked away. "It was a mistake."

Speech had never been so difficult for Beatrice. She spoke slowly, postponing the moment she feared, when the Judge's gentle touch would tense, when his open hands would clench and his expression become rigid. As he worked, his hesitations said things he refused to say aloud. Human to human, physical contact was as eloquent as song.

So Beatrice edited. It was Eyni's skin he felt, but the Judge had never heard Eyni's name. It was her duty to say it, but she delayed because then Eyni would become a barrier between them. We want contact, she told the Judge. We try to be gentle, but disease is part of what is exchanged, too. We do our best. His hands fell into the rhythm of her words; her tone matched his careful motion. "I believe you," he said once. She hadn't realized until then that her tone had begged for his confirmation.

She had intended to tell him everything, but she didn't. All life is at the mercy of death, she said. A world might stabilize its situation, but change, any change, often brought disease. Intelligent life could disguise that fact with philosophy or religion, but the true gift that intelligence gave its bearers was the ability to make contact with each other, to know they weren't alone. That was the Friends' philosophy. That was the mission of the Ship.

The Judge listened without comment. He continued cleaning her wound. She waited for his touch to become like Pritchard's: hard and binding. It didn't.

Beatrice felt that the two of them had become an island in the Earth, a piece of the Ship. Although the Ship machinery was silent, the background mechanical hum from outside the hut substituted for the backdrop of voices that formed the white noise on the Ship. The Judge understood when bits of her story were told in song. She understood when he moved her hair and let it slide against his bare skin, between the coverall and the glove, as he reached for bandages. "Were you forced to do this?"

He wanted to give her an excuse. She ached to take it. "No. I chose to come." She looked into his grave face. "Friends die, too, and some of us on the Ship. It's as if these viruses are a bridge between species, a grim kind of song."

His hands dropped to his sides. "Who are these 'friends,' Beatrice? They aren't human?"

She didn't know how to answer, and didn't need to. He knew, but for both of them the words were ugly and inconclusive. What did it mean to say that Friends were alien? That they therefore couldn't possibly be friends? "You'll meet them when the Ship comes. It's on its way."

He frowned. "It hadn't moved from its orbit around Jupiter when I came into the cave."

"The call went out."

He glanced at the ceiling as though he might see up to the Ship. They were underground, he'd said, in the same cave where the two of them had met. It explained the dampness, the darkness, and the difficulty of her rescue.

"The call was made too soon," Beatrice added. "They shouldn't have done it. I didn't think they would."

"Your friends? Syne, Emit, and Talley? They did it without you?"

She hummed an affirmative, because it was easier than human speech and she was too tired to explain that only two minds were necessary, and that she doubted one of them had been the Fox.

He placed gauze against the wound. Her bleeding had been slowed by a powder he applied, but the white gauze was immediately soaked. The Judge didn't seem to notice. Distractedly, he taped it in place. "How did they call? They didn't mention it."

"Pritchard must have forced them to do it," she said. "He can't have understood the beacon, though we had guessed he did."

"The Adjusters—I mean, Pritchard—knew all this?" His tone was sharp, but the anger wasn't directed at her.

"Not everything, but he invented Numerica. There is no such place. We live in the Ship. We have for all the generations since we left Earth." She didn't mention how the Friends had acquired her ancestors as passengers.

The frown turned on her as though he sensed that she had withheld information. His eyes examined her with the deliberation of a judge, although his Open Court must have vanished with the Assembly. She felt their peace slipping away and reached for it with her voice. "I fear for the Earth," she said in mixed words and song, "but all life is change. Earth will adapt, however difficult it seems at first. If we hadn't called the Ship, it would have left, but isolation is dangerous, too. It's what creates the danger of contact." She was talking too much.

The Judge looked down at the unfinished bandage. His shoulders had slumped. He reached for more tape, and set methodically to work. The poetry was gone from his motion. Even so, though he was quick, he wasn't brutal.

"Do you understand?" It was unlike Beatrice to seek confirmation, yet she did.

He pressed a piece of tape against her skin, but his gloved fingers didn't seem to touch her. "You want me to judge you," he said. "You want me to say that what you've done is right. I can't. You and your friends have taken a chance with our lives. However you justify it by claiming contact was inevitable or that you were careful, what you did by coming to Earth was to remove us from the decision. And then you conspired with Pritchard to hide the truth."

The door squeaked. "Judge?" The man who had brought the lantern stood in the doorway. He blinked, adjusting to the light. "Judge? You've been a long time," he said. "Is everything all right? We'd like to get out of here."

The Judge patted the end of the tape down over the top of her shoulder. "I just finished," he said, stepping back from Beatrice.

"Good." The man opened the door wider.

"Judge ..." Beatrice reached for him, and managed to clutch the edge of his coverall.

"I'll be out in a minute," the Judge said, dismissing the intruder, who left quickly, then the Judge turned to Beatrice. His expression was pained, that of a disappointed man.

"You forget," she said, letting her tone recall their previous rapport. "I'm human. All four of us are. And we're volunteers. The Friends let Earth choose, through us."

The Judge glanced at the door, then back to Beatrice, as though he had questions, but not time enough to ask them. He pulled the plastic gloves off his hands, turning them inside out. They were dark with her blood. He grazed the side of her cheek with his bare thumb, just once, in a gesture from which she took some hope. "It will be all right, Beatrice," he said.

She doubted that and thought guiltily of the Assembly. It wasn't disease alone that would transform the Earth. She smiled though, grateful for the reassurance, which told her she hadn't become a monster in his eyes.

She was relieved that she wasn't the one who had called the Ship; others had made the decision.

He unzipped the front of his dirty coverall, exposing rumpled clothes. "Put this on," he said, beginning to take out an arm. "I'll help you. It will keep you warm."

"It'll be too big," she protested, wanting the warmth and the intimacy of sharing his clothing but repulsed by the shabby, stained garment. "I couldn't walk with it on."

"Judge!" The voice from outside was impatient.

He looked out the door, then back, and shrugged back into the coverall. "I'll get you something better," he said. "Wait here." His tone made it an order, though he seemed unaware of the forcefulness of his voice and smiled as though by obeying she was doing a favor. She knew the truth. He was protecting her, keeping her away from men outside who might harm her. He went to the door, but hesitated before walking through it. His back straightened. He took a deep breath.

"They didn't need to kill those three men," she said, aware of the reason for his unease.

"I know."

Stefan had been invulnerable. It was an unspoken benefit of being a ticker. No harm could come to anyone with constant access to the Assembly without its being known instantly throughout the world by a dump. For the first time in his adult life, Stefan knew the possibility of physical danger. He was alone in a cave with twenty clansmen who felt no loyalty to him and who had already killed three strangers. So Stefan smiled at John Junior as he left the hut. "We should investigate this site before we leave," he suggested.

"They'll send investigators back. Nothing can disturb this place in the meantime." John Junior had slung a rifle over his shoulder again, though he hadn't carried it into Beatrice's hut. He rested his arm comfortably on it, but it seemed ready for use.

Stefan wondered if Denning's son had shot, or merely ordered the shooting. Beatrice's news he put aside; it didn't tell him who was behind her kidnapping. "You're right, but I'm going to look around before we leave," Stefan said in a friendly, reasonable way. "I probably won't be back myself, and it could be important to my judgment. I want to do everything possible to free your father."

John Junior shrugged. "All right."

Stefan didn't like that he was being given permission; it meant permission could have been denied, but since it *had* been given, he didn't push the point. Someone was moving about inside the other hut. The shadowy figure was visible through the partially translucent walls. "What is that humming noise?" Stefan asked as he walked toward the hut and the noise became louder.

John Junior cleared his throat. "You said you like my father," he began, as though beginning a speech.

Stefan cut him off. "I was telling the truth."

"Then why didn't you free him? If you believe it, that's enough. That's what the Open Court is for."

John Junior, a local policeman and a politician's son, shouldn't have been so naive; Stefan hoped that his misplaced confidence didn't reflect John Denning's own attitudes toward what the Open Court could accomplish. "I can't," he said. "Not unless I have proof that he's innocent." The boy stared earnestly. "The Adjusters are involved. I can only be sure of making one more dump, the moment I connect, so everything has to be exactly right."

"Then you won't connect until you're certain?" John Junior seemed eager to know.

Stefan nodded. He hadn't mentioned the loss of Assembly contact to the clansmen and was glad he'd kept that to himself. He distrusted John Junior. Like his mother, Marta, he was secretive. Stefan continued toward the other hut. John Junior followed, but when Stefan went inside, he stayed at the door.

A very young clansman, his face still pudgy and nearly unmarked by tattoos, was seated on a stool, reading a handcopy book reminiscent of those in Romaric's collection, except it was smaller. He looked up as Stefan en-

tered, then beyond him to John Junior. John Junior
motioned the young clansmen to leave with a jerk of his
thumb and the boy placed the open book, spine up, on
an anonymous piece of machinery, got hurriedly off the
stool and walked out of the hut, sidling past Stefan.
Stefan went farther inside without questioning what the
young man had been doing there.

Near the door was an abbreviated living area: a camp
stove, a clothes chest, shelving with foodstuffs, more
bedding, and two stools. Beyond the living area were a
group of boxy machines. They were freestanding, in
new-looking plastic cases. Although their operation was
not revealed by their shape, in style they reminded
Stefan of Marta's computer system. Visible machinery
seemed as awkward as a man on crutches, and was similarly embarrassing. The Assembly's hardware was out of
sight in the Southlands; its codes and connects were as
simple and personal as prayer.

Stefan picked up the book the young man had left.
The New Way. He'd never heard of it, but unlike Romaric's books this wasn't fragile and yellowing. Printed
on new paper, it had stiff binding and smelled of fresh
newsprint.

John Junior walked inside.

"Does this belong to your man who was here?" Stefan
asked, holding out the book.

John Junior took it from Stefan, glanced at its cover,
then tossed it to the ground. "Judge, you know it
doesn't. That's an UN-Assembler tract."

"Why was your man reading it, then?"

John Junior shrugged, hitching the rifle farther up his
shoulder. "Curiosity. Danny's young."

Entirely plausible. Stefan continued to the rear of the
hut. There the room lost its damp, underground odor
and smelled of new plastic and ozone. The mechanisms
included a maintenance meca wall, though no mecas
were detached. That installation had been expensive. Beatrice's kidnappers were wealthy. He had heard many
things said of the terrorist UN-Assemblers, but not that.

It was difficult to fund a cause without recourse to the Assembly.

The tallest machine seemed to be the source of the insistent hum. Stefan studied it with his hands behind his back. He didn't recognize the function of any of them. Possibly a gadget-happy clansman might, but Stefan didn't ask John Junior. The hum was a low-pitched vibration that nagged at Stefan; it had a subtle rise and fall of pitch and tone, a slow drummer's rhythm.

John Junior glanced self-consciously down at his rifle, now cradled in his arms, then out the open door, before speaking. "I don't think we'll find out what these are. We looked at them while you were with the Traveler, and no one had a clue. Unless you know." John Junior was smiling affably, but Stefan didn't believe it. The son wasn't as smooth as the father, and Stefan heard the sharp edge of a question. *What do you know, Judge?*

Stefan shrugged, and continued studying the tall machine. There was an alphabetical keyboard. Reasonable, if the designers were UN-Assemblers or deadheads. Near it was a round black switch with a red line turned entirely to one side. There was a red button. Nothing was labeled.

Stefan reached out through his connect one more time. The Assembly was gone, as if it had ceased to exist. A failure of his connect was possible, but Stefan didn't believe that was the cause. The kidnapping made much more sense if the kidnappers could hide from the Assembly. Pritchard was traceless; why not a place where people were shielded from the Assembly? It would explain a great deal, including most importantly that the clans were involved in Beatrice's kidnapping. The gadgeteers of the Northern Sister continent had built a shield machine, and placed it underground where no passersby would notice the gap in the Assembly. Clansmen, possibly including John Denning, had taken part in the kidnapping, and Kaim Pritchard had compelled them to do it. The kidnapping had not been an either/or situation. Both the clans and Pritchard, acting for the Adjusters, had done it. Finally, it made sense.

"You're right." Stefan turned away from the machine and faced John Junior. "An expert needs to study this; I don't know what I'm looking at. Can you radio for a specialist to be sent—I can't use the Assembly, as I mentioned."

John Junior slung his rifle back on his shoulder. Like his father, he couldn't keep entirely still. "We've already radioed the surface. They're sending a full team, including a doctor for her."

"We can't leave her behind, alone. I won't."

"We don't want her with us, Judge."

"I'll stay behind with her." He said it evenly and without aggression, but let John Junior know, absolutely, that he would stay or Beatrice would come with them out of the cave. He would not leave her. Stefan rather hoped the clansmen would go. It would give him more time with Beatrice; he needed to understand the things she had left unsaid.

"No, sir. I can't allow that. You're too important. She'll be safe enough down here. It won't be for long." John Junior spoke in quick staccato bursts, trying to convince Stefan.

A tattooed man peered in the hut's open door. "Everything all right?" he asked John Junior.

Fatigue, fear, and the underground had heightened Stefan's sensitivity. He made an intuitive leap. John Junior had just been asked whether or not it would be necessary to kill Stefan.

"Fine," John Junior said.

"Good." The man smiled genially at Stefan. "You all right, Judge? You look tired."

"I am," he said. The man left.

There was only one reason for John Junior to kill Stefan Acari. Some or all of the Waterman Clan, and probably other clans, such as Orion Nash's Woodmakers, were UN-Assemblers. They had been blackmailed by Kaim Pritchard into doing what the Assembly wanted done: draining Beatrice of information. They would kill a Judge before letting that news into a dump. "No,"

Stefan whispered. He truly had liked John Denning, and the man fronted for terrorists.

"Okay, Judge?" John Junior grinned, a poor imitation of his father. "Ready to go?"

"With Beatrice."

John Junior scowled, glanced at the machines, then nodded. "Okay."

Apparently it was better to walk through the tunnels with a disease carrier than to leave Stefan alone with these machines. "I'll stay here until you're organized," Stefan said. "I can probably find something for her to wear." He motioned at the clothes chest, then walked to it, away from the machines.

John Junior was visibly reluctant to leave Stefan in the machine hut. If Stefan was right, the young man was cold-blooded enough to murder three of his own co-conspirators to preserve their secrets. Stefan's only protection was that the clansmen thought of him as gullible, or as an ally. If that changed, Stefan could easily have an accident underground. "Don't be too long." Stefan made his voice weak. He yawned. "I'm barely awake. If I sit down, I'll probably fall asleep." The effete Ropan.

John Junior wasn't ready to act directly against a Judge of the Open Court, or he assumed they still might use him. "Okay."

Stefan didn't answer. He opened the chest, looking through the dead men's clothing for something to fit Beatrice. John Junior hesitated, then left, taking the light with him, so the room became as dim as Beatrice's. The advantage was that they wouldn't see him move about. Stefan waited a moment in case John Junior returned, then went back to the machines.

The tall machine was humming. He had a hunch that if a shield against the Assembly was derived from anything in the hut, it was from this contraption. He needed to know. He needed to connect and dump. Stefan didn't trust the clansmen not to kill Beatrice. He decided to call Pritchard, a known quantity. The wildmen were not. Let the conspirators keep each other honest and Beatrice alive.

The machine had a keypad, a round, black knob, and a red button. *Which one is off?* he thought. *Guess.*

They'd want to turn it off quickly, if strangers came. Not the keyboard.

The round knob had a gradient. The signal strength? Not an on/off switch for an emergency.

He pushed the red button.

The humming slowed. The machine trembled. The hum ended.

Through his connect, Stefan reached out to the Assembly. He found it.

Stefan's connection was automatic and joyful. His sense of the Assembly was unusual, however, almost at arm's length. He ignored the difference. The Assembly still existed. Civilization would not crumble. The life of the world rushed through him and he had the satisfaction of knowing, though he couldn't feel it, that his mind had dumped into the Assembly. The world now knew what he knew: The Travelers brought mixed blessings to Earth, one of them the possibility of disease. The Ship held aliens. It was coming to Earth. Pritchard and the Adjusters had interfered with truth and hid information from the Assembly. They had used the Northern Sister Clans as scapegoats; those clans knew how to block Assembly access. Beatrice was safe.

Stefan hesitated on the Assembly margins, reaching for the reflected emotion of the many million minds within; the sensation wasn't as thrilling as usual.

Inlander. The Assembly called him. No, this call came from Kaim Pritchard.

Just who I want, Stefan sent, as though they were on a call. Then, truly pleased by the knowledge, he added, *You're alive.* The new Traveler disease wasn't invariably deadly. Stefan noticed that they did seem to be on a call, though Stefan hadn't made or answered one. He saw the glare of yellow sunlight on green trees and was startled by the colors. Pritchard was outdoors, though Stefan didn't see Pritchard himself. In relief from the constant gray of the caverns, Stefan thought that no sky

had ever been more blue. *Get us out of here,* he told
Pritchard. *Your allies are undependable.*

Allies? Pritchard was sardonic. *No one will believe
that.*

John Junior rushed into the hut, followed by two other
running men. "You did it," John Junior yelled. "You
worthless, clanless, bastard Ropan! Kill him!"

The two men aimed their guns at Stefan.

"I'm in the Assembly," Stefan said, calm with his customary aplomb. "Killing me won't hide anything. The
entire world knows whatever I see and I'm looking
squarely at you." It was difficult to stare at the men and
not into the deadly apertures of their guns, but Stefan
managed it. He was safe, connected.

"Traitor," John Junior yelled.

An odd charge, Stefan thought.

Pritchard answered. *You're their friend.*

What's going on? The oddity of the call with Pritchard
distracted Stefan even from the weapons pointed at his
chest. He hadn't willed himself to speak to Pritchard.
Words had apparently become unnecessary. Their exchange was on a different level: thought, not language.
What kind of connection is this?

John Junior looked at the machines. "We've got to
get out of here! Just leave him. He's dead." They ran
from the hut.

"Good. Come and get us, Pritchard." Stefan sat on
a stool.

"Get out of the cave, now," Pritchard told him. *"You
can't wait for help. That was a self-destruct you switched
on. Look."*

Stefan turned. The bottom of the tall machine seemed
foggy—that was his first thought, until the acrid odor
of burning plastic made his tired brain realize the fog
was smoke.

"Get out," Pritchard said. *"A fire in a cave is
dangerous."*

Stefan saw an image from Pritchard's mind of a fire
inside a cavern. It had been impossible to extinguish; it
had burned for years, heating the underground, draining

oxygen, until the fuel had been exhausted. Saltpeter, an inflammable ingredient of gunpowder, was mined in Man Mouth Caverns. "All right," Stefan said aloud, absorbing the gestalt as easily as though his own memory had been evoked. The memory left traces from Kaim Pritchard himself behind. The traces were ugly.

Inlander. Pritchard heard Stefan's thoughts and commented mentally. Stefan shuddered. It was as though sewage had been dumped into his mind.

Just then the fire reached a critical point. With a loud whoosh, a sudden burst of heat and an immediate stench of burning metals and plastic, the rear of the hut exploded in flame. It spread in seconds toward Stefan.

"*Go!*" Pritchard screamed inside his head.

Stefan jumped up, ran, and passed through the door barely ahead of the fire, which raced along the melting plastic walls. The cavern air would quickly lose its oxygen and become saturated with poisons released by the burning plastic; he had to escape fast.

Outside, the clansmen were running. They yelled at their stragglers to hurry as they headed away from the tunnel through which their group had first come, and into the dark.

A secret tunnel, Pritchard said. *Go. Follow them, Inlander. Go. It will be faster.* The last clansman disappeared. Stefan chased after him. The biting odor of burning plastic was already thick in the air. Hundreds of dying bats were dropping from the ceiling, some onto Stefan. Then both Stefan and Pritchard shared a thought. *Beatrice.* Her hut was behind Stefan.

Too late, Pritchard said.

No. Stefan stopped. He covered his nose with his right forearm and turned back. The squalid smell of the coverall battled the chemical stench; the chemical odor won.

The cavern had never been so bright. Stefan ran to the light, toward Beatrice's hut. He passed as wide of the flames as possible, but the heat seared his face and the dense smoke made him gasp. Beatrice was already at her door. She came to him, clasping her blanket-dress to keep it on. He grabbed her free hand and pulled her back the way he'd been. They stepped on dead bats.

The fire, for all its intensity, was oddly stationary. There was no blowing wind to spread it; noticing that, Stefan felt confident, but then he saw creeping flames. The gray, grainy floor was beginning to burn. The odor of burning flesh added to the stench.

Smoke was more the enemy than fire. The upper reaches of the dome were filling with toxic clouds. There was no atmosphere into which it could dissipate. Stefan's eyes teared and sight was difficult despite the brightness. Their coughing slowed them. He tripped on a dead bat and Beatrice's grasp of his hand kept him upright, but he was uncertain which way to go. The clansmen had disappeared.

He knew the tunnel through which he had entered the cavern. That way was a long trip back to Quinn's headquarters and meant recrossing the smoky cavern. The smoke was worsening; they might not make it, but he didn't see a tunnel in the direction the clansmen had gone. He set off anyway, pulling Beatrice, hoping he'd find it.

A huge explosion—a cache of armaments?—sent bits of twinkling flame fluttering down on Stefan and Beatrice, as if the cave was raining fireflies. A burning plastic flake landed on Stefan's arm. His coverall began to burn. As he ran, drawing Beatrice with him, Stefan pressed his sleeve against his chest, smothering the flame. New fires began throughout the cave as the tiny flares ignited additional sites on the floor. Fire spread as if saltpeter was moldy wood, first blackening, smoldering, then bursting into flame.

They were dodging sections of burning ground, but Stefan kept hold of Beatrice's hand, afraid that if he let go, he would lose her in the heavy smoke. He could barely see anything less bright than the fire. Even through his shoes, his feet were hot as he stamped on bits of kindling ground to pave a way for Beatrice; her feet were bare. He was glad of the mud caked on on his shoes for its usefulness as insulation.

Beatrice went one way when he went another. Her hand slipped free of his. Stefan looked back. She was a dark figure against the bright outline of hell. He slowed, turned, and reached for her. She grasped his hand again. They ran.

A spark caught the edge of her blanket-dress. Immediately the skirt had a fringe of flame. Stefan released her hand and yanked the blanket off. It dropped, flaring brightly and igniting the ground.

He looked ahead. In the surge of light from the burning blanket, he spotted a darker place. The kidnappers' tunnel. Choking on chemical fumes, they ran. Their lives were at stake. They reached it. The tunnel wasn't burning yet.

There still was smoke, but not much. The atmosphere cooled. A breeze brought them fresher air, as the fire sucked clean, oxygen-rich air through the tunnel into the burning cavern. Coughing and gagging, half asphyxiated, but recovering, they had outrun the fire. It was dark in the tunnel. Stefan remembered his extra light and patted his pockets, searching for it. He found the handheld electric torch and flicked the light on.

"Are you all right?" he asked when he could talk.

She made a small, low sound. He heard her deep, indrawn breaths as she struggled to fill her burned lungs with clean air.

"We should hurry. The fire will spread, and if this is a short way outside, then the fire will come through here, reaching for more oxygen."

He moved the light to illuminate her face. She was bent over, still coughing. She raised her head and blinked like an owl, slowly. Her face was darkened with soot. Lines from tears marked her cheeks like thick tattoos. Her coughing lessened, though her chest still heaved as she tried to breathe.

She squeezed his hand and, briefly, between gasps, smiled. He smiled back. They started walking, using the paltry light cast by the handheld lantern to choose their way. Whenever he didn't need it to pick a path through the dark, he kept it oriented where she would set her feet. His shoes wouldn't stay on her tiny feet, so he didn't offer them. She was naked, but the darkness clothed her and he did nothing to strip her with light. It was important that they get out of the cave as quickly as they could.

The fire was no longer at her heels and the smoke was in their lungs, but not the air. Stefan felt exhausted, yet he was jubilant at their survival. Life was the sweetest gift. He looked down, watching Beatrice's ankles and feet in the circle of light. She didn't walk as though her soles were burned; he thought of yogis, who still practiced skills that predated the Old Moderns. It could also be that they'd moved so quickly through the cave that the burning floor hadn't had an opportunity to scorch her. In any case, he was glad.

They didn't talk. He said nothing of the clansmen who had passed this way, and might even now be hiding in the passage hoping to ambush them. It would do neither of them any good to worry.

The tunnel walls became unnaturally smooth. The floor changed from stone to poured concrete. They rounded a corner. Ahead was an oval of natural light. The cave mouth. He was reminded of their return to the Waterman party. Perhaps she also thought of that. She did not hurry eagerly forward. "I'm sorry," she said. "We—I—didn't understand our own arrogance in believing we could decide Earth's future." Her voice was hoarse.

He had been harsh. "I'm sorry, too," he said. "You did what you believed was right. I'm sure there will be a gain to Earth from contact with your friends."

"For the survivors." She sighed.

He felt the impulse and for once couldn't control it. He reached around her and, careful of her injured shoulder, he embraced Beatrice. She leaned against him. "Thank you," she said.

He pulled back a bit, remembering the filthiness of the coverall, and thinking of Liada. He was able to connect with the Assembly again. He would have to deal with Liada and the consequences of their divorce to Tepan—but he intended to divorce her.

Stefan looked at the cave mouth. It was closer than he'd realized. The entrance was small. A shadow, the silhouette of a man, stood waiting for them. Without having to think about it, he was certain it was Kaim Pritchard. "Pritchard's out there," he warned Beatrice. "He's all right; he survived."

No, I'm here, Pritchard said inside Stefan's mind. *I never left.*

Stefan hadn't terminated the call. Immediately, he tried to snap the connection.

Here I am, Pritchard gloated, still present inside Stefan.

"Get out of my head," Stefan said both aloud and by interior monologue. He used his code to break off the Assembly connect.

Why is an audience of one any different from an audience of millions? Pritchard laughed.

"What?" Beatrice asked. She looked at the cave mouth, where Pritchard stood with his hands on his hips, waiting for them—Stefan knew it as well as he knew his own stance—and she pulled back on Stefan's arm, reluctant to leave the cave, though it had been her prison.

His duty was done. Stefan wanted to disconnect. He couldn't. Over and over he tried to terminate their connection but Pritchard's leering presence permeated his thoughts.

Pritchard laughed at each failure. *Here I am, Inlander,* he said. Pritchard's thoughts dumped into Stefan's mind. Stefan felt him as though the two of them had become the same man, and knew, for a repulsed instant, every dirty thing Pritchard had done, and why. He knew what Pritchard had done to him.

Stefan ran at the dark outline ahead that was Kaim Pritchard, intending to kill him. Pritchard continued to pour his thoughts like sludge into Stefan. *Get out! Get out! Get out!* Stefan screamed at Pritchard, wanting to drown the ugly insight.

Stefan burst out the cave mouth. Sunlight washed over him, stunning him with its beauty and the loveliness of the world outside the cave. He came to a stop and stared, awestruck, then finally looked at Pritchard, about two meters ahead.

Pritchard was in the light. His skin was shiny and the color of cooked crab; it was also peeling. His eyes were pink. He'd lost weight and his peacock clothing hung loose, but his genuine improvement was obvious as he shifted to a fighter's stance. "Is this what you want?" Pritchard said aloud. He had heard Stefan's thoughts as easily as Stefan had them.

Let go of my mind! Stefan said. "I won't let this invasion continue."

You'd miss me if I left. Pritchard laughed, and Stefan felt the foreign flash of nasty humor in his mind while the sound itself echoed back into the tunnel. Pritchard looked there. Beatrice had followed Stefan and stood naked at the border between darkness and light.

Through some web doctoring or Adjuster magic, Pritchard had a constant link into Stefan's mind. Stefan received spillover of Pritchard's thoughts, too, but more a seepage of emotion. He knew, because he felt it, precisely what Kaim Pritchard felt as he gazed at Beatrice's naked body.

For days, perhaps for all his life, Stefan Acari had done his duty as others defined it. He'd led a narrow, proper life, and kept his private reflections buried so deeply inside that he rarely consciously knew he had them. He didn't think this time. He bypassed thought for action. Seemingly without volition, his right hand balled into a tight fist. Despite his fatigue, or because of it, he raised that fist. Only as he swung and felt the clean, slicing movement of his hand through open air, did he become aware of what he did. His fist connected with Pritchard's face. Impact was satisfying.

Chapter 9

Stefan lost the fight.

Pritchard was already turning aside as Stefan swung; Stefan's fist landed glancingly on Pritchard's left cheek. The impact stunned Stefan, who had never done such a thing, but Pritchard just grinned and stepped back.

Stefan assumed the fight was over. He felt childish but relieved, as though the idiocy of physical combat had calmed him. He stretched his fingers, which seemed more hurt than Pritchard's face.

"Brawling with a nixt mirko, Stefan?" Pritchard spoke like a teacher chastising a usually obedient student. His face was a peeling patchwork of pale, flaking skin, red welts, and fading bruises from his illness. The grin didn't help his appearance. "Let me show you how it's done," he said, and in one smooth movement, Pritchard kicked outward, from his side, straight into Stefan's groin. Stefan gasped and bent over, too hurt to make a sound. Pritchard's fist swung at him casually. Stefan might have avoided it if he'd had breath and sense to try, but instead the fist landed just under his chin in an upper cut that even Stefan sensed Pritchard had reined in. That knowledge hurt as much as the punch, which sent him sprawling backward on the open hillside, staring up at the beautiful blue sky. Pritchard stood over him.

"In Zona, the next move against someone stupid enough to start a challenge he can't win might be this." Pritchard raised his booted foot and held it a few inches above Stefan's face, then slowly settled it just where Stefan, on Pritchard, had landed his blow. "It's symbolic, don't you agree, to grind a challenger into the dust? An Inlander lives a life full of symbols. The tenants' annual gifts, the curtsies and bows. An estate ring from the Oblander. All those *good* things."

Everyone on the hillside was watching: the clansmen Pritchard had arrested as they'd run from the cave, Pritchard's ID agents, and worst, Beatrice. Everyone could see the depth of Stefan's humiliation. They would feel it in his next dump, just as Pritchard knew it now.

Pritchard removed his boot from Stefan's face. Stefan didn't stir. He felt the dirt on his cheek even through the dust and soot from inside the cave. Pritchard was still watching him. "But my education isn't just from Zona," Pritchard said. "This is what I learned at school." Pritchard's foot hovered over Stefan's groin, then the toe of his boot tapped Stefan's side without hurting him. "Kidneys," Pritchard said. He raised the position of his foot. "Ribs. Nothing too visible. Never let it be said that Per Ezio isn't noble. How fine a man he is to have never left a mark!" Pritchard put his foot down without having kicked Stefan.

"I don't believe you." Stefan's voice was rough. His throat ached from the harsh smoke inside the cave. *I don't believe Romaric did anything to you,* he said into their joined minds.

Then look.

Stefan saw Romaric Ezio through Pritchard's eyes, the eyes of a friendless charity student. Tall, thin, and elegant in his customary black, often accompanied by a pack of hangers-on, Romaric was a threatening villain. To Pritchard, Romaric seemed to have made tormenting him his mission. School was a memory blur of insults and minor beatings. Poupey had not been so much terrified as cowed into submission by the knowledge that he could not win. It would not be permitted for a charity student to harm, even in self-defense, any noble student.

Stefan turned away.

Pritchard chuckled. "You're tired, Inlander," he said. "You're not thinking. This isn't the way Per Stefan Acari behaves. Assaulting a sick man! Get up and apolo-

gize for your unprovoked attack. You and your dear
friend Ezio can set the dogs on the traceless nixt
mirko tomorrow."

"I never did anything to you," Stefan said aloud.

You never helped, either. Pritchard extended his hand.

Grasping Pritchard's hand took as much force of will
as Stefan had. He intended to submit, but a streak of
stubbornness came over him. Stefan breathed deeply just
as Pritchard once more invaded his mind, taunting Stefan
with his helplessness; it triggered an animal reaction. Stefan was free of the cave. He wanted to be free of Pritchard's intrusion. More: he wanted to win. As Pritchard
helped him up, Stefan yanked Pritchard with all his
might, pulling Pritchard toward him, off balance. Stefan
kicked up with his legs. He connected, barely, with
Pritchard's chest. It was a glancing blow, but surprise
sent Pritchard reeling backward, though he didn't fall.

Stefan jumped up, pleased he could move so nimbly.
"Get out!" he snarled. A physical attack was so unlike
him, Stefan felt that he was watching another man, yet
he was proud of what he'd done. Whatever the justice
of Pritchard's complaint from their school days, Pritchard now was entirely wrong. Stefan faced him man to
man, upright, not supine on his back like a submissive
dog.

Pritchard's aquamarine shirt, a foppish thing made
garish by silver threads gleaming in the sunlight, had a
clump of cave-mud clinging where Stefan had kicked
him. He made a show of dusting himself off. "You shock
me, Inlander. Truly."

Pritchard was thinking through his next move. Stefan
felt it inside his head and knew he wouldn't win a physical confrontation. "We can continue this . . . jousting,
Pritchard, or you can do as I've asked. Disengage your
call. It's pointless. You already know everything."

"There's a point, Per Acari. It prevents you from entering the Assembly. My answer is no."

Sweat was pooling along Stefan's spine. Outside the
cave it was a hot afternoon. He unzipped the coverall
but didn't dare take his eyes off Pritchard or his thoughts

away from the seepage leaking from Pritchard's mind, Stefan's only clue to Pritchard's intentions. "When this is over, Kaim Pritchard," Stefan said in a low voice, so no one else would hear, "I will still be a Judge and an Inlander. Do you want an enemy? I give you my personal pledge, the sworn word of Acari, which you *know* is good, that I won't enter the Assembly until whatever truth you want to hide from the public is safe to reveal. I'm having no difficulty staying out, whatever they say about tickers' addiction. Now, free my mind."

"No."

Perhaps if he hadn't just experienced Pritchard's memory of abuse at the hands of Stefan's school friends, Stefan would have reacted differently. For an Inlander's sworn word to be rejected was enough provocation that the Oblander's Grand Appeals Court in Ropa might have pardoned Stefan even if he had taken a gun and shot Pritchard down where he stood. Pritchard was Ropan; he knew. Therefore, he had to have a good reason. "Why not?"

Through the link between them Stefan felt Pritchard's own frustrated discomfort at the crossing over of his emotions into Stefan. "It isn't you doing this?" Stefan asked.

Pritchard hesitated, then shook his head. *The Adjusters. They don't want you to dump. You haven't, except into me.*

The Adjusters had excluded him from the Assembly, and tapped into his mind via a traceless ID agent. Stefan glanced around the hillside. The armed men were all Pritchard's Independent Defense agents; the clansmen were under guard, and weren't friends of his, anyway. Stefan was as defenseless as he had been in the shielded cave. "For how long will this continue?"

Pritchard shrugged.

Outrage was useless. Pritchard didn't enjoy the link, either. They had effectively become two bodies and one mind. He imagined Romaric's advice: kill the nixt mirko.

Pritchard's eyes narrowed. "You can try again, Inlander."

Stefan glanced into the cave. Beatrice was at the mouth, just in the sunlight, watching them from slightly above. Soot or the dappled light had darkened her amber complexion, making it olive. Uneven tufts of her hair stuck up in several places, like feathers on a newborn chick, soft-looking and fragile. Her eyes were too big for her face, and they made her seem innocent. She was naked, and so slender that she reminded him of one of the malnourished survivors of the generations of the Great Deaths. Pritchard was watching her, too, but his erotic inclinations, which had enraged Stefan before, this time were sufficiently muted by fondness that they merged fluidly into Stefan's own sensibility. "If you feel that for her," Stefan said, "why don't you show it?"

The breeze ruffled the top of Pritchard's coiffured hair and the lace edges of his cuffs. His expression was blank, but his emotions roiled at the question. Of all the varieties of affection, his was among the most distasteful; Stefan shuddered at its echo. Pritchard liked Beatrice in part because she did not like him; he liked her more now, because Stefan did; he despised her because she was foreign; he was intrigued for the same reason, and condemned himself for that. His combination of attraction, contempt, and guilty self-disgust would never interfere with his duty to the Adjusters. *I do my job,* was Pritchard's underlying thought.

"Their ship is coming." Stefan said it without thinking, as a protective gesture, reminding Pritchard that Beatrice was important.

No it isn't. It hasn't left Jupiter orbit. I've checked. She lied to you, just as she lied about the disease. It isn't extraterrestrial. Dr. Felipe says it's a cousin of Red Death, and Red Death has been around for hundreds of years. The Travelers are trying to scare us. That ship is probably a huge, empty balloon.

Stefan had heard truth in Beatrice's voice. He had recognized it from his own speculations. Beatrice could be mistaken—perhaps her ship hadn't left Jupiter orbit—but she hadn't lied. Whether it was Pritchard's illness or another, she had brought disease to Earth.

Pritchard was so absorbed into the larger psyche of the Assembly that he didn't even know where he ended and the Adjusters' manipulation began. He didn't know when *he* was lying, or being lied to. He didn't care. Truth or fiction were the same to him.

Pritchard grinned, but Stefan's sudden compassion for the lost man that was Kaim Pritchard went so far that, having just fought him, he extended his hand. "We can work together on this."

Pritchard ignored it and started away, toward his men. As he left, he said, "You sent a good doctor to me."

Stefan nodded as if Pritchard had thanked him, as in his way he had, then without another word, Stefan turned, too, and went to Beatrice.

The Judge smelled rank and looked exhausted, but he obtained what he considered proper clothing for Beatrice—a clean pair of pants and a more difficult to locate shirt—for which she was grateful. He stood beside her while Dr. Felipe rebandaged her shoulder, watching as though supervising the work. He stepped out of his heavy coverall, pulling the legs over his dirty shoes only with difficulty and staggering as he did. His suit was wrinkled and stained with perspiration; while it had perhaps once been discreet, it would never have been flattering. The Judge seemed to ignore that he was a body as well as a mind.

"Pritchard will want to ask you questions, Beatrice," the Judge said. When he spoke her name he lingered on each syllable, and the sounds came from deep in his throat. "Questions are proper," he continued, "but you needn't return to the Lodge with him. I'm staying in Bowl; you can come there with me." He glanced across the road to where Pritchard was assembling and briefly interviewing his captives. Pritchard turned at the same moment, then both men quickly looked away from each other.

"My friends are in the Lodge. I should go to them." She had watched his confrontation with Kaim Pritchard in amazement, measuring the fury that would drive the

Judge to violence by the lack of skill he showed. Unlike Kaim Pritchard.

"I think it's prudent for you to come with me to Bowl," he said. "I'll see that your fellow Travelers are told you're safe, but then Pritchard won't have you, and all information about your ship, hostage."

Beatrice was sure Pritchard would not release her from his custody and every armed man on the hillside was his. The Judge must have realized it, too. He wanted another confrontation with Pritchard. "Thank you, but I prefer being in the same jeopardy as my friends. And thank you, too, for saving my life, Stefan."

He'd asked her to use his name, and his enjoyment at hearing it made his enunciation stilted, an endearing trait, Beatrice thought. "It was my pleasure," he said and bowed. She liked the way he did it. Even tired, when the courtesy could have been automatic or sloppy, he kept his attention on her, fully aware of whom he saluted. What she did with her voice, he did with a tight control of gesture.

He cared for her. It had been obvious in the way he touched and refrained from touching her as he washed her wound; it showed in his voice and in his eyes. Nevertheless, her mission was a barrier between them. He was not a man who would excuse her for his own convenience or even from affection, so it was imperative that he approve. She wanted to convince him that her mission was right. "The Ship should be here soon."

He seemed surprised. "Your ship? It hasn't left Jupiter."

His certainty made her suspicious. "Are you in the Assembly?" She reached out for the beacon; she found it.

The Ship was *not* on its way to Earth after all. The call hadn't been sent. She was disappointed; a choice remained to be made. The Ship's arrival might have been all right: Pritchard had survived the most virulent of the diseases. The Ship's coming wouldn't destroy the indigenous civilization—except that it depended on the Assembly. There was no help for that.

"No." The Judge glanced at Pritchard. "I've been cut off from the Assembly by the Adjusters." He explained about the shielded space in the cavern where she had been held, and his new connection with Kaim Pritchard. She was amazed at human cleverness, and appalled.

It was their first meeting in sunlight. She watched him as he spoke. The Judge's—Stefan's—hair was darkened by dirt and matted after hours wearing a helmet. His face was smeared with grime and streaked by tears induced by the smoke. Beneath that, a stubble showed. She liked the way he looked. His touch would be deliberate. He wouldn't rush. In the cave, bandaging her shoulder, his hands had never strayed from the exact requirements of their task. She imagined him without his self-control quite so tightly wound, a bit dirty and disheveled, and she reached farther toward him than was comfortable with the awkward bandage and the ache from her wound. "It will be all right," she said. Once the Ship was called, all the Adjusters' tricks would be worthless, but because she didn't want Kaim Pritchard to understand the connection between the Assembly and the Ship, she couldn't explain it to the Judge. If Pritchard knew before the call was sent, then he might kill her and her fellow Travelers to prevent it.

"Don't move again," Dr. Felipe ordered Beatrice. He was taping her wound much more tightly than the Judge had done.

"If there is a problem, Doctor, or any complication, then inform me immediately," the Judge said, using such a commanding tone that the doctor drew back in clear offense, but the Judge, who took his authority for granted, seemed not to notice.

"*You* aren't the patient, Judge Acari," Dr. Felipe said. He studied the Judge, frowning at what he saw. "But you're liable to become one. Go home and rest."

Beatrice stared down at her hands to prevent herself from smiling. The two men would bicker and never know why they had. "Stefan, it's all right," she said.

The Judge nodded brusquely at Dr. Felipe and watched in silence as the sour doctor finished, put his supplies in a black case, and walked to one of Pritchard's vehicles, parked up the hill.

"He's right," Beatrice said. "You're more tired than I am. Get some rest."

"When I know you're safe."

"No one is ever safe, Stefan." Beatrice briefly closed her eyes. The daylight was so bright that light wasn't stopped by her eyelids. Her throat still hurt from inhaling smoke and words weren't sufficient to explain. It needed song, yet she tried. "All life is risk. Isolation isn't safety, it's only delay." He seemed unmoved by the Friends' platitudes.

Until the Judge turned to him, Beatrice hadn't noticed Kaim Pritchard's arrival. "My *better* half," Pritchard greeted the Judge. "I don't need to detain you; I know everything I need. A coach will take you into Bowl." He gestured up the road. Beneath his flayed skin, Kaim Pritchard's face glistened like scar tissue.

"I'm glad you're well." Beatrice was reluctant to needlessly antagonize Pritchard when, if he realized the truth about the beacon, as he may have had the puzzle pieces to do, the Travelers' lives might be in his hands. She had survived the kidnapping, but needed to survive her rescue.

Pritchard gazed at her for a moment without answering. The Judge began to speak, but then Pritchard interrupted. "You claim that the Travelers brought new diseases to Earth, so is it fair to say that you made me ill?"

Beatrice looked at the Judge, but he was watching Pritchard. "Yes."

"What? No apology?" Pritchard was jovial in his disbelief.

"Why should she apologize to her kidnapper?" The Judge came aggressively closer to Pritchard. "The clans were your tool."

"Go away, Inlander. You've become superfluous." The connection between the two men was audible in a subtle commonality of intonation. Both had focused on her, as if she were a prize in a contest between them.

"Go rest," she urged Stefan. Beatrice would be safer with Pritchard once the Judge left. "You need it."

The Judge ran his hand through his sooty hair in a gesture suggestive of Pritchard. "He won't do anything to hurt you," the Judge told Beatrice. "We're in regular contact. For now."

Pritchard snickered.

The Judge pretended to ignore Pritchard, bowed to her, then walked away in the direction Pritchard had indicated. He stumbled once on the uneven ground, probably from fatigue.

Pritchard waited until the Judge was out of sight around the curve of the road, then he bowed and took her hand in a gesture he probably meant to be gallant, but he held her so tightly it hurt. His peeling fingers looked like blind, wormy, wriggling creatures in caves. She jerked free.

"I have never wanted to hurt you, Beatrice, but you act as though you expect it. I suppose *he* is your hero, a man who is no more than a bundle of habits tied together with twine made of good manners. Believe me, I know him much better than you can."

"Then you know that isn't true."

Pritchard pursed his lips and glanced in the direction the Judge had gone, then gazed at Beatrice longer than was comfortable. "He's angry because his wife disappointed him. What do you think he feels for a person who claims to have betrayed the Earth?"

There was no advantage in conversation with Kaim Pritchard. On the Ship, dealing with a Kroni, she would have simply ceased to acknowledge his existence, but although he controlled his reaction, Beatrice guessed shunning infuriated Pritchard. "I haven't betrayed anyone," she said.

"You're right, you haven't." He stroked the back of her hand with his fingernail, lightly scraping it against her skin; she forced herself not to pull away. "You can't. You're not quite human, are you, Beatrice? Your Friends have changed you."

*   *   *

A soft, warm hand gently shook Stefan's shoulder. "Sir, Sir. Wake up." A woman; whispering, she sounded a bit like Beatrice. He savored the moment, pretending she was.

Years had passed since Stefan had lain in bed quietly daydreaming without the Assembly available to supplement his thoughts. The linens had a starchy, commercial feel that crept into his consciousness, and the hotel bedroom was scented with cleaning solutions disguised by floral fragrances, but he was comfortable alone. "Later," he said.

She leaned near enough that he felt her breath against his ear. "Sir, please. It's important."

He yawned and opened his eyes.

As an adolescent exploring the Assembly, Stefan had discovered pornography. "You don't have to imagine anything, it's all there," he'd eagerly told Romaric. There it was. Full, round, tanned, and hanging before him waiting to be touched, the maid's lacy, white apron bib—the erratically puritanical wildman hotel's idea of formal livery—hid nothing.

Inside his mind, Kaim Pritchard leered and laughed.

"Get out!" Stefan shouted.

The poor girl jumped back. In tears, she said, "It's almost two o'clock in the afternoon! Sir, I need to make up the room."

An explanation would only confuse her. "Is that what you wanted?" he demanded gruffly, to hide his embarrassment. He kept the sheet around himself and sat up in the bed.

She bit her lip and looked around as though someone might be hiding in the room. There was an eavesdropper, but Stefan had no power to evict him.

"I have a message," she said, whispering again. "You're to go to the Clan Hall."

Stefan studied her tattoos, but couldn't read whether or not she was a member of Denning's clan. "The Waterman Clan Hall?" Weren't all the Waterman clansmen arrested?

No, Pritchard said. *Why bother with a headless horse? I have Denning and the worst of them.*

The girl nodded. "She'll meet you there."

"She" could only mean Marta Denning. "Why not here?"

The girl glanced at the floor, as if to indicate the management on the hotel's lower levels. "They wouldn't let her. All of us are under suspicion. Will you come?"

He imagined Marta pretending innocence and pleading for help; he was sure she'd known about the Waterman conspiracy.

"Sir?" The maid hesitated. "She said to tell you one other thing. She says she's sorry you've been involved in this, but that you *are* involved. Mr. Pritchard has sent for your wife and son. They're on their way here already, in an unscheduled Throw from Paris. She said to meet her at the Clan Hall as soon as possible." The girl spoke quickly and scarcely breathed throughout the speech, but gained composure as she progressed and was standing taller when she finished.

You bastard! Stefan raged into his connect, but he was talking to himself. Pritchard had evaporated from Stefan's mind like water when heat is applied, making Marta's accusation ring true.

The image of Tepan in the clutches of scum like Poupey, who thought childhood was an inadequacy more quickly overcome by proper application of terror and force, frightened Stefan. He had to protect his son. And Liada. Whatever his own mixed feelings of regret and dissatisfaction, he wouldn't subject her to what Pritchard might do to an Inlandres for sport and revenge. "I'll be there," Stefan told the maid. "Now get out, and let me dress."

"Yes, sir," she said brightly. "I'll only leave the meca." She rushed away before he could object.

He flopped back against the pillows. With his mind clamped tightly around Stefan's, why had Pritchard needed extra security?

Coward! Stefan shouted into the void that was Pritchard's missing presence, Stefan's own former entryway into the Assembly.

No response. The protocols of Zona did not require an answer to every challenge.

The door opened again. A smooth-surfaced meca rolled into the room, identical to the one Stefan had watched a few days earlier. It turned its attention to the chair on which Stefan had dropped his filthy clothing. Carefully, as if the ruined suit was fabricated of spun glass, it lifted the clothes and placed them on its second arm, holding them extended on its own clothesline while it cleaned the chair, then it meticulously folded them and repositioned them in a neat pile.

The Old Moderns had lived deluged by mechanized gadgets; waste was one of their greatest sins. The Assembly had purged them from most of the Earth. The UN-Assemblers wanted them brought back. Civilization would change without the Assembly, but perhaps it wouldn't collapse.

His back ached. He arched it, hoping to relieve it, then hurried to the bathroom, where he shut and locked the door, though modesty in front of the meca was silly, like hiding from a dustbin.

Another day had passed. Beatrice was in Adjuster custody, and so was John Denning. Stefan was ready to enter a preliminary judgment—against Pritchard *and* the Waterman clan—but couldn't.

After dressing, Stefan went to the deadhead access booths near the hotel lobby. He used his emergency access code to the Open Court—it was entirely physical, meant for a failure in his connect—typing it in with one finger, careful to be exact.

"Access denied," a mechanical imitation of a woman's voice said. "Invalid code."

Stefan tried again, just to be sure. And again. "Access denied. Invalid code," it said each time.

The Open Court was refusing his call.

Poupey? Where are you? You can't hide forever.

Pritchard didn't answer.

Drom Hanzin wouldn't refuse his employer's call. Stefan typed in his steward's code.

"Per Acari?" Drom had his dummy up again; it bowed, a puppet on a blank stage. "I hadn't expected to hear from you so soon."

Stefan grinned, stupidly grateful to have gotten through. "I'm on a deadhead access again, but I'm here."

"Ah." It was a noncommittal, politic sound. "Per Acari, I understand—everyone will—that you've been under pressure, and that can lead to imperfect judgment. If you're concerned about the tenants, then you needn't be. As for the Open Court, the tenants don't care if their Inlander is on it or not. Most actually prefer not."

Stefan had intended to discover how Pritchard had managed to get Tepan and Liada away from Acari. He had no idea to what his steward was referring. Poor judgment? The most ill-advised thing he'd done recently was to try to connect and dump from the cave, but no one could know about that. "Explain yourself," he ordered curtly.

There was a hesitation. The dummy froze into an awkward pose and embarrassed smile. "Your dumps are always reviewed in our region, Per Acari," Drom's dummy said. "I make it a point to register them in my personal updates; people are such gossips. You were wise to get your wife away first, so there wouldn't be a scene."

Exasperated, Stefan shook his head. "What are you talking about?"

"I only mean that while this episode might irritate the Oblander or scandalize some indwellers, it is insufficient grounds for tenants to break obligations to Acari. Your social position will suffer, although there may be sympathy because of your wife's infidelity."

Stefan felt sick fear laced with cold, hard anger; its name was Kaim Pritchard. "Drom, I haven't made a dump in three or four days—I've lost count. I've spoken with you since then. What are you talking about?"

There was a long silence. "Per Acari," he said finally,

"it isn't necessary to be embarrassed. I am committed to the service of Acari. I don't intend to resign."

Drom, resign? For him to even say the word was shocking. There were few positions anywhere that would give Drom so much authority. Because Stefan was a Judge, Drom Hanzin was the Inlander of Acari in all but name. "I'm not embarrassed, Drom. I haven't done anything of which I'm ashamed." Stefan had to stop speaking momentarily as his anger nearly broke through his apparent calm. "Tell me, what am I supposed to have done?"

Drom Hanzin, a cosmopolitan man, had trouble making a clear, direct statement about it. He hemmed and hawed and only after Stefan shouted did he believe that the "facts" needed to be spoken. "You were seduced by the Numerican woman, and arranged with her to blame a supposed kidnapping on the Independent Defense agent instead of the wildman clan she had hired to help her escape his lawful custody. They bribed you to protect them—John Denning did—by offering to kill Pera Acari, and by providing a web doctor to cover your actions, but their web doctoring didn't work. The Assembly Adjusters corrected their intervention and restored the truth."

I'll kill you, Kaim Pritchard, Stefan thought savagely. There was no response, not even a chuckle. Kaim Pritchard wasn't the real problem, anyway. An "adjustment" had been made to Stefan's supposed dump, an adjustment that had incriminated him and was well beyond Kaim Pritchard's power. Stefan cleared his throat. "None of that really happened, Drom," he said.

The dummy's expression didn't change. Angry as he was, Stefan's shock was worse. Despite mounting evidence to the contrary, he had believed in the honesty of the Assembly itself, truly and deeply believed. He had supposed the matter of the Travelers was a special circumstance, and that the Adjusters' reaction had been colored by their unfortunate choice of on-site agent, Kaim Pritchard. "Drom, the dump is a lie. You've known me for twelve years. Is it in character for me? Is it reasonable?"

From nowhere, a pipe materialized in the dummy's hands. The dummy lit it, a delaying tactic. Only when it was going did he answer. "Per Acari, unhappiness can change a man. For several years, I've been aware that you were ... dissatisfied. Sir, I will of course pursue any action to which you direct me, but I must advise you that it is best if you simply walk away from the Open Court, quietly, now that they've ... released you as a Judge. If you don't, then there could be further repercussions for Acari."

Meaning Stefan could be relieved by the Oblander, and a regent for Tepan installed in his place. How could anyone counter the instinctive, gut-level trust the Assembly engendered when it placed lies directly into a person's mind? Were truth and rationality ever enough? Romaric was right. People *believed* the Assembly. Unwilling to listen any longer to the concealed contempt in his steward's voice, Stefan pressed the key that broke the connection and terminated the call.

I'll kill you, Kaim Pritchard, he sent again, meaning it, but Pritchard was still hiding. Ice priests, cold as their home in the Southlands, the Adjusters had done this.

There was no utility code to reach the Adjusters. They were met inside the Assembly, at their discretion, not that of Assembly users, even its tickers. Stefan stared through the empty frame at the blank wall on its other side. *Tell them I want to talk to them,* he sent at Pritchard. *Call Amicus Curiae. I have something to say.*

Pritchard didn't answer, but that didn't mean he wasn't listening. Stefan felt Pritchard's constant weight against his mind, as once he'd sensed the Assembly connection, but this was a foul breath over his shoulder, a dark shadow dogging his heels. Stefan waited for the blinding light of Amicus Curiae.

Stefan knew Pritchard was amoral and that he was the Adjusters' chosen agent, yet the Adjusters had chosen Stefan, too, and placed him on the Open Court. He wanted to be able to trust them again. *Please answer me,* he begged.

The wooden chair legs screeched against the tile floor as Stefan pushed the chair back from the deadhead access. After that, the silence was oppressive.

Had he been able to connect with the Assembly, Stefan might have sought out an Adjuster. Had he been able to connect, there was research he could have done, too: the origins of the Great Deaths, for example. He was curious.

"Stefan." The voice came without visual fanfare. The frame remained blank. Stefan almost thought it was inside his mind, but when he tried to answer there, Pritchard sullenly said, *Aloud, Inlander. I'm not your courier.*

"Stefan Acari." Stefan recognized this Adjuster, too; he had labeled her the Companion. Although they rarely met, he had often sensed her presence with him at the Assembly margins. He stood. "Ma'am?"

She laughed. It reminded him of Beatrice's laughter, not Liada's, and made him smile as he sat back in the chair, but his smile vanished quickly. "Why have you done this to me? Lied about me to the entire world?"

"This is a serious matter. You were warned."

"I was threatened and bribed, not warned. Tell me what is going on. Make me understand. I can help." Stefan closed his eyes since there was no image in the visual frame and the empty deadhead access booth was distracting. Without sight, he felt closer to connection in the Assembly.

"You have doubts," she said. "Some of us believe you are disloyal." Like Beatrice, her voice was smooth. It encouraged him to want to please her, but that voice, so reminiscent of Beatrice's, was something manufactured by the deadhead booth, a soothing trick designed especially for him.

"When did loyalty become a condition of a connection in the Assembly?" he demanded. "Why should the Open Court hide truth?"

"Since our world has been threatened by aliens. Possibly invaders."

"Beatrice's 'friends'?"

She didn't answer his question. "There are some issues for which the Open Court is not the proper forum. The ship is dangerous. Prove yourself, Stefan. Go home. Leave the Northern Sister and go back to Ropa now. Immediately. Do that, and I'm sure the rest of this can be straightened out." She spoke as if the false dump were a story draft that could be corrected by revision. An adjustment.

"You won't tell me anything?"

"Go home. There is a throw to Ropa scheduled in two hours."

"My wife and son are on their way here because of your agent, Pritchard."

Pritchard spoke inside Stefan's head, but his tone and texture were that of the Companion: *Pritchard will do nothing to Liada and Tepan without our consent. Return home. They will immediately follow.*

Pritchard—Poupey—truly was a puppet, a mask the Adjusters wore, and the Adjusters were the only players on the stage. From years of dumps, Stefan had long practice in stilling his thoughts. He quelled his horror; there was nothing mankind could make that could not be subverted. At the Lodge, Pritchard himself had done a similar thing with his men. "Pritchard is loyal," Stefan said.

"We don't expect that depth of loyalty from you, Stefan." The Companion spoke aloud in the booth. "There is no need. You can be trusted, but not in this. Go home."

He would be damned before he'd dance a shorter version of what they had just forced Kaim Pritchard through. The Adjusters had made Stefan a Judge and thought they could unmake him one, too, but judgment didn't depend on their appointment. They knew his thoughts, so he deliberately sent them through the sieve that was Kaim Pritchard. *You imagine that because justice sometimes requires concealing the truth, that justice can exist without first discovering truth. It can't. I am a Judge. I will decide for myself.* He terminated the call by manual disconnect. The Adjusters could only speak to him through Pritchard.

Pritchard: Poupey. The name had been prescient, Stefan thought in compassionate contempt.

I don't need your pity, Inlander.

Stefan had wanted to check on Romaric and Maja, but other things came first. He would meet with Marta Denning and see about finding a web doctor.

Chapter 10

Sunlight came through windows like a blessing, leaving pools of warmth on Beatrice's bed and gilding her amber-colored arm as it lay on the pale covers; starlight had entered the Ship's window as cold as the surrounding darkness; it had illuminated nothing. In light, Earth held the advantage; in darkness, the Ship.

"It doesn't matter, even if it is true," the Fox sang.

"How can it not matter?" Beatrice winced as the doctor adjusted the position of her arm. Immobility had stiffened it. Dr. Felipe glanced at her, but was not nearly as solicitous for her well-being as he had been a day earlier, on the hillside. Beatrice did not visually indicate the doctor, but sang, "He knows something about us. Look how he acts. Listen to his tone when he speaks." The doctor frowned as she sang.

The Fox turned away from the window, politely facing the doctor. "How is she?"

"Her healing is progressing normally." He sounded tart.

"But?" The Fox expressed in human words the reservation implicit in the doctor's tone.

Dr. Felipe looked at both Beatrice and the Fox, hesitated, glanced at the listening guard, who stood impassively in the doorway, then compressed his lips and began applying an astringent salve to her wound.

"Is it serious?" the Fox went closer.

Dr. Felipe scowled at his work. "No. She was lucky."

Beatrice sang for privacy and to add emotional flavor. "You see? He's afraid of both of us, and he actively dislikes me."

"Is there anything else?" the Fox asked Dr. Felipe. He stood opposite the doctor across Beatrice's bed.

"Why did you come to Earth?" The explosion of words burst from the doctor in one breath.

"I don't understand." The Fox sounded puzzled and innocent. "We came as guests, hoping to be friends."

"Friends!" The doctor returned to his work. Despite the tension in every other part of his body, his hands bandaged Beatrice's wound steadily and professionally. He looked only at what he was doing. "That Judge was a decent man—I reviewed his file when he first asked my help—and look what she did to him!"

"What did I do?" Beatrice's bewilderment was genuine. She amended her question. "What does Pritchard say I did?" She had endured a long interview with Pritchard after their return to the Lodge. She had told him whatever he asked about the kidnapping, except anything to do with the beacon and her rapport with the Judge. Her emotional response to a man was irrelevant to either the kidnapping or her mission to Earth.

"Mr. Pritchard didn't ruin the Judge," Dr. Felipe said darkly. "You did. His own dump convicts him."

"The Judge." The Fox clarified as a way to draw information from him.

Dr. Felipe placed the last tape over the bandage and stepped away from the bed. With Beatrice no longer his immediate patient, he glared down at her. "He loves you. What did you do to make a man like that feel so much so quickly? Some alien trick, probably. And he doesn't even know the truth." He picked up Beatrice's hand and held it as if for comparison with his own darker, duller skin. "You're alien."

Kaim Pritchard had called her an alien, as Beatrice had just told the Fox. "That isn't true," she said. "I am human. What you're seeing is a covering. *It* is alien, but the four of us are not. It isn't really our skin." She let him hold her hand a moment longer, then she gently withdrew from his grasp.

Dr. Felipe gathered his paraphernalia into his bag. "Your differences are more than skin deep." He closed the bag and stared into Beatrice's face for a moment. "Your people have changed."

"That isn't so."

The guard, no doubt relaying every word they spoke directly to Pritchard, had entered the room, but he stepped out of Dr. Felipe's path as the doctor walked deliberately away from Beatrice. At the door, he turned. "Only an alien could have transformed the Judge like that."

So she was a villainess in a drama concocted in the Assembly, and the Judge was a "ruined" man. She felt ill, and couldn't show it. The guard was looking. His eyes were cameras for Pritchard.

The Fox returned to gazing out the window. He seemed to be daydreaming, which meant nothing on the Ship, but Beatrice had acquired some local habits and was annoyed. She had told him, in song, about her capture, the weird examination using images, followed by the questions in the hut in the cave, and of how she had believed the Ship was on its way. She'd told him about her rescue by the Judge, and in song it was impossible not to let emotional shadings enter a description. "They take elements of truth and twist them," the Fox sang in commiseration. "The Judge cares for you, and the Judge is dangerous to Pritchard. So."

Beatrice was troubled by the accusation that the Travelers were no longer human. Such genetic drift would be immaterial to the Friends, but not to the people of Earth, and not to the Judge. She began a lament.

"You know the rule," the guard said. "Talk in a real language."

They ignored him, as they did all such orders, but Beatrice ceased singing. The sunlight now felt too hot. A medicinal odor remained from the doctor. "I wish it had been true, in the cave, that the beacon was down. If the Ship were here, our mission would be over. There would be no decisions to make."

"I'm sorry," the Fox sang in tones of great regret. "I chose you to come, if anyone did. In the Ship, you acted from thought, not habit." He returned, and sat on the edge of her bed, taking her hand, the one Dr. Felipe had displayed as a comparison with his own. The Fox's color was the same as hers, the color of the Friends. His skin was smoother than it had been before they'd come on the mission; his wrinkles had vanished beneath the alien skin. His blue eyes were the same, and his graying hair was the same, but were they human? The skin was an alien cloak, but Dr. Felipe said that beneath it there was also an alien. "Only the four of us know both sides: Earth and the Friends. We need to decide whether to call the Ship."

"We should tell the people of Earth," Beatrice said simultaneously with the Fox's singing. "They should decide."

"Hush. Beatrice, you're tired, you're young, but we're here; we can't cede the decision to others. I wouldn't press you, but there may not be much time. Do they know about the beacon?"

"Hey," the guard said. "I told you to talk our language."

"Listen!" The Fox issued a command. "When you thought the beacon was down, what did you tell your Judge?"

She realized her error, and according to the doctor, the Judge had dumped himself into the Assembly. "They might know that the Assembly is made from a beacon of ours. I'm not certain exactly what I said." She had jeopardized their lives.

The Fox took her hand, for comfort, and made a defiant sound. "It's time to decide if the Ship should come. If the answer is yes, we should make the call now. Pritchard survived his illness. It's enough. Charles and Mariyo will take too long to make up their minds. If we wait, Pritchard may kill us before we can call."

It was her fault if their secret was discovered. She'd talked too openly to a man who allowed his mind to become public. In the dim cave, when she had supposed the beacon was gone, his Open Court had seemed extinct. "We'll call now." The mission parameters said to call the Ship if, in their judgment, both Earth's population and that of the Ship could survive contact relatively unscathed—if the benefits outweighed the deaths.

"I mean it truly," the Fox said. "We need to *choose*. Is destroying what they've built right?"

Disease was the deciding factor, not the Assembly. They hadn't even known of the perversion of the beacon until after they had arrived on Earth.

"Paul," she said, then hesitated because she so rarely used his given name within song. It, like all human words, made an awkward stop, but it was also intimate. "The Assembly wasn't part of the mission parameters." To sing the obvious made it a question.

He stared into her eyes, a rare, intimate contact on the Ship. "Do you trust the Friends?"

"This is the last warning," the guard said. "Mr. Pritchard has gotten stricter."

"Don't you?" she asked in human language, to placate the guard, so he wouldn't send the Fox away. "I told the Judge that contact was for the greater good," she said. "You don't believe it is? You?" The Fox was the closest human friend to the Friends. He must trust them. Then she realized she'd used human speech; the guard's eyes widened. He went to the doorway and glanced into the hall, but stayed inside the room.

The Fox went to the window, and stood observing the sunny afternoon cynically, as if for deceit. "One last story, Beatrice.

"A fox and an ass swore eternal friendship," he sang. "They went walking in a wood, like this one here." He waved a hand toward the trees. "A lion crossed their path. The fox volunteered to go to the lion, saying to the ass, 'We must make terms with him, and get him to join our friendship.' So, the fox went to the lion, but instead of doing as he'd told the ass, he offered to help the lion trap the ass, provided his own life would be spared. The lion agreed, quite willingly. So the fox steered the trusting ass into a great pit and trapped him for the lion. As soon as the lion saw the ass was trapped, he sprang upon the fox, killed and ate him, leaving the ass to be eaten later, at his leisure." He turned back to

Beatrice. "Tell me, are we betraying this world and leading the lion to the ass if we make the call and close the beacon for the Friends? Can we let the Friends destroy the Earth again?"

"The Friends don't try to destroy anyone," she protested.

"The Friends hurt no one, as long as they get their way. Their way is contact. They're relentless in pursuit of it. So, Beatrice, am I a foolish fox, or a wise one to believe it's best for Earth, too, to do what they want? To call the Ship. What do you choose? The end of the Assembly or their perpetual isolation?"

Kaim Pritchard walked into the room. He jerked his head at the guard and the man followed him farther inside. "You two sound thoroughly confused," Pritchard said. "I want to know what it's about and I want to know it now."

Pritchard had dressed more soberly than usual, in darker colors and with less flash, more like the Judge. His skin was peeling, but the new skin underneath was duller then before, less like scar tissue. His ugliness was in his voice.

"Listen to him," the Fox sang. "Is this the person to whom you would defer your decision? Is this man human and I'm not?"

Pritchard strolled to the window and joined the Fox there. "I don't know what you said, but I don't think I liked it." Pritchard turned slowly to face the Fox, who continued to gaze out the window.

Beatrice sensed a change in Pritchard's stance just before he moved. She shouted, "No!"

Pritchard wrenched the Fox around to face Pritchard, then slapped him, openhanded but hard. A slight ruddiness was left on the Fox's amber-gold skin. He still didn't look at Pritchard.

"I've come to one conclusion," Pritchard said. "Do you want to hear it?" He spoke to the Fox, who didn't answer, but to forestall another attack, Beatrice said, "Yes."

"I've decided that your Ship doesn't give a damn what

happens to you. You're expendable. Am I right?" He turned to Beatrice. "Am I right? I can do anything I want." Pritchard kicked the Fox in the side. The Fox only grunted, but he had to grab the windowsill to prevent himself from falling. Now, he watched Pritchard.

Beatrice pushed away the covers and jumped off the bed. "Please, no. Stop. Kaim, please!"

In a parody of charm, Pritchard smiled at her and bowed. "Who can stop me? Not your precious Inlander. Not your Ship. But you can, if you tell me what I want to hear."

"You're right, Kaim," Beatrice said soothingly. "The Ship won't come here to protect us. If you beat Paul it won't matter except to him, to you and to me. Please, don't do it."

Pritchard smirked, as though surprised at an unexpected success. He took a step away from the Fox. "But you can call your Ship if you want? Isn't that why you have connects? Your plan is to use our Assembly?"

The Fox said nothing. Beatrice swallowed hard.

"I can do anything I want," Pritchard reminded her, "and Beatrice, while I don't want to hurt you—any of you, particularly—I do not worry about my conscience if necessity requires it."

"Yes," she said. Inspired, she added, "If two of us enter the Assembly, then the Ship will immediately come." That should prevent Pritchard from trying to force them to connect with the Assembly, and it was close to the truth. Too close for comfort.

Pritchard clapped his hands, applauding either Beatrice or himself. "That wasn't so difficult. Tomorrow we'll do more."

"This is dangerous," the Fox sang.

Pritchard kicked him again, moving so swiftly that Beatrice only saw it as he connected. The Fox doubled over. "No more of that," Pritchard said. "From now on, you will all speak so I can understand.

"Tonight," he continued, "since you've been so useful, Beatrice, I have a special guest for you to meet. We'll dine together. Just you." At some unspoken command, the guard took hold of the Fox and tugged him toward the door. "We'll leave you to get dressed," Pritchard said. "Wear your best." He bowed to Beatrice. "I'll return for you in ten minutes."

The outer door of the Waterman Clan Hall clanged shut behind Stefan with a sound like a prison gate closing. Stefan scanned the lobby; he and Marta were alone. In only a few days the place seemed to have acquired a thin layer of dust. The Great Gathering Room was dark. "Where is everyone?"

"Home, trying to scrape away their clan tattoos," Marta said bitterly. "That Independent Defense agent is framing us, the entire Waterman Clan."

Like the awareness of someone reading over his shoulder, Stefan sensed Pritchard worm his way back into joint consciousness. He shook his head as if he could shake Pritchard out, then decided to ignore him. "You're lying," Stefan said impatiently. "Your clan was involved in the Traveler's abduction. Her rescue was a sham. You're a clan officer. If you weren't a deadhead, Pritchard would have arrested you, too." He should have sympathized with Marta's situation. Her son, as well as her husband, were in custody; her clan was being destroyed around her, but Marta Denning stood with her hands on her hips like an angry housewife while sending him messages about things she shouldn't have known. "How did you find out about Liada and Tepan?"

"I still have a few friends."

"That isn't an answer." Though it probably wasn't so mysterious. Pritchard would have wanted Stefan to know, and most likely had leaked the news purposely.

She sighed heavily, her chest heaving, then smiled with the strain of trying to make a new start. "Stefan, I'll tell you everything I know, but let's go to my office, where we can sit."

There were chairs in the Great Gathering Room, but Stefan acquiesced and followed her to the elevator. He wondered when Liada and Tepan would arrive in Bowl, and what Pritchard intended to do with them. *Are you listening?* he sent. *Why have you brought them here? What use are they to you?* But Stefan knew precisely why his family had been seized. The Adjusters wanted hostages to his loyalty. Liada and Tepan's safety depended on his good behavior.

The third floor's coolness reminded Stefan of the caverns, but instead of sour memories of the rescue, he pictured Beatrice standing at the cave mouth, just into the sunshine. He would divorce Liada, if she didn't divorce him first. His falsified dump would provide sufficient grounds. Before anything, however, he had to protect her from Pritchard. He owed her that. Then there was Tepan. To protect him, Stefan had to clear the Acari name.

He could go home. The Adjuster Companion had more or less promised to clear him if he did. Walking through Bowl on his way to the Waterman Clan Hall, Stefan had considered that: a falsified vindication after a false dump. If he agreed to walk away, he could not be a Judge again. Whatever provision against truth the Adjusters made, he would never believe in the Assembly or himself. He would have failed to discover the intent behind the Travelers' arrival; he would have given the Adjusters unfettered power in the Assembly, and sacrificed Beatrice to it. Most of all, he would have abdicated the greatest responsibility there was, the responsibility to judge—and do—what was honorable and just.

His alternative to bending to the Adjusters' coercion was to clear his own name. That put Liada and Tepan at risk, as well as Stefan himself. It meant finding such allies as he could, like Marta Denning, and fighting outside the Assembly.

They entered Marta's office; her computer was on and humming, though at a higher pitch than the device in the cave. He sat in a comfortable chair near the window and she sat opposite him, not at the desk. "Pritchard came to us," she said immediately. "He needed us to use the free zone."

"The Assembly shield?"

"Yes. ID was getting nowhere investigating the Travelers, waiting for the information they'd volunteer, but Pritchard was afraid to use any coercion, especially any that might become known in the Assembly. I don't know why. John guessed that the ship out there can eavesdrop on the Assembly, or that Pritchard thought it could.

"He flattered us. He said the clans were better able to understand technical information about that ship. He threatened. We've done some things . . ."

"You're UN-Assemblers."

She frowned, and Stefan wished he'd kept silent. Voluntary confessions were rare, and he sensed this one was truthful. He'd get more by simply listening.

I didn't threaten them, Pritchard whispered silently. *I didn't have to. They offered their help when I told them I knew their secrets. John Denning is an ambitious man; he preferred a clandestine alliance to prosecution. And I promised Independent Defense wouldn't interfere in Denning's campaign for President of the Region. A carrot is often more effective than a stick.*

"We want the Assembly limited," Marta continued. "That's no secret. But Pritchard went too far. He promised that John would be the next President of the Northern Sister. After that, we were sure he'd double-cross us, but how could we refuse Independent Defense? We couldn't. It was John's idea to invite you here. He said we needed someone Pritchard couldn't corrupt, with authority Pritchard couldn't ignore or preempt. John tried to get you interested in the Travelers, when the kidnapping didn't go off as first scheduled, but you refused to become involved. We only wanted you here to be sure Pritchard didn't make us his scapegoats. He did anyway. Right after Pritchard had the Traveler woman kidnapped, he called John to the Lodge and arrested him."

"Pritchard didn't kidnap Beatrice." Stefan was certain Pritchard wouldn't have chosen Beatrice as the kidnap victim, and the complaint from his mental rider confirmed it.

"All right, we did it, but it was part of the agreement. It was his plan."

It seemed long ago that John Denning had claimed

Stefan wasn't cynical enough. "The Traveler barnacles were a lie you planted so you could pretend to trace Beatrice once you were done questioning her. That way you could find her, and not wait for Pritchard to do it and blame you."

"Yes." She was twisting her hands around each other as though washing them. "We're not proud of this, Stefan, but we had no real choice. Once the Assembly is involved, no one does." She looked directly at him. "You know what I mean. That dump they've done of you." She shook her head.

He wouldn't be sidetracked. "Why the delay? You could have 'found' Beatrice as soon as John was arrested."

"He *had* John." A tear trickled from the corner of her eye, and she patted it with her hand, erasing the wet line it had made across her Waterman tattoos. "He wanted information. We had to get it for him."

Crocodile tears is the local expression. Pritchard's voice was acid in Stefan's mind. *That woman is colder than I am.* Pritchard's amusement was an expanding bubble. It burst, drenching Stefan. Involuntarily, because of his connection with Pritchard's emotions, Stefan smiled. When Marta glanced up and saw it, he was mortified. Whatever else he doubted, Stefan did not doubt Marta's love for her husband.

Stefan cleared his throat. More gently than he had spoken earlier, he said, "There's no physical proof of Pritchard's involvement. We can't rely on testimony, because the Assembly can pervert it. ID has John and the other clansmen, but no one can charge Kaim Pritchard." He didn't mention the Adjusters; better Marta not know they'd become directly involved. "I'm sorry, Marta, you and John should have come openly to me when you were first threatened by ID."

"We couldn't." It was as close as she had come to admitting they were UN-Assemblers.

By involving him, John Denning had brought Stefan down with them, but they'd done him one service. They'd opened his eyes.

Are you becoming an UN-Assembler, Inlander? Pritchard laughed at him. *I think you'll have difficulty entering any secret society, with me listening whenever I want.*

Stefan stood. "Thank you for telling me the truth," he said. "I'm sorry, but I can't do anything to help you. I'm not a Judge. I can't even enter the Assembly."

"I know," she said. "Please stay. There's one more thing. Pritchard trusts you. So do I. You're honest. Will you be our emissary to him? The information he wanted didn't all go up in flames in the cave. I have it." She nodded at the computer.

Stefan sat back in the chair. "About the Travelers?"

"Yes. And it's formatted so he can't get it without me; I've been careful. And I'm a deadhead. He can't use the Assembly on me. No one else knows any of it. He has my husband and son, your wife and son, and members of my clan. I'll trade information for their freedom and to clear us from all criminal charges."

Find out what she knows. Pritchard was eager.

"That information was wrongfully obtained," Stefan said.

"You won't do it?" Marta seemed caught between outrage and disbelief. "This can help you, too."

Let her tell you what she has. Pritchard wanted the data. *The Adjusters will appreciate your help. So will I, Inlander.*

Stefan sensed the undercurrents in Pritchard's mind. He would do something for the Inlander, if the information was useful. He didn't really need to harm Stefan further; he was already satisfyingly bruised, and it was better to deal with an Inlander, who was at least civilized, than a wildman clan. "Pritchard will double-cross you again," Stefan told Marta. "Don't tell me anything. Pritchard is tapped into my mind somehow, through the Assembly, and can eavesdrop on everything that you say to me. Besides, he has a personal grudge against me. You're better off negotiating with him on your own, but be very careful. He doesn't think that he can ever free John. John's popularity makes him too dangerous to the Assembly. Even this bribery and kidnapping they

claimed against him in my false dump hasn't swayed the
Assembly consensus in the Northern Sister very much.
They're more cynical of the Assembly, and it's *my* dump;
the information seems secondhand."

Quiet! Pritchard screamed inside Stefan.

"I see," Marta said. "And besides his being in your
head, you're getting a line from him, too?"

Marta did understand. A bit shaky from the foreign
flood of anger sent by Pritchard, Stefan closed his eyes
and leaned against the back of the chair. "Yes."

"You *are* honest." She sounded surprised. "You could
have sold us out to him."

Stefan opened his eyes and saw her studying him. "It
truly didn't occur to me." He shrugged and the movement hurt, as though Pritchard was a headache riding in
his brain. "I'm stupid, I suppose. All those years of believing in justice and the Assembly. The worst is that in
a way I still do."

Her smile was faint, but real. "You want to clean it.
Reform it. It's too late for that, Stefan."

Pritchard was still too enraged for coherence.

"He wants your information," Stefan told Marta. "My
best guess is that the Adjusters are very disappointed in
him." Stefan got up again, but didn't turn to leave.
Marta watched him with the same calm she'd shown
throughout their discussion. Curious, with both husband
and son held by Pritchard. She must have a plan.

"He needs it," she said. "I'll tell him this much—he
knows it, I think—that ship is alien. They're an
invasion."

Stefan didn't believe Beatrice was part of an invasion,
but he had no evidence that would convince anyone.
"Beatrice calls them friends and I believe her," he said.

"Stefan." Marta glanced down at her hands. "That
woman isn't quite human. Her responses were
different."

"Their *lives* are different," he interrupted. "It doesn't
mean anything." He put his reminiscence of Beatrice's
naked body, and her strange skin, out of his mind before
Pritchard could seize on it. "I have a request," he said.

"For myself. John mentioned a web doctor as if he knew one. I'd like the name, and how to reach him."

"You want Pritchard out of your head."

He nodded slightly. "Pritchard is listening, of course. I'd have to act quickly. Please, Marta, if you know how I can contact the web doctor, tell me. Maybe, without Pritchard eavesdropping, I can clear myself and find a way to help us all."

"Telling you will lead Pritchard right to the web doctor."

"I suppose so," he admitted.

She nodded. "Then we understand each other." She got up and went to her desk, then sat in front of her keyboard and began to type, hitting the keys with light, staccato jabs. Stefan imagined the many layers between those tapping sounds and the meaning created inside a reader's mind, a long line of possible misinformation. The Assembly was wonderful, if only it could be kept honest. It was global civilization. As she worked industriously at her typing, Stefan realized her comment had been a rejection and dismissal. He felt foolish, still standing and waiting. "You won't help?"

She paused in her work. "This is your fault. You could have freed John that first day, but you were afraid of Pritchard and Independent Defense."

"That isn't true," he protested. "I had no proof, nothing and in fact, John *is* guilty. Pritchard knew it. The Open Court needs ID to enforce its judgments and he wouldn't have obeyed any ruling I tried to make." He wasn't getting through to Marta. "I'm not afraid of him."

She shrugged and continued typing. "Good-bye, Stefan," she said.

He walked out of the office. The line of closed doors in the dim corridor reminded him of how much the Waterman Clan had lost; he forgave Marta her last-minute venom. His life was also a shambles. What should he do if he didn't return to Ropa? Hang about Pritchard's gates and hope to learn something useful? He pressed the button to call the elevator. It seemed to take a long while, though it should still have been on the third floor. No one else was in the building.

He shared an adversary with the Waterman Clan, but he couldn't work with Marta, not with Pritchard eaves-dropping. Stefan felt him, still there, like the hot breath of an animal riding on his shoulder. Then, too, the Waterman Clan had given in to pressure. John Denning was a true politician. When trapped, he had compromised and worked with the Adjusters. Unlike the Waterman Clan, Stefan couldn't pretend to submit.

Stefan remembered Romaric. Not only would he be pleased by Stefan's conversion, but he could be a useful source of information.

Per Ezio is dead.

"What?" Stefan's voice echoed in the empty corridor. The elevator finally arrived. The door opened and Stefan automatically stepped inside. *What?*

Despite what you're thinking, I had nothing to do with it, Pritchard said. *If you want to blame someone, blame Beatrice. It was the Traveler illness.*

Pritchard was gleeful. From his delighted tone, he was also truthful. Light-headed, Stefan leaned against the elevator wall.

Good riddance, Pritchard sent. *The man was a fraud. He used his peerage and counterfeit scholarship to hide the fact that his morals were no better than mine. Why do you think that snake wrapped himself so hard around you, Inlander? He envied the real thing.*

Get out! Tears were forming in Stefan's eyes. His chest was tight. He had known Romaric all his life.

Grow up, Inlander. You always suspected the truth about your dear friend, even though you wouldn't con-sciously admit it. Why else didn't you insist that Liada tell you who fathered this bastard child she's carrying? You knew the father. Romaric Ezio, your best friend.

Stefan's vision blurred. He felt groggy. It was a simple matter to turn Pritchard out; the world itself seemed to be fading. His eyes ached. He did notice that the indica-tor showed the elevator still on the third floor. He reached out to push the button again. Was the elevator stuck?

Running away from the truth, Inlander?

Stefan's arms seemed to take forever to reach the button for the lobby. When it did, his hand slipped off. He tumbled to the floor.

Inlander?

Kaim Pritchard took longer to return for Beatrice than he had said he would. She stood at the window while she waited. Even Beatrice, a stranger to worlds and armies, recognized that the Lodge had become a fortress since her capture. Three vehicles the color of drab, mottled foliage drove past. One had a gun mounted atop it. There were more sentries than previously, and they walked in pairs, always with weapons, alertly studying the woods. She watched as darkening clouds gathered and gradually cooled the air. Pritchard's return coincided with her recognition of the gloom. He was taciturn, though he made a modest effort to be pleasant.

"You look well in blue," he said as he escorted her down the long corridors to his suite. "It suits your complexion."

Uncertain whether his comment was a compliment or an insult—so much of what he said was just to please himself—she only smiled, as insincere as he, and let him clasp her left hand through his right arm. They strolled like lovers through the Lodge. Walking beside him, Beatrice could not help but compare Pritchard with the Judge. Pritchard was shorter, but thickly muscled. His hands were wide and hard. Pritchard was heavily perfumed, while the Judge smelled only of himself, as a man should. Both men were graceful, but in different ways. The Judge was diffident and polished; Pritchard was athletic and strong.

Possibly as a consequence of the activity outdoors, the Lodge interior seemed deserted. They were alone.

"Were you trying to make us sick?" Pritchard asked suddenly. "Is that why you Travelers cared so much about our illnesses? Your tattooed friends say so." He nodded in the direction of the older building, separate from the rest of the Lodge, where the captive clansmen were kept. "Is that why you've come?"

"No! Death isn't why we've come." She was lying. They'd expected death, and hoped for acceptable mortality levels, but since they'd seen Earth, no death seemed quite acceptable.

"Were the Great Deaths supposed to make us extinct, and since they didn't, you've come to finish the job?" He was evidently now aware of the Ship's previous visit: the Adjusters must have told him.

"Kaim, this is *less* virulent. Our Friends gave Earth time to recover and grow resistant so they could stay and meet you—us."

Pritchard worked unsuccessfully to suppress a grimace. "Thank you," he said. "So they do intend to stay?"

She saw what he meant. "Not as invaders. They're friends."

"Friends who will come only if you call them. And it takes two of you to make the call, through the Assembly."

She didn't answer. He knew dangerously much and, as the Fox said, he twisted it. If he knew everything, he would never let them call. The threat wasn't of invasion but it was real; there would be radical change on Earth without the Assembly.

They were in the huge lobby, near his suite; he stopped. He'd mentioned guests, so Beatrice guessed these questions weren't ones he wanted overheard. "If you don't call," he said, "they'll simply go away. That's what you people first told us. Pardon me, Beatrice, if I don't believe that. These creatures are going to come. If everything was as pleasant as you claim, then you would speak freely."

She wished she could consult her friends, but the time for honesty had come. "The Ship came once before." Her voice was feeble. She cleared her throat and raised it. "You know that. It came in order to take people aboard. My ancestors. The Friends needed interpreters. The Great Deaths were accidental, the result of two separate ecosystems meeting. It's not shocking. Humans have done it to each other—the contact with the Americas, for one."

"I'm not shocked, although I wouldn't call something your Friends seem to have expected precisely an accident."

Beatrice reached out for the beacon. She felt it, but none of her fellow Travelers was listening, so she couldn't join with them to make the call. Even if she provided the beacon with proper codes and explanations, a call required two singers. It had been built by Friends, who did nothing alone. She withdrew, but even the brief contact had brought tears to her eyes.

"Why have they returned now?" Pritchard asked.

That answer came suddenly to Beatrice, born of her fears. The Friends had grown accustomed to the shipborn humans; they weren't strangers anymore. In human terms, they'd become too alien, too like the Friends. She stared; had contact made her less human?

Pritchard bowed very deeply, and she guessed he was parodying something or someone outside her experience. "Enough for now. Beatrice, I'm pleased you've been so forthcoming. Perhaps your stay with the wildmen was productive, after all. Come, I'm sure you'll enjoy meeting my other guests."

From exuding menace, he was abruptly charming. Everything about this man was a lie. He had no interior life, just whatever was expedient, or whatever the Assembly chose to put into him. He knew what they wanted him to know. He led her to the private dining room where he had twice entertained the Travelers. None of her friends was there, and no food was on the table.

A voluptuous, richly dressed woman turned to them; she seemed to have been pacing. A young boy sat slumped on a chair, his head on the table. The woman, seeing Beatrice and Pritchard, frowned and spoke a foreign language at them. The boy sat up. The woman walked a few steps closer and spoke to Pritchard again, haughtily. Beatrice recognized it as Ropan.

The sleepy boy climbed down from the chair and went to the woman, while keeping his attention warily on Pritchard. His eyes were bleary. As Beatrice watched, he rubbed them and yawned. "Maman?" he whispered. The woman hushed him and prodded him slightly behind her.

Pritchard didn't reply. He led Beatrice to a place on the far, long side of the oval table—four places were set, one at each of its sides—pulled out a chair and helped her into it. Only then did he answer the woman, sharply, in her own tongue. He spoke at length.

As Pritchard spoke, the woman observed Beatrice without the least care that Beatrice was also watching her. Gradually, she pulled the boy closer. Unlike the local women, she wore a thin, satin and lace blouse, as well as a layered, full skirt rather than the Sisters' loose pants. The woman's shining black hair was done up in a complicated arrangement of drooping waves, which emphasized her long neck, as did her exquisite necklace: a large red stone set off by alternate rows of gold and diamonds. Her shoes were elaborate concoctions designed to hinder, not help, her stride. She had swayed slightly when she'd walked, but seemed accustomed to the inconvenience.

Beatrice's face became warm. Each movement of the woman's eyes across her body was an indignity. Beatrice regretted having worn a rather simple, sacklike dress that had been easy to slip over Dr. Felipe's bandage. On the Ship, elaborate outfitting was a sport in the human shelter, one she had neglected, but of which she knew enough to realize she had badly lost this competition.

"An interesting group," Kaim Pritchard said. He grinned, but he was flushed, as though his fever had returned or he was tense.

The woman pressed her flawlessly outlined lips together so firmly that, momentarily, her mouth disappeared into a single thin line. She wore her clothes a bit too tightly, Beatrice decided.

"Hello." Beatrice smiled at the stranger, and was ignored.

Pritchard had brought them together in order to humiliate her, or perhaps both of them. He made some light, sardonic comment to the woman in the other language. He bowed, and then sat down at the end of the table opposite to where the woman stood. His deference affected a mocking tone, but the mockery was false. While Pritchard wasn't precisely afraid of her, he was unwillingly respectful. The complex mix of attitudes reminded Beatrice of Pritchard's attitude toward the Judge and she suddenly knew who the woman was. These were the Judge's wife and son. Pritchard would delight in such a confrontation. Beatrice looked for similarities between the Judge's beautiful wife and the Judge. She saw distress but no kindness in the woman. It was difficult to imagine how they had chosen each other. "Kaim," Beatrice said, holding her head high, "aren't you going to introduce me to Stefan's family? Is he coming? You're not keeping him away, are you?"

"You expect Stefan?" the woman asked. Through her difficult accent, she seemed troubled. Beatrice was pleased they could understand each other without Pritchard translating.

"Let me introduce you, Pera Acari," Pritchard said with a slight bow from the chair. "This is Beatrice Whit, your husband's lover." He said it straightforwardly, without the smirk Beatrice would have expected.

"No," Beatrice said. "He only rescued me. Nothing more."

Kaim Pritchard should have been enjoying their uncomfortable situation much more than he was. "When will the Judge arrive?" she asked.

The boy coughed from deep inside his chest. The cough went on, horrifying Beatrice. Not the Judge's son, she thought. The boy's mother turned to him with obvious concern. She spoke. He shook his head, unable to answer; the cough itself had stopped.

Pritchard nodded accusingly at Beatrice and spoke in the foreign language. The Judge's wife glared at her, but she sat down at the table, sending the little boy off to the fourth place, across from Beatrice, with a gentle push.

"I've gathered you together to make an announcement," Pritchard said, when they were all seated. "An unfortunate incident has occurred. While Per Acari was engaged in an illicit search for a web doctor, he was assaulted by his fellow malefactors." Pritchard lingered over the word, then smiled. "Per Acari is dead."

Chapter 11

Marta Denning enunciated her words in staccato taps, which made her wildman pronunciation into an accusation. "You said he'd be alert by now."

Awake, but with his eyes closed, lying idly on the bed, Stefan groggily pondered the gossip Marta's presence in his bedroom would create. He didn't recall their return to the hotel. He didn't care. Stefan knew his apathy was peculiar, but. it didn't trouble him. "You shouldn't be here," he finally said.

"His short-term memory is returning." It was a man's voice, slightly familiar, sounding both placating and yet irritated.

"Nash," Stefan said as he identified the voice. "Orion Nash." They'd been introduced at the Waterman Clan Hall. He was president of another wildman clan and an unpleasant xenophobe.

"This is ridiculous," Marta said. "I won't go through the same conversation a third time. You used too much."

Stefan supposed he shouldn't remain so passive around a woman he didn't trust. He opened his eyes and struggled with his body in an attempt to sit up. His legs felt loose and his arms felt disconnected. "What's going on?" He didn't recognize the modest room. The damp smell of a cellar contrasted oddly with the bedroom furniture: the bed, a night table, a battered wooden armoire, and two upright wooden chairs, neither of which was being used. The light came from an overhead fixture; there were no windows. Stefan was fully dressed, supine on the bed.

Marta rolled her eyes. "Think. We've been over this before."

A shadow memory insinuated itself. They'd drugged him so Pritchard wouldn't know where he'd been taken. "But Pritchard will know where I am the moment I do."

Marta smiled, not at him but at Nash. "Not anymore."

Stefan gaped at her and managed to raise his head. His shoulder ached when he rested his weight on his elbow. He remembered falling in the elevator.

"Good." Marta nodded a curt dismissal at Nash. "I'll take it from here."

Nash looked grim. "I still don't think we should rely on an outsider."

"Who better? He can get close to Pritchard; none of *us* could. Besides, John trusted him, and no one's a better judge of men than John."

Stefan rubbed his temples. His head hurt and it remained difficult to focus on their conversation, but disjointed memories were rearranging themselves as he forced himself to concentrate: John Denning, at his party, grinning, had said, "Tonight we're cavemen!" Denning enjoyed playing with hidden truths. Beatrice, in pain from her wound, looking to him for aid, had lightly stroked his cheek in her cave prison when he told her he wasn't in contact with the Assembly. "Of course not," she had said. How had she known?

"Pay attention, Stefan." Marta came close to the bed. She smelled of lavender, but was wearing loose pants and a man's work shirt rather than the dress he remembered from their meeting.

"We're in a cave," Stefan said. "Pritchard will know."

"There are hundreds of miles of caves around these parts," Nash said. "Many, many tunnels."

"I'll tell him," Marta insisted. "I'll call if I need you."

Nash made a performance of his reluctance to leave, repeatedly hesitating over his departure. In John Denning's absence, his co-conspirators against the Assembly were jockeying for position, but Nash finally left the room, though he kept the door open a crack as if to suggest he would be listening.

Marta left the bedside once Nash was gone. She leaned against the armoire and studied Stefan. "I knew about the false dump, and that Pritchard had annexed your mind before you told me. I'd been expecting it." She grinned with a rather masculine relish of her own words. "You see, Stefan, I'm not a deadhead. I can use the Assembly just fine. I'm a web doctor. Pritchard doesn't know."

He does now, Stefan thought. Shock after shock. He would never have guessed, despite her confidence and competence. All her elaborate equipment was merely a cover? But such a good one. Who would suspect a deadhead of being a web doctor?

She crossed the small room and sat in one of the wooden chairs. Her bulk hid all but its legs. He looked into her face and saw strength there, and determination, and a very female tenacity. "I need your help in freeing John, Johnny, and the others," she said. "We're going to attack the Lodge tonight."

"Pritchard knows what you tell me."

"No, Pritchard is gone from your thoughts. You have your privacy again, such as it is after all your dumps, although you're still annexed to Pritchard. His mental clamp is stuck around your mind. It's a reflex; it'll last until one of you is dead—he didn't tell you that, did he?—but he can't spy on anything you think or do or say. Unfortunately, you can't enter the Assembly, either."

He had first patted his head, expecting a bandage, and that they'd surgically removed his connect, but there was nothing. She had finessed an end to Pritchard's intrusions: web doctoring. "You're sure?"

She smiled, pleased as a self-satisfied cat. "I'm very good at what I do. For twenty-two years I've fooled the Adjusters. I'm traceless, even to them. I guarantee you're hidden. They won't know you're alive unless you show yourself physically, or if Pritchard dies and you enter the Assembly. That's our plan."

"You want me to help." He wasn't a member of her family or clan. She wasn't doing this for him.

She nodded. "You're a major problem for the Adjusters: too important to just disappear; too honest and too rich to bribe; too smart to fool. They've disgraced you, but if ever you made a real dump, it would expose their fraud. That's why Pritchard annexed your mind before they took any action against you. Even so, I'm guessing that their next step would have been to stage your suicide, or your murder by the clans. So we did it for them." She grinned just like her husband. "They think you're dead. If you reappear and you're outside their control, it will frighten Pritchard. So you're going to go to the Lodge, free John, and once he and the others are safe, we'll dump your story into the Assembly, unaltered. After that, no one will ever trust the Assembly again."

"That means killing Pritchard."

"Does that bother you, Stefan?"

To kill was wrong. He knew it, and yet he felt for the first time that killing might be an inescapable necessity, if truth was to survive. Marta was observing him.

The Assembly itself was not evil. He'd sensed the melancholy on Assembly margins and experienced the joy of contact too often not to believe that, in whatever sense the Assembly was independent of its users, it cared for people. What had happened in Bowl was unusual, because of the Travelers, and even so the aberration was a subversion of the Assembly's spirit by Adjusters who should be rooted out. Life without the Assembly was unthinkable; the Assembly without the Adjusters, though, was another thing entirely. "No," he said. "But it isn't supposed to be like this."

She seemed satisfied by his response. "It never is, Stefan. The trick is to plan for when it becomes 'like this' anyway. The Assembly needs a counterbalance; it's too powerful alone. We need more than one source for our information."

She seemed poised to launch into a speech. "What about the Travelers?" Stefan interrupted. "You made some accusations; I won't let you harm any of them." He struggled until he was sitting upright on the bed. He pulled his knees up and rested his head on them, but his body felt somewhat under his command.

She shrugged. "While I was in your head I saw how you feel about that woman. Don't let your emotions color your good sense. She's different. They've brought diseases purposely, to test us." She held out her hands in a gesture meant to show inoffensiveness. "But harming them isn't our plan; we just want our people."

Stefan didn't trust her.

Marta stood. "Will you help us get our men back?"

He wished for certainties about life again and wondered if he could be a judge without them. Whatever he felt about the Assembly—and he suspected he'd been so much an Assembly insider that he had never seen it clearly—the Waterman Clan and its allies had committed criminal acts. As Stefan hesitated, Marta added, "Your wife and son are at the Lodge. You'll need our help to free them, just as we need yours."

If Pritchard thought he was dead, there was no political reason to hold Liada and Tepan; he should already have sent them home. Pritchard had left traces behind in Stefan's head. The envy/desire/resentment/contempt Pritchard felt for an Inlander was magnified by sexual hunger when he imagined women of Stefan's class. He had kept Liada, and Tepan, the heir to a Ropan estate, in his possession. "I have no other choice, do I, Marta? You've manipulated me from the beginning."

She didn't deny it, and only accepted his agreement with a nod. "Rest awhile. You'll feel better soon."

Physically, Marta Denning hadn't changed. She was still overweight, still plain, still outwardly unimportant, yet she'd shed whatever it was that made her seem ordinary. "I see what John sees," Stefan said.

She blushed, though he hadn't meant it as a compliment.

Kaim Pritchard couldn't have planned an entrance into the Lodge better designed to humble Stefan. Confined in an underseat storage compartment of a crowded private van, his face pressed against a cutout opening through which he saw a selection of poorly shod feet, Stefan gagged on the combined stench of cheap floral perfume and dust. He forced his gag to become a cough, which was muffled more easily by road noise.

"We're almost at the gate," one of the girls warned.

He held his breath and the gag reflex subsided.

The van's meca driver didn't bother to avoid bumps. The girls, sitting upright, rode them easily, but Stefan was on his side, his legs pulled into a nearly fetal position. Each time the girls rose slightly in the air, so did he. He would bounce against the dilapidated fabric-covered wicker-work bench on which they sat, only to be pressed down again by gravity and the bump of the girl's buttocks landing back on the seat; then the revolver Nash had given him jammed into his thigh.

The ride gave him too much time to think. He remembered Pritchard's last contact. Romaric was dead. Pritchard's happiness made Stefan certain of it; Pritchard's parting shot made Stefan unable even to grieve for his best friend. If it was true that Romaric had deceived him with Liada, then he had been betrayed twice. He could not believe it of Romaric, and yet he couldn't disbelieve it either. Romaric had always been able to rationalize.

"All right," the leader said to her girls. "Tonight is why we've been coming here for two weeks. Check everything."

The odor of saltpeter from the caverns, used in making gunpowder, mingled with the scent of sweat and flowers as they inspected their weapons.

The girls' job was to subdue the barracks, restricting Pritchard's resources to his men on active duty. Once the breakout point in the Hilltop Lodge grounds opened and the attackers shot a flare, the girls were supposed to put Pritchard's men to sleep. They carried gas grenades and masks. Battles fought by women; wildmen were shameless. Wild women, Stefan corrected himself, and smiled.

They'd known he was there, and that knowledge had spiced their conversation. They'd each tried to outdo the others, engaging in a wild, tag-team verbal seduction of the man hiding beneath their bench. After all, these women had already given their bodies for their cause. Still, he didn't begrudge them their lewd conversation. They were warriors going into battle; they might die, yet several times they'd emphasized to each other that they needn't kill the men they would be visiting, only incapacitate them. He respected them for that and wished them well.

"Here we go," the leader said.

Feet moved as, in anticipation of arrival at the Lodge, the women gathered up their paraphernalia. The girl seated nearest Stefan's airhole had kept her legs considerately splayed and her feet wide throughout the trip, but now she forgot. One of her scuffed heels bisected his view. He smelled her stale feet.

The van stopped. A side door opened. "Hi, Freddy," the girls sang out like a chorus.

"Good evening, ladies." Freddy sounded young and as though he were trying to be suave. This would be one of Pritchard's men.

"Too bad you're on duty tonight," one girl blatantly flirted. "Gonna be a good party."

Freddy must have leaned into the van. There was a moment's silence, then he said, "Seven of you tonight?"

"Lanney's sick," a girl said.

Lanney, confronted by the moment of truth, had backed out, or so Stefan understood from what he had overheard.

"Yeah, a bad case of old boyfriend," another girl said. They giggled.

"Well, I'll be by later," Freddy said. "I get off at ten."

After a round of cheerful good-byes, the van drove away down the Lodge's long, wooded drive.

"Poor Freddy."

"He's not so bad."

"Yeah, but he's hooked in," the leader said firmly.

"Gotta do it."

"Yeah."

Several sighed, then they were silent.

Stefan closed his eyes against the sight of the feet of

these women warriors, planted firmly on the floor in high-heeled shoes. "Good luck," he said.

"You, too," they called, seemingly cheerful again.

The van stopped. They clambered out. He heard their voices, and the voices of Pritchard's men, discussing the disposition of the van. "Oh, it knows where to go," a girl said insouciantly. "Come *on*, honey. Just leave it."

Pritchard's eager young men did so, as they had on other evenings. A few minutes passed, then the van moved, driven by its meca, toward the parking area, where, on Nash's signal, it would explode and disable some of Pritchard's vehicles.

Careful to keep low, Stefan climbed out of the bench. So briefly that it seemed a hesitation of the mechanism on the drive uphill, the van stopped at the point in its route nearest a side door of the main Lodge. Stefan slipped outside, leaving the van door only partially closed so he wouldn't need to slam it. This was the most dangerous portion of his trip, but no sentry was nearby and no alarm was raised as he ran on tiptoes up the gravel path to the door.

The light above this side door was broken, as he'd been told to expect. The door itself, however, was locked. Far to his right a pair of sentries stood motionless, looking out at the trees for intruders. Near them a floodlight mounted on a tall pole lit the grounds. In its light the shadows of tiny insect wings fluttered in time to the sound of crickets. A line of unattended vehicles formed a perimeter of its own. The van crept toward them.

Stefan jiggled the doorknob while pressing his body against the door to try to move it, and to keep himself in shadows. A small cart carrying a single guard drove by; it was badly tuned and noisy. After it passed, a sound on the other side of the door made Stefan stop his attempt to force the door. He listened. A creak. Something close. He kept his hand on the doorknob and felt it turn; he let his hand ride the doorknob as the door was unlocked. The door didn't open, though he moved slightly aside, expecting someone to exit, all the while keeping hold of the doorknob so it didn't return to its former, locked position. He readied an explanation—he'd come here to see Pritchard—but time passed and no one came.

He opened the door a crack, only as far as he needed to get in, went through and closed it after himself quickly, so as little light was shed outside as possible.

A housekeeping meca had placed its tow in the corridor at the room entrance nearest this outside door. The meca itself was no longer in sight, but Stefan heard vacuuming in that room. Pritchard distrusted the clans, so he used mecas to clean the Lodge, but mecas weren't Assembly driven. A wildman had tinkered with this meca's programming. Know your tools.

Beatrice's supposed rescue from the cave had been bungled. Stefan had worried that this assault on the Lodge would be poorly planned, but it seemed to be proceeding well.

He'd been told no one was using the ground floor of this wing. Apparently, that was right. The Lodge seemed almost too quiet. There was no human activity. Denning's room was upstairs, isolated from the Travelers and the more recent detainees, including his son.

Stefan straightened his rumpled clothing. The bench interior had left lint on his dark pants, but he couldn't do much about it. The heavy revolver barely fit into his jacket pocket, and it distorted the tailoring, but from a distance he would look sufficiently respectable that he probably wouldn't be shot on sight. As he walked past the meca and down the long hallway to the interior set of stairs, he kept his right hand in his pocket and hoped to seem merely casual as he disguised the gun's presence. A descendant of warrior strongholders, Stefan had handled rifles since childhood; he'd hunted, but never with intent to kill a man. The handgun made it obvious that had changed.

He tensed as he entered the stairway enclosure, but no one was guarding it. The stairs were carpeted. He climbed them without making a sound. At the landing, he stayed back from the doorway. He felt like an assassin as he brought the gun out of his pocket, but his hand was steady. The textured grip was warm.

Stefan gingerly opened the hallway door. Denning's room was near this end. Stefan entered the corridor as if he belonged there, but moved quietly, with his right arm, holding the gun, behind his back. There was a guard, but he was looking into an open room, Denning's room, eavesdropping on a barely audible conversation. He didn't notice Stefan. That was an advantage Marta had given him—he didn't register on a geographic search via the Assembly.

Almost on tiptoes, Stefan moved lightly and barely breathed. He shifted the position of the weapon in his hand and brought it forward.

When Stefan was only two steps away, the guard turned. He saw Stefan. Arm raised, Stefan leapt at him. The guard lifted his hand to protect himself. Stefan brought the handle of the gun down, as hard as he could, on the side of the guard's head. The blow was glancing, intersected by the guard's hand.

"Hey!" the man said. He moved backward, bumping against the open door. He reached for his own weapon, but with his injured gunhand. He flinched when it hurt, and hesitated too long.

"What?" called someone in the room. Not Denning.

That first strike dispelled Stefan's inhibitions. He remembered Pritchard, taunting him while he lay on the ground. As the guard moved, Stefan clubbed him with the gun again. He hit the man in the temple. The man crumpled. Stefan himself staggered to stay upright against the force of his own blow.

He looked down. A depression the size of the gun's handle marred the man's forehead. Blood seeped from the wound and trickled out the man's ear. First pleased at his success, Stefan next was horrified by what he'd done, but like an automaton he remembered the voice from Denning's room. *You must do this,* he told himself.

He took a breath while turning the gun so the barrel faced forward again. He felt for a safety, but there wasn't one. His index finger poised on the trigger, he entered the room.

Tom Chantry, Pritchard's second in command, had left his interview with Denning to investigate the guard's outcry. As he entered the narrowest part of the standard hotel room, near the bathroom, he looked up in puzzlement from the guard's fallen body. He saw Stefan. At the same time, Stefan saw him.

The man would warn Pritchard. Pritchard had Tepan. With no further thought, Stefan squeezed the trigger.

The recoil on the Sisters-manufactured revolver was worse than Stefan had expected. He couldn't have shot an accurate second round. It wasn't necessary. He'd aimed automatically and well. A gaping hole in Tom's chest went directly through the heart.

The body tumbled as though there were some spirit left, first to its knees, then finally down, head first on the ground.

Stefan's thoughts were detached from his having killed. *Now I'm an outlaw; I'll never be a Judge again.*

He heard movement in the room and tensed. Sickened, he nevertheless readied himself.

"Don't shoot! It's John." A moment later, hands held above his head, John Denning came into sight. "Stefan?" Denning dropped his arms. "Stefan?"

Their danger kept Stefan calm. He nodded as though he'd met Denning in passing on the street, then backed up and returned to the hallway. He looked up and down. No one else had appeared. No one was running to investigate. The Independent Defense agents felt safe because of the Assembly, but he was a menace the Assembly couldn't see. Stefan knelt and reached for the guard's neck. He found a pulse. *Thank God,* he thought. He hadn't killed this man.

John Denning stepped over his interrogator's corpse; he was gaping at Stefan.

"Help me drag him out of sight," Stefan ordered.

Suddenly Denning grinned. He took the man's two hands and towed him into the room's short hallway himself. Stefan staggered slightly as he got back on his feet and followed the guard's body. It trailed blood on the carpet.

Tom Chantry seemed to be kowtowing to Stefan. The bullet that had killed him had passed through him. A bloody red hole was in his back. Stefan didn't want to step over the corpse so he didn't go farther.

"Well." Denning, still grinning, stood between Stefan's two victims. He shook his head as though the fact that Stefan had rescued him was amusing. "What has brought a Judge to this?"

Stefan leaned against the side wall, opposite the bathroom entrance. John Denning had been held so long that the Stefan Acari he remembered may as well have been another man. "I've been expelled from the Court," he said by way of a perfunctory explanation.

"You?" Denning laughed. "Well, so then Marta hired you as a gunman? She always was a good judge of talent."

Denning's crude humor made Stefan want to hit him. Appalled at his quick shift toward violence, he looked at the revolver in his hand, but didn't return it to his pocket. The thing was soiled by the guard's blood and flesh.

The shot had seemed loud to Stefan, but this Lodge was too large for Pritchard's needs, and people were thinly spread. "Do you think he sent a warning to Pritchard?"

"I don't think there was time. They're not tickers; they don't dump." Denning was more subdued.

Mention of Tom Chantry caused Stefan to glance at the body. It had toppled facedown, but because the knees had hit the ground first, its ass was in the air. The indignity death inflicted was not new, but Stefan unaccountably felt that this, his first murder, deserved better. He stared, thinking that he should straighten the corpse, then noticed a nauseating stench of blood and bowels rising from it. He swallowed several times, then gave up the fight. He was going to retch. He pushed past Denning and entered the dark bathroom. He vomited into the sink.

Denning followed him in and switched on the light. He waited in silence. When Stefan stopped retching, Denning leaned over and turned on the tap. The water washed the vomitus away. Denning left the water running and stepped aside.

Stefan rinsed his mouth.

"Better?" Denning asked.

"Go look." Stefan gestured in the direction of the corridor. Denning nodded at the order, and left.

Stefan still clutched his gun. The butt was sticky with blood. He rinsed it under the faucet, careful to get only the revolver's exterior handle wet. His hands were steady. This didn't feel like his real life, but it was.

Denning returned about thirty seconds later. "No one." He was carrying the guard's weapon, a self-loading rifle. Stefan wished he'd picked it up, instead of leaving the weapon for Denning.

Stefan was feeling better, although embarrassed. Denning actually looked well. Beneath his tattoos, his face had color. He glanced around the bathroom like a tiger caged in a zoo, and turned to look into the other room as though anxious to leave. "So, what's the plan, Stefan? How do we get out?"

Stefan wiped sweat from his forehead with the back of his hand, and picked up his revolver from the counter. "I've just come from Marta." In as few words as possible, he appraised Denning of the situation.

"My cavemen," Denning said affectionately. He seemed to recognize the plan. At Stefan's questioning look he said, "Why else did the land local give *this* place to Pritchard? Hilltop Lodge is undermined by caves. So, what's the diversion?"

"I think I am."

He hadn't meant the statement to be funny, but Denning laughed, and after a moment, Stefan smiled. It *was* funny, a Judge breaking criminal conspirators out of Independent Defense's detention; it was only horrible that the Judge was him.

"We need to get moving," Denning said. "We've got to make trouble for Pritchard."

"I want to find my son."

Denning nodded. "So do I." He clapped Stefan on the back. The implied familiarity didn't feel awkward. "You've come a long way, Stefan. Are you on our side?"

"You mean the Assembly?" Whose side *was* Stefan on? He remembered the man he'd just killed. Was there ever any justification for taking a life? Was there such a thing as a greater good?

"Never mind," Denning said. "You're still a judge. With or without a court. Give yourself credit for doing right." Denning seemed serious.

"Let's go." Stefan hurried out of Denning's room. The guard he'd struck with the gun butt hadn't moved. The man was likely either dead or dying.

"A diversion means that Pritchard is diverted," Denning said. "That means he has to know we're here."

Tepan and Liada were safe for the time being. Stefan, when he concentrated, could remember Pritchard's distorted mixture of envy and contempt for his social superiors. He would spend considerable time trying to impress Liada with his power. "We need to free the Travelers," Stefan said. "After that, we'll find Pritchard."

"That isn't what Marta planned, is it?"

Stefan didn't answer. They hadn't encountered any of Pritchard's men in the corridors. There were none in the lobby, which they'd just surreptitiously entered. Even with the Assembly to protect them, it didn't seem right that Pritchard would have posted no one on guard.

"Maybe he does know we're here," Denning said. "Maybe he wants us."

Stefan felt a chill down his back and made an instinctive attempt to connect. Nothing, just as Marta had claimed.

The lobby was dim; they could see outside through the large windows. The front of the Lodge was dark, except for searchlights, but through the rear windows, the older Lodge building, where the captive clansmen were kept and the clanswomen had gone, was brightly lit. The lighting wasn't of the type Stefan would have expected an erotic party to generate, and armed men were searching the exterior of the building and the nearby woods. "Damn it!"

"What?"

The girls, who had made him smile while teasing him, had been discovered. Because of them, the main Lodge guards had been called away. He couldn't do anything for them, and didn't want Denning to try. "The Travelers' rooms are down that corridor. Pritchard's suite is here in the main Lodge. I'm going for the Travelers." Stefan stepped out of the shadows and into the lobby. Nothing happened, so he ran across the open space to the other side, down a short hallway, and into the enclosed interior stairway for that wing.

Denning followed, moving heavily. "All right," Denning said when he arrived. "I'll take them to the clan for safekeeping. Tell me, Stefan—is it the woman?"

No one would review Stefan's dumps again—or perhaps, just once more—and so, paradoxically, he didn't feel a need to guard his privacy so strictly. "Partly." To admit to acting even in part from personal emotion felt like coming clean of a great secret.

"Ah. And the wife is over there." Denning nodded sagely to himself, eyes sparkling.

Stefan didn't understand how Denning could be rude and intrusive, and yet have people like him, as Stefan himself did. "The Travelers are usually guarded," Stefan said, ignoring Denning's observation.

They were in the carpeted stairwell, a duplicate of the one near where Denning had been kept. The door had no window. Denning pushed Stefan aside while getting his rifle into firing position, braced against his shoulder. The rifle was a better weapon for the job, so Stefan didn't protest.

Denning burst into the hallway alone, shot twice, and stood waiting. Stefan shrank from looking, since he expected at least one body on the floor, but when he followed Denning, no one else, dead or alive, was there. It had been irresponsible to shoot randomly; the Travelers could have been in the hall. "Target practice?" he asked sarcastically.

"Diversion," Denning said.

Ten doors—fewer than in Denning's hallway, so apparently these rooms were larger—lined the corridor. Every door was closed.

"It would be nice if they'd come out to us," Denning said. "Why don't you call to them?"

After Denning's shots, it would be difficult to get the Travelers to open their doors—if they were even in their rooms at all. Stefan started toward Beatrice's door, but just then he heard footfalls on the stairs. He turned and grabbed for the rifle. Denning let him have it. "In there," Stefan hissed. He twisted the doorknob of the nearest door. It opened. He shoved Denning inside and closed it, then ran farther down the corridor and turned, holding his hands in the air and the rifle in his right hand. Pritchard's agents found him like that a moment later. "I want to see Kaim Pritchard," he shouted, and threw the rifle down.

Beatrice decided she would not have liked Liada Acari even if the woman hadn't been the Judge's wife. She was spoiled, and seemed relieved by the Judge's death. She was willing to play up to Pritchard, too, using Pritchard's social insecurity to her advantage.

Their conversation was in the Ropan language, preventing Beatrice from comprehension of details, though the inflections, tonalities, and pitch told more than the speakers supposed. Pritchard thought he was toying with Liada, but she was handling him expertly, using the meal to reveal his inadequacies, while seeming to regret their exposure under the guise of enjoying the food. It was a cat-and-mouse game between two cats.

Beatrice spent the dinner watching the boy and remembering the Judge. Obviously unwell, Tepan struggled to conform to a standard of behavior better suited to healthy adults. He tried to eat and to appear attentive to the conversation, all the while stricken by sickness and grief. He often looked at his mother. She would smile at him, and he would return the smile with a puzzled expression. Once, he asked aloud if his Papa would come. Pritchard answered with a laconic no. "Stefan is dead, and so is Per Ezio."

The boy stared at his plate.

To share food was, like the sharing of sex, one of the universal expressions of goodwill; among creatures of social intelligence, it was also the frequent occasion for displays of authority, temper, and repressed animosity. It happened on the Ship, too.

The Friends had given a farewell feast for the four Travelers before they left. Very little of the meal had been to her taste, or that of any other human. Such negligence was not usual among the Friends, who lusted for contacts with others, craving strangeness in the way humans craved family, and so Friends normally were sensitive to alien desires. "Why?" she had asked the others on the short one-way shuttle trip from the Ship to Earth.

"To show solidarity with them," Mariyo had said. "To show we're one with the Ship."

The Fox had given a different explanation. "It's the beacon," he told Beatrice. "It puts them in a foul mood. They want to spur us on to get rid of it. Klini"—the Fox's special Friend, in the way Eyni had been to Beatrice—"told me that when we returned, we should bring Earth foodstuffs to the Ship. She said she wanted to learn how to prepare them."

Beatrice wished that the Judge could have met the Friends. In her defense of them she had made them sound unreasonably like saints. They weren't. She thought he would have judged them ... human.

"Back from the dead, Inlander?" Pritchard said as Stefan was shoved into the dining room.

"My death was fabricated." Stefan bowed, very correctly, as though Pritchard were his equal, well aware of Tepan, Liada, and Beatrice in the room and that their safety might depend upon him. The three of them gaped, but Pritchard, doubtless forewarned by his men, seemed unperturbed.

Pritchard's dining room attempted an extemporaneous grandeur in the same failed way Pritchard's clothing attempted luxury and grace. An oval table, too large for the room, had been set with four places. A formal white linen tablecloth covered the table, but the tablecloth was cut for a rectangle, and the corners hung too long. Stefan and his escort had entered at one of the room's two doors, the one near the foot of the table, adjacent to Liada; the other was near its head, where Pritchard sat. A buffet table was situated along the wall between the doors. It wasn't large enough for the overly generous number of dishes prepared for Pritchard's dinner party, and which should have been set out in separate courses. Two platters—one with a beef tenderloin garnished with parsley and herbs, the other a stuffed, whole snapper—had perforce been placed on the main table, as if for guests to help themselves, yet guards turned awkward waiters stood at either end of the room, ready to serve and protect. Both seemed young and startled by events.

The room was warm, but in addition to the electric chandelier, Pritchard had lit candles in a candelabra on the table. Although the tall windows were open wide, what little breeze existed was trapped by the sheer curtains. They billowed slightly, displaying waterstains.

"Papa!" Tepan shouted, pushing his chair away from the table with his hands and scraping the polished floor. He jumped off the chair, pulled a bit of tablecloth with him—but not so much that anything came crashing down—ran to Stefan and threw his arms around his father's waist. Stefan lifted and hugged him, pressing him against his body, savoring the physical warmth, rubbing his face gently in Tepan's thick, brown hair and delighting in the boyishly untidy scent of his son.

Beatrice got to her feet. She stood clutching the edge of the table and staring at him with Tepan. Stefan smiled at her. Even if he hadn't reached the other Travelers, at least he knew she was well. He squeezed Tepan one more time, vigorously, and carried him back to his chair.

Tepan stood on it with his one arm around Stefan's waist and his head resting against Stefan's side.

"Hello, Stefan." Liada spoke as if from a regal distance.

"Now that the pretty scene is over," Pritchard said, "we can talk seriously. Well, Inlander, what did the wildmen do to you? And how did you arrive?"

Stefan wished Pritchard had managed to get the dinner right. It was painful, having felt Pritchard in his mind, to know that Pritchard would suspect he hadn't, but wouldn't know where he'd gone wrong. Why didn't the man consult the Assembly for protocol and etiquette? Stefan knew the answer. He recalled the flavor of Pritchard's uneasy arrogance, and saw Pritchard's watchful attention on Liada. Pritchard must regret Stefan's reappearance.

Stefan thought of the party girls and didn't look too directly at Pritchard, the way a brazen liar might. "I walked in through the woods," he said. "You don't keep a very tight perimeter." He wanted to send help to the guard he had clubbed while the man might yet be saved, but debated warning Pritchard that Denning was loose while Denning might be recaptured; he stayed silent.

"No, you didn't. You came in with those whores." Pritchard smiled at Stefan's lie.

The girls had indeed been found out. The clansmen attack was badly damaged.

"This is all your fault, Stefan," Liada cried out in their own language.

Liada was sitting artificially tall in her chair, and looked every bit the noblewoman. "What? That you were forced to dine with a nixt mirko?" Stefan immediately wished he hadn't said that in front of Pritchard.

Liada colored slightly, but continued. "None of this business with wildmen and Numerica was any concern of yours. You were so self-righteous with me, but look what you've done." She gestured loosely at Beatrice.

"Keep her out of this!"

Pritchard was listening avidly again, his attention going back and forth between them as though watching a close soccer match. "Sit down, Stefan," he said, overly familiar, and indicated Tepan's place. "I owe you a dinner."

Stefan hoped he was being sufficiently diverting. He glanced outside. These windows faced even more directly onto the Lodge's partially enclosed yard. The curtains obscured the view, but they would be able to see enough once the clansmen attacked.

One of Pritchard's waiter-guards stepped forward as if to force Stefan to comply. Stefan picked Tepan up again. "Come on then," he whispered softly to his son, "you'll sit on my lap." He sat down directly across from Beatrice and smiled.

"I'm glad to see you." Her lovely voice was shy. The warm candlelight tempered her unusual complexion and made her eyes seem large.

"I'm glad you're well," Stefan said.

"She's the wrong choice, Inlander." Pritchard wore the smirk of a bully who'd had his way. "She isn't human."

Stefan suppressed the urge to look at Beatrice. To do so would give credence to Pritchard's accusation. A waiter-guard brought Stefan a fresh plate, though Tepan's appeared untouched, and served him vegetables and game. Stefan accepted the service automatically.

"Her ship has visited Earth before," Pritchard continued. "We have Beatrice's friends to thank for the Great Deaths."

Stefan chanced a look; Beatrice was studying her plate. "That would have nothing to do with Beatrice," he said.

She raised her eyes, but not her head.

"Alien abductions." Pritchard sounded amused. "They stole people while infecting Earth. There was a literature on the subject. It's a shame Romaric is dead. He might have been able to supply some clues from his old books, but she killed him."

Stefan despised how Pritchard showed off his intimate familiarity with Stefan's life, and Romaric's, but did as he'd always done. He ignored his own emotion.

He did notice Beatrice's. Something more than this situation was bothering her. She had the same strained expression he'd seen in the cave when she had claimed her ship was on its way. It hadn't been; she simply hadn't heard her ship's beacon in the cave. Then it occurred to him to wonder if the beacon was from the ship. What was the beacon? Her mistake had occurred at the same time the Assembly signal was shielded. Were her beacon and the Assembly connected? If her ship had visited Earth before, could the beacon be located on Earth?

Pritchard shifted tacks. He observed Stefan while speaking ostensibly to Beatrice. "How much have you Travelers been changed, Beatrice? Have these friendly aliens tinkered with your humanity? Selected for certain traits? Tell me, Beatrice, are you an alien?"

"No!"

Pritchard was hounding Beatrice for Stefan's benefit, to hurt him. Romaric had claimed that people were being selected for Assembly talent; there was an ongoing natural selection. If Beatrice were part of a similar process, what did it matter? She was watching him across the table. He moved Tepan to the side, balancing him on one leg so he could see her better, and hummed a cheerful bit of noise he'd heard from her, or perhaps one of her fellow Travelers; her eyes widened, then she smiled.

He had given John Denning sufficient time to escape. "By the way, Kaim," Stefan said in Pritchard's own falsely friendly manner, "there is a guard outside John Denning's room who needs a doctor."

Perhaps Pritchard checked on Tom Chantry and didn't find him. "And where is Denning?" he asked after a moment.

"Last I saw, he was running south, toward Bowl."

Pritchard was silent, and his expression was withdrawn, as he went deeply in the Assembly. He came out from it frowning. "Who's the web doctor?" Pritchard stood and walked around the table toward Stefan. "I can't get into your mind. Who did it?"

The best way to get back at Kaim Pritchard was to

frustrate him. He was accustomed to easy targets. Stefan took his cue from the Travelers and didn't answer.

Pritchard came closer, smiling like an attentive host. "What makes you believe that the only thing the wild-man web doctor did was keep me out? Why should they hold themselves back, when they had free range throughout your head? Tell me, Inlander, have you been acting like yourself? Killing? Maiming? Are those your usual repertoire?"

"I did what had to be done."

Pritchard stood so close that his cologne irritated Stefan's throat, which was still tender after the cavern fire. He picked up Stefan's fork, jabbed a piece of carrot, and ate it. Tepan's hands tightened on Stefan; he rubbed his son's back, comforting him.

"You're not eating, Stefan." Pritchard speared another piece of carrot from Stefan's plate and for a moment Stefan feared Pritchard would try to feed it to him. "You should. So should all my guests. Everyone deserves a decent last meal. We have here the three most important people in your life. Pick one."

Stefan's arm tightened around Tepan. He glanced down as the boy squirmed.

"A good choice. He won't be missed." Pritchard dropped the fork and grabbed Tepan's collar, yanking him out of Stefan's grasp. Liada screamed. Stefan started to reach for his son. The waiter-guards suddenly held weapons. Tepan kicked and cried for Stefan. Pritchard held the boy at arm's length, as if his sixty kilos were as negligible a weight as his life was insignificant to Pritchard.

How could he have forgotten the latent viciousness in Pritchard's mind? Pritchard wanted exactly this.

"Tell me where Denning is and all about the wildmen plan. Tell me everything I want to know, or Acari doesn't have an heir."

Liada screamed that Stefan should answer him.

"Now, Inlander," Pritchard said. "Those women weren't acting alone."

Stefan closed his eyes, but there was no escape into

the Assembly. He opened them and watched Pritchard as he spoke. "I came into the Lodge in the van with the women. I left Denning in the wing where I was found; we were leaving. The wildmen are attacking through the woods, tonight at midnight."

"How much of that is true?"

Tepan had quieted, and was watching his father from the height of Pritchard's arm. "All of it. You know me, Pritchard. I don't lie." Only a man who'd been a fool for too long could have made that statement and been believed so easily.

Pritchard dropped Tepan back in Stefan's lap. The boy's leg came down on the plate of food. It crashed to the floor.

Through the open window, the night brightened into brilliant fire, as if the sun had exploded in the sky. The air filled with an explosion and gunfire so loud that it drowned out Kaim Pritchard's scream.

Chapter 12

Stefan clutched his son against his chest and dove for shelter under the dining-room table, followed a moment later by Beatrice, Liada, and Pritchard's two waiter-guards. Pritchard didn't move, despite battlefield noise so great that the heavy wooden table trembled. The electric lights went out, though the room remained lit by candles. They flickered from shock waves produced by explosions just outside the windows.

Even having known the plan, Stefan was startled by the ferocity of the battle. Some of the noise was wildman machinery bursting through the earth; some of it was hastily armored vehicles arriving from the road; some of it was death. In such an onslaught, it would be easy for bullets to stray in the wrong direction. "Keep down," he shouted over the battle sounds, and even so was barely heard. The women nodded.

Marta had said there would be no special mission to rescue him or his family from the Lodge, but that if they got away from Pritchard, the clans would defend them. Stefan did not trust the wildman rescuers, however. John Denning was a generally honorable man, but Stefan wasn't certain he would have charge of the battle. Orion Nash, or Marta, might well decide to blow up the entire Lodge hoping to kill Pritchard and the Travelers. Since Denning was probably out of the Lodge, Stefan, and those he cared about, needed to escape the building, too.

The sounds lessened as the battle lines between the attacking clansmen and Pritchard's guards were drawn. The clansmen hesitated, waiting for the girls' work in the other building to have freed their brothers and sons. Instead, the girls had been taken.

Stefan passed Tepan to Liada. He glanced at the two guards to see if they would try to stop him, but neither seemed to care what he did. Stefan scrambled out from beneath the table.

Kaim Pritchard had sunk into the chair at the head of the table. He gripped the chair arms with tremendous strength and stared straight ahead, eyes wide in the wavering candlelight, focused on nothing. The glare from a burst shell outside the window lit his pale, peeling face. He looked dead, but wasn't. He blinked once. Pritchard was in shock so severe he couldn't function.

It was vital to any possible success that the clans deploy one of their Assembly shields to set up a "free zone." They had done so. Pritchard was cut off from communication with the world beyond the Lodge, and from the inner world of the Assembly files, minds, and Adjusters. He couldn't issue mental orders to his men. He probably hadn't been so alone since becoming a peripheral. Even Stefan, who knew the loneliness outside the Assembly firsthand, was startled by the degree of Pritchard's personal incapacitation. He had expected Pritchard to anticipate the clans' use of a shield.

The fighting had definitely lulled. Stefan signaled to the others that it was all right to get out from under the table; he helped Liada with Tepan. The boy was shivering. Pritchard's guards worriedly observed their silent, immobile superior. Both were still armed; one glared at Stefan as though he might have caused Pritchard's predicament.

"What's the matter with him?" Liada asked, moving her eyes to indicate Pritchard.

No one who hadn't played, worked, and even lived inside the Assembly could comprehend the anguish Kaim Pritchard must be undergoing at his loss. Stefan had left the Assembly voluntarily; besides, he had never maintained the low-grade constant contact Pritchard had. The man was crippled by having been reduced to his own mind. Would the entire Earth be as broken as this, without the Assembly?

Beatrice echoed Stefan's thoughts. "A hollow man," she said.

The guards were also cut off from the Assembly, from Pritchard, and from each other. Stefan had to use this chance. "He has surrendered," Stefan told them. "The Assembly is gone. Put down your weapons. If you don't, the wildmen will kill you when they come."

The guards looked at each other, then at Pritchard.

Another explosion rattled the room as the battle's pace picked up again. Shrill, savage, triumphant shouts came from the wildmen outside. Smoke from the battlefield drifted in through the windows, bringing the stench of gunpowder, blood, and death.

"Go! Run!" Beatrice said in tones that chilled Stefan. "The wildmen are coming."

"Papa!" Tepan shook free of Liada and flung his arms around Stefan's legs for protection.

One of the guards looked at Pritchard, then, keeping low and out of direct line of sight with the windows, he ran for the nearest door. The other scuttled closer to it, but didn't leave. He had a powerful gun, identical to the one Denning had taken from his guard. It wasn't aimed at anyone, but it was available for use. Stefan guessed that if rushed, he would shoot.

With an eye on that remaining guard, Stefan disengaged his son and went to Pritchard. "Kaim, the Assembly's gone. It's over."

Stefan hadn't expected Pritchard to react—he'd been speaking for the benefit of the guard—but Pritchard's attention flickered across Stefan's face, though his eyes seemed disconnected from his mind. Air hissed between his clenched teeth. Stefan thought Pritchard might survive his amputation from the Assembly after all. That wouldn't be good news for Stefan or the clans. As he spoke, and under the guise of comforting Pritchard, he put his arms around Pritchard and tried to feel if Pritchard was carrying a concealed gun. If so, he intended to take it and use it against the guard. "I've been through this," he said, to keep talking and lull the guard. "I know what you're feeling, but you'll recover, Kaim."

Stefan didn't feel a weapon on Pritchard, which stood to reason since he'd been inside his own perimeter, though it was disappointing. Stefan rested his hands on Pritchard's shoulders. *I should kill him,* Stefan thought. Marta had told him to do it, and killing Pritchard would be prudent, but Stefan uneasily remembered Pritchard's claim that Marta had tinkered with his mind. How had it become so easy for him to use trickery and violence? Even now he didn't regret killing Tom Chantry, and possibly the other guard. Was it Marta, or had bits of Pritchard himself oozed into Stefan's mind when they had been connected? Perhaps leaving the Assembly had unleashed something already in him? Causes were irrelevant; actions mattered. How would he judge himself if he killed Poupey? Stefan stepped back. Pritchard's eyes followed him.

Stefan pretended to ignore the guard's gun, and spoke generally to everyone as though they were all on the same side. "We've got to get out of here before the wildmen come." As he spoke, he picked up Tepan again, then walked to the door. Liada and Beatrice were coming. Indecisive, the guard looked between them and the violent scene through the window, discounting Pritchard; the guard showed no disposition to interfere.

"Stop." Pritchard sounded as though his throat were rusty from disuse. He cleared it, then said again, louder, "No. Stop them."

The guard, probably relieved at having received an order, raised his gun and aimed at Stefan.

The flares outside were gone, though there seemed to be fires burning, but the main source of light in the dining room was the candles. The flickering, smoky light they shed made the room eerie. Pritchard's attention moved restlessly between Stefan, Liada, and Beatrice as though he was uncertain who they were and what he should do with them. Stefan recognized his problem: disconnected from the Assembly, Pritchard felt stupid.

"You have to run, Pritchard," Stefan said. "You have

to get out of here before the clansmen find and kill you."
The door was only a step away but he didn't move. The
guard's gun was on him.

"You." Pritchard seemed to have difficulty finding
Stefan's name. "Inlander. This is all because of you."
His attention fixed on Stefan. Slowly, he rose to his feet.
"I remember. No one was ever good enough. Not me.
Even in the Assembly, I couldn't be a ticker. And he
wanted to kill me, but he couldn't because you would
notice. But he's dead now, isn't he, Inlander?" Pritchard
wore a look of animal cunning.

Stefan wet his lips. The guard's rifle hadn't moved
from him, though Pritchard was clearly irrational. Softly,
like gentling a skittish animal, Stefan said, "That was a
long time ago, Kaim. Romaric is dead from the Traveler
illness and I'm sorry, truly sorry, if he wronged you. But
it has nothing to do with the clans. You need to get
away from here, outside their shield, to where you can
reach the Assembly again."

"The clans." Pritchard looked outside, then back at
him. "You're their friend. What's their plan? Tell me."
The flatness of Pritchard's tone matched the blankness
in his eyes, but at least he was back in the present.

Of his own accord, the guard gestured roughly with
his rifle.

"This is all your fault, Stefan," Liada cried. "These
wildmen, this danger."

Pritchard turned his attention on Liada. "The Inlandres. So soft and squeamish."

Liada gasped. "Tell him what he wants to know!"

"They want their people," Stefan said. "That's all. Let
them take the prisoners. They'll leave, and you'll be
back in the Assembly." More than anything else, Pritchard should crave a return to the Assembly.

Pritchard's attention flit from one thing to another.
He looked at Beatrice, and briefly his expression
warmed. "You want her," he said, "but so do I." Pritchard spoke to Beatrice without pausing between thoughts
or sentences. "These wildman will hurt you. I have to
keep you safe." He reached for her.

She shrank away from Pritchard. "I need to find my friends." She spoke more to Stefan than Pritchard.

The rest of the Travelers might be in danger, but with Pritchard unbalanced by the loss of the Assembly, the threat to the four of them in the dining room was immediate. "You need to connect," he told Pritchard. "You've got to get away from here. Go. The wildmen will be coming." He put every inflection of fear he could manage into the speech.

The guard looked anxiously at the door, but Pritchard seemed scarcely to notice. "Come with me, Beatrice. I know a way out through the woods." He advanced toward her.

When Stefan had started out of the room, it had been to the door near the head of the table, where Pritchard had originally sat, and closest to where he now stood, but Beatrice sprang away as Pritchard grabbed at her. She ran for the second, rear door. As Pritchard followed, to catch her, Stefan moved into the way, blocking him and also blocking the guard's ability to shoot at her. Pritchard shoved Stefan aside. Stefan lost his grip on Tepan, who cried out in fear as he fell to the floor. Meanwhile, Beatrice had yanked open the rear door and was escaping.

"Shoot him," Pritchard shouted at the guard as he chased out of the room after Beatrice. Their footfalls echoed as they ran down the hallway toward the lobby.

The rifle barrel faced Stefan like the blind eye of death. He didn't move. If he tried to help Beatrice, the guard would certainly kill him. That he hadn't done so yet showed his wariness of Pritchard's rambling talk and odd behavior, or perhaps some innate decency. Pritchard, the old Pritchard, had cared for Beatrice in his distorted way. Even disoriented, he hadn't meant to harm her, and was unarmed. Stefan needed to save himself.

The guard stared at Stefan, with occasional worried glances at the open door, but didn't fire. "The clans are winning," Stefan said. "He's not in any shape to stop them. They'll come here looking for him. What do you think they'll do to any ID agents that they find?"

"Shut up," the man said, but his heart wasn't in it. He wanted to hear what else Stefan had to say.

Stefan picked Tepan up again, and used that as an excuse to move a step closer to the guard. "I'm a friend of John Denning's. I can protect you. You know who I am. Stefan Acari, a Judge of the Open Court, an In-lander. You're not going to shoot me in front of my wife and my son." Stefan held out his hand. "Give me the gun, and let's get out of here."

The man hesitated, then lowered his weapon. "Go on," he said. "But the gun's mine."

It was the best offer Stefan had been given all day. "Thank you," he said sincerely. "Come on." He gestured at Liada and carried Tepan out of the room in a quick walk just short of running.

If they went to the clansmen and the clansmen lost, Pritchard would have them again. For the Adjusters, who wouldn't want witnesses to this incident, it would be easiest to kill them all and blame the wildmen. Since Stefan had never believed the clansmen had any chance of long-term success—the Assembly controlled too much, and the Adjusters couldn't allow their control to be eroded—the best protection for Stefan and his family was to get far away and hide until things quieted down. Once killing an Inlander and his family wasn't so convenient, Stefan might come to terms with the Adjusters through some agent other than Pritchard. Pritchard had too many unresolved old grudges against Stefan, apparently courtesy of Romaric. Stefan needed to find a coach that the clansmen hadn't destroyed or commandeered and get away from the Lodge, but first, he had to find Beatrice.

Beatrice had seen the ease with which Pritchard fought the Judge outside the cave. She'd felt his raw strength whenever he touched her. She wasn't strong enough to outrun him, even while he was recovering from an illness. She could never fight him and win. Her choices were to hide, find help, or remain confined by a man whose soul had been lost inside a machine.

Beatrice sprinted for the lobby, thinking of its windows and its doors. The fighting might help provide cover; the attackers might help her. At least she'd be away.

Pritchard's heavy footfalls were close. She stretched her legs to increase the distance she covered and reached the lobby just ahead of him. She aimed at the door—the one she'd left through days earlier. Outside, the night was lit by gunfire and explosions.

Pritchard's fingers grazed her shoulder. His nails ripped a seam in her dress. Fear added a burst of strength. She would have to slow to open the door. He'd have her. Beatrice raised her good, left arm to shield her face and raced straight at the glass window. Unlike the Ship, windows could be exits on Earth.

"Mr. Pritchard!" exclaimed someone inside the lobby. "Sir."

Beatrice didn't look, but Pritchard dropped a bit behind as he did. If Pritchard ordered it, she'd be shot. Her throat, still rough from the smoky cave, burned as she gulped air. Her panting was louder than her heart. "Stop her!" Pritchard shouted.

She smashed against the glass. It was like running headlong into a stone wall. It didn't break. Instead, she bounced off, stunned, and collapsed onto the ground, wheezing and dazed.

Pritchard was standing over her, looking down. A few seconds must have passed because she didn't remember his arrival. She rolled away so he couldn't put his foot on her face, as he had done to the Judge. A second pair of booted feet ran to them and stopped beside her.

"Bullet-proof. Shatter-proof. We're quite safe." Pritchard sounded more normal than he had in the dining room, as though the chase had revived his old instincts and self.

Still dazed, Beatrice looked out on the battlefield she'd tried to reach. Her safe haven.

The grassy field was glutted with bodies. As she watched, a group of tattooed men ran across it shooting at the darkened old building. Gunfire came from Pritchard's beleaguered garrison. The wildmen yelled, gleeful at the killing, in war whoops muted by the thick glass, but so bestial they might have been a source for the dark song of the Kroni. She turned away.

Pritchard studied the carnage outside without expression.

She wished there was light in the lobby, so his enemies might see his silhouette and pierce the glass with their guns. She'd heard his last order, to shoot the Judge.

"Get up," he said. His voice was still flat.

"What about our men?" The questioner was the guard who'd come up to them, the same man who had run out of the dining room.

"I can't help them without the Assembly." Pritchard pushed Beatrice with the toe of his boot, encouraging her to get up without much hurting her. "First thing to do is contact the Adjusters."

Winded, bruised, with her right arm bandaged, it was more difficult than it would normally have been, but Beatrice sat, then stood up. She received no help from either man.

Pritchard sighed. "He hasn't shot the Inlander."

"What?" The guard didn't understand. Beatrice did. She hoped the Judge had escaped in the confusion. Pritchard reached down and removed a tiny handgun from inside his boot. He examined it, checking its mechanical condition. His hands held the silver gun as though contact with it brought physical pleasure.

"Stay here," Pritchard said to his agent. "Don't let her get away, but don't harm her." He was going to murder Stefan.

Beatrice's eyes were excellent in dim light. She noticed movement in the shadows nearest the dining room, the right size and shape for human beings. Pritchard hadn't seen them yet because he was still facing her. Beatrice screamed as loud as she was able, which to her song-strengthened voice was very loud, even despite her sore throat. To warn the Judge, her scream wasn't merely noise, but a message in song. "He's dangerous. Get away. Run." It was probably futile, but the Judge had used song once. Perhaps he would understand. She didn't know what he could do, however.

Pritchard stopped. He gazed at Beatrice, gun in hand.

Any normal person would have guessed her scream had been a warning to someone, but Pritchard seemed puzzled. He snapped at the guard, "I didn't want you to hurt her."

"I didn't touch her," he protested.

When the battle had begun, Beatrice recognized that Pritchard had lost connection to the Assembly. She had known because she herself had reached for the beacon and failed to find it. After her experience in the cave, she knew better than to conclude that the call had been sent—it seemed unlikely, since only the Fox had been ready to do it. This was part of the wildman attack, a temporary and local disturbance in the beacon. For the duration, Pritchard had been emptied of those parts of his mind that were adjuncts of the Assembly. While he now seemed more vulnerable than he ever had, what was left of him also seemed less empathetic, as though he had forgotten how to be human without the Assembly's constant flow of advice. "Don't leave," she said, using undertones of sexual innuendo. "I'm sorry I ran from you. I was afraid. Earlier you'd been so . . . hard."

"I don't want to hurt you." His muttered comment was spoken as if to himself.

"But you like the Judge," she said, "and you want to hurt him." She moved closer and provocatively placed her hand on his arm—not the one in which he held the gun, that would be too bold—meanwhile inflecting her voice with all the liking for Kaim Pritchard she could muster. She'd never voluntarily touched him before.

"If I don't survive, then he can't," Pritchard said as though explaining something elementary.

"You will." She made it sound as though she wanted him to live. In truth, she didn't want him dead. There had been too much death about this mission. "Let him go."

Pritchard seemed to accept her friendly conduct at face value. He was less devious than he had been. He glanced in the direction of his suite, but didn't leave. "You were in the cave," he said. "How far did the Assembly barrier extend?"

It was a dangerous question, though Pritchard hadn't intended a trick. "I don't know. I'm not in the Assembly."

"He'd know. The Inlander." Pritchard glanced down at the gun in his hand.

The guard, apparently impatient with Pritchard's new inadequacies, and without the Assembly to supplement his loyalty, if that was what it did, said, "Sir, our men are dying out there. What do you plan to do? Will the deadhead access work?"

The Judge stepped out alone from the shadows and walked forward with his hands held high in the air. Beatrice bit her lip at his audacity. He didn't glance at her. He bowed, but only at Pritchard. With his raised arms, it seemed more of an obeisance than usual. "The deadhead access won't work. The Assembly still can't reach here." The Judge spoke to Pritchard, but was answering the guard. He walked toward Pritchard. Nonplussed, Pritchard let him approach until the Judge was only at arm's length. The Judge pointed out the window. "Look," he said. "That's ground zero. They have their device there, in the tunnel where they broke through. See how heavily it's guarded."

Pritchard hadn't aimed his gun at the Judge, nor ordered the guard to kill him. He moved a careful distance away from the Judge but looked where he indicated. "So you think I should surrender to them." Pritchard sounded bitter.

"You never did before," the Judge said, which Beatrice didn't understand. "I admire that, Kaim. You only bided your time."

Pritchard was motionless, listening intently.

Beatrice had supposed the Judge had left his wife and son behind, that he was acting only to protect them, but wasn't sure. He indicated the battlefield again. Beatrice looked, but it seemed a jumble of bodies, fire, and men. "If you can't eliminate the shield—and it doesn't seem that you have manpower enough in position—then it'll take you too long to walk outside its range to do any good. They told me its reach is about three or four miles; this one is much larger than the other. You need a vehicle; you've got to get out of here and get reinforcements before they break into the other building. Once they do, they'll vanish into the caves again, or disappear into the town. Their web doctor is good."

It sounded sensible, and it sounded as if the Judge's advice was in Pritchard's best interests. "You have no reason to tell me this," Pritchard said suspiciously. "You're lying."

The Judge turned to him, while continuing to ignore the presence of Beatrice and the other guard. "I came into this on the wrong side because you were defensive and refused to cooperate with the Open Court. Then the Adjusters intervened, but, probably on your advice, they distrusted me. They threatened and offered a bribe; it didn't work. Kaim, you've never forgotten who I am. 'Inlander,' you call me. We've had Romaric between us, but he's dead."

The guard was restless. "Shouldn't we get going?" he asked.

The Judge nodded. "Yes. We can talk on the way." He almost put his arm around Kaim Pritchard's shoulder, then seemed to think better of it. Pritchard smiled. The Judge gestured toward the wing where Beatrice and her fellow Travelers had been lodged.

"I don't trust you," Pritchard said to the Judge, but he put his gun back inside his boot.

"Yes, you do, Kaim." The Judge was solemn. "You've been inside my mind. You know me from school. What these wildmen really want is the destruction of the Assembly. That's not my goal. It would bring ruin to the Earth again, maybe worse than the Great Deaths. Kaim, don't confuse me with Romaric. You opened my eyes to his bullying. We both know why he did it. Jealousy. The only things he had were inherited, like this." He had been twisting the heavy ring he wore on his left hand; he pulled it off. "Here," he said. "Take it. I don't care about it. This can't let a man connect. What matters is the thing you and I share, the Assembly. Without Romaric, perhaps the two of us would have been friends." Even with her command of song and understanding of human tone, Beatrice wasn't certain the Judge was lying.

Pritchard's eyes were on the ring the Judge had extended to him. It usually looked dull, but in the flash of gunfire, the stone gleamed like molten gold, sometimes yellow and sometimes orange. "Taking it won't make me an Inlander."

"You want to be one? What good has it done me?"

The guard shifted his rifle from one hand to the other. Pritchard stood indecisively, looking at the ring, then the Judge, then the ongoing battle outside. The Judge pressed the ring into Pritchard's hand, even closing Pritchard's unresisting fingers around it. "You should go," he said. "These wildmen can't win here today. Can you imagine the chaos if everyone could create pockets outside the Assembly? There'd be wars again. Go on. You're the only one who can stop them."

Pritchard looked at the ring in his hand, but placed it in a pocket, not on his finger. "You'll come with me, Inlan ... Stefan. I don't trust you, whatever you say, but the wildmen do. You might be useful." Pritchard's yearning for the Judge's appeal to be true made his voice tremble and his cautious words irrelevant.

The Judge glanced back at the shadows in which he'd hidden his wife and son. He didn't bring them out. He was playing a role with Pritchard. Beatrice was almost certain.

An explosion shook the besieged barracks. There were no lights visible inside, but the traces of gunfire coming from the building showed the ID agents were still fighting, although a corner of the building was on fire.

"We'd better hurry," the Judge told Pritchard.

Pritchard put his hand around Beatrice's upper left arm, holding her tightly, and started dragging her toward the Traveler rooms upstairs in the other wing.

"Just leave her," the Judge said as he hurriedly followed. "She's useless for what you have to do."

Pritchard chuckled. "I'd almost believe you, except you're so concerned for me. Remember, I *have* been in your mind. And you'd protect your son and Beatrice with your last breath. But never mind, Stefan. I have reasons for wanting you alive, and maybe there's a grain of truth in what you've said." Pritchard glanced back sharply at the guard, seemingly confused for a moment that he wasn't following. "Come along!" he said, then to the Judge he added, "This is inconvenient."

"I miss it, too."

They were talking about the Assembly.

"What happened to the guard I ordered to kill you?" Pritchard spoke companionably, as though he and his victim were old friends, and all the while he continued to pull Beatrice to the corridor.

"He didn't have the nerve, without the Assembly to back him."

"And Pera Acari?" Pritchard's hand tightened on Beatrice.

"The cold bitch was sorry I wasn't really dead. I left her behind, with Tepan. They're safer there, for now."

"You've changed, Inlander. Stefan. I like you better, and that means I should not trust you. You go first."

Beatrice watched the Judge. Pritchard was right. He had changed. He wouldn't have been capable of this elaborate deception when she'd first met him. He'd lost his innocence—as she had on this mission.

They entered the lower level of the wing containing the Travelers' rooms. It was dark without the electric lights, but she could still see fairly well from the faint line of light that entered the hallway beneath each door. She imagined Charles, Mariyo, and the Fox, probably huddled together in the Fox's room, listening to the explosions and the barbaric shrieks, uncertain whether to run or stay. Pritchard was a survivor, and for now, they'd be safer with him than with anyone else. "What about my friends?" she asked Pritchard. "You need them, too."

"I don't need anyone." Pritchard wasn't boasting; he was stating his belief.

The darkness slowed Pritchard's pace. The Judge got farther ahead. He stopped at the heavy door to the outer stairwell leading upstairs to the Travelers' rooms. "Stefan," she called, "get my friends. Please!"

He didn't answer, but he entered the stairwell. The door creaked; as it opened it let in light from a window.

"Inlander! Wait!" Pritchard sounded angry, yet uncertain whether his anger was justified. The door closed behind the Judge before Beatrice, Pritchard, or Pritchard's man arrived. "Damn it." Pritchard tried to hurry her, but Beatrice slowed him, purposely tripping once, and taking her time in getting up, trying to give the Judge an opportunity to get upstairs and call her friends. She listened, but didn't hear his voice.

When they reached the door, Pritchard warily ordered the guard to go through first. He did, then returned. "Nothing," he said. "Acari isn't here. He must already be outside."

Pritchard pulled Beatrice into the stairwell. "What's he doing?" Pritchard muttered. He stood in the dim stairwell, then tried to peer through the window. He brought Beatrice with him, and though she strained, all she could see was the darkness lit by occasional flashes from the sporadic explosions.

The outer door opened. The guard jerked his rifle into firing position. "There you are," the Judge said cheerily. "We're out of sight of the battle. Hurry. There's a row of coaches just across the drive."

Pritchard signaled and the guard went through first. Pritchard hesitated, as though he had expected a report, but the guard didn't return. The Judge still held the door open. Pritchard, pulling Beatrice, left the Lodge. She tried to hang back, to exit more with the Judge than with Pritchard. There had been strain in the Judge's tone as he urged them outside.

"One of their vehicles will be best if we can get one," he continued. "They'll think of it as theirs, and ..."

Four tattooed men surrounded Pritchard, their guns

aimed at him. The guard was already prone on the ground, motionless. The Judge stopped talking as he came outside, just behind Beatrice. He let out a long breath. "Tie Pritchard up. And he has a gun in his boot." He reached his arm around Beatrice's shoulders, leaving it to the wildmen to deal with Pritchard, and pulled her close. She felt his released tension in his trembling. "You're safe," he said.

"I'm going back in," Stefan told the oldest of the four clansmen Denning had stationed at the door to wait for him. *Thank God Denning is an honorable man, and a careful one,* he thought. After getting the three other Travelers out, Denning had posted guards at all the doors so Pritchard didn't escape, and given them orders to help Stefan. "My wife and son are inside."

"John said to bring you to him."

Stefan shrugged, which didn't leave room for discussion. "Then shoot me. But I'm going in and I'd appreciate a gun. You owe me that much for bringing Pritchard out."

Inside the yard, out of sight of this doorway, someone shrieked as he died.

One of the four tossed Stefan his carbine. It seemed too light to be worth much, and was an unfamiliar, local design, but Stefan nodded a grateful thanks. "I'll wait ten minutes," the same man said. The others agreed.

Pritchard and his agent had been disarmed and were under guard, but Stefan had made sure it was understood that Beatrice was an ally and his particular friend. They treated her with respect. As they started back toward the breakout point, the clansmen headquarters, Pritchard didn't curse or threaten, yet his set expression showed that if Pritchard survived, he would make Stefan pay. "Now you're like me," he said.

Was Stefan's true self like Kaim Pritchard? "I'm not a puppet," Stefan said, but he felt guilty. However he rationalized that Pritchard was an evil man who let himself be used by corrupt Adjusters, Stefan knew that he had betrayed whatever frail innocence had remained in

Kaim Pritchard after all the years. Stefan watched them leave while wondering how he had become so morally reckless. He had been a Judge of the Open Court, a careful man, prissy, perhaps, and unable to use deceit as a weapon. Now, Pritchard had walked into a trap Stefan had set.

Stefan nodded further thanks to the guard who was staying behind. The door squeaked as Stefan reentered the Lodge. He winced at the sound, went through the stairwell, then walked only a few paces down the dark corridor; he stopped. He had never intended to go on. It was pointless to bring Liada and Tepan here, where there was danger. Better to get a coach first and drive it closer to where he'd left them. Stefan didn't believe the clansmen would let him leave the area, however. If Liada and Tepan had been with him, they all would have been forced to go to the wildman camp. He had to steal a coach and evade the clansmen.

He sat down, leaning against the wall. His back ached. His head hurt. He held the carbine out for a tactile examination; his hands were shaking. Within the space of an hour, he'd rescued John Denning by killing one, or possibly two men, had talked an ID agent out of shooting him and had bluffed Kaim Pritchard, but despicably, using Pritchard's weakness for acceptance by an aristocracy of which he could never be a part. And he had saved Beatrice, for the time being. He had also abandoned his wife and son, albeit to protect them, and now he was planning to steal a coach and escape from his own supposed allies, leaving Beatrice and the Travelers behind, while rationalizing that they were too important to be harmed, and disregarding that certain clansmen believed they were alien spies.

This would make a very interesting dump.

It couldn't be him. In spite of everything he'd done, he didn't feel guilty. What would the Judge he'd been have ruled? Judge Acari of the Open Court would have called murder murder. So why did Stefan Acari feel horrified, but right? If justice could be tempered by mercy, were there also other, greater goods? Did morality have an emotional level beyond logic or justice?

The old Stefan Acari wouldn't have sat in this corridor waiting for the clansman who'd given him this gun to go away—or even wondering whether time was so short that he should shoot him. He would have been honest, and either gone for Liada and Tepan, as he'd claimed was his intention, or tried to bully his way into getting a vehicle from the clans. He wouldn't have used subterfuge. Damn it, he was that man. Stefan stood. He started down the dark corridor toward where he had left Liada.

He wasn't careful. Pritchard's men had already either run away or tried to join their fellows and been cut down. Anyone left in the Lodge was cowering, waiting for the clans to leave and the Assembly to return. Stefan went into the lobby as openly as he might have a week earlier, calling Liada's name.

"Stefan?" Liada was hiding with Tepan, but she came out of the shadows.

"Come with me," he said. "We're getting out of here."

She picked Tepan up from the ground and walked to Stefan, cradling their son in her arms as if he were a sleeping baby. "What happened to the others?"

He didn't want to explain. Inside the Assembly, explanations were never necessary. One simply *knew*. Romaric complained that such knowledge was unnatural, but he had never truly experienced it. Romaric. Stefan needed time to think long and hard about his friend. Light from outside lit the room with an unsteady red glare. It shone in Liada's black hair and warmed her pallor. She was very beautiful. He didn't want her. "Come on," he said gruffly.

Stefan didn't take Tepan, because to do so would have kept him from using the carbine. Tepan was deeply asleep. It was late night in Acari, from which he'd just come, a night in which he hadn't slept. He didn't move when Liada rearranged his weight.

"I'm sorry, Stefan." Liada wasn't apologizing for anything that night. Her tone was unlike the aggressive voice in which she'd said those same words before. "I know you did your best, but . . ." Her voice trailed off, still not speaking the reasons for the emptiness between them. "I'm sorry."

She was having difficulty walking quickly in her silly, stylish shoes. He slowed his steps. They had been heading to the Travelers' wing, but he wondered whether it might not be better simply to try to walk away through the woods. Safer, too, with the battle raging outside, and both sides likely to shoot at anything that was trying to escape it. As long as they weren't taken by the Assembly forces. Could she manage the woods in those shoes? Unlikely. He continued toward the coaches.

"What are you going to do?" she asked.

It took him a moment to realize she was speaking of their marriage, not of fleeing the Lodge. "There won't be a repudiation," he said. "If Drom mentioned it, he was acting without authority. After that dump, you can divorce me and get your dowry back. But wait, Lia. It's possible I won't survive this, or not for long. Then you can be regent for Tepan."

"I don't want you dead, Stefan."

"I never thought you did." Stefan had one last chance to retain a measure of his former life. If he tried to reconcile with Liada—a reconciliation might be convenient for her, too—perhaps that would convince the Adjusters that he was loyal, and they would let him return to Acari, ignore the world and lead a diminished, provincial, private life.

Stefan stopped walking. No. He couldn't turn his back on everything he'd learned. "It was Romaric, wasn't it?"

Liada had a nasty laugh. "Your sainted friend."

"He's dead. I don't blame him any less than I do you."

"You'll excuse him, though. He's not here and pregnant. Men! And so you have that scrawny creature instead of me."

"She's not my lover!"

Liada laughed again. "Of course not. You're too virtuous for anything so physical. I never believed that stupid dump."

There was no use talking to her; there never had been. "You take Tepan. He's too heavy for me." She thrust the boy at Stefan.

Tepan's small body felt hot. Worried, Stefan looked down. The light was too poor to see much. He raised his son's head higher and moved closer to the window, but fighting had slowed; there wasn't much light. His face seemed dirty. He felt Tepan's forehead; it was too warm. "Has he been coughing?"

"Not much. What's the matter?" Liada felt Tepan's head, too. "A fever." She gave a startled cry. "There's blood on my dress!"

Stefan sniffed and smelled blood. Tepan had a nosebleed. Red Death was a hemorrhagic fever. Pritchard hadn't bled out, but his eyes had been bloodshot. Romaric? It had begun with the same symptoms. Stefan couldn't speak to curse or pray.

"What is it?" Liada's voice was rising. "Please!"

She knew, but wanted him to say it so she would have someone to blame. "He has the sickness that killed Romaric."

"God! No! I've held him." She came close, however, and stroked Tepan's head. She looked up at Stefan. "It's from them. Your bitch friend."

"He caught it at Ezio," Stefan said, as though that excused Beatrice. He started walking determinedly for the battlefield. The glass door was the closest access.

"Stop. Stefan, where are you going?" Liada tugged at his arm.

"The closest doctor is probably with the wildmen. Or at least they'll give us a coach now." Red Death should be quarantined. He was wrong to bring his son's feverish, bleeding body where there were others, but if Tepan was to have any hope, he needed medical care immediately. Liada was hanging back. "Are you coming?" Stefan had reached the door; he went out without waiting for her.

The clamor of voices and confusion reached Tepan; he moved in Stefan's arms and mumbled. How had Liada not noticed the obvious? Stefan shifted his son's position and stroked his forehead, trying to soothe him. Beatrice was with the clansmen. Good. Perhaps this was best.

The gunfire had stopped. As Stefan walked to the edge of the battlefield, he remembered the dash through the cave with Beatrice. She had been different with him, much more open, at least in part because he wasn't connected to the Assembly. In fact, when he had told her the Assembly was gone from the cave, she had already known it. He stopped again, puzzled. How had she known? She refused to connect.

"What are you doing?" Liada hobbled to him, finally catching up. "These wildmen will shoot us!" She was crying. "Come back! Come back inside!"

In the cave, Beatrice had known the Assembly was gone. She had also said she couldn't hear her ship's beacon, which somehow meant that her ship was coming. She hadn't been any more right than he had been concerning the Assembly.

It all came together in Stefan's mind.

When the Assembly was blocked, so was Beatrice's beacon. When the beacon was gone, her ship would come. The beacon wasn't on the ship at all; it was on Earth. The beacon and the Assembly were the same thing.

"What's the matter?" Liada shook his arm; Tepan mumbled incoherently.

Stefan loved his son, but the Travelers were the most important people on Earth. If the Travelers signaled their ship to come—probably by using the Assembly, or rather, the beacon—then the beacon/Assembly would end, worldwide and perhaps forever.

The Travelers could terminate the Assembly. The Assembly itself, the source of Earth's civilization, was an alien artifact.

Chapter 13

John Denning had a politician's welcoming smile in place as he walked out from the clansman position, crossed a field that only minutes earlier would have been impassable, and met Stefan and Liada. "Stefan! Welcome. And just in time. They want a truce. They're ready to negotiate and you're an ideal mediator."

"John, I need a doctor for my son." Stefan looked for the Travelers, but didn't see them.

Tepan stirred in Stefan's arms. "Your son?" Denning asked. "Poor kid, he's tired." He stooped slightly, to bring his tattooed face to Tepan's eye level, then made peculiar expressions at him, sticking out his tongue, rolling his eyes, twitching, until even though he was sick, Tepan giggled at an adult engaging in such antics. Success achieved, Denning straightened. "The Numerican disease?" he quietly asked Stefan.

"I think so." Stefan's personal respect for Denning had just gone a notch higher. Denning hadn't backed away or shown anything but compassion.

"Come on." Denning clapped Stefan on the back and used his hold to draw Stefan closer to the clans' position. "And you must be Stefan's wife," he said, looking sideways at Liada. "Welcome."

She didn't respond.

"Does she understand?" Denning asked.

"Answer him," Stefan demanded in their own language. Liada was pouting, too absorbed in her own distress for common courtesy, but she briefly nodded.

Denning muttered something under his breath, then glanced at Stefan. "We have a doctor back in the tunnel.

Your wife can take your son to him, and you'll negotiate. This is it, Stefan. Don't give them anything but their lives, and they give us our people. All of them. We're winning, but we've got to get out of here before the Adjusters notice our free zone and send reinforcements."

Stefan scanned the field, remembering it as it had been, a grassy yard. When this was over, it might be one again, and no one, seeing it, would quite understand how the battle had been fought. The cease fire had given the clansmen time to regroup and reposition themselves. Most had come through the tunnel, but armored trucks had brought more clansmen into the compound. A group of lightly wounded men were being loaded onto one of those trucks as he watched, along with six or seven inert, covered bodies. The fallen ID agents had been left on the field like garbage.

"Come on," Denning urged. "Let's get out of the line of fire in case all hell breaks lose again. They've still got ammunition."

Stefan, carrying Tepan, allowed himself to be led toward the clans' headquarters position, an area between the tunnel breakout point and two armored trucks strategically deployed to prevent Pritchard's garrison from a clear shot. Liada scurried closer and stayed on Stefan's far side from the garrison. "You have the Travelers?" Stefan asked.

"Yeah." Denning frowned. "I've got to tell you, Marta's not too crazy about them." He nodded at Tepan. "I'm surprised you aren't furious, too."

"Marta's wrong, John."

"They don't cause the disease?"

Denning sounded willing to hear another side, but the Travelers *had* brought disease to Earth. It was their motive that needed to be understood, yet could any motive possibly excuse them? He almost blurted out to Denning the reason for the Travelers' importance, how they could bring down the Assembly, then stopped himself. Until he knew what was going on, silence was best.

They reached the clan's sheltered position. Marta

Denning's bulk was obvious in the dim light; apparently she didn't trust anyone else to retrieve her family. Orion Nash was there; he greeted John while ignoring Stefan. Another man, young, agile, and armed, guarded Kaim Pritchard, who sat on a folding camp stool, his hands bound behind his back, and stared dully at the ground as they approached. Stefan was uncertain Pritchard had noticed them, then he spoke. "The happy family," he said.

"Don't trust him," Stefan said. "I've been inside his mind, John. He'll do anything the Adjusters ask. He's entirely their puppet."

"We're not naive. I want my son back, or Pritchard's a dead man."

Rock and dirt were scattered around the breakout point. The clansmen had placed a ramp up to the surface, making passage between the surface and the tunnel system easy. The underground was lit. Bodies, living and dead, lay on tables or the ground. A field hospital, as Denning had said. The effect was like looking into hell.

Most clansmen wore thin wires around their heads that plugged into their ears. A small bulb-shaped device was at their chins. Radio headsets. Stefan had seen them on other visits to the Sister Continents and had thought of them as toys, not weapons of war, but communications were important to any battle. Marta wore one. John had one low, around his neck. None was offered to Stefan. He was a marginal ally. "Where are the Travelers?" he asked.

"Down below." Denning looked past Stefan, and said to Liada, "Pera Acari, please take your son into the tunnel, where he can be examined in safety."

Denning used the proper form of address, but his tone lacked respect. "Is Dr. Felipe there?" Stefan asked.

"Who? No. Dr. Anders."

"I'll take Tepan to him." Stefan started down the ramp. Beyond Tepan's urgent need for treatment, Stefan needed to verify that the Travelers were alive, and learn how they, including Beatrice, were being held. Clansmen had kidnapped Beatrice once before, and held her in a cave; they'd killed their own men to disguise it. Given Marta's attitude, Beatrice might be unsafe.

"Look! Someone's coming out!" a clansman shouted.

"Stefan, wait!" John Denning grabbed him. "We need you."

Tepan stirred in Stefan's arms and whispered in his ear, asking about the tattooed men; he said he was hot and tired and wanted to go home. Stefan kissed his head and whispered back that it was all right, that he should sleep.

Marta seemed to notice Tepan for the first time. She came over, her expression softened, and she seemed a wife and mother, wildly out of place on a battlefield. "What a beautiful little boy," she said, bending close and speaking like a newly introduced neighbor.

Tepan tightened his grip on Stefan's shoulder and buried his face in Stefan's neck. He was getting heavy. "I need to bring him to the doctor."

"First things first," John Denning said. "Pera Acari, take your son." It was an order, and as he spoke it, John Denning lifted Tepan from Stefan's arms. The boy shrieked, a thin, wailing sound of distress, almost a whistle. Stefan reached to take him back. "All men have fathers, Stefan," Denning said, turning away to prevent it. "There are lives you can save out there." Stefan hesitated, then Tepan was gone, deposited in Liada's arms by Denning. She grimaced, at Tepan's weight, at his illness, or simply at Denning, but she took her son. He was still whimpering.

"Let's go," Denning said.

Stefan delayed. Liada scowled at him, then she went down the ramp accompanied by Marta. He turned to Denning. "A Judge isn't a negotiator. I don't think I should do this." Stefan wanted to see the Travelers. This battle was beginning to seem peripheral to the important issues: the Travelers' ship, the Travelers' illness, and the continued existence of the Assembly.

"We need you to end this, Stefan," Denning said.

"He doesn't like your son," Pritchard yelled at Denning. "He's not on your side; he has his own. An In-lander." Pritchard spat.

Denning rolled his eyes at Stefan, dismissing Pritch-ard. "The lives you can save are real, Stefan, but do as you choose." He started walking to where a young man had come out from the garrison building and now stood alone, unarmed, holding a piece of white cloth in his hand.

This wasn't a job for a Judge, but Denning had asked as a father and friend. Stefan felt an obligation to help not only him, but all these men. Reluctantly, he followed.

"Thanks. I knew you'd come." Denning slowed as Ste-fan caught up. "I forgot that you've met Johnny," he said. "I apologize for the circumstances. We were in a difficult position, thanks to him." He jerked his head to indicate Pritchard, now behind them. "And I apologize for the invitation to Bowl, but if you hadn't been here, Pritchard would have killed us all once we'd wrung that poor girl dry of information for him."

Stefan didn't acknowledge the apology. It was John, acting the politician. Still, he had been allowed to keep the carbine; perhaps Denning did view him as an ally or a friend. "One thing. Is this negotiation real, or are we buying time?"

Denning grinned. "You've gotten cynical. Don't worry, everything is real."

They reached the ID agent with the white flag. The clansmen had trained a floodlight on him. The man, about the age of John Junior, was sweating. His eyes darted nervously around the dark field, which was con-trolled by his enemies. Before that night, he'd probably never considered that he had so many. An ID agent was not threatening to law-abiding citizens of any continent. Though local regimes varied, the Assembly was not an adversary of any of them, nor an occupying power. Or so Stefan had believed.

"I'm John Denning," Denning introduced himself. "Send out all our people, then we'll go away. Simple. This is Per Stefan Acari, an Inlander from Ropa, and a

Judge of the Open Court. He's here to corroborate our sincerity, and yours." Stefan bowed.

"An expelled Judge," the man said. "Without any authority."

"What's your name?" Denning asked sharply, as if there was a protocol to the negotiation that this man had already violated.

He licked his lips, and glanced back at the garrison building. "Nur Samiya." He was a thin man with a sparse mustache and a long chin; his accent was Outbakan, giving him a strong, competing English Speakers' Empire pronunciation. Stefan couldn't recall having noticed him and doubted Nur Samiya's prominence in Pritchard's organization, but the young man held his head up and looked Denning in the eye as he spoke.

"Mr. Samiya," Stefan said. "The clansmen are holding Kaim Pritchard and all four Travelers. Those people are important to Earth and to the Assembly. As an agent of Independent Defense, your duty is to secure their safety and connect with the Assembly to report. Your prisoners, though important to no one but their families, give you your only basis for negotiation. I will walk back with you and confirm that your prisoners are alive and unharmed. If that is so, this negotiation can proceed."

Samiya turned and waved his hands wildly at the garrison, as if concerned that his message would not otherwise be understood. An ID agent, he had depended so long on the Assembly for instant, exact communication that it apparently was difficult for him to trust any other arrangement. Almost immediately, a clansman was thrust out the front door of the garrison. The man hesitated, blinking as the floodlight swung from the negotiating group to him. Stefan didn't recognize him. The man waved, and first hesitantly, then eagerly, he ran to the clansmen position.

Someone on the field called a name, and the released man shouted back. On the far side of the field there was a wild, whooping, enthusiastic yell.

"A show of our good faith," Nur Samiya said. "But no one comes into the garrison."

Stefan exchanged a look with Denning. "Then you've killed some of your prisoners," Stefan said, working to keep his tone flat so it wouldn't be hostile. "What about the women?"

Samiya didn't deny the accusation. "The whores?" he said. "They're asleep, doped by their own gas."

The girls might be dead, too. Stefan remembered their high-heeled shoes and their courage; he no longer felt the respect for Nur Samiya that he'd been developing. Such brave young men.

"Send out your prisoners," John Denning said. "All of them. Now. We're not taking them one by one."

"What do we get?" Samiya asked. "And with what assurances?"

"You get your lives," Denning said. "We can blow that building at anytime. You have our people in there, so we haven't. Yet."

"What about Mr. Pritchard and the Numericans?"

Stefan put a hand on Denning's arm. "John, back off. Let me speak with Mr. Samiya alone."

Denning looked quizzical, but walked about ten paces away. When he was gone, Stefan said, "Whatever has happened since, you know me from my dumps. I am, or was, a ticker and a Judge. I tell you, Samiya, the wild-men will do it. They will blow up that building even with their own people inside it. They killed three of their own men in that cave with the Traveler. These people are not entirely rational, and they're running out of time. You were wise to negotiate; do as he says or his people will massacre you."

Samiya shifted his weight. "We can't."

Stefan pressed the carbine to his side. "How many of their people have you killed?"

Samiya looked directly at him as though about to protest, then sighed and looked down. "Three girls, and two of their men. One of those was from their own gunfire. It was his son." He nodded at Denning. "We wouldn't have been stupid enough to kill him."

It was better than Stefan had feared, but worse than it might have been. "I'll tell him, and I'll also tell him that you're going to cooperate with everything he's asked. I'm going to say that you want them to leave the Travelers behind, unharmed, when they leave. They'll probably agree." Stefan started toward Denning.

"How many sides are you playing, Judge?" Samiya called.

Stefan went over to Denning. "He'll do what you want, but he needs the Travelers."

Denning shrugged acquiescence. "How'd you manage that? Not that I wasn't sure you would." Denning raised his radio headset onto his head and whispered into it that their people would be coming out.

"I told him you wildmen were terrorists, and crazy."

Denning chuckled. "Revolutionaries, not terrorists." He started back to Samiya, but Stefan caught his arm. "John, one other thing." He thought of Tepan being examined by the doctor and remembered his father, bleeding out, effectively dead before his heart and brain finally stopped functioning. *Not my son,* he thought fiercely and impotently, knowing John Denning was thinking the same thing. He didn't want to be the one to tell another man his son was dead, but it was his duty. "John . . ."

Denning looked at him, waiting, forcing him to say it. "John Junior is dead."

Denning released his breath. "How?"

"He *says* from shots fired by your men outside."

Denning didn't change expression. Stefan wished for comforting words to say, but couldn't find them. Pritchard, having seen into him, was right; Stefan had disliked John Junior. He did like John Denning and he identified with a father's pain. "I'm sorry, John," he finally said.

Denning nodded and started for Nur Samiya, moving without any apparent threat though he was armed. Stefan followed. Denning turned. "Go see to your son," he said.

"Are you all right?" Of course he wasn't, and might never be again, but Stefan had really asked if he could continue dealing peaceably with Pritchard's agents.

"Fine." Denning seemed cool. "There are other fathers waiting. I'm all right, Stefan. Go on to your son."

"Should I tell Marta?" Stefan didn't know what was
proper.

"I will," Denning said, "when the time is right."

The boy would be all right. Beatrice had recognized his
symptoms as soon as his mother carried him down the
ramp. It was a flash fever, not the gradual kind; children
his age nearly always survived. "The Judge's wife and
son," she whispered to the Fox.

"Then he must be nearby," he said.

Charles showed his fear of the wildmen by compli-
ance; he told the Fox to be quiet. Despite orders from
their guards to be silent, Beatrice had explained the
events in the dining room to her fellow Travelers. These
armed clansmen were guards. They didn't even try to
pretend otherwise.

Beatrice felt ungainly on the high stool. She shifted
position again and watched as the Judge's family was
led to the makeshift hospital by Marta Denning, whom
Beatrice recognized from the Waterman party. The hospital wasn't far from the Travelers.

The cave was man-made. The walls and floors were
smooth and well-lit by lanterns hanging from hooks in
the walls. It was really only a broadened opening in a
tunnel that went away into the earth. That tunnel was
lit with yellow lights that reminded her of the Waterman
party. Mechanical humming sounded from down that
tunnel; it was the same humming that had permeated
her kidnappers' camp. Beatrice and her fellow Travelers
had tried and failed to contact the beacon. The four of
them were as isolated as she had been while in clansmen
hands before.

Marta Denning stayed with the boy and his mother
while they waited for the doctor to complete his surgery
on one of the clansmen wounded in the battle. She whispered comforts to the boy that he could not understand
and that the Judge's wife ignored. When the doctor was
ready for them, Marta spoke to him briefly; then, as he

turned to examine the boy, Marta glanced about the cavern, and went to the Travelers. "That's what you want for us all," she accused. "That poor child is sick because of you."

The other Travelers simply gazed at her, so Beatrice did the same. Marta Denning crossed her arms and stared back, focused only on Beatrice. It was uncomfortable to be singled out, especially when she already felt guilty.

"Why are you fighting?" Beatrice whispered. Natural death could be gruesome. It often seemed untimely. Violent death, however, the hand of one intelligence raised against another, was depraved. On the Ship, every human had feared the Kroni, but in all her life, Beatrice had never heard of any violent act a Kroni had committed against a shipboard companion. Human fear was an innate reaction to them, like the revulsion she'd felt at seeing her first cockroach, a perception and not a truth.

The doctor, seeing the bloody nose and bloodshot eyes of the Judge's son, pulled away with almost that aversion, then seemed to steel himself and return to examining the child. Fear, but fortitude could conquer fear. She remembered: It was the same on the Ship.

"Why don't the Friends cure him?" Beatrice had asked as she stood beside the Fox, both of them within the circle of watching Friends. Inside that circle, Eyni was dying. Beatrice had used the human language to ask her question, ashamed of her own resentment. Eyni had heard her voice and raised his head.

"They can't cure it," the Fox had said, "but they would have prevented it if they'd never taken any humans aboard."

Eyni was dying of a hypervirulent influenza from a world of Friends. An illness from Earth, it had mutated repeatedly and rapidly through the centuries. The strain had become harmless to humans, but endemic among the Friends.

Eyni had looked at Beatrice. "Sing a lament," he'd told her. "Make it the first one sung on Earth."

Beatrice had cried, which Friends didn't do, though

they felt as strongly as anyone. That moment she'd sensed a great circle of connections. Ships left the worlds of Friends because it was natural to them, as inescapable as death, but to a Friend it was the essence of real life. They enlarged the sphere of contact, touching and connecting others with song, yet knowing death would sometimes occur. That circle of inevitable connection had brought humans among Friends, and it led to Eyni dying of human disease in a circle that included her. One could keep separate, safe and alone or one could expand and grow: for an individual or a race, the gamble was the same. It had been at Eyni's deathbed that she had decided to go on the Earth mission.

Beatrice sighed. Marta Denning scowled. "You want to know why we're fighting? It's because of you," she said. "If you hadn't come, then no one, none of us, would be here. No one would be dead."

A Ship—Beatrice's Ship, in fact—had touched Earth, setting off illnesses that adapted to Earth's ecosystem, and began the Great Deaths. The Ship had captured her ancestors: enigmatic, half-savage creatures who had been unable to communicate, and were relegated to a human shelter that then was little better than a zoo. As years passed, Friends observed Earth; the Shipboard humans had learned to sing. Contact made, they were used to calibrate the beacon; other humans had set it on the icy, seldom visited south continent. Then those humans had been abandoned by the Ship, which had no longer been able to approach Earth because of the functioning beacon.

Beatrice rarely thought of those other humans sent on a one-way mission to Earth by the Friends. How had it seemed to them? Only a few generations removed from living on that world, had they told themselves that they were protecting Earth from strangers and aliens, rather than from disease, as they established the beacon? Perhaps, with the Friends still unfamiliar with human song, those sent to Earth had hidden their true feelings. Perhaps they'd hated the Ship and were glad to safeguard Earth from contact. Those abandoned messengers must have been the ones who established the Assembly; only they knew how to connect with the beacon. They must have felt they were doing right, or doing something harmless. Had they been the first Adjusters? Had they kept the truth of the beacon's origins from Earth's citizens even as they began using it to create the truth-telling, truth-seeking Assembly?

Under heavy guard, Pritchard came down the ramp. He saw the Travelers and tried to have his guard set him among them, but the guard resisted and brought him closer to where the doctor was still examining the Judge's son. It was farther from the exit ramp.

"Are we pets to the Friends?" Beatrice asked the Fox in song.

Mariyo made a loud, rude sound at the Fox and Beatrice both. "Would you keep a pet that killed you? We're *their* Friends."

"Quiet," Charles said again.

Marta's jaw had dropped. She had never heard song and stared as if Beatrice and her fellow travelers were insane. Beatrice suppressed an urge to jump at Marta, or bark, or bite.

"Aliens," Marta Denning said. She shuddered and stared. There was menace in that look.

"We're human," Beatrice said.

She snorted. "We did tissue tests. I know better."

Beatrice's right arm, still in a sling, ached; her fingers were slightly swollen. That distorted the color of the skin. Her left hand had a definitive amber color. A skin graft, performed by the Ship's skilled surgeons when she made her decision, the skin was from Eyni, a gift taken shortly before her Friend's death. "That's my Friend," Beatrice said, rubbing the skin. If she closed her eyes she could pretend it was Eyni's cool, smooth self, not a remnant of his life. She had yet to sing his lament.

Beatrice's legs dangled above the ground; the stool was too high. "I've chosen," she sang to the Fox as she swung her legs. "As soon as their shield is gone, we'll summon the Ship."

"It isn't time," Charles protested. The Fox said nothing; it wasn't necessary, since he agreed with Beatrice.

Marta Denning looked at one of the nearby armed men. "Keep them under close guard," she said, "and don't let them make any more of that alien noise."

Beatrice didn't protest, though Marta's look was a challenge that she do so.

Marta returned to where the doctor was examining the boy. The Judge's son was more infectious than any of the Travelers. Even Marta Denning probably knew it, but she went to the Judge's wife, the boy's mother, and put her arm around the woman for comfort, though Pera Acari had carried her bleeding son.

The Judge's wife glanced into Marta Denning's tattooed face, tried to disguise revulsion with a false smile, then she stopped trying and pulled away. Kaim Pritchard said something to her. She glanced coolly at him, but he'd spoken in their foreign language, and Beatrice didn't understand anything but the tone of shared arrogance. Liada Acari hesitated. She looked at the tattooed men and Marta, at Beatrice and her fellow Travelers, at her son, then she shrugged delicately and spoke briefly to Pritchard. The lesser evil, apparently, Pritchard smiled graciously and said something about the boy, because they both looked at him.

"He'll live," Beatrice said. "He's young, just the right age. It looks more serious than it is."

The Judge's wife studied Beatrice, unconvinced but wanting to hear more.

Pritchard spoke to the Judge's wife again in their shared language and she turned away from Beatrice. The Judge's name—Stefan—was repeatedly said.

Marta Denning pressed her finger against her ear, pushing the earpiece of her radio device deeper, to listen better, and hurried up the ramp, whispering into the mouthpiece.

These clansmen were in some sense the Judge's friends. He had given Beatrice into their custody and sent his wife and son into their keeping. John Denning had come to the rooms of her fellow Travelers and asked them to voluntarily come away with him, for their own safety, using the Judge's name. Beatrice trusted the Judge, but in view of the antagonism between him and Pritchard, and considering his incomplete knowledge of her mission, she wasn't certain his view of matters was right.

She and her fellow Travelers had to get away to where they would have access to the beacon again. That was what Pritchard would want, too—access to his Assembly. Thus, Pritchard needed to win. She hummed a brief statement of intent to the Fox.

"Don't interfere," he said. "We don't really understand what's going on."

"Stop that," a guard said.

"Sorry." Beatrice slipped off the stool; she thought she understood enough. Now that Marta was gone, she might push the situation a bit. She pretended to stretch, as though stiff, then rambled in Pritchard's direction. The two men guarding the Travelers exchanged a look, and one turned to watch her, but neither told her to stop; nor did Pritchard's guard. Pritchard watched her approach, and didn't comment.

He was much recovered from when the Assembly had vanished and his cunning had been jarred awake by the Judge's deception. With his attention still on Beatrice, he spoke to the Judge's wife in her own language; his tone was lazily sardonic. She smiled.

"I'm sorry," Beatrice said quietly. Her guards weren't close enough to overhear. They watched, but didn't listen. His guard didn't seem to care.

Pritchard gazed at her without expression.

Aware of Liada Acari, Beatrice pitched her voice only for Pritchard. "I'm sorry I ran away when you wanted to protect me, when the attack began. I was frightened."

"The Inlander's trick won't work twice," Pritchard said skeptically. "I don't believe you."

She may as well not have spoken. Then she saw a way to help both the Judge and herself. "You believed him because so much that he said was true. I'm telling the truth, too. We want to get away from these people. We'll help you."

Pritchard said nothing.

Beatrice sighed. They'd been sent to Earth to determine whether or not contact was biologically safe, and weren't trained in human politics. The human shelter was run casually, mostly by women. This was different. Men conducted these affairs, which had more to do with power than with breeding.

"If the Judge comes down, then take his gun from him." Pritchard was watching his feet, not Beatrice, as he spoke. The sound was barely audible. "Give it to me. I'll get you out."

Pritchard looked up. He smiled slyly. He knew exactly what he was asking. Betray the Judge, for him. The request was a fair one, after her offer, and possible. The Judge would let her approach closely enough that she might do it.

Did she need to pay so high a price for immediate access to the beacon? The Adjusters apparently did not know enough about the beacon to guess that a call to the Ship would shut the Assembly down. No one else seemed aware of the connection between the Assembly and the beacon. She could wait. What would Pritchard do with a gun, anyway? His hands were bound. If he managed to get free, he would have to shoot his way through the guards, up the ramp, and through the field in order to escape. His first shot might be at the Judge.

The doctor had left the Judge's son and was treating a clansmen wounded in the leg. They joked together. The boy seemed forgotten. Beatrice walked hesitantly closer. The doctor glanced at her. "Stay back. He needs to have his electrolytes and fluids monitored, but I can't do it here." He watched to be sure Beatrice went no closer, and in fact showed greater concern over that than he did for the boy, who lay sweating on the makeshift bed of the field operatory. His eyes were reddening as blood from the broken capillaries filled them. His nose had stopped bleeding, but dried blood caked his face. His mother watched from a slight distance. Periodically she spoke brief words of encouragement to him in their language. When Beatrice began a low, cheerful song, a true human song from Earth, the Judge's wife interrupted. "You did all this," she said. No expert at song could have put more hatred into four syllables.

Stefan saw Marta, looking grim, walking toward the aboveground clan headquarters. Uncertain whether John had told her about John Junior's death, he avoided her. It was cowardly, but he didn't know how to sympathize with a woman who'd done as much as anyone to kill her own son.

He went straight into the tunnel, then hesitated at the bottom of the ramp, looking for Tepan, finally spotting him on a folding table not far from the entrance. Liada and Beatrice were both nearby. So was Kaim Pritchard.

Beatrice's presence with Tepan made him uncomfortable. He only nodded at her. Liada was watching and it was their son who was ill. Besides, his new insight made him wonder what the Travelers were planning. According to Beatrice, calling their ship was the essence of their mission, yet they hadn't done it yet. Why? There were three sides in this, not two. Four, if he counted himself.

"How is Tepan?" he asked Liada in their own language, detaching Beatrice from the conversation.

Pritchard answered before Liada. "He'll be fine, Stefan." His use of Stefan's first name sounded like a calculated reproach. "The doctor says it's nothing. Fatigue and a bloody nose."

Relief and suspicion mixed equally in Stefan's mind. "Is that true?" he asked Liada.

She glanced at Pritchard, then came closer. "I wish it were." She extended her arms to him as though in need of his comfort.

"No!" Beatrice shouted. She made a noise Stefan didn't understand, but which raised his hackles. He turned on her, angry and astonished. "She'll take your gun," Beatrice said. "She's working with Pritchard. He asked me to do it, too."

Liada turned angrily to face Beatrice, then Stefan. The lanterns made her pale complexion ghostly; her eyes were dark. "I would never conspire with the nixt mirko against you."

The carbine was heavy on Stefan's shoulder. Liada couldn't have gotten it; Beatrice must be wrong. Both women were waiting, both were trying to make him choose between them, to judge whom he trusted. At that moment, he didn't care for either of them. He went to where Tepan lay. "Doctor?"

The doctor was a fleshy man whose tattoos had faded and spread with age; he left a patient to come to Stefan. He seemed respectful, perhaps because of the trust implied by Stefan's possession of a gun. "I'm not sure what it is," he said. "I have nothing here to use to treat him. I told your wife, he needs hospital monitoring, fluids, and rest. I'm a surgeon, not a medicant, but I did what I could."

He had done nothing. Tepan needed Dr. Felipe, who disdained surgeons. "Thank you."

"Stefan, he will be all right," Beatrice said. Her tone was sure, but he couldn't believe any reassurance. Tepan was feverish. His face was a flushed, unnatural red. Stefan scooped him up in his arms. "I'm taking him into Bowl," he announced. "Liada, come along." The Travelers had to be kept safe, especially Beatrice, and that was best done out of clan hands; he regretted adding that to the alleged garrison demand, and decided to ignore that he had done so. "Beatrice, you and your friends accompany me, too." He didn't wait to be sure they came, but walked for the ramp.

Just then, Marta started down. It was obvious, seeing her, that she knew her son was dead. She carried a rifle, which she hadn't done before.

They met at the base of the ramp. She nodded. "Stefan. Where are you going?"

She was ready for a fight, any fight. Stefan lowered his head slightly and spoke calmly, as a friend. "I'm taking my son to the hospital in town. He'll die if he isn't properly treated."

Her eyes went from Stefan to Tepan; they didn't relent. "No one leaves until we all do."

"I'm neutral, Marta." He'd almost said innocent, then he'd remembered the man he'd killed. "Let my son live."

His voice must have told her he knew about John Junior. She flinched. "No one is neutral. The Open Court gives legitimacy to the rest of the Assembly. You'll wait with us. Get back. Take a seat by your son until the doctor moves his patients out. It'll be soon."

He sensed Liada behind him, and Beatrice. He had intended to call Marta's bluff, but something about Marta Denning at that moment made him change his mind. "All right," he said instead, "but we'll wait outside, in the open air." The confines of the tunnel felt claustrophobic and, with Pritchard present, dangerous.

"Okay. You, your son, and your wife. Those four will stay." She pointed the rifle at the Travelers.

Stefan looked. Not only Beatrice, but the other three were behind him. He had told them to come and the guards had allowed it. The three Travelers were a separate cluster about four meters from Stefan, his family, and Beatrice. Marta thought the Travelers were alien invaders. She wanted to kill them, and Pritchard, and she'd placed them all in the tunnel. The shield device was there. The other one had been booby-trapped. Stefan suspected that the Lodge would not survive the attack, and neither would the tunnel. "Don't forget, Marta, they're part of the deal with the garrison."

Just then a low boom echoed down into the tunnel from above. It caused the tunnel lanterns to vibrate. "What was that?" Stefan asked. He couldn't see over the lip of the ramp.

Marta grinned. "Gas grenades."

A few scattered gunshots erupted, then stopped.

Marta listened with satisfaction. She nodded at the ensuing silence. "That building had too many rooms; they had to be gathered together in a few. Now they're asleep. It'll speed things up."

"Asleep?" he asked. "But they'd agreed to send your

people out." The negotiation had been a ruse to maneuver the agents into a setting where they could be gassed. He wished he'd had no part in it, and couldn't even claim that he'd suspected nothing. "Are you going to kill them?"

She looked away. "You're neutral, Stefan, remember? Go up if you want. When we leave, we'll bring you and your family with us. Pritchard's men and the Numericans are none of your business."

Tepan stirred. Stefan had a responsibility to him, but it couldn't be paramount to his responsibility to the Earth; that had to be Stefan's side in this. "Listen, Marta, the Travelers are important. I can't explain how, but you must not hurt them."

She remained impassive, but Pritchard got to his feet. His guard pushed him, but Pritchard allowed himself to be shoved slightly backward, against the wall and wasn't forced to sit down.

John Denning was coming; Stefan heard him moving through the clansmen positions with a politician's invariable grace, indulging in a smattering of his ready, and now congratulatory, banter, but he must be coming to be with Marta.

"Come, Stefan." Liada walked out from behind him and started up the ramp.

"Wait," he said. Liada stopped, and eyed Marta nervously; she stayed next to Stefan. "This has nothing to do with Beatrice herself," Stefan told Marta, but he was also speaking to Liada. "Let the Travelers come with me. It's extremely important." He wanted to keep her talking until John arrived. John was a voice of sanity in comparison with the rest.

"We did extensive tests," Marta said. "The nonverbal examinations are slow to correlate, but the results are powerful. Do you know what's on that ship, what her friends are? Nocturnal things that hunt humans."

"That isn't true!" Beatrice cried.

"She's not human. Forget her, Stefan."

"John," Stefan shouted as Denning appeared at the top of the ramp.

Denning hurried down. He put his arm around his wife, but there was no significant lessening of her fierceness or tension. "Let Stefan go," John said quietly.

"I already told him to go up. Him and his wife and his son. He wants to take the aliens, too. I won't let him."

John glanced back, probably at Beatrice, then shrugged slightly at Stefan as if he were helpless in the face of his wife's decision.

"Listen, John." Stefan turned his back slightly on Marta and lowered his voice. Pritchard was inching closer to the ramp, trying to hear. "The Travelers are important. Why else has the Assembly coddled them? If you hurt them, you'll be harming all of Earth."

"If you know something, then tell us," Marta said. "Otherwise it's none of your business. I'm sorry you care for the girl, but she stays here."

"John, trust me on this." He couldn't say more without Pritchard hearing too much. Pritchard had been inside his mind. He knew what Beatrice had said in the cave, when the Assembly was gone. He might have made his own conjectures. The Adjusters could suspect something; Stefan was glad Pritchard was out of contact with them.

"Trust *us*," John said. "There isn't time to indulge you."

Beatrice hummed something cautionary, a warning he felt in his bones, but if he didn't speak, the Travelers could die. The Travelers didn't really grasp the rancor their introduction of disease aroused. "If they call the Ship, John, then it terminates a beacon they placed on Earth a few centuries ago—when they were here before." He could not say the word *Assembly* with Pritchard listening. "You see, don't you, that if their goal was invasion, they could have done it then. They didn't."

"That's your theory," Marta interrupted. "Not mine."

"You miss the point." Stefan hesitated and looked at Kaim Pritchard, worried that he had already said too much in Pritchard's hearing, though it hadn't been enough for the Dennings. Pritchard's arms were behind his back, but the angle was wrong. "Check Pritchard,"

Stefan said. "He's trying to free himself. And come up with me. I'll explain there." He started up the ramp.

Pritchard vaulted forward, crashing into his guard. Stefan turned back. Pritchard was using his legs, while pulling his arms free of the rope. The guard went down. Pritchard stooped as though to check on him just as one of the Travelers' guards raised his rifle and fired. The shot missed. Pritchard came up holding his downed guard's gun. He shot the two men who had been guarding the Travelers. Both went down, though one of them was alive; he was writhing and making a high-pitched whining sound.

Marta raised her weapon. She shot, but Pritchard was already moving and her aim was poor. She didn't hit him. He raked the doctor's area with random shots. The doctor and his patients dove to the ground. Pritchard didn't hit any of them. He turned to the Travelers.

Kaim Pritchard had not missed the point. He was acting to save the Assembly without first consulting the Adjusters.

"No!" Stefan shouted. His arms were encumbered by Tepan. He couldn't reach for his carbine. Marta hesitated. John was no longer armed. Stefan thrust Tepan at Liada. She grabbed him automatically, holding him too low, head down. He cried out. Beatrice ran back toward her friends, screaming.

Pritchard shot the three Travelers farthest from Stefan. These shots were different from his others, aimed, precise and accurate, but nearly as rapid as had been his automatic-mode firing. The three Travelers fell silently. Pritchard hesitated, and rather than shoot Beatrice, he turned his barrel to point up, at Stefan and the Dennings.

"Three is as good as four, isn't it, Inlander?" Pritchard said. He seemed exhilarated. "I'm afraid though, that you'll win our contest since I've shot her friends."

Pritchard's gun was loaded with heavy bullets. They had ripped into the Travelers and his other victims, opened their insides wide and scattered bits of raw organs throughout the bottom of the ramp.

Beatrice wailed. Her horrible, grieving noises were as alien as they were human. The tunnel had the stench of a butcher shop, a mix of offal and raw meat. Pritchard's attention wavered for a moment as he glanced at her.

Stefan raised his gun, then Pritchard ran, this time sideways, to where the doctor's post had been. With that one move he was able to cover them all with his gun. John Denning was closest. Marta gasped and didn't shoot. Stefan stepped back, and up the ramp, to get a sight on Pritchard.

"It doesn't matter now," Pritchard said. "The Assembly is safe. This little group of conspirators is doomed, whatever happens to me." As he spoke, he came closer.

Stefan brought his gun up and shot at Pritchard. He hadn't aimed—there wasn't time—but he had expected to track Pritchard's movement and shoot again. He didn't get the chance. After his first shot, the gun jammed. One shot and he'd missed. Pritchard had been lucky in his choice of borrowed weapon; Stefan hadn't.

Pritchard vaulted forward like an acrobat. Wrestlers weren't supposed to be so graceful. He landed near Marta, and kicked up. Her rifle flew out of her hands.

Liada screamed and ran up the ramp, lugging Tepan. Beatrice's keening never wavered.

John Denning ran forward to tackle Pritchard, but Pritchard evaded him, then shot at John. Marta shrieked. She ran to John. Two clansmen rushed down the ramp. Pritchard ran at them. Unbalanced by the incline, the first was an easy target for one of Pritchard's kicks, then he was past the second and above them on the ramp. He ran away, out of sight over the edge of the ramp.

"John," Marta was screaming. "John."

Beatrice's wailing hadn't stopped. Liada was out of sight but Tepan's crying sounded near. More clansmen were coming, shouting questions.

Stefan threw down his useless carbine and chased up the ramp, after Pritchard. By the time he reached the top, Pritchard had vanished. Stefan stood motionless, surveying, trying to decide where Pritchard would have gone. The moon was out. The clans were using lanterns now that the garrison was subdued. Strange, elongated shadows moved, but Stefan searched in vain for the figure of a fleeing man. Everyone he saw was running toward him. Kaim Pritchard had escaped.

John Denning struggled up the ramp to Stefan. "Get out of here," he said as he waved a clansman away. Blood ran from his right leg, but the wound didn't look serious. "Marta's going for the switch. We have five minutes to evacuate, and then the entire hilltop explodes. It's going to be big. Pritchard's on foot. It's the last chance to kill him." He hobbled away. Over his shoulder he shouted, "Hurry!"

Chapter 14

Beatrice's lament filled the underground and rose up, out into the night, but it would never reach the Ship. Its lonely sound prefigured the solitary future of human life. Of her life. The decision was irrevocable; the call could not be made. Earth would live alone, a spinster world, warning off potential suitors with its mournful beacon. She lamented that. She cried out for her murdered friends. She mourned Eyni, whose death would not only be the first death of a Friend lamented in song on Earth, it would also be the last.

Marta Denning slapped Beatrice. "Stop that caterwauling. Help the doctor get his patients aboveground, or we'll leave you behind. Probably should anyway."

Startled from the light trance that was integral to a lament, Beatrice blinked and faced Marta Denning's unreasonable antagonism with dignity. "The dead need a cloak."

"The living need a hand," Marta answered. "This place explodes five minutes after I start the countdown, and I'm doing that now."

In her grief, Beatrice hadn't noticed what occurred after Kaim Pritchard murdered her friends. The Ship moved for the Friends' reasons, but each other species made its own journey. The human one had ended before it rightly began. There would be no synergy, no chance of new companions. There still was life, however, and so she went to the doctor. Two men were carrying the last stretcher, with a wounded man, out of the tunnel. The doctor handed her a rolling cart loaded with boxes.

"Forget the supplies!" Marta called from farther down

the tunnel. "If you're done with the men, then get up. There's five minutes. I've set it."

The doctor frowned as he gazed around his makeshift surgery. No wounded remained on any of the frame tables. The doctor nodded and trudged up the ramp, with his hands clasped behind his back. Only his long gait showed any hurry. Beatrice dropped the handle of the cart. It rolled downhill, then stopped. She followed the doctor. He strode off toward a waiting truck, but she hesitated, wondering if she should leave with these people. If she stayed, she'd die. For the first time she grasped the clansmen intentions. Men were running and shouting, frantic to depart, but there were others who were motionless. Gas grenades, someone had said. Clansmen were hauling inert bodies from the garrison and dragging them onto trucks, but she was sure they concentrated their efforts on their own people. Violent death was selective, a matter of tribal boundaries. The Assembly was a false remedy for human insularity.

Earth had become her real and future life. Welcome home. She couldn't hear the beacon crying, but after the explosion she would forever more.

"Beatrice!" It was the Judge. She spotted him near a small coach, waving and beckoning her. "Come on! We have to go." When she didn't come, he ran toward her.

To the side of the ramp lay the dead bodies of her fellow Travelers. The Fox had met his lion; it was another man. She remembered the fiery explosion in the other cavern and almost craved the peace of death, as Eyni had, near the end.

The Judge grabbed her. "Thank God," he said. "Beatrice, mourning them can come later. We have to get away!"

His touch awakened her. There still might be good in life. She ran beside him to his vehicle. His proud wife was visible through the window, sitting stiffly upright in the back, not looking for the Judge, only waiting. She would have betrayed him; Beatrice was certain. The coach had a nearly triangular shape, so it was roomy in that one rear compartment—they wouldn't have to sit too close—and very plush, a car for a wealthy family. Pritchard had sometimes used it. There was a detachable driving meca; it was missing. Pritchard liked to drive.

"Get in," the Judge ordered her. She slid in next to his wife. He yanked open the door to the driver's compartment. The motor was already running.

"Just in the nick of time," Pritchard said from the front. "I was thinking I'd have to drive this myself, up where they'd see me. Get us moving, Inlander."

Pritchard crouched in the cramped storage area beside the driver's seat, positioned so his rifle was aimed at Stefan and he was out of sight. "Drive," he said. "And remember, I'd just as soon shoot, Inlander."

Stefan was "Inlander" again. He was lucky Pritchard hadn't immediately shot him. To a man of Pritchard's narrow vision, Stefan deserved it for betraying Pritchard to the clans, despite the fact that minutes earlier Pritchard had ordered a man to kill Stefan. Stefan heard the click as Pritchard took the safety off. Stupid. He'd only cause the subcoach to crash, but Pritchard supposed the gun would intimidate Stefan; that was how he thought.

Stefan pushed the power lever. The subcoach jerked, then sped forward toward the road. "Where do you want me to take you?" His own composure surprised him.

"Just go! Faster! Get out from their shield."

Two trucks, racing side by side down the Lodge driveway, were behind them. They'd overrun the subcoach, or force him off the road, if he didn't increase his speed. Stefan pushed the lever farther. The subcoach seemed to hesitate, then to leap into the air before accelerating into breakneck motion. Stefan turned sharply. Pritchard yelled for him to slow down. The rifle flew from Pritchard's grasp, going sideways, away from him, and up over the plastic barrier between the front and rear compartments. Pritchard grabbed for it but was too late; it was gone, lost in the rear compartment. Stefan jerked the subcoach again, out of the path of the trucks. He watched through the compartment mirror-monitor as Tepan crashed to the floor and cried out, awakening in fear. Liada shouted angrily and bent forward to help Tepan, banging her head cruelly on the compartment divider. Beatrice grimaced and clung to the armrest. Next to Stefan, cramped in his movements by the storage chest, Pritchard clung to its edge.

How far would the clans' explosion reach? Would it cover a larger or a lesser area than their shield device? When the explosion came, or they drove outside the free zone, Pritchard would contact the Adjusters. If Pritchard were dead ... Stefan stopped that thought. He would not kill again. *Ever?* He wondered.

The clans knew what they were doing. Those trucks had a plan. He slowed and let his subcoach be passed.

"Damn you, Inlander! Get out from their shield!" Without his rifle, Pritchard couldn't enforce his demand.

The trucks barreled past. Stefan pushed power in again but went slowly. The long drive finally ended. How far did the shield extend?

The trucks turned left on the main road, away from Bowl. Stefan followed. He thought he understood. A hill stood between them and the Lodge, a kind of earthen work against the explosion.

Lights of another truck approached from behind, and were quickly closing the gap between them.

Pritchard was probably continuously trying to connect with the Assembly. Stefan let the other truck gain on them.

It felt like hours had passed in the subcoach. How long until the blast freed Pritchard to contact the Assembly? He wouldn't kill Pritchard, but if Stefan rendered him unconscious, they'd have more time.

Flinching even as he did so, Stefan increased speed to the maximum and yanked the steering lever sideways, running the subcoach off the road, moving it back closer to the Lodge. The tires crunched first gravel, then the underbrush, which slowed their passage only slightly. Trees came up fast. A startled deer darted away. Stefan concentrated on avoiding a collision. He steered the subcoach between two looming oaks. A small tree trunk scraped across the subcoach's right side. The lights on the truck that had been behind swept over them, paused, then continued past.

Abruptly, the subcoach lurched and stopped, caught in a gully too deep for its wheels to climb. The interruption of their movement threw Stefan and the others forward, then back. Beatrice tumbled off the seat, on top of Tepan; both cried out in alarm. Pritchard yelled a Ropan obscenity, but Stefan smiled. He raised his head. His neck ached. He forced open his door. Pritchard's anger meant he had not yet connected with the Assembly. Stefan jumped out of the coach.

"Damn you, Inlander!" Pritchard was already climbing out of the front compartment, chasing after Stefan.

Stefan yanked the rear subcoach door open to search for the rifle. The subcoach lit with a courtesy light that seemed too bright in the dark woods. He saw the gun. It was loose on the floor, in the middle, but nearest Liada. "Get it!" he yelled, reaching inside the coach.

Beatrice righted herself. Tepan screamed as if he were wounded. Blood poured from his nose.

Liada gaped at Stefan as if she didn't know him, then she realized what Stefan wanted and grabbed for the gun. Her fingers closed on it.

Beatrice called out a warning, not in human language but her own sounds. Stefan understood. Pritchard was outside and coming. Pritchard kicked, but for once he didn't connect. His boot thudded hard against the fiberglass subcoach with a dull sound; it must have hurt. Stefan had lurched out of his way and fallen into the subcoach, onto Liada. She wriggled, attempting to free herself.

Stefan tried to get out of the compartment but Pritchard pushed him down, among Tepan and the women's legs. Then Pritchard slammed the compartment door, crushing it against Stefan's left leg. Stefan reached for the gun, hoping to turn and stop Pritchard, but Liada held onto it. "Shoot!" he yelled instead.

Beatrice, meanwhile, pushed open the opposite door of the rear compartment. Stefan's legs were caught. He couldn't even climb off his crying son. Stefan could only watch Beatrice—he met her eyes—as she slipped out of the subcoach and with a troubled backward look, ran away into the dark woods.

Pritchard wrenched open the door, freeing Stefan's legs. He grabbed both legs and dragged Stefan out of the coach. Stefan's head banged against the door frame. He couldn't move his left leg. "You stupid fool," Pritchard said. "You keep trying to fight me, but no matter how much confidence you picked up from my mind, you don't have my training or my talent."

"There's nothing of you in me!"

"No?" Pritchard stooped, made a fist, and rather casually punched Stefan. Stefan barely felt it.

Liada shrieked. Tepan cried out for his father. Dazed, Stefan didn't see what happened next, but Liada must have realized that she held the gun a moment before Pritchard also did. Randomly, wildly, she fired it. So close to Stefan's ears, the sound was deafening. The interior light in the coach went out. The plastic barrier between the front and rear compartments shattered like shrapnel. A piece grazed Stefan's head. It did nothing to Pritchard.

Pritchard planted a foot in Stefan's midsection as he stretched to reach Liada and the rifle. The foot twisted as he turned. Stefan rolled instinctively, as much to help himself as Liada, but Pritchard's balance was good. He didn't topple.

The sky in the direction of the Lodge lit up as though struck by lightning. A half second later the sound of the detonation hit them, a tidal wave of noise in which nothing else was audible. The sound of Liada's gunshots disappeared.

Pritchard came off Stefan. He glanced down, then seemed to discount him as a factor. The rifle was firmly in Pritchard's two hands, but Stefan didn't know what he had done to get it. The noise faded. Pritchard stood still, just a step away from Stefan, grinning as if he expected something wonderful to reach out to him.

It did. Pritchard grunted like a self-satisfied boy after

his first orgasm. It had become too late to stop him from connecting with the Assembly.

In the aftermath of the explosion, the woods were still. Tepan and Liada were quiet. Pritchard kept some attention on Stefan, but did nothing as Stefan inched his way to a sitting position with his back against the side of the subcoach. "Liada?"

She didn't answer. He imagined her terror. These events must be a mystery to her. He placed a hand on the edge of the door frame and lifted himself onto its ledge. Pain in his left leg brought tears to his eyes. He bent forward—his gut hurt as he did, no doubt bruised by Pritchard—and felt along the length of the leg. No bones protruded, so he supposed nothing was broken. "Liada?" he said again.

"She isn't worth having, is she, Inlander?" Pritchard said. "Pretty, but not someone like us." His legs were spread in a triumphant posture, and he held the rifle loosely in his hands.

"Count me different from you, Pritchard." Stefan ached as he twisted to look inside the subcoach. The sky in the direction of the Lodge was bright enough to light it. Liada slumped across the seat. Tepan was partly on the seat and partly on the floor. Neither was in a comfortable position. "Liada? Tepan?" Stefan touched Liada, the closer of the two. Her body was warm. There was a pulse in her arm. "Thank God," he said.

"Did you think I'd killed them?" Pritchard laughed. He was ebullient, doubtless an effect of his return to the Assembly. "They're your family, and too important for easy solutions like that."

"You're going to kill us all anyway."

Pritchard shook his head. "You always underestimate yourself, Inlander. You still have uses, and I'd be sorry to lose you just when we've become so . . . intimate. But I'll kill you if I have to, and the boy will die if he isn't treated soon. Give me your word, your personal pledge, that you won't make more trouble for me and that you'll help me get away from any wildmen we meet. If you do, then I'll have the new ID team bring a physician for Tepan. Perhaps Dr. Felipe. A good doctor, as we both know."

Pritchard was entirely himself again, a self that depended on the Assembly, and he knew precisely how best to persuade Stefan.

"I understand your hesitation." Pritchard used the rifle to indicate Liada. "I've been inside your mind. We're two sides of the same man, and we're neither of us comfortable surrendering. But get used to it, Inlander. I own you, or you and your son are dead. Make the pledge." One-handed, as he continued to hold the rifle trained on Stefan, Pritchard fished the Acari estate ring from his pocket. "Swear on this; then your son will get medical treatment, and you'll live. If not, all three of you are dead because I don't have the time to watch my back. Decide."

Kaim Pritchard would do it. People were convenient or inconvenient to him. "All right. You have my word, the pledge of Acari, that I'll help you escape any clansmen we meet. Nothing else, and only if you send medical help for Tepan."

"Accepted." Pritchard placed the Acari estate ring on his little finger, but his fingers were much thicker than Stefan's and even there, it did not slide all the way down. He extended his hand. "Kiss it."

Only a tenant pledging fealty need kiss his Inlander's ring. Pritchard expected Stefan to protest, but whatever satisfaction Pritchard received from the perceived humiliation of the ceremony was worth Tepan's survival. Stefan leaned forward, inadvertently groaning as his bruised gut hurt, and kissed his own ring.

Pritchard pointed the rifle at Stefan's head. The barrel seemed huge. Pritchard grinned happily. Stefan refused to cower or beg. Pritchard pulled the trigger. It clicked.

Nothing happened.

"Empty," Pritchard said. He chuckled. "She used it up. Stupid woman. I don't have ammunition to reload. Of course, I could have killed you with my hands."

"Of course." Repelled by Pritchard's easiness with violence, Stefan remembered his own death count. Two men, since the second must have died in the explosion. Two lives. *There is no residue of Kaim Pritchard left in me,* he told himself. *What I did was necessary.*

There wasn't much wind in the forest, but smoke from the burning Hilltop Lodge was drifting into the sky and toward them. It was visible above the glow of the fire, a dirty cloud against the night. The frogs, the owls, and other night creatures gradually resumed their croaks and screeching. Pritchard was deeply connected inside the Assembly, Stefan supposed, since he had become motionless and silent.

Stefan used his arms to raise himself to the point where he might have stood, but the slight weight he placed on the leg hurt. He didn't do more. Pritchard observed him a moment, then returned to his Assembly proceeding.

Stefan glanced once in the direction into which Beatrice had vanished, grateful Pritchard seemed to have forgotten her. Her ship would depart the Solar System after whatever scheduled time her friends aboard decided was enough, the beacon secure, its warning unbroken. The beacon was a lighthouse warning ships away from dangerous shores; it was an alarm, not an invitation. It also warned strangers of the kind of race that had been found. Earth housed a people who had created a despotism from an alarm.

"Get up. Let's go, before someone comes." Pritchard leaned across Stefan to peer into the subcoach. "They're fine," he said.

Stefan didn't move.

"Well? Is your leg broken? I'm not going to examine it myself, Inlander. You're no challenge, but I don't feel like tumbling around in the woods with you."

"I'm not sure." Stefan was tired. He wanted only to sit and wait for Tepan's doctor to arrive.

Pritchard sighed heavily, and knelt on Stefan's left. "I warn you, Inlander. No games." Pritchard examined his leg with expert, practiced hands. "Probably a fracture. Not a bad one. I'll make a splint, and you can walk."

"Where?"

"You gave me your pledge to help me through the clansmen. We're walking out of here, parallel to the road. You'll do exactly as I tell you." Pritchard had gotten up and was walking about in the vicinity of the subcoach, studying the ground.

Stefan looked into the rear of the subcoach again. Neither Liada nor Tepan had stirred, but he balanced on his right leg and lifted Tepan to a more comfortable position. The boy whimpered at his touch, but didn't awaken. His skin was slick with perspiration. "After the doctor."

Pritchard paused in his search. "We're leaving. The doctor won't arrive for three hours. Every agent in the area was at the Lodge."

Three hours was much too long for Tepan. Pritchard had tricked him. "Bowl is just down the road, Pritchard. The doctor can be here in fifteen minutes, if you call."

"That would warn the locals that I'm alive." Pritchard returned. He kicked the subcoach's open door. "Damn, do you know how hard it is to find something rigid enough to make a splint in a dark forest? I shouldn't have been so rough with you." He was cheerful.

"I'm not going anywhere if there won't be help for my son."

"There's help, but it's on my timetable. The boy will be fine. Beatrice said so."

"No." Stefan wondered just how far Pritchard could be pushed. What value did he place on Stefan Acari?

Pritchard shrugged. "All right. As soon as we're far enough away, I'll send an anonymous accident report; someone will investigate. I'm traceless; I can do it. Satisfied?"

"Yes." He had a high value, apparently. Why? Pritchard seemed confident, yet he couldn't be too popular with the Adjusters after the fiasco at the Lodge. His replacement might already be on his way.

Pritchard, after grumbling over the difficulty to which Stefan had put him, found a broken branch that was sufficiently strong and straight. He tied it to Stefan's leg with straps from the storage chest in the subcoach. He worked methodically enough to appear competent. It hurt when Stefan stood, but he could stand, and with a bit of practice walking stiff-legged, he could hobble.

"Let's go," Pritchard said. "Beatrice went this way, too." He pointed toward the road.

He'd remembered Beatrice after all. "You said you'd get emergency help for Tepan." Stefan strained, but for him, the Assembly was as absent as it had been at the Lodge. He would be unable to verify that Pritchard did as he promised.

"I will. Come on." Pritchard carried the rifle, though it was empty. He looked at Stefan, then came back, and helped him start to walk by supporting his left side.

"The Assembly is doomed, Pritchard." Stefan spoke to keep his mind off the pain. It took willpower to place weight upon his leg. Each step felt like the bone was a knife pressing into his flesh, and burning. He wanted to hop, but the uneven ground and the dark wouldn't allow it. "There are miles of woods and caves. They have friends in town. They'll escape, then too many people will know it's possible to make shields against the Assembly. Eventually this group, or some other, will bring the Assembly down. The Adjusters will have killed it."

"Is that what you want, Inlander? It won't happen. The only real threat to the Assembly was the ship and the Travelers. I think the Adjusters knew about the Assembly's origin; that made them afraid. But now, the Assembly is safe. The ship won't return for generations, if ever. Would you really want it to?" Pritchard sounded congenial and curious, a product of his pleasure at reunion with the Assembly. "Without the Assembly there would be nothing to prevent the rich and strong from taking whatever they want."

"Like you do?" Stefan asked.

Pritchard laughed. "I only do what has to be done."

"There would be laws and government. There were, before the Great Deaths."

"We do better now." Pritchard was right. Before the Deaths, history had been a catalog of wars and empires.

"I've been in your mind, Pritchard. You're not sincere."

"Do I need to be sincere, Inlander, in order to make the Assembly virtuous in your eyes? I'm a tool. That's all. I don't need to care about the worms in order to act on their behalf. I'll do the dirty work and leave morality to you." He stopped, and since Stefan was leaning on him, Stefan also stopped. "You need a cane. I won't carry you to Bowl."

Pritchard walked off, leaving Stefan effectively stranded as he searched the area for a suitable staff.

The road wasn't far. Stefan saw several trucks pass, heading in the direction of Bowl. He looked up. Through the leafy branches, stars were visible. The moon was bright. Somewhere out there was Beatrice's ship, waiting for the warning to stop so they could visit.

Pritchard returned with a heavy stick. "This will do," he said. "Lean on it."

"A tyranny can be comfortable and safe," Stefan said. "It can appear good, but it's not freedom. We should be able to meet new friends from the stars."

"Whatever you say, Inlander. As for me, I just wanted to get out of Zona. Though school was no better."

They didn't speak for a while. What did Stefan want? To make the world better? It sounded romantic and naive. Without the Assembly, there would be chaos. The makeshift cane was awkward on the even ground. Stefan started counting his steps, anticipating the pain each time he put his left leg down, feeling the way with the stick so he wouldn't slip in a depression in the ground. "Romaric said you used the Assembly to cheat on exams."

Pritchard chuckled, but made no other response.

Stefan waited for a footfall on his right leg. "Did you?"

"Would you believe me if I said no? No one else did. They assumed anyone from Zona was unfit. And don't bother to ask about the girl—I saw Ezio's slander when you dumped into my mind. Think whatever you want; I don't care."

"That's a lie, anyway." Pritchard had learned more

from Stefan when their minds were joined, but Stefan did know that Pritchard had, and still did, yearn for approval, not precisely from Stefan but from what he represented to a man who'd escaped Zona only to discover he never could.

"You're just like me," Pritchard said. "You think of other people as worms, too. Remember? You *play God*?" Stefan had struck a nerve in Pritchard. "The only difference between us is that you lie to yourself and pretend you care about them."

"How can anyone who spends as much time as you inside the Assembly lack all empathy? John Denning is right; so was Romaric. The Assembly is a vice for you and me; the Adjusters use it to poison the world. Eventually, Denning will bring it down."

"John Denning is nothing." Pritchard stopped. He waved a hand, indicating the road and the way into Bowl. "We *gave* his clan the shield. Independent Defense did. We wanted them to use it on the Travelers. The only surprise was that they'd made a second one."

Pritchard wasn't lying. It explained why he hadn't expected a shielded attack from the clans. Even the battle the clans had won had been rigged by the Assembly. Stefan limped on, as Pritchard directed him, without continuing the conversation.

Tree branches caught at Beatrice's dress; the uneven ground tried to trip her, and she felt the lumpy forest floor through her thin-soled shoes. It was much worse than walking the path. The place reeked of damp decay, wild creatures, and malodorous plants she would never identify. Stray, screeching sounds startled her. She felt clumsy and frightened and knew there was no comfort in any direction.

Her friends were dead. The Ship was far away. It hadn't been disease that prevented the call, unless violent behavior was an illness. Perhaps it was. The tattooed men and Pritchard contrived gleefully to kill everyone in their paths. The Judge was the only person she trusted, but he was a captive of Pritchard, who had already murdered her friends.

Three is as good as four, Pritchard had said. He thought he had saved the Assembly. He was probably right. She couldn't make the call alone. Two healthy, sane adults who could use song were needed; only one Traveler was left.

The mission protocols claimed none of the Hosts could do it. Beatrice hoped the protocols were wrong.

Song was the foundation of the Assembly's grammar. Generations of humans on Earth had been selected naturally for the ability to work within the Assembly, as on the Ship her ancestors had been gently selected for facility with song. Time and the widening applications of the Assembly had favored those who inclined to a better grasp of the Assembly's primitive quasi-song. An Assembly adept might be capable of making the call. Most would not do it, if they understood what was being done. The Judge might be an exception.

After she ran from the crash, when Pritchard didn't chase her, Beatrice had stayed nearby. She listened as they argued. Though she couldn't hear their words, what she could hear displayed their different philosophies of life. The Judge spoke with passion, trying to make contact with Kaim Pritchard on the level of his emotions as well as his mind; Pritchard spoke to get what he wanted done, enjoying his power.

She only saw that the Judge was hurt when they left the wreck. She was able to follow in silence, despite the unfamiliar forest, because of their slowness. She stayed as far away as she dared without the risk of losing them.

There was elegance in her solution. Ever since she had met him, Beatrice had wanted the Judge's approval of the Travelers' mission, and endorsement of the Friends' purpose in contacting Earth. If he agreed to call the Ship, she would have it. A call made under such circumstances, one Traveler and one Host, felt intuitively good. She trusted him. If he refused to try, then maybe the call had never been right. He would be the judge.

If it was possible to do it, she would see the Ship again. After trading, after taking on passengers and disembarkation of some Friends, after the thrill of a second contact had passed and the Ship left the Solar System, she could be on it. So could the Judge.

Beatrice told herself to stop daydreaming. Even if the Judge wouldn't or couldn't call, he was the only person alive on Earth whom she cared about. She watched over Stefan as Pritchard bullied him. She heard pain in his voice and wished she could help, but knew she couldn't free him from Pritchard and didn't try. Something would turn up.

They nearly reached the road, then they stopped. Their argument was in low tones that didn't carry.

The Judge called her name a few times, but his voice told her not to answer. She didn't. They waited, then started walking again, following the road, but not on it, though it made travel more difficult for the Judge. They walked in the direction of Bowl, but at this rate, they wouldn't arrive until midday.

She knew where they were going, and could afford to let them get farther ahead. Beatrice crouched among the trees and bushes, resting, and reached out for the beacon. She felt it, a bit of song and a lament for home. There was no euphoria. There was no joy in the beacon; just the opposite. Her feet firmly on the ground, Beatrice felt weightless, but not light. The song was a wail. She accepted it. The lament for Earth washed over her, the only lament she could give her own dead.

Pritchard kept his word to Stefan. After they had paralleled the road about a kilometer, a yellow emergency vehicle came searching and found the gash in the foliage where the subcoach had sped into the woods. Then the road curved and Stefan was no longer able to see them, but Tepan and Liada must have been brought into town; the vehicle had passed Stefan and Pritchard at top speed, heading back with its lights flashing. They hadn't stayed to search for the subcoach's missing driver. Either Pritchard had managed to deflect them, or these locals were unwilling to look for outlaw survivors of the Lodge's mysterious explosion.

"What will happen to me when ID comes?" Stefan asked.

Pritchard helped him over a fallen tree trunk. The jolt of pain at every left footfall had settled into an unpleasant but tolerable routine. "I'll argue," Pritchard said, "as I already have, that you're easily controlled, because of your son. You won't be killed. You're too well known, and there will be no one to corroborate your story once we catch the clan leaders. You'll still be Inlander of Acari." He removed the Acari estate ring from his finger and handed it to Stefan. "Here. This isn't mine."

Stefan didn't believe Pritchard's sudden, if rudimentary, empathy and was suspicious of the gloom that had replaced Pritchard's earlier euphoria. Stefan stopped as he twisted the ring onto his finger, with the *ad hoc* cane balanced against his leg. There had to be an advantage to Pritchard; that was how this man survived. Then Stefan understood. "As long as I'm alive, the Adjusters need you alive, too," Stefan said. "Otherwise I could dump into the Assembly faster than they could stop me. You must be in deep trouble, Pritchard." He had to have been bluffing when he threatened to kill Stefan.

Pritchard didn't answer for a long time. He continued to make the way easier for Stefan as they resumed walking, even occasionally helping him over an obstacle, always without any sense that he was doing it for a person, rather than a plan. "I should have killed Beatrice," Pritchard eventually said. "It isn't necessary, but it would have been safer. They know my reasons. I'm not traceless to them. It was a lapse of judgment, they say. Disloyal."

Pritchard felt some murky, bottled-up emotion for Beatrice that had caused him to spare her life; the Adjusters were angry because he was human. Stefan didn't know whether Pritchard's current malaise resulted from his need to kill Beatrice after all, once she was found, or from the fact that he was in disgrace for failing to do so earlier. In any event, Stefan was very grateful that Beatrice hadn't responded to his desultory calls.

Stefan chose his words carefully. He knew Pritchard's deep fears from their mutual mental infiltration. "I've been inside your mind. I know you're not just an adjunct of the Assembly, a dummy that the Adjusters use and program." It was an image stolen from Pritchard's fears. "Let her go. She's helpless. She can't call her ship. If you kill her, it's totally unjustified by a need to protect the Assembly. I'm not a Judge of the Open Court anymore, but I still know when something is wrong. Don't do it. If the Adjusters order the death of innocents, then there is no justice at all in the Assembly." Justice wasn't an important concern of Pritchard's. "The Adjusters are wrong." Neither was morality of interest to him. Stefan searched for a way to reach him, knowing that whatever he said, he had to be sincere. Kaim Pritchard knew him more intimately than from a dump; he'd lived inside Stefan's mind. Stefan looked down at the ring Pritchard had given back. "Save her life—reason with the Adjusters— and it's a new start between us, without Zona, Acari, or school. Do it and you'll have my respect."

It sounded pretentious and had probably been futile. Stefan waited for a sarcastic sneer from Pritchard, but Pritchard was quiet. Stefan feared saying too much, so they continued in silence.

Beatrice was out there. The area had small, scattered villages. Some were dependencies of Bowl while others were homes of outlaw or subsistence farmers, the outliers of the Assembly system, much more common in the two Sister continents than elsewhere. There might be a refuge for Beatrice in the hills, if Pritchard didn't track her, though the likelihood of a clanless fugitive finding sanctuary was remote.

A truck was approaching. The sound was impossible to miss amidst the woodsy silence, but there were no headlights. As it neared, they saw that it was shining lights into the forest margins. "Get down," Pritchard said. Simultaneously, he pulled Stefan into the off-road swale they'd been following. Stefan's leg twisted; he lost his cane. He yelped involuntarily. The truck was too far away to hear him. Pritchard's hands were at his neck. Those hands were efficient weapons. "Don't move," Pritchard whispered.

So close, the last traces of Pritchard's cologne were discernible even through the crushed foliage odor of the ditch. It was a scent that Romaric sometimes had used.

A stranger on the truck was calling Stefan's name. They knew about the crashed coach, and suspected he'd survived. Denning must have sent them.

The truck passed them slowly, still calling. Once it was out of earshot, Pritchard released his grip, but didn't help Stefan up, and didn't get up himself. "They'll be back," he said.

"They think you're dead," Stefan whispered. "They aren't searching for you, only for me. Marta wanted me to make a dump. She thinks I'll be more convincing than clansmen."

"She's right. That's why if I'm in any danger, you die first."

They lay side by side in the ditch. Boredom and tension were an odd combination, but Stefan felt both. The pain from his leg came in surges. His gut, where Pritchard had stepped on him, was a constant dull ache.

The rumble of the returning truck could be heard earlier with their ears so close to the ground. Stefan shifted position slightly.

"Don't even think about it," Pritchard said.

The truck came closer while Stefan considered how he could attract its notice without being killed by Pritchard. He leaned closer to Pritchard. Several times he had attacked this man, always without success. If Stefan chose, seriously, to kill him now, would he be physically able to do it? Was he morally able? Since he was not, could he simply get away? "I'll keep my pledge," Stefan said. "If they have me and not you, then I'm useless to them." Stefan knew the answer to that: if he was useless, it was only because Pritchard was alive. They'd search the woods much harder.

"Shh."

The truck was very close, when suddenly it stopped. Since it was behind them, Stefan couldn't see the cause. The clansmen were no longer calling his name, yet he heard voices. Beside him, Pritchard edged forward, trying to see. Stefan squirmed in his way, to prevent it. There were several reasons why the truck might have stopped; the most likely was that they'd found Beatrice.

Chapter 15

"Run," Stefan whispered to Pritchard. The clansmen were searching the roadside for them. They called to each other—three voices—and to Beatrice. "A bit farther," Stefan heard her say. "Be careful. He has a gun."

Wind ruffled the trees overhanging their position in the ditch; the air smelled of ethanol from the truck engine, which the clansmen had kept running. Stefan was sure they would be discovered, but Kaim Pritchard didn't move. He didn't even threaten Stefan, as if he believed in the sincerity of Stefan's pledge, though it was unlike Pritchard to trust anyone. If Stefan stayed quiet, then when they were found, Pritchard might kill these men, while if Stefan startled them while they were at a distance, Pritchard could escape without killing. Stefan's pledge didn't require him to help Pritchard commit murder.

He started to roll away from Pritchard, but Pritchard grabbed him immediately and forced him back. They were face to face and eye to eye. Stefan might have shouted for help, but he didn't.

Pritchard stared as though eyesight could enable him to read Stefan's mind. Stefan stared back, trying to remember Pritchard well enough to penetrate his plan. Perhaps ID agents were nearby; it felt as though more than Pritchard's three hours had passed. Unconsciously, Stefan struggled to connect, as though Pritchard and the Assembly were one and the same.

They weren't. Pritchard allowed himself to be a puppet of the Adjusters. He gave himself away, he wasn't taken. Stefan remembered their forced mental connection, before Marta ended it, as a filthy thing, yet they had actually coexisted in relative peace, their responses to events not so opposite as either of them might have perceived at the time. It had been the intrusive connection itself, not Pritchard specifically, which had infuriated Stefan. Pritchard's emotions and the tenor of Pritchard's thoughts had been sardonic, full of anger laced with contempt for everyone, including himself. His justification for his life had been similar to Stefan's: *whatever I am, I do good.* Just as Stefan had, Pritchard believed in the Assembly. It had rescued him from Zona. The fundamental evil afflicting Pritchard was that he had the ability to choose but accepted a master and let them, the Adjusters, determine his choices.

The clansmen were close. Their feet kicked up last year's fallen leaves and raised a moldy smell. Stefan wanted to tell Pritchard that he should judge for himself. He opened his mouth.

Pritchard shook his head and raised his eyes to signal that the searchers were too near. Stefan hesitated. While he had been contemplating Pritchard's life, Pritchard had probably been deciding how best to kill the clansmen.

"Now," Pritchard murmured. He thrust Stefan away and up, helping him to his feet at the same time that he propelled himself away, into the woods.

"Here I am!" Stefan shouted, waving his arms like semaphores as a distraction from Pritchard's movement. He stumbled closer to the road. His body had stiffened while lying in the ditch and everything hurt. "Here! I need help!" He'd sworn to aid Pritchard's escape.

All three clansman ran toward Stefan. All had guns. "He's gone!" Stefan shouted. "I'm safe." He hobbled awkwardly forward to meet them, having lost his improvised cane.

"He's getting away!" The clansmen were intent on chasing Pritchard.

"It's me you want." Stefan stumbled into their direct path to Pritchard. Two hesitated, but one continued, then a second followed. The one who stayed was older and panting.

"Judge?" he asked. "That was Pritchard?"

There was no point in lying, and Stefan didn't.

Shots rang out from the direction the clansmen had taken. Pritchard's rifle was empty. Voices shouted, checking position and quarry.

Stefan had pledged to help. "We should leave quickly," he told his rescuer. "He's in the Assembly again, and they'll send ID agents. We have to get away."

The clansmen looked into the woods where, apparently, from the shouts and confused shooting, their prey still eluded the hunters. Stefan suspected that if they didn't have him yet, they never would.

"Go to the truck," the older clansman said. "Marta needs us to get him if we can." He set off determinedly into the forest, but the man was clumsy. Pritchard would get away. Stefan hopped a meter onto the roadway. His body loosened up as he moved. It was almost a pleasure to walk the level ground of the road.

Beatrice peered out from the covered rear deck of the truck. Moonlight whitened her hair and shadows gave her thin face a skeletal cast. Smudged across the white linen of her bandaged arm was a smattering of forest litter, mostly bits of leaves and dirt. Her thin blue dress was ripped along the lower right side. She jumped down gracefully and hurried to Stefan. "I told them he had you captive," she said. "I showed them where. Did I do right?"

"You did exactly right," he said. She hadn't given a pledge. "Beatrice, the Adjusters want him to kill you."

She nodded solemnly, but also seemed pleased. "They're afraid. I might still be able to call the ship, if you help me." She took Stefan's hand. Her fingers were cool. She smelled of the woods they'd just left, but she had a residual earthy aroma, one Liada would have disguised with perfume, as Pritchard did. "My friends are dead." Beatrice's fingers tightened around his. She rushed through her words as though they burned her mouth, telling him what he already had guessed about her ship, the beacon, and the Assembly.

Stefan had fallen under the spell of her expressive voice in the cave. He remembered that first encounter as a rare moment of understanding between two people, and for him, a personal moment of truth. After that moment in the cave, he had unconsciously sensed that the Assembly might not be necessary, that there were other ways of reaching truth and trust, because he'd felt both for Beatrice, an emotional rapport he couldn't explain. *Call it love,* he thought, and put his arm around her shoulder, careful not to disturb the bandage, while he listened with complete attention. She briefly described song, the basis for interspecies communication on her ship. Even when she spoke a human language, there were elements of song in her speech. Her pauses, the animation and inflection, even the sound of the words she chose were influenced by a sensibility that went to the essence of thought, directly to emotion. Her eloquent speech was the music of her mind. According to her, he might share that music because he knew the conventions of song; they were the Assembly's.

His leg ached from standing. There were tarpaulins in the rear of the truck, and a few boxes, but no bench. He led Beatrice to the side of the road, where a flat-topped guard rail was the right height for a seat. The metal rail was cold, but sitting was a relief. She wanted him to choose whether the call should be made, though it would destroy the Assembly. She wanted him to judge her mission.

"The Assembly is a tool," he said. "Any tool should be discarded when it becomes a crutch, and certainly when it's a barrier to progress. But not if it's a defense." She began a protest and for once he hushed her. True, the beacon was her Friends' own construct, and the Assembly a distorted use of it, but even her Friends had thought a defense against themselves was necessary. Refusal to open the door to the rest of the universe could be cowardly or it could be a provident protection. Tepan was ill. Stefan might be stricken, as Pritchard had been.

"Tell me about your Friends," he asked. "Are they worth the cost of meeting?" For there would be an immense price, the destruction of the civilization built upon the Assembly.

"I'll tell you about my life," she said. The combination of sounds in which she conveyed it only touched on human words, but he recognized her meaning in the same way he would have recognized information in the Assembly, intuitively, with the fuzzy edges providing deeper significance than simple, finite words.

He learned of the human shelter, where no Friend or other went, so that there was a place of safety from strangeness. With few words and much emotion, she described the mercurial Eyni, a baffling friend but a true one, and his death of natural, human causes. She admitted to being frightened of the Kroni; she mentioned the doubts the Fox had held. She described the window that looked into the dark. They sat side by side on the rail between the forest and the road, while the clansmen searched for Pritchard. In words where necessary, whenever song was too alien or subtle for him to understand, but whenever possible in tone and song, Beatrice conveyed her life, as she viewed it.

Forced to concentrate, Stefan forgot the woods and the chase. Just as was the case in the Assembly, meaning was compressed into shorter passages than it could have been expressed in language alone. It was as though she made a dump of her life and asked him to judge its worth. *Is there a price too high to pay for the future?* she seemed to ask. *Life on a reservation is a waste. I left the human shelter. I cannot thank my ancestors for being captured by the Ship and bringing me to this moment, but those events made me, even the deaths. This future is good.*

If asked to judge the propriety of the initial contact, Stefan didn't think he could have approved it. Humans had different imperatives from those of her Friends. The contact had occurred anyway, however, and every death since then attributable to it—human and Friend—would be meaningless if they didn't give them purpose by attempting the call. And yet, if Tepan died . . . ? Still, he would choose to go forward. The Adjusters' Assembly could kill civilization, too, and leave no alternative.

"Get in the truck," a clansman called as all three trudged back, tired and without Pritchard. "We're leaving."

"Stefan?"

He understood her minimalist question. "I can't," he said as he limped back to the truck with her. "As long as Pritchard is alive, then I can't connect with the Assembly, or the beacon. He did something—the Adjusters did." Just as Stefan had disappointed Beatrice, he now would disappoint Marta Denning. He couldn't make the dump she wanted as long as Pritchard was alive. The two of them were bound into one creature, both protecting and repelling each other.

"Too bad they didn't catch him. They meant to kill him." Beatrice had seen her friends murdered in cold blood; she had no sympathy for Pritchard. Stefan wondered why he did, after all that Kaim Pritchard had done, yet a self-image of persecuted Poupey, the target of the Inlanders' sons, had been indelibly deposited in Stefan's mind, a legacy of their joining. Stefan's guilty acknowledgment of his failure to help, his obliviousness to another's suffering, made him unable to want Pritchard's death. He owed Kaim Pritchard something.

There was a solution. If Pritchard could be maneuvered into a free zone, where there was a working Assembly shield, while Stefan stayed outside it, then, perhaps Stefan could enter the Assembly. "I don't want to kill him, or set someone else to do it," Stefan said quietly to Beatrice. "But I'll try to call the ship with you, if ever I can."

She sighed with relief. "Thank you." Beatrice kissed him, not passionately, but as her arms slipped around his back, they both pressed closer. Stefan stopped analyzing her voice, stopped pondering the future, and relished the human heat of physical passion with a person about whom he cared, an absolute good among the shadings of wrong and right.

"Hey! Get in," the clansman said. "Marta wants you."

They moved away from each other. Stefan, at least, was embarrassed. Beatrice reached with her one good arm to help Stefan climb onto the flat bed of the truck, and followed him inside. The truck was intended to carry cargo, not passengers. It was dusty and smelled of pine shavings. Stefan sat in a rear corner, and watched Beatrice settle into the other.

One of the two younger clansmen came around the back of the truck and hopped in easily. He banged on the sidewall. "Let's go!" he called.

The truck moved slowly at first. The loose tarps and scattered boxes rattled noisily, so that it was impossible to talk. Stefan stared out at the road, half expecting Pritchard to run out of the woods and jump inside, but as they picked up speed, it became impossible. They left the area and headed toward Bowl. The Dennings had pursued a bold strategy, apparently. Whatever happened, the entire town would know, and the Assembly couldn't easily conceal the truth known to so many minds.

Pink light shone through the trees as the sky lightened toward dawn. It didn't seem possible that the night had already passed. Independent Defense had never come. If the Adjusters had decided to abandon Pritchard, then they would kill him, but only after Stefan himself was dead. Just in case, though, Stefan tried to connect. Nothing.

With time to think, Stefan became anxious about Tepan's condition. He looked at Beatrice. Her eyes were closed, but she opened them as he watched her. They couldn't talk through the rattling noise and motion, but she flinched as though she knew his thoughts. What right did her shipboard Friends have to dispense illness like an inoculation, knowing some of the infected would die? The greater good was too amorphous a justification. He worried that he had chosen to call her ship on the basis of emotion, yet there was little else upon which to decide in a situation with so many unknowns. So, he trusted Beatrice. He relied on her truthfulness and her assessment of her Friends, while accepting that the ultimate responsibility was his. That was the difference between a puppet and a judge.

The sun was up when they entered Bowl. It was empty and shuttered, like a coastal town awaiting a hurricane. The storm would come. Independent Defense would sweep down on the wildmen. Even the dump Marta wanted him to make wouldn't have prevented it. Only one thing would stop them, and that was the end of the Assembly. For better or for worse, he was ready.

The Judge believed the call was right; that knowledge fortified Beatrice's decision. She reached for the beacon and found it. Entirely aware that it was impossible, she tried to call the Ship. Her mental voice sang the codes that would eliminate the beacon if two minds sang them. The Friends might even have heard her as an additional note in the perpetually mournful song of the beacon, but the call to the Ship didn't occur. The Friends couldn't approach any closer to Earth than they were.

The call couldn't be made alone. Stefan was trapped by Pritchard, but he would try if given an opportunity. Beatrice had to give one to him.

The Judge was studying her. He smiled. Relieved that his somber examination of her was finally over, she returned the smile. She had kissed him from gratitude so strong it required a physical expression, but the kiss had become more, a promise for the future. He was so close she could easily touch his hand. She didn't. Their future would be decided in the next few hours.

He could do it. She was sure that he could use song as well as a shipboard child, which should be enough—if only he could reach the beacon with her. She'd never wanted to kill, but Pritchard had to die. Frustrated, under cover of the noise of the moving truck, she sang a bit of that frustration aloud.

He tapped her knee. They leaned close, so she could hear him over the rattling truck. "If anything happens to me," he said, "Marta Denning might be able to do it. She knows the Assembly."

Marta Denning. Beatrice shook her head at the Judge and looked out the open rear of the truck. What kind of message to the Friends would Marta Denning send about the people of Earth? She didn't want anyone but the Judge to join her call. They both had to survive.

The truck entered Bowl. The town's stillness seemed unnatural, even so early in the day. The driver must have thought so, too, because the truck slowed with each block they passed, and finally stopped. One of the two men in front ran back. "I can't raise anyone on the radio," he said.

He and the clansman with them in the rear compartment looked at the Judge as though he might have answers. The Judge accepted the role, and nodded. "Independent Defense must already have arrived. They'll be at the Waterman Clan Hall." To Beatrice, he added, "It's just around the corner." The Judge stood, having to stoop under the low cloth ceiling. "It's probably too late for us to get away. Let's see what they're up to." He extended his hand to Beatrice.

She took his hand and they helped each other out of the truck. The gray dawn made everything look pale, but the sky was clear; it would be a sunny day. Beatrice had never before appreciated the efficacy of sunlight, but it made her feel suddenly more hopeful that they could survive.

"The walking wounded?" the Judge said, apparently a joke. He chuckled, stretched, and looked up at the sky. Beatrice didn't want to fail him, but she found playfulness difficult.

The clansmen waited for them on the empty street. Their guns seemed to make them jumpy without giving them any comfort.

"The three of you should leave," the Judge said to the clansmen. "There's a good chance they won't bother chasing you. It's the two of us they'll want."

The oldest man glanced at the other two, then shrugged. "We'll stay, Judge. Just in case there's something we can do."

The Judge seemed surprised, though Beatrice wasn't.

They had implicitly accepted him as their leader. He shook hands with each of them, then they all started walking to the Waterman Clan Hall. The Judge had difficulty, so they went slowly. A sense of his dignity kept the three men from offering help.

There were buildings on all sides. Beatrice had looked through windows, but had not been viewed through them before. She never saw anyone observing them as they passed, but an occasional disarranged curtain or a shade hastily pulled down magnified her awareness of being on stage. She didn't like it.

"Cowards," muttered the man who'd been in the truck bed with them.

"Hush," the older one said.

"If they came out and joined us, it would tell the bastards something."

Bowl was an occupied town. Invaders had landed and most inhabitants just wanted the trouble to go away.

The street opened into a wide square; they stopped immediately after rounding the corner. More than a dozen men were standing around four trucks. These were newer, sleeker vehicles than those the clans had used. A hoverplane had landed in the open center of the square. Several more men were gathered around it. Even from such a distance, Beatrice recognized one as Kaim Pritchard.

As they watched, a group of six people were led uncomplainingly from the clan hall to a truck. Every one of them was wearing a cap and had his hands bound. The Assembly was their jail.

Beatrice turned to the Judge. The three clansmen were armed. The distance wasn't as far as the men had shot during the firefight at the Lodge. He might still call the Ship with her if they killed Pritchard.

"One of you, give me a rifle," he said. "A good one."

Stefan wouldn't let anyone do what he was unwilling to do himself. These men had submitted themselves to his command, making their lives his responsibility. He didn't want to kill Kaim Pritchard, but it might become necessary. He asked for a gun.

The closest clansman handed Stefan his rifle, then dropped his hands to his sides as though he didn't know what to do with them.

The square was full of ID agents, all linked through the Assembly, and able to act as one. Metallic shimmers from the rooftops indicated that they were covered on all sides. Whoever shot Pritchard would be committing suicide. Stefan moved slightly forward of the others.

"Kill him," Beatrice whispered.

If he raised the weapon, the ID agents would certainly kill him before he got off a shot. "Do you know if there's a shield—a free zone—in Bowl?" Stefan asked the clansmen without turning to look at them.

They didn't know.

Pritchard walked slowly toward Stefan, alone.

It seemed to Stefan that Marta would have installed a shield device in her clan hall. Perhaps ID agents had swooped down on the disorganized clansmen before she had time to trigger it, or perhaps Independent Defense had stormed the hall despite it, but Stefan felt reasonably confident that there would be one, probably on the third floor, among the machinery of Marta's office. If he could maneuver Pritchard there . . . and stay outside himself . . . Or was he rationalizing his failure to do the necessary but evil thing: murder?

"Stay here," he said. "The four of you. Protect Beatrice at all costs; she's the last Traveler." He didn't have time to explain to them why that was important, but he glanced at Beatrice. She was watching him, waiting for him to act. Her skin glowed in the morning sunlight. A leaf from the forest clung in her hair like a flower. Her face was wan. "Keep ready," he said and smiled as though he believed in their success.

"Inlander," Pritchard shouted across the distance between them. He had stopped walking. "Throw down your guns. I know you won't shoot me, but they don't." He gestured, and by the artificial magic of colluding minds, a troop of eight uniformed soldiers appeared from behind the trucks. They formed a row like a firing squad, all weapons trained on him.

Stefan and his small band couldn't win by force. He tossed the rifle to the pavement.

"All of you," Pritchard shouted.

Stupid, to have led these men here. He should have ordered them to run away. Their clansmen were being loaded into the trucks like zombies, who had lost their will and minds.

The troop of soldiers advanced.

"Do as he says," Stefan called over his shoulder. This was much worse than his hillside fight with Pritchard. That had been foolishness; this was for high and very real stakes. He raised his hands over his head and limped toward Pritchard in order to keep him away from Beatrice. It would be a hot day. The air already was humid. His leg hurt, but the pain was so well established that it was an annoyance, not a disaster. Worse was his pervasive fatigue, his dirtiness, which seemed to increase under the scrutiny of the spotless Independent Defense agents, and most of all, his sense of utter failure.

"Inlander, I've been waiting for you." Pritchard looked grimier than most of those in the square, but he'd changed into clean clothes since their flight through the forest.

Stefan tried to smile and fall into Pritchard's style of sardonic banter. "They searched the woods a long time."

"I had my own transportation." Pritchard indicated the hoverplane with a hand gesture. It bore ID's rarely seen insignia in modest black.

"Kaim, how is my son?" Pritchard's first name slipped out naturally as Stefan spoke.

"He's doing very well. Dr. Felipe expects a full and complete recovery."

"My wife?"

"Fine. Impossible, according to Dr. Felipe." Pritchard smiled slightly. So did Stefan, recalling the sour but eminently capable Dr. Felipe. "The first thing she did when she woke up was to file an application with the Oblander to divorce you." Pritchard said it lightly, with shared humor. He knew how little regret Stefan would feel.

"The Dennings?"

"What is this, Inlander? If you want a report, apply for Assembly access."

"Kaim, please promise me you won't hurt Beatrice." Stefan hoped Pritchard might be susceptible to begging from an Inlander.

They were only about a meter apart, but Pritchard glanced over his shoulder, then came a bit closer. His sham joviality disappeared. "Inlander, you have no room to negotiate. Absolutely none. Do as you're told and you'll survive. That's the best you can hope for."

A tall, thin, hunchbacked man of about fifty was approaching from behind Pritchard. Stefan had never seen him before. He looked strikingly unlike the athletic ID agents in the square. He walked without any particular sense of authority. As he neared, Stefan saw his sallow complexion and sunken eyes. He seemed tired and his black suit was rumpled. Without appearing to have noticed him, Pritchard stepped to the side, transferring command of the situation. "Enough," the man said wearily. His voice was husky. He didn't look at anyone when he spoke.

"Sir." Pritchard bowed very deeply.

"You've caused great trouble, Stefan," the man chided, though he barely glanced in Stefan's direction. "But the Open Court is a noble institution and you are an honorable man. We believe you deserve another chance."

"You're an Adjuster." Stefan had never met one. "I thought all of you stayed in the Southland." He was buying time, but also curious. Which one was this? The timbre of his voice meant nothing. Though Beatrice called her beacon commands song, and used the same term for her audible alien speech, there was no actual sound inside the Assembly except on a call, and even that was a reproduction, susceptible to use of dummies.

"You think the worst of us, yet didn't we choose you for the Open Court?" the Adjuster said. "Trust that we aim at what's best for humankind."

Stefan recognized the manner of speech from the Assembly in the way one recognizes the color of a particular thread in a multicolored cloth. "Amicus Curiae," Stefan said.

"Just so. Like you, a judge. We have fuller information. Stefan, let us decide this case." He didn't look at Stefan.

"Are you going to kill Beatrice?" Stefan tensed, and a sharp pain went through his left leg and up his spine. He steadied himself on his good, right leg. He was sweating. He thought he could feel Beatrice watching from the corner where he'd left her.

"We don't want to kill anyone. We hoped that the new arrivals would join our Assembly. We regret their deaths. We didn't order them." The Adjuster didn't glance at Pritchard. His failure to physically address his listener, or to use significant body language during the conversation reminded Stefan of the Travelers, but it also could disguise lies.

"You evaded my question. What will happen to Beatrice?" Stefan was expendable, but Beatrice wasn't. As long as she lived, there was a chance that the Ship would be called. He looked back. The soldiers had removed the clansmen's weapons, and stood guard on them, but Beatrice was with them and unharmed.

"Stefan, we've known that one day the ship would come." The Adjuster's voice broke, like that of an adolescent boy, or someone who seldom spoke aloud. "When they deposited the first mission on Earth to establish the beacon, our understanding of them was incomplete. Now we know they'll cancel all we've done and abolish the Assembly. We can't allow that. We don't need them. They'll leave eventually, probably soon, and they won't return—unless a call is made. Beatrice is dangerous. However changed they are, she and the other captives on that ship are still human. She is our enemy because she's capable of calling, and training others to call with her."

The Adjusters had always known the truth of the origin of the beacon. The Assembly was founded on a lie. It wasn't a human invention; it was a gift.

"Remove her connect," Stefan said. "Then she's as harmless as I am."

Pritchard chuckled, but his amusement ended abruptly, probably at Amicus Curiae's command.

"Like heeling a dog," Stefan said.

Pritchard flushed. Amicus Curiae seemed not to notice. "There are always caps. Stefan, I can unravel what the web doctor has done to you; I know much more than that woman. I can adjust the imagery of your dumps and let you connect with us again. Prove your loyalty and I will."

Distrust of the Adjusters had not erased Stefan's yearning for the Assembly itself. He would connect and it would surround him like a long separated lover. Stefan felt an ache, the mental equivalent of phantom pain for a lost limb. All he had to do was let Amicus Curiae adjust his mind to fit the reality the Assembly required— and let Beatrice die. "No."

"Kaim," the Adjuster said. It was an order, and there was undoubtedly more said through the Assembly.

Pritchard bowed. "Bring Beatrice here, Inlander. It's your only choice. You can't help her no matter what you do, so you may as well survive."

That was how Pritchard lived, pragmatic amorality eased by the nirvana of connection with the Assembly. Pritchard truly did not want to kill Beatrice, but he would allow it to be done. There were armed ID men throughout the square. All had a subtle commonality, a dishonest mixture of tension and assurance. They told themselves that they were fine and right, but like Pritchard, they didn't believe it. They didn't even believe it mattered anymore. "All right," Stefan said. "Walk back with me to her." Pritchard would be in constant contact with the Assembly. Everything they said would be overheard, at the very least by this Adjuster, but this was Stefan's last chance at persuasion.

Pritchard nodded. "I don't believe you intend to cooperate," he said as he started walking beside Stefan toward Beatrice, "but step by step the end result will be the same." He moved too quickly and had to wait a moment for Stefan to catch up. "You should have kept that cane I made you, Inlander."

Sickened, Stefan realized Pritchard was correct; this was how it could begin. He was leading Beatrice's intended executioner back to her. "How much trouble are you in? Will killing Beatrice really cure it?"

"She's never liked me, anyway." Pritchard glanced at Beatrice, who was warily observing their approach.

"You don't like yourself. Kaim Pritchard, for this once do something that you yourself will respect. Poupey."

Pritchard's head jerked up from watching Stefan's difficult progress.

"You didn't surrender to Romaric. Amicus Curiae is just another bully." Pritchard said nothing.

They'd arrived. "Stefan?" Beatrice looked from him to Pritchard and back. There were tears in her eyes.

Pritchard bowed to Beatrice. Entirely suave, he said, "The ship hasn't moved in the slightest. They have no idea what's going on here, do they?"

"Any call to her ship requires two callers," Stefan answered for her. He faced Pritchard. He would have to kill Pritchard bare-handed. He didn't know how. He didn't have a weapon. His leg was broken. He doubted his quickness and his ability to surprise. Even if he succeeded, the ID agents would shoot him, probably before he could complete the call. He would fail, but he would try.

"Don't, Stefan," Pritchard said. "You've been given your life."

The windows were keeping Beatrice alive. Once she was out of public view, an order would be given and she would die. She was terrified. She had been in danger since arriving on Earth, but even during her abduction she had never felt the immediacy of her death so acutely as while listening to Pritchard and the Judge talk around its edges. The Judge had been unable to persuade Pritchard to spare her, and so he had decided that he, too, would die. She couldn't stay passive.

"I don't want to die." She startled both men, who,

though they were discussing her, hadn't considered that she would act independently.

Pritchard squinted at her, as if the light was in his eyes, but didn't answer. She had needed it said; she wanted it in Pritchard's heart, a tiny revenge, whatever happened.

"Please, Kaim." The Judge's quiet dignity was entirely wasted. Pritchard had made up his mind a long time ago. The death he regretted was that of the Judge.

They had isolated the Judge from the Assembly, but she had never indicated a desire or an ability to enter it. The Adjusters had discounted her. She could connect with the Assembly via her implanted connect, which was meant to reach the beacon. She could not call the Ship, but she might call the Earth.

Beatrice felt for the beacon. It was there. Then, like inching her way into cold water, she poked at the Assembly. It was permeable to anyone with the right commands. She held her breath, jumped, and entered. She felt the rush of pleasure the Judge had described as she met all the connected minds throughout the Earth. She was with them. They were with her. To dump her mind: it sounded deviant, but it was as simple as the will to survive. She forced herself on them.

She felt their surprise, like a huge intake of breath all over the world played out in her mind. She experienced their interest and watched as they absorbed the memoir of her life.

"No!" Something screamed in her ears and her mind.

The world around Beatrice hesitated. Pritchard turned. He stared. His eyes met hers, then he started to turn away, toward the Judge.

The Judge hadn't noticed, quite. Of everyone in the square, he was the only one not inside the Assembly with her.

"Kill her!" The command was so powerful, she wanted to die.

Kaim Pritchard threw himself on top of Beatrice, and fell with her onto the ground.

*   *   *

Stefan sensed an alteration of the atmosphere in the square. The word "sudden" was too slow. He had been waiting for a change, any change, as a distraction, but as he readied for the leap—he would go for Pritchard's throat—he saw Pritchard gape, slack-jawed, at Beatrice. Beatrice was staring up into the sky.

"No!" Amicus Curiae screamed. Even from halfway across the square, his piercing shriek caused Stefan's pulse to race, and filled him with thoughts of death.

Pritchard's eyes moved to Stefan. Stefan started forward on his right leg, to intercept Pritchard. Pritchard leapt at Beatrice. Stefan stumbled, but stayed upright.

Shots were fired, from all around the square. Pritchard's body exploded with wounds.

Astonished and bewildered, Stefan did the thing that was, for him, most natural. He connected with the Assembly. And there it was. He was inside.

Kaim Pritchard was dead.

Stefan's dump was automatic and unstoppable. He felt it, although usually he didn't. It released the pressure in his mind, but connection lacked all its usual joy. He shared with the world his awareness that this connection had been brought about by death, perhaps by suicide.

Stefan was immediately hailed from inside the Assembly. He hadn't yet taken any action, although options surrounded him like a glittering arcade. For once he didn't lose his sense of self. He identified his caller easily by her vivid interior voice, so like her voice outside. He was astonished. *Beatrice?*

They were on the Assembly margins, where the melancholy was greatest. It made her response mournful, though she answered with only a brief command. The Adjusters were gathering. They must call the Ship.

I don't know how to call.

Follow-the-leader.

Stefan could not fathom how their dialogue was being facilitated. When forcibly linked with Pritchard, they had been inside each other's mind. Stefan had never encountered this instant, but external, mental communication. He had no impression of Beatrice's surroundings, though

he could see her, buried beneath Pritchard's inert body.
There was no dump of himself into her mind, or of her
into him.

Now. Do as I do.

Stefan listened. This universe of the Assembly outside
the files was featureless, soundless, and lacking any other
impression, yet he perceived what Beatrice performed:
a series of commands, each dying as it was completed.
He scurried to keep up. It was a game of follow-the-
leader through a few images, but mostly a series of what
seemed to be thought-emotions. Twice Beatrice started
again. It had to be perfect, and he needed to hurry.
The Adjusters. He was drained when she finally stopped,
not exhilarated.

Do you hear it?

What?

We're outside the Assembly system.

He was glad. The Adjusters tried to follow and disrupt
them, but Stefan suspected that beyond the Assembly
confines they had built, their power would be much less
than Beatrice's.

Do you hear it?

He tried. This universe seemed empty. Beatrice enjoyed the dark, but he was uncomfortable in it. His mind
skipped a beat. Someone was beside his real body, talking aloud. He blinked and ignored it. *That?* He knew it
wasn't what she meant. Then he heard it.

Very softly, someone was crying.

The word alarm had made him imagine something
loud and frightening. Instead, quiet misery kept ships
away from Earth. *Yes. I hear it.*

Stefan had assumed that the beacon would disappear
when the commands were given, yet he remained aware
of the misery. The sadness reflected back to him. They
hadn't reached the Ship; the beacon wasn't gone. *Why
do I hear it? Did we fail?*

*No. We need to deliver the mission statement. This is
the hardest part, Stefan, the reason only a person who
knows song can make the call. Be careful. Be concise. I'll
go first.*

He felt that she wanted to say more, but resisted.

The mission statement. As he listened to Beatrice, he understood the reason the Assembly so readily received dumps from its adepts. This wasn't an automatic deposit of the contents of Beatrice's mind, however, it was measured song, the difference between random noise and a symphony. He could not do this.

He had supposed from Beatrice's comments that extinguishing the beacon was a matter of codes, like erasing a file. That was wrong. The beacon would not have been so flexible that humans could use it as their Assembly if it had not also been complex. The beacon had judgment. It would decide whether or not there was adequate cause for its own termination, and whether there was truth in what was sung. The alarm was an open court; the beacon was a justice machine. It warned ships away from danger. In doing so, it also protected the Earth.

He listened to Beatrice. She sang of the Ship and of the embrace of different peoples. The richness of her description of the Ship contrasted sharply with the lack of fullness in her understanding of what it would touch, the Earth. Her experiences of Earth were paltry. Nevertheless, he understood her to say that contact was right. A progression, she called it. Stefan thought, though embarrassed by his criticism, that Beatrice's song could have been composed on the Ship, there was so little of Earth in it. What there was mostly concerned him.

As she sang, he understood something else. She had not been intended to sing alone. Two voices were desired, side by side, just as the two of them had together opened the gate to the beacon's choice. She hoped that he would add something to the call. Haltingly, he tried to echo those aspects of her song that he understood best. She made room for him eagerly.

Beatrice was happy; despite her losses, she was calling her home. Stefan's song was somber. He wasn't sure he was doing right. He trusted Beatrice. When he sang of the Assembly, he didn't commemorate the Adjuster ordering death, he remembered his own joy. Those dead

of disease—an important element in Beatrice's song—
were not merely necessary sacrifices, they were people
he knew. She sang of few casualties; he sang of Tepan,
now in recovery, and of the death of his flawed friend,
Romaric. He remembered the multitudes he had
touched in the Assembly, but there was one he remembered best: Kaim Pritchard. He felt his song veer into
a lament.

Pritchard had known exactly what he was doing when
he protected Beatrice. His twisted life had been straightened by one fine and final act. As intimately as they had
been bound during Pritchard's last days, Stefan didn't
know why he had done it.

I am a Judge, he sang. His song echoed the message
of the beacon, even to its sadness. *This call was my
choice.* The weight of responsibility entered every phrase
of his song.

Stefan stopped. Beatrice had.

"Do you hear it?" she asked.

The bright sunshine, which Stefan had never stopped
seeing yet hadn't noticed, glared in his eyes. The three
clansmen from the truck, who had used their bodies to
shield his, stepped aside.

"What have you done?" someone wailed. Amicus Curiae, and many of the Independent Defense agents, had
fallen into a stupor like that of Kaim Pritchard during
the initial phase of the clan attack on the Lodge.

"Judge?" It was the older clansman. The ID guards
were staring vacantly ahead, aware of the clansmen, but
uncaring. Beatrice, covered in Pritchard's blood, was
pulled from beneath his body by the three clansmen.

"Do you hear it?" Beatrice asked again. She was the
living person, smiling at him, and not the disembodied
articulation with whom he had recently shared a trial.

He listened. The wind was picking up; it whistled
slightly as it entered the square. Far away, a bird
chirped. A door opened; a man's footsteps sounded loud
on the concrete walk. Across the square, prisoners in
caps began shouting as they were loosed from the grip
of their artificial tranquillity; they yelled for someone to

untie them. Amicus Curiae whimpered. The agents of Independent Defense who were not in a daze, strained, as Stefan did, to hear that which was gone. The Assembly had vanished. The beacon had stopped its alarm. Wherever it had once been, there was silence.

"The welcome of silence." Beatrice opened her arms to him. "We did it. The Ship will come."

He embraced her. They both smelled of blood, but the Earth was no longer crying.

ROC BRINGS THE FUTURE TO YOU

☐ **THE IMMORTALS by Tracy Hickman.** The United States in the year 2010—ravaged by disease and slowly stifled by martial law. Though fear runs rampant across the land, one man, Michael Barris, dares to challenge the government's tightening grip. This powerful cautionary tale paints an engrossing portrait of the near future. (454022—$19.95)

☐ **THIS SIDE OF JUDGMENT by J.R. Dunn.** In a dark, new twist on the Frankenstein theme, three men—a madman drunk on power, a hunter weary of bloodshed, and a protector who can no longer protect—come together in a debut novel that is part sci-fi thriller, part high tech, and part page-turning madness. "A page-turner!"—*Publishers Weekly* (454863—$5.99)

☐ **KNIGHTS OF THE BLACK EARTH by Margaret Weis and Don Perrin.** Xris, top human agent of the Federal Intelligence Security Agency, finds himself joining forces with his oldest enemy in a desperate attempt to halt the seemingly unstoppable Knights of the Black Earth—a fanatical group determined to sabotage the current government and revive Earth supremacy. (454251—$18.95)

☐ **DEATHSTALKER by Simon R. Green.** Owen Deathstalker, unwilling head of his clan, sought to aovid the perils of the Empire's warring factions but unexpectedly found a price on his head. He fled to Mistworld, where he began to build an unlikely force to topple the throne—a broken hero, an outlawed Hadenman, a thief, and a bounty hunter. (454359—$5.99)

Prices slightly higher in Canada.

The Roc Frequent Readers Club
BUY TWO ROC BOOKS AND GET
ONE SF/FANTASY NOVEL FREE!

Check the free title you wish to receive (subject to availability):